Praise for

Grown Ups

NEW YORK TIMES BESTSELLER

SHORTLISTED FOR THE 2020 AN POST IRISH BOOK AWARD FOR POPULAR FICTION

"Sensitive, funny, wonderful, immensely touching." —Nigella Lawson

"I LOVED *Grown Ups* so much. It's SUCH a treat. I felt like I was rolling in PURE JOY throughout." —Caitlin Moran, bestselling author of *How to Build a Girl*

"She's only gone and done it again! I love Marian Keyes's books with a passion, and now she's got a fabulous new one . . . Brilliant as ever." —Jane Fallon, bestselling author of *Tell Me a Secret*

"It is charming, funny and poignant. But also profound, heartbreaking. If you already love Marian, this is her best yet. If you haven't read her, this is the one." —Nina Stibbe, bestselling author of *Reasons to Be Cheerful*

"THIS BOOK. Reader, I LOVED it. Funny and thoughtful, and such brilliantly drawn characters I am genuinely bereft that my time with them is over." —Hannah Beckerman, bestselling author of *If Only I Could Tell You*

"A novel that is warm and witty, but never afraid to tackle the big stuff." —Elizabeth Day, bestselling author of *How to Fail*

"Marian Keyes's gift for storytelling is utterly magnificent. I feel like I've met every single character in this book. I may even be a character in this book. Nobody nails chaotic families like Marian." —Liz Nugent, bestselling author of *Unravelling Oliver*

"Over the past twenty years, Marian Keyes has built a reputation for breezy fiction that also tackles difficult and, at times, controversial subjects, and *Grown Ups* is no exception. . . . Keyes's literary skill lies in taking themes that in different hands might be rendered portentous or oppressive and making them accessible. *Grown Ups* is a warm-hearted, wise and highly entertaining portrayal of how families behave; of our tendency to idealise the notion of extended family gatherings, and of the love and tolerance required to sustain our closest relationships." —*The Guardian*

"Beautifully drawing an extended family that's beset by rubbish parents (each of the brothers struggles with the legacy of their critical mum and dad), complex behaviours (overspending, cheating, bulimia) and the natural disorder that comes with being each other's nearest and dearest, this is Keyes at her best: capturing everyday voices with humour and empathy with writing that you'll devour in a weekend. Just pure and simple joy." —*Stylist*

Praise for

MARIAN KEYES

and her previous books

"Keyes is the real thing." —*The Globe and Mail*

"Clever, hilarious, poignant. . . . Gloriously funny." —*The Sunday Times*

"Everything this woman touches turns to comic gold." —*Cosmopolitan*

"Fabulously entertaining. The queen of intelligent women's fiction." —*Sunday Mirror*

"Wildly funny, romantic and nearly impossible to put down." —*Daily Mail*

"Keyes is an international treasure. The ultimate choice for a binge read." —*Stylist*

"When it comes to writing page-turners that put a smile on your face and make you think, Keyes is in a class of her own." —*Daily Express*

"Keyes writes about women who are absolutely themselves, even when society tries to insist they are something else." —*Irish Times*

Also by Marian Keyes

FICTION

Watermelon

Lucy Sullivan Is Getting Married

Rachel's Holiday

Last Chance Saloon

Sushi for Beginners

Angels

The Other Side of the Story

Anybody Out There

This Charming Man

The Brightest Star in the Sky

The Mystery of Mercy Close

The Woman Who Stole My Life

The Break

NON-FICTION

Making It Up As I Go Along

Under the Duvet: Deluxe Edition

(*Under the Duvet* and *Further Under the Duvet*)

Grown Ups

MARIAN KEYES

Anchor Canada

TORONTO

Anchor Canada edition published 2021

This edition is distributed in the United States of America by
Penguin Random House Canada Limited.

Library and Archives Canada Cataloguing in Publication data is available upon request.

ISBN 978-0-385-69724-8

Cover illustration by Gemma Correll

Printed in Canada

Published in Canada by Anchor Canada,
a division of Penguin Random House Canada Limited,
a Penguin Random House Company

www.penguinrandomhouse.ca

10 9 8 7 6 5 4 3 2 1

For my husband

The Family Tree

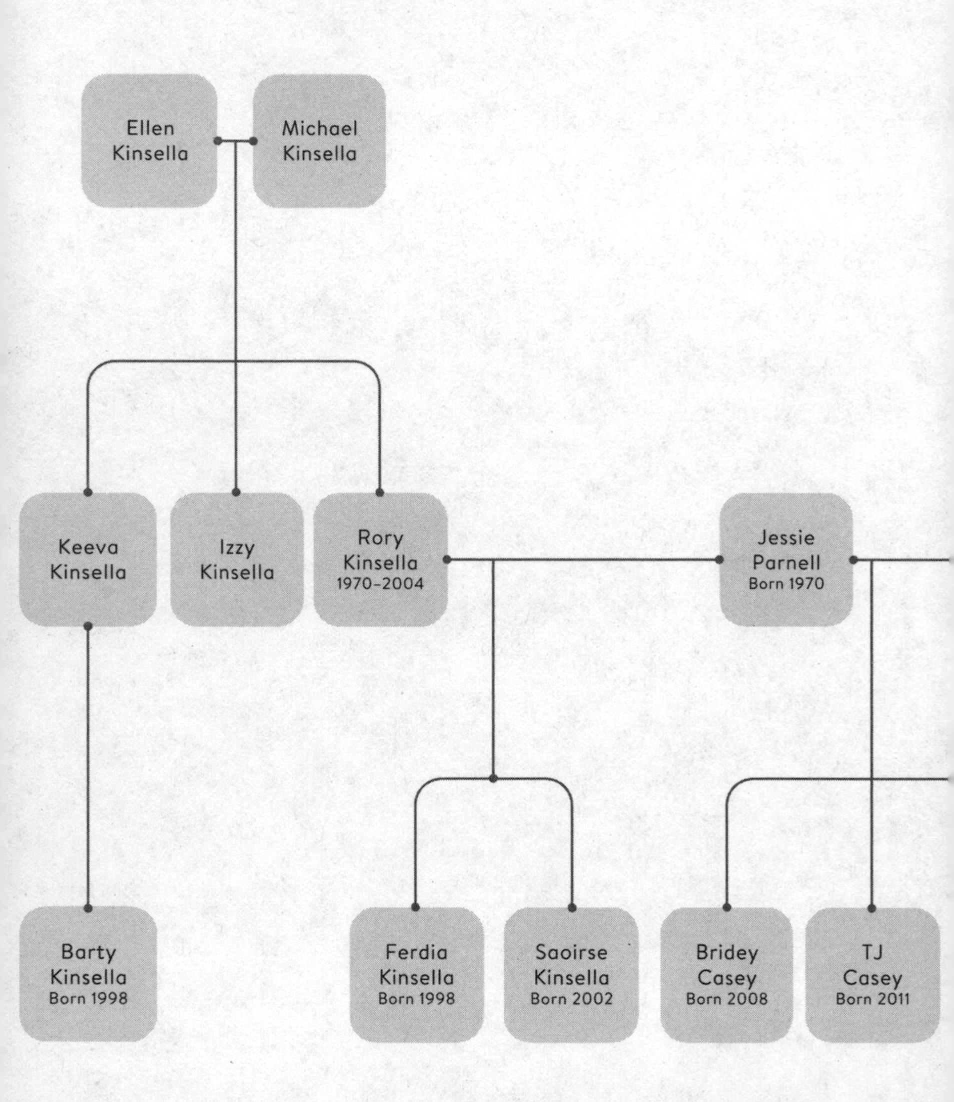

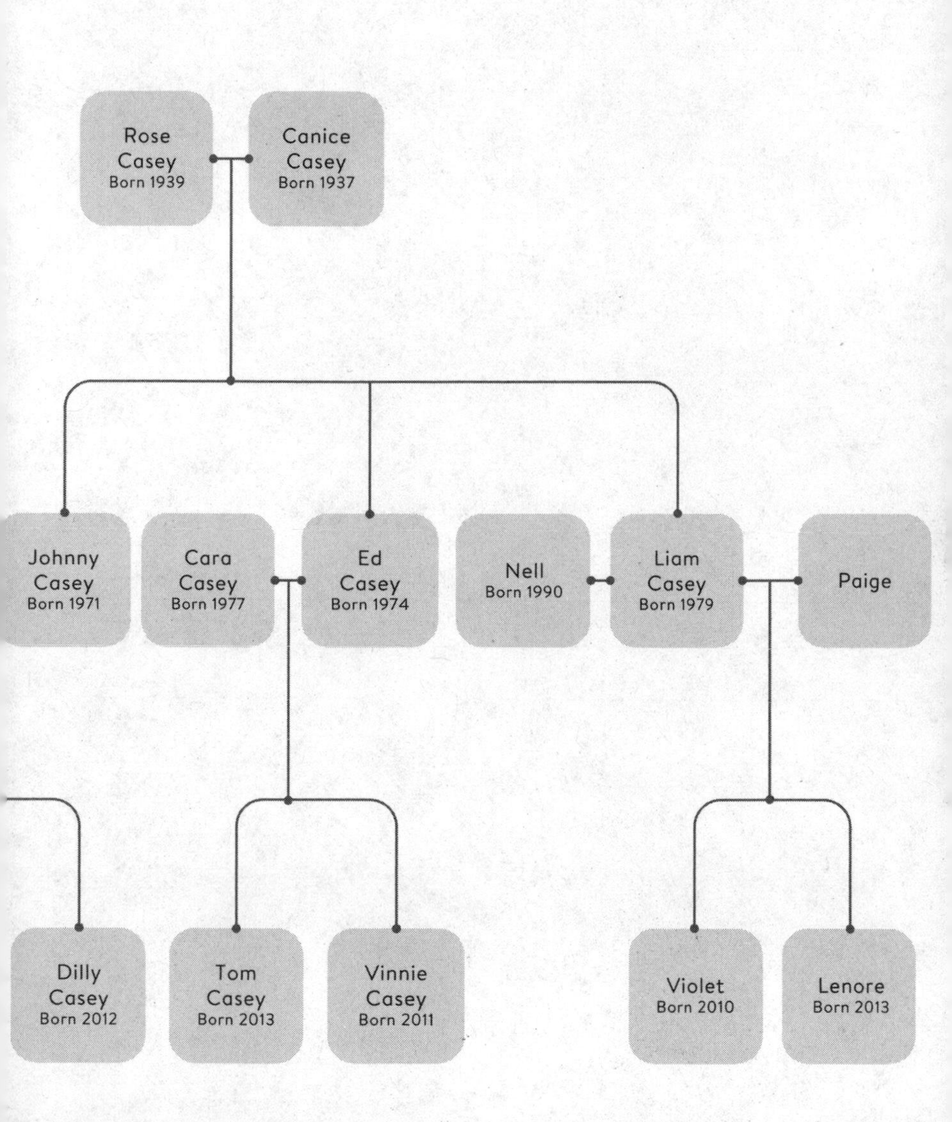
Rose Casey Born 1939
Canice Casey Born 1937
Johnny Casey Born 1971
Cara Casey Born 1977
Ed Casey Born 1974
Nell Born 1990
Liam Casey Born 1979
Paige
Dilly Casey Born 2012
Tom Casey Born 2013
Vinnie Casey Born 2011
Violet Born 2010
Lenore Born 2013

'When we were children, we used to think that when we were grown-up we would no longer be vulnerable. But to grow up is to accept vulnerability . . . To be alive is to be vulnerable'

Madeleine L'Engle

Prologue

Johnny Casey launched into a fit of energetic coughing—a bit of bread down the wrong way. But the chat around the long dinner table carried on. Lovely. He could die here, literally *die*, on his forty-ninth birthday, and would his brothers, their spouses, his *own* wife, Jessie, or any of the children, even notice?

Jessie was his best hope but she was off in the kitchen readying the next elaborate course. He could only hope he survived to eat it.

A sip of water didn't help. Tears were streaming down his face and *finally* Ed, his younger brother, asked, 'You okay there?'

Manfully, Johnny waved away his concern. 'Bread. Down the wrong way.'

'Thought for a minute you were choking,' Ferdia said.

Well, why didn't you say something, you useless tool? Twenty-two years of age and more concerned with Syrian refugees than your stepfather expiring!

'That'd be a shame,' Johnny croaked. 'To die on my birthday.'

'You wouldn't have died,' Ferdia said. 'One of us would have tried the Heimlich manoeuvre.'

Someone would have needed to notice I was dying first.

'You know what happened recently?' Ed asked. 'Mr Heimlich? The man who invented the Heimlich manoeuvre? Finally, at the age of eighty-seven, he got to do it on someone for real.'

'And it worked? He saved the person?' This was from Liam, the youngest of the Casey brothers, right down at the end of the table. 'Be a bit mortifying if he did it, then the person snuffed it.'

Liam tended to bring the snark to any situation, Johnny reflected. Look at him there, lounging back in his seat with a careless grace that made Johnny's teeth itch. At forty-one years of age, Liam was still propelling himself through life, using only good looks and swagger.

The cut of him, with his surf-y hair and half the buttons open on his crumpled shirt.

'Like Mr Segway,' Ferdia said. 'Invented the Segway, said they were totally safe, then died on one.'

'In fairness,' Ed said, 'his only claim was that you'd never fall over on one.'

'So what happened?' Johnny, despite his resentment at the lot of them, was interested.

'He accidentally drove one off a cliff.'

'Oh, God.' Nell, Liam's wife, dissolved into giggles. 'Started believing his own publicity? You know, they were a bit safe, so he got fooled into thinking they were bullet-proof?'

'Got high on his own supply,' Ferdia said.

'You'd know about that.' Liam threw his nephew a dark look.

Ferdia glared in return.

So the feud between those two is on again? What is it this time?

He'd ask Jessie. She kept tabs on the various Casey alliances and grudges—it gave her life. Where was she anyway? Right, here she came. Carrying a trayful of, by the looks of things, sorbets.

'Palate cleansers!' she declared. 'Lemon and vodka.'

'What about us?' Bridey piped up. She was twelve years of age and operated like a union rep for the five youngest cousins. She policed their rights with vigilance. 'We can't *possibly* have vodka, we're *far* too young.'

'On it,' Jessie said.

Course she was, Johnny thought. Fair play to her. Never dropped the ball.

'Just lemon for you guys.'

Sometimes Johnny didn't know how Jessie did it. Even though Bridey was his first-born, he sometimes found her insufferable.

Bridey issued stern instructions to the younger kids that if their sorbets tasted 'in any way funny' they must desist from eating them with immediate effect.

She actually said those words. 'Desist.' And 'with immediate effect'.

It was at times such as these that Johnny Casey wondered at the wisdom of sending children to expensive schools. They created *monsters.*

Jessie resumed her spot at the head of the table. 'Everyone okay?' she asked.

Cheerful noises of assent rose, because that was how things rolled in Jessie's world.

But when the hubbub quietened down, Ed's wife, Cara, said, 'I have to say it, I'm bored out of my skull.'

Good-humoured chortles followed and someone murmured, 'You're funny.'

'I'm not joking.'

Several heads jerked up from their sorbets. All conversation ceased.

'I mean, *sorbets*?' Cara asked. 'How many more courses do we have to sit through? Couldn't we just have had a pizza?'

Okay, Cara had one or two issues. To put it mildly. But she was a sweetheart, one of the nicest people he'd ever met. Johnny's gaze went to Ed: it was his job to keep his wife under control. If that wasn't a very sexist thought and, yes, he admitted it was.

But Ed looked stupefied with confusion. 'What the hell?' he asked. 'Jessie, I'm sorry!'

Jessie was dumb with shock.

Trying to pull things back to normal, Johnny adopted a light-hearted tone. 'Ah, come on now, Cara. After all the work Jessie's done . . .'

'But she did nothing! The caterers did it.'

'*What* caterers?' several voices asked.

'She *always* has these things catered.'

Jessie would never use caterers. Cooking is her thing.

Up and down the table, the mood was of scandalized commotion.

'How much have you had to drink?' Ed asked Cara.

'Nothing,' she said. 'Because I had that bang—'

'—on the head!' Ed finished her sentence and his relief was audible. 'She got a bang on the head earlier. A sign fell off a shop and hit her—'

'That's not what happened—'

'We thought she was okay—'

'You *wanted* me to be okay,' Cara said. 'I knew I wasn't.'

'You should go to the emergency room!' Jessie was struggling to recalibrate to her default personality of Nurturing and Bossy. 'You're obviously concussed. Go this very moment, why are you even here?'

'Because Ed needs Johnny to loan him the money,' Cara said.

Right on cue, Jessie asked, 'What money?'

'From the other bank account,' Cara said. Then, 'Oh, God. I wasn't meant to say that.'

'What bank account?' Jessie asked. 'What loan?'

'Cara, the hospital, right now.' Ed stood up.

'Johnny?' Jessie locked eyes with him.

He knew the drill: she'd say no more here, but there would be hell to pay later. However, he still had something in his arsenal. 'Jessie? What caterers?'

Unexpectedly, Ferdia glared at Johnny. Angrily he said, 'You're really doing this to her?'

'I'm entitled to know.'

Ferdia paused. His tone towards his stepfather had many layers. 'You? You're entitled to nothing.'

In Johnny's stomach, dread slithered, like eels.

Everyone else was still watching Jessie: did Superwoman really use caterers?

'We shouldn't be exposed to this,' Bridey said, in an undertone. 'We're children. It's inappropriate.'

Pinned by the collective gaze, Jessie's eyes flicked back and forth. She looked panicked. 'Yes, okay, yes!' She sounded exasperated. 'Sometimes. So what?'

'And that was the day my childhood ended,' Bridey murmured.

'How did you know?' Liam asked Cara.

'I used to do Jessie's accounts,' Cara said. 'A hefty payment to the Cookbook Café popped up each time we had another of these endless dinners. You don't need to be a rocket scientist—'

'I have five children, between eight and twenty-two!' Jessie cried. 'I run a business, there are only so many hours in the day and, Johnny, you're never here and—'

Cara stood up. 'I'd better go to the hospital,' she said. 'Before I fall out with every one of you. Come on, Ed.'

'Hey, Cara, do you *really* like my new hair?' eighteen-year-old Saoirse interrupted.

'Oh, sweetie, don't!' Cara said. 'You know I love you.'

'That means it's bad?'

'That fringe makes your face look like the moon.'

It did *make her face look like the moon! Cara was spot-on. All the same, you can't say that to a teenage girl.*

At Saoirse's devastated expression, Cara looked sick with remorse. 'I'm so sorry, Saoirse. But it'll grow back. Come on, Ed.'

'Before you go?' Liam's eyes were narrowed. 'Did you *really* think that massage I gave you was . . . What was the word you used?'

'"Dreamy"? No. I hated it. Forget being a masseur. You are *terrible*.'

'Hey!' Nell jumped in to defend her husband. 'He's doing his best.'

'Why are *you* bigging him up?' Cara asked.

Suddenly, Liam was energized. He smelt blood. 'Why wouldn't she back me up? Tell us, Cara, come on, tell us.'

'No, Cara.' Nell's voice was sharp.

'Tell me,' Liam ordered.

'Don't!' Nell said. 'Cara, it'll come back on you too.'

'Tell me.' Liam's tone was urgent.

Then, because Cara was concussed, confused and long past caring, she told them everything.

Six Months Earlier

APRIL

Easter in Kerry

One

Just after 7 a.m., Cara's internal line rang.

Oleksandr, the doorman, spoke. 'The eejit has landed. ETA three minutes.'

Cara turned to her trainee. 'Vihaan. Showtime.' She tugged at her skirt once more and ran a hand over her chignon. 'Remember—'

'Shadow you. Keep smiling. Say nothing.'

'Don't show any shock, no matter what he comes out with.'

'I'm *way* excited for this. I hope he's heinous.'

'Stop.' First Oleksandr being irreverent, now Vihaan. In this job, you shouldn't even *think* these things.

Flanked by Vihaan, Cara took her position, facing the front door, in the flower-filled lobby. She summoned her warmest smile and stepped forward. 'Welcome back to the Ardglass, Mr Fay.' Her welcome was sincere: she loved the hotel. 'I'm Cara Casey, and this is my assistant Vihaan—'

'I don't care what you're called, just take me to my room.'

'Certainly, sir.'

'Get my bags up to me. Now. Not in fifteen minutes. I mean *now*.'

Cara made urgent eye-contact with Anto the bellboy. *Go, go, go*. 'The elevator is this way, Mr Fay.'

In the elevator, Cara asked, in a deliberately soft voice, 'How was your journey here this morning?'

'Long. Tedious as fuck.'

'Where have you come—'

'Stop. Talking.'

Outside the suite, the electronic door key worked. The Ardglass keys always did, but sod's law would have had it failing today of all days.

'Welcome back to the McCafferty Suite,' Cara said.

Of the fifty-one rooms in the Ardglass, this suite on the third floor was her favourite: the long sash windows overlooking the leafy trees of

Fitzwilliam Square; the original Georgian coving; the bathroom with its claw-footed tub and underfloor heating . . .

'Here's your luggage!' Anto and his trolley hurtled in.

'The best hotel in Dublin,' Mr Fay said, sarcastically.

But it *was* the best: the best bed linen, the best food, the best spa. However, what elevated it above all the others was the service from its multicultural staff: intuitive and seamless, respectful but relaxed. Everyone, from skint honeymooners enjoying just one glorious night, to high-net-worth habitués of luxury hotels, was made to feel special.

'Where would you like your bags, Mr Fay?' Anto asked.

'Why don't you just stick them up your butt?'

'They wouldn't fit, sir.' Anto's shtick was cheeky Dublin humour.

'They'd fit up hers.' Billy Fay pointed at Cara. But as the burn landed, she'd already bundled the pain away, before she felt a thing.

Anto hurriedly heaved the suitcases onto the luggage rack, then scarpered.

Cara refreshed her smile. 'Although you've stayed here in the past, would you like me to explain the room's features to you again?'

'Just get out, you fat bitch.'

Vihaan gasped.

Cara would have to have a word with him later.

'Can we send anything up to you, Mr Fay? Coffee? Tea—'

'Like I said, get out and take your little Isis lapdog with you.'

'Certainly, sir.'

They left the room and headed for the back stairs.

'Wow. Ling wasn't wrong. He is the *worst*,' Vihaan muttered.

'He's been travelling for maybe eighteen hours. He's tired.'

'He made Ling cry last time. That's why you're in so early, right? You're the only one who can handle him? And what's he mean with the Isis thing? I'm *Hindu*.'

'Vihaan, sweetheart, no. Don't let him get to you.'

'And another thing! You're not fat!'

Their eyes locked, in sudden mirth. 'But,' he said, 'you *are* a—'

She tried to put her hand over his mouth. He wrestled himself away, both of them giddy from the release of all that tension. Still laughing, they came into the reception area.

'Bad?' Madelyn asked.

'Oh, yeah. I'm in Isis and—'

'I'm a fat bitch.'

After a furtive scan to check there were no guests around, they laughed away the remainder of the stress.

'So?' Madelyn interrupted. 'The competition winners, Mr and Mrs Roberts, their ETA is one o'clock. Which room have they been allocated?

'Not sure,' Cara said. 'I'll know when I see them.'

Now and again, in a radio phone-in, a lucky duo won a couple of nights in the Ardglass. They tended to be people who couldn't ordinarily afford a stay. Cara and her team got very excited on their behalf: they wanted them to experience the full wonder of the hotel.

'What do we know about them?'

They always did a discreet social-media search on expected guests to ensure that gaffes, such as gifting a complimentary bottle of champagne to a recovering alcoholic, didn't happen.

'Not much. Married couple. Paula and Dave Roberts. Mid-forties-ish. From a small town in County Laois. Looks like they have two teenagers.' Some competition winners were *totally* on for the penthouse. But others, unused to five-star hotels, were more relaxed in a regular room. But Cara never knew for absolute sure which way to go until she'd met them.

Two

One hundred and eighty kilometres away, in the Lough Lein hotel in County Kerry, Nell read from the laminated mini-bar list. 'Seven euro for a beer? Three euro for a can of Coke?' She paused, shocked. 'They're having a laugh. There was a Lidl by that last roundabout—we could buy stuff for, like, far less than this.'

Liam shrugged. 'No need. Have anything you want. Jessie's paying.'

'I don't feel okay about that.'

'Look, the cost of our room—all the rooms—will dwarf anyone's bar bill. Even yours. Anyway, Jessie doesn't judge. She's not like that.'

Nell considered how many rooms Jessie had booked and enumerated them on her fingers. 'Jessie and Johnny, Cara and Ed, you and me. Then there's the kids—Ferdia and . . . What's his buddy's name? Barty. Okay, them. Saoirse and Bridey. TJ and Dilly. Cara and Ed's pair. Is that all of us? I'm running out of fingers . . .'

'So, seven rooms. But she books way in advance and gets a discount.'

'Four nights, five-star hotel, the top floor, view of the lake, Easter weekend. Liam, they must be loaded.'

'She works hard. They both do.' They'd talked about this too much. It was starting to piss him off.

Without any real interest, he switched on the TV and speedily clicked his way through an afternoon chat show, a technicolour cartoon, a rugby match and a news report of desperate-seeming crowds, standing in the rain, behind coils of barbed wire . . . The camera focused on a small boy sitting on his father's shoulders, wearing what looked like a Tesco bag to protect his head from the downpour. Immediately Liam hit the off button—but it was too late, Nell had seen. 'Let's check out our balcony,' he said quickly.

He slid open the glass doors and stepped outside. To his relief, Nell followed. In silence, they leant on the railing, looking out over the muted navy blue of the lake and the craggy grey-green mountains on the far side. Three storeys below, in the grounds, shrieking children ran around.

'Beautiful, right?' Liam prompted. 'Very Instagrammable.'

'Ha-ha.' Nell reached for her phone and clicked off a flurry of shots. 'Yeah, it's stunning.'

'Now are you glad you came?'

'Hah! Like I had any choice.'

Liam shrugged. When Jessie issued her decrees, people tended to fall in.

It was five months since he'd married Nell. To begin with, Jessie had given them space, but in the last number of weeks, she'd invited them to several family events. Pressure had really been brought to bear for this weekend.

'I've litch never met a human with such a strong will,' Nell said.

'You're not exactly a pushover yourself. My money would be on you,' Liam said, and was relieved to see her smile.

Further along the corridor, Johnny was disappointed to discover that he and Jessie were billeted in a two-bedroomed suite, sharing with their two youngest daughters, TJ and Dilly. This weekend, he'd been hoping to have sex with Jessie, without fearing the sound of small feet running out of their bedroom and bursting into his.

A locked door was his idea of freedom.

But Jessie had said that Dilly was still too young. 'Maybe next year, when she's eight.'

'She'll be eight next month. And she's sharing with TJ. TJ's nine, she'll take care of her.'

'Shut it.'

Speaking of which, here came TJ, trailed by Dilly. 'Mum, I've unpacked my case. Applause, please.'

'You're a legend. It's more than your father has done.'

'Why would I,' Johnny said, 'when you do it so much better than me?'

'Do it, you lazy feck!' TJ said.

Johnny laughed. 'Wonder who she heard saying that.'

'It was Mum.'

'I know, hon. It was a rhetorical question.'

'What's that?'

'"Rhetorical" means it doesn't need an answer,' Bridey explained loftily.

Where had *she* come from?

'Your suite door was open,' Bridey said. 'You really need to be more careful. I could have been anyone.' She turned to TJ and Dilly. 'Right, kiddos. Let's inspect this room of yours.'

Johnny began to hang up his clothes. 'Bridey's bound to find some safety issue. She's a pain in the hole.'

'Johnny, no. Don't say that, she has ears like a bat. Anyway, that officious thing, she's only twelve, she'll grow out of it.'

He'd paused in his unpacking. 'I brought a *suit*? We're supposed to be *relaxing*.'

'Saturday night, we're having dinner in the fancy restaurant.'

'I don't want to wear a suit.'

'No one's making you. It's there if you want the option.'

Yeah, right. 'Okay, Mission Control, give me my schedule.'

'Tonight, casual dinner in the Brasserie, six thirty, nice and early. Afterwards the kids go to the movie and the rest of us have a few drinks. Tomorrow, Good Friday, day at leisure.'

That just meant she hadn't organized any big lunches or dinners. He'd still be made to go for a hike. Or to meet friends from Dublin who were also down in Kerry. And what was the point of that? They could see them at home any time. He was meant to be on a *break*.

'Tomorrow, people can get room service,' Jessie said. 'Have toasted sangers in the lobby, whatever they like.'

'Even go into Killarney for chips?' Bridey asked. She, along with TJ and Dilly, had shoaled back into the room.

Johnny could see that Jessie wasn't keen on that idea. She liked everyone on the premises, where they could be summoned at a moment's notice. If she could have made them wear electronic anklets she would have.

'Mum, Dad, are you aware that their window *opens*? Might I remind everyone, we're on the third floor?'

'It opens literally two inches,' Jessie said. Her phone beeped and she picked it up. 'No *fecking* way!'

'What's up?'

'Ferdia and Barty missed their train.'

'Pair of flakes.' TJ sounded uncannily like her mother.

'They were at some protest.' Jessie pressed buttons, then clamped her phone to her ear. 'Ferdia, what the hell?'

'Oh, yikes.' Dilly put her hands over her ears.

'Really? Well, listen—no! No. You are *not* bailing on this weekend. With rights come responsibilities. This is your family.' As she'd been speaking, she'd been clicking on her iPad. 'There's a train at one p.m. tomorrow, gets into Killarney at four forty-five. Be on it.' She ended the call.

Rancour lingered in the air.

Dilly asked, 'Mum, can Auntie Nell come out to play?'

Jessie shooed them away. 'Bridey, show her how to ring Liam and Nell's room.' She sat in uncharacteristic stillness, clearly mulling something over. 'Someone will have to collect that pair of eejits from the station tomorrow,' she said. 'Which might interfere with—'

'I thought tomorrow was "day at leisure"!'

'Yeah, but . . .' She flashed him a guilty grin. 'I was thinking . . . We've never done the jaunting car thing. At the Gap of Dunloe?'

'No, babes, no. Only American tourists do that.'

'It would be fun.'

'Jessie.' He abandoned his unpacking. 'The shame would end me.'

'We're making memories.'

'Seriously. I'll need therapy to recover from a memory like that.'

'Auntie Nell's here!' Dilly squealed from the hallway. 'And her hair is pink!'

Dilly dragged in her newest aunt. Nell's long thick hair was indeed pink, a pastel wash rather than a fluorescent eyesore.

'Oh, my God, you look amazing!' Jessie jumped to her feet. 'Not just the hair, but all of you!'

Nell wore loose navy overalls, Dr Martens and a scarf tied in a big bow on her head—she looked as if she'd been painting a shed. And perhaps she had. Her job involved building theatre sets, so Johnny found it difficult to distinguish between her work-wear and her normal get-up. Jessie, Johnny knew, approved strongly of Nell's look. She thought, as a family, it gave them 'texture'.

'Thank you for this . . .' Nell gestured awkwardly. 'Our room, this hotel. Liam and I could never stay somewhere so beautiful.'

'Oh, honey,' Jessie said. 'You're so welcome. We're all so happy you're here.'

'Thanks.' Her face flooded with colour.

'Can my hair be made pink?' Dilly asked.

'Probably not, bunny,' Jessie said. 'You're too dark.'

Seventeen-year-old Saoirse, twelve-year-old Bridey and nine-year-old TJ were Jessie mini-mes: tall and blonde. Dilly, the youngest, a solid little unit with tangled brown hair, was undeniably a Casey.

'Ooh! But what about you, Mum? Your hair is light. Get yours made pink!'

'I'd kill to look even a tenth as cool as Nell, but there are more chemicals in my hair than in the whole of North Korea. If I add anything else, it'll fall off in my hands.'

'Not to mention causing uproar at work,' Johnny said.

'Yeah.' She sighed. 'Oh, Nell! Listen, have you booked a spa treatment for this weekend?'

'Um, no . . .' Nell squirmed. 'I've never had a massage.'

'What? No! That's not right.'

Nell smiled. 'I dunno if it's my sort of thing.'

'Please, you must have one. Just charge it to the room. Oh, God.' Anxiety seized Jessie. 'They might all be booked out. We'll do it now. Johnny, ring down to the spa.'

'Don't,' Nell said. 'Please.'

Halfway to the phone, Johnny froze. Which woman was he more scared of?

He was saved by TJ. 'Are we going, or what?'

'Going,' Nell said. She, Bridey, TJ and Dilly hurried from the suite.

'Oh, Johnny.' Jessie was aghast. 'She's never had a massage.'

'She's thirty, a millennial. They've no money.'

'I know. Like, I *know*. But—'

'Get a hold of yourself! You're talking like she's never seen a banana. Carry on telling me the schedule for this "relaxed", "relaxing" weekend.'

'It *will* be relaxing!' She giggled. 'God, the state of me—the beatings will continue until morale improves, right?'

Three

At about one o'clock, a man and a woman, stiff with self-consciousness, advanced reluctantly into the Ardglass reception area. Cara hurried from behind the counter, wearing her biggest smile. 'Mr and Mrs Roberts?'

'Um. That's us.'

This was *definitely* not a penthouse situation. These poor people were terrified. Dave's suit had been cut for a younger, slimmer man and Paula's too-formal dress had probably been bought specially. The Ardglass's regular guests tended to breeze in dressed down in running shoes and unstructured athleisure wear, the muted tones and casual air belying hefty price tags.

Gently she guided the Robertses to a cluster of armchairs. 'Can I offer you coffee? Tea? A glass of champagne?'

'We don't want to be any trouble,' Dave said.

'It's no trouble at all. But we can have it sent to your room as soon as we've checked you in. We'll do that, will we?' She smiled again, desperately keen for them to enjoy this. The Honeymoon Suite was also a no-go, she decided. They'd likely be embarrassed by its sexy implications. But she wanted more for them than a regular room. Click, click, click, went her head, mentally scanning all the bookings over the next few days. 'Let me just get your check-in details.' She went to the reception counter and threw, out of the side of her mouth, 'Corrib Suite', at Madelyn.

'*Perfect*,' Madelyn breathed, and picked up the phone, straight into action.

Cara kept the Robertses talking while the Corrib Suite was quickly kitted out with champagne, flowers, handmade chocolates and a welcome card from Patience, the deputy manager.

High in the eaves, it was smaller than the other suites. The cream and pale gold décor of the sweet little sitting room was attractively cosy. The bedroom was bright, simple and straightforward—no four-poster complications to scare them.

Paula looked around. 'This is nice.' She seemed marginally less terrified.

'How about that cup of tea now?'

Paula scanned the room. 'Kettle?' she asked.

'The rooms don't have kettles,' Cara said. 'But anything you'd like, anything at all, just ring down.'

'Okay,' Paula said quickly.

Cara suspected she wouldn't. Paula and Dave were humble people who were more likely to try to sleep with every light in the room blazing than to bother someone to explain how to turn them off.

Cara rang for the tea, then said, 'Seriously. Those lads downstairs in room service need to be kept busy or else they'll be out of a job.'

Dave's attempt at a smile was more of a grimace.

'You won't be putting anyone out.' She directed this next bit at Paula. 'Let someone else wait on you for a change. I don't know about you, but I've two boys and I seem to spend my entire life standing at the hob, frying fish fingers.'

Was Paula starting to understand that there was a real person behind Cara's uniform and name badge?

'I feel as soon as they finish one meal,' Cara said, 'it's time for me to start cooking another.'

Now Paula smiled.

'I've been lucky enough to stay here a couple of times,' Cara said. 'It took me a while to relax. Then I got the hang of it. They really know how to take care of you—they *want* to do it. Now, let me show you the features of the room.'

She talked them through the lighting and the sound system. 'Room-service menu here. But basically they'll do anything you like, cheese on toast, curry chips, even if it's not listed.'

A knock on the door announced the arrival of the tea. As Gustav, the young uniformed waiter, delicately poured from the silver pot into the china cups, Dave hovered, as tense as a board, a fiver clutched in his fist.

At his first opportunity, he thrust the note at the boy and blurted, 'Thanks, son.'

'Thank *you*, sir,' Gustav murmured.

Dave turned away from him. He looked spent. And that wouldn't do. The Robertses seemed like big tea drinkers. If Dave had to go through that every time they wanted a cup, he'd be dead from the stress of tipping by the end of the day. Not to mention stony broke.

She was already formulating a solution when her internal line rang. It was Hannah the hair. 'Excuse me,' she said to Paula and Dave. 'I need to . . .'

Out in the corridor, she said, 'Hannah?'

'Cancellation. You want your hair blow-dried? Got to be right now, though.'

'You *serious*? What time is it? One thirty? I'm already off the clock! Be with you in ten. *Thank* you.' First, though, she raced down to the storeroom in the basement. 'Any spare kettles?' There were bound to be. All kinds of peculiar abandoned things lived there. A functioning kettle turned up in moments. In the kitchen, she assembled a tray with a silver teapot, a strainer, china cups, all the paraphernalia necessary to make tea, then hurried back up to the Corrib Suite.

Paula opened the door. 'Oh!'

'You can have all of this,' Cara said, 'if you promise to order everything else your heart desires.'

Then Dave appeared. They both looked so relieved she wanted to cry. 'Grand,' he said. 'We'll do that. Like, thanks.'

Downstairs, Cara cut across the garden to the glass and sandstone spa, where Hannah was waiting. Dressed in black combats and a black top, she looked more like a sniper than a hairdresser.

'You're not doing me a sneaky favour?' Cara asked suspiciously.

'Nah. Guest cancelled. Ten minutes' notice. They still get charged, I still get paid. Weekend away, you'll have a better time with good hair. Jump up there till I shampoo you. Get rid of—'

'That terrible chignon.'

'Yeah.'

'You're so right. Good hair makes everything better.' Cara brimmed with sudden levity, as Hannah massaged her skull. 'I've sort of been dreading this weekend.'

'Why's that? All those kids?'

'Ha-ha. No, but now that you mention it . . . My own two boys are the most amazing kids ever born. Like, *obvs.*' She joined in with Hannah's grim laughter. 'And their cousins are lovely. But . . .' It was the boredom she couldn't handle. Half an hour spent taking care of a gang of eight-year-olds and she began to panic. It made her desperate to dive into her phone but unable to fully surrender because, without her constant surveillance, one of the kids was likely to fall into a fire or break their leg jumping off a table.

At the mirror, Hannah switched on her hairdryer, with the same grim purpose as a person revving up a chainsaw. 'Boho waves do you?'

'God, anything. Yes.'

After the dryer, Hannah did some magic with a GHD. Cara watched as lengths of shiny, dark-brown waves tumbled around her face and wondered why she could never manage this at home.

But Hannah was a genius. She was so good at hair that the Ardglass management were prepared to overlook her less-than-sunny manner.

Finally, Hannah ran her fingers through Cara's waffle-like waves. 'There you go. Done.'

In the mirror, Cara's suddenly shiny hair was all messy, on-trend glamour. The rest of her really needed to up its game to be worthy of it. More make-up. Better clothes. 'You're *amazing*, Hannah.'

Hannah regarded her dispassionately. 'You look good. Breaks my heart that all your great hair is hidden in a *bullshit* chignon.'

'Look, I've nothing to give you—'

'Hey! You're my friend. I don't—'

'—right now. But I'll wine you on Tuesday.'

'Off you go. Don't kill any kids. Or do. It's your weekend.'

She put in her earbuds, found Michael Kiwanuka on her phone, and stepped out into the spring day.

Even though it was only two thirty, the Luas home was crowded, maybe because it was the Thursday of the Easter weekend and people were already knocking off.

She'd finished early because she'd started early. Her usual start time was 10 a.m. but today she'd come in at six to wrangle Billy Fay. They were good employers, the Ardglass, so it was only fair.

When she got home, the boys had to be fed—*more* fish fingers, *more* oven chips, *more* baked beans. Then Baxter needed to be dropped over to her parents before they started the drive to County Kerry. They'd get to the hotel just in time for dinner.

Her feelings about the upcoming weekend were decidedly mixed. On the one hand, four nights in the dreamy Lough Lein hotel: everyone—even people who, unlike Cara, weren't obsessed with hotels—would kill for less. On the other, Jessie and Johnny paying for all of them made her squirm. But on the third hand, Cara and Ed could never have afforded it and Jessie really *did* insist and—hey! A man had stood up: a precious seat had become free.

As she dived, so did another woman. Both had their hand on it, both had equal claim. They locked eyes in a silent battle of wills. Cara looked at her skinny-jeaned adversary. *I'm as deserving of that seat as you are*, she thought. *Right now I have the best hair in this entire city*. Then she remembered what Billy Fay had called her. *Fat bitch* . . .

An upsurge of self-loathing burst its banks and rushed through her every cell. She moved back into the jostling throng, surrendering the seat to the victor.

Four

'Oh!' Jessie's tone made Johnny pause.

'What?' he asked.

'That profile in the *Independent*. It's already up online. I wasn't expecting it for a couple of weeks . . .'

Shite. 'It'll be fine. Forward it to me.'

In silence they both read.

Jessie Parnell is late. By three minutes. She sweeps into the PiG Café, on full charm offensive: a finance meeting had overrun, parking had been tricky and she hopes I haven't been worried.

(A friend of mine has a theory about punctual people—they either have excellent manners or they're monstrous control freaks. I wonder which Parnell is? Perhaps both?)

Parnell is whippet-lean, tall, easily five nine or ten, and her fitted white coat is pristine. She looks rich. Probably because she is.

The success story of Parnell's International Grocer is familiar to Irish people. Back in 1996, Jessie Parnell, a fresh-faced 26-year-old from County Galway was just home from a holiday in Vietnam. A passionate cook in her spare time, she decided to recreate *gỏi cuốn*, a dish she'd fallen in love with there. But it proved impossible to source most of the ingredients in Dublin.

'These were pre-internet days,' she reminds me. 'Ireland wasn't multi-cultural the way it is now. If they didn't have the stuff in Super-Valu or Dunnes, you simply couldn't get it. I saw a gap in the market.'

It's everyone's dream: sitting at your kitchen table and coming up with an idea for a killer business. All the best ideas are simple ones, but maybe you need Parnell's dynamism to act on it.

'Around then, Irish people were starting to travel to the Far East, places like Thailand and Japan, and sampling what my dad would have called "food with notions". I felt they'd want to start cooking those cuisines.'

So how did she set up her business?

'I was working for a food export company, I'd met a few key people, so I knew where to source products.'

At the time, she had two years under her belt as a salesperson with Irish Dairy International.

Parnell getting a job with IDI was no mean feat: back then, their biggest customer was Saudi Arabia, who had a policy of not negotiating with women. In light of this, IDI had been reluctant to interview her.

But, according to Aaron Dillon, head of HR, as soon as Parnell walked through the door, he knew she was special. 'Full of energy and optimism, very much a team player. Always smiling, always sunny.'

(Photos from the time show a healthy-looking young woman with fair hair, freckles and big teeth. You couldn't call her beautiful, but she was bursting with vitality.)

'Not everyone liked her,' Aaron Dillon admitted. 'The word "pushy" was used, but I reckoned she'd go a long way.'

Two people who *did* like her were two men who began working for IDI that same year—Rory Kinsella and Johnny Casey, her first and second husbands respectively.

'That pair made a great team. Rory was the solid one and Johnny had the charm,' Aaron Dillon confirms. 'Both brilliant at their job.'

And both in love with Parnell, if the rumours are to be believed.

Parnell won't be drawn on that. But, as Johnny Casey has been quoted as saying, 'I was in love with her for her entire marriage to Rory', it's probably safe to say that they are.

Parnell drew up a business plan for her proposed business, which she cheerfully admits was a fiction. 'I did a five-year projection,' she laughs, 'but I had no idea if I'd survive the first month.'

Nevertheless, she must have talked a good game, because she got a bank loan.

'In fairness, in those particular days,' she reminds me, 'banks were very keen to lend.'

In late 1996 in a small shop-front on South Anne Street, Parnell's International Grocers opened their doors for trading. Much has always been made of the look of the store. Over the lintel, the old-fashioned mirrored sign with curlicued gold-leaf lettering looked simultaneously novel and as though it had always been there. Instantly, it guaranteed confidence.

Inside the store, Parnell featured recipe cards and cooking demos. The staff was knowledgeable about what to cook with those adorable little jars of Saigon cinnamon or Burmese salt-cured anchovies.

Of course, Irish customers paid a hefty premium for the privilege of buying these ingredients, which could have been picked up in the markets of Birmingham or Brick Lane for a tenth of the price.

Parnell is unapologetic. 'I was paying the carriage, the Customs duty, and I was taking all the risk.'

From the very moment it opened, PiG (as it quickly became known) enjoyed a brisk trade. From today's vantage point, it seems a no-brainer that Parnell's International Grocers would be a success—a newly sophisticated population, richer than at any other time in their history.

But Parnell says it was nothing of the sort. 'I'd given up my job to work full time on getting the business off the ground and my flat was my guarantee for the loan. I could have lost everything. I was petrified. It's an audacious thing to set up your own business. Plenty of people would have been happy to see me fail.'

When I demur, she's insistent. 'Not everyone likes an "ambitious" woman. When it's said about a man it's always in a good way. But a woman? Not so much. If I'd failed, the embarrassment would have been as painful as the financial loss.'

But she didn't fail. She insists—correctly—that a large factor in her success was timing.

In 1997, when she married Kinsella, the Cork branch was up and running. At this point, Kinsella left Irish Dairy International to work as a salesman for his wife's company and, less than a year later, Johnny Casey joined them.

By the early days of the new millennium, there were seven stores nationwide, three of them—Dublin, Malahide and Kilkenny—featuring cafés. During this time, barely seeming to break stride, Parnell also had two children: her only son Ferdia in 1998 and her eldest daughter Saoirse in 2002.

When the crash hit in 2008, PiG had sixteen outlets around the country, including a fine-dining restaurant next to the original site on South Anne Street.

In some circles, PiG was known as 'The Land That Recession Forgot'. But Parnell is quick to disabuse me. 'The recession hurt us, the way it hurt every business. Eight of our premises shut.'

The recession may have passed but the world has changed beyond all recognition since PiG first opened its doors. How has it remained relevant when the most obscure ingredient can be sourced on the internet and your local Centra stocks Scotch bonnet chillies?

'Very high-quality exotic fresh produce and diverse cuisines. In the last five months, we've showcased Uzbeki, Eritrean and Hawaiian food. We've also featured Gujarati cooking, instead of generic Indian, and Shandong instead of Chinese. And every launch is supported by the cookery school.'

Ah, yes, the cookery school, perhaps Parnell's greatest achievement. It's a mystery how she continues to woo highly strung, over-scheduled, big-name chefs to little old Dublin, but continue she does. In the last month, Francisco Madarona, the chef-patron of Oro Sucio on the Yucatan peninsula, did two days—immediately sold-out—of demos of his Modern Mayan cuisine. Considering that Oro Sucio is fully booked for the next eighteen months, this is quite an achievement.

So how did she manage to bag Francisco?

'I asked,' is her reply.

Hmm. I suspect it's not as simple as that. However, she has a unique combination of charm and dogged determination. It may not hurt that she's a very attractive woman. She's grown into her youthful toothiness, her hair is a sharply cut bob in an expensive-looking golden blonde and, considering she's forty-nine, her skin is flawless, not a wrinkle in sight.

She's refreshingly up-front about her forays into cosmetic surgery. 'No Botox, but I'm a devil for the laser. I got all my freckles lasered off—it hurt like you wouldn't believe but it was the happiest day of my life. Now and again I get the face zapped off me to stimulate collagen. Excruciating but no pain, no gain.'

Speaking of pain, experts agree that if she'd sold PiG in 2008—apparently three buyers with deep pockets made overtures mere weeks before the worldwide crash—she'd have made an eye-watering amount. But she turned them all down—too much of a control freak?

Or perhaps she's not motivated entirely by money. It's common knowledge that her staff are well taken care of. Which may explain, despite her reputation as 'a benign dictator', the almost cult-like loyalty she inspires among her employees.

It seems as if she lives a charmed existence, but we must remember that her first husband died when they were both only thirty-four. They'd been married less than seven years and had two young children.

Rory died of an aneurysm. 'It was so horribly sudden.' Her face clouds. 'I can't describe the shock.'

Since then, perhaps she finds it hard to trust that happiness will last? It would certainly explain her non-stop drive.

She has never spoken about when her relationship with Johnny Casey started. He was working for Parnell when Kinsella died, and she's credited Casey with keeping the business going during those months after her bereavement.

It was only when Parnell became pregnant with her third child, less than three years after the death of her first husband, that she went public with Casey. They married that same year, a low-key register office affair, compared to the 120-person extravaganza of her wedding with Kinsella.

According to several sources, Rory's parents and two sisters, Keeva and Izzy, have never forgiven her. They declined to contribute to this piece.

I ask Parnell what it's like working so closely with her (current) husband.

'Handy,' is her immediate answer. 'If something crops up about the business, I can address it there and then. I've been known to wake him in the middle of the night to ask if he's remembered to do something.'

Managing a demanding career with five children—how does she do it?

'With a huge amount of help. I've a housekeeper who comes in every weekday. He does the laundry, housework and after-school childcare.'

Hold up. '*He*'?

'Totally. Why not?'

You have to wonder why. This is the woman whose first husband was her employee, then her second. And she didn't take either of their names.

So how does she unwind? If ever?

'My kids and I pile into my bed and watch TV or just catch up. I'm all about family and I'm at my happiest when we're all squashed in there together. I adore children. I was nearly forty-two when I had Dilly. I'd have loved more but Johnny threatened to go for the snip.'

Without checking her phone, she knows when our allotted hour is up. I'm treated to a warm, fragrant hug, and then she's gone, click-clacking away in her pristine coat, changing the world.

'It's fine,' Johnny said.

'It's mean. Like, going on about my coat. It's only my North Face cold-weather thing—it's *practical*. It's only white because all the black ones in Large were gone. And I'm not "whippet-lean", I'm average-sized.' She flashed a trying-hard smile. 'And I'm *not* a control freak.'

Johnny raised an eyebrow. 'Babes . . .'

'Not in that way! He makes me sound like a monster! And I'm only five foot seven. Like, why has he exaggerated my height? And that thing about you being in love with me for my entire marriage!'

'I know.' Johnny had said it as a quip, a long time ago. But it was one of those things that was trotted out every time a new interview was done.

'Now it's treated as hard fact, like the moon landings. He makes me sound like a man-hating, two-timing, slutty, white-coat-wearing giantess-who-sleeps-with-chefs. And his shite-y attempt at psychoanalysing me, it's *pathetic*.'

'C'mon. Don't let it get to you. It's fine.' In fairness, he thought, it could have been a lot worse.

Five

Outside Newcastle West, with less than an hour to go, Ed suddenly said, 'Did we pack the Easter eggs for Jessie and Johnny? I don't remember putting them in.'

Cara laughed. 'Oh, *I* remember. It was such a relief to get them off the premises.'

For the past four days, seven hand-crafted artisanal Easter eggs had lurked in the garden shed, bought as paltry thanks to Johnny and Jessie for this weekend. None had been purchased for their own two boys, because they'd get so much chocolate over the next four days that it would surprise no one if they collapsed into a diabetic coma.

It was a matter of deep shame that she felt so conflicted about this upcoming weekend. What nobody would understand was that she found Easter nearly as bad as Christmas. So. Much. Food.

Even at home in her own house it was difficult, with all that sugar knocking about. But staying in a hotel, with Jessie at the helm, the next few days would be just one meal after another: giant breakfast buffets with an obscene array of irresistible choices, leisurely lunches featuring wine, then elaborate three-course dinners every night. Sometimes she joked to Ed that she wouldn't be surprised to be woken at 2 a.m. to be forcibly fed to ward off 'night starvation'.

She might be able to duck out of a couple of the lunches but Jessie liked big family get-togethers at dinner time. Attendance was borderline mandatory.

In addition to the many meals, sugar would be *everywhere*.

There was the giant egg hunt on Easter Sunday morning, where overexcited children swarmed through the grounds snatching Creme Eggs from hedgerows and flinging them into small buckets. (Last year Vinnie had found eleven and Tom got sixteen.) In addition, the hotel distributed full-sized eggs to everyone, adults and children alike.

As daunting as the tsunami of food was this weekend's compulsory sociability. She didn't want to see people. Or, rather, she didn't want people seeing her. She wished she could hide herself away until she was thin again.

'You're okay?' Ed asked, squeezing her knee.

'Fine.'

'You'd tell me if you weren't?'

'Course!'

He was a good man, the best. But she refused to offload on him because the boys—*and* Ed—were so happy. For the past month, Vinnie and Tom had talked of little else: the swimming pool, the kids' movies, hanging out with their cousins. They'd literally been crossing days off the calendar in the kitchen.

Bottom line, the next four days were precious and the least she could do was try to enjoy them.

'We have our own TV!' Vinnie yelled from the interconnecting room. 'Literally our own actual TV!'

'And our own key!' Tom raced into Cara and Ed's bedroom to wave the card at them, then scooted away again. 'We're grown-up now.'

You had to hand it to Jessie, Cara acknowledged. This was exactly the right age for the lads to have their own space. Vinnie was ten, Tom was eight: they were thrilled with their independence yet reassured by their proximity to herself and Ed.

'Nearly time for dinner,' Ed announced. 'This is your three-minute warning.'

Bracing herself, Cara stepped before the full-length mirror. This wrap dress was . . . grim. Even with the sucky-in underpants. But at least it fitted. Her jeans had cut into her for the entire drive from Dublin, a pain that was almost pleasant because it felt suitably punitive. She could have eased the discomfort by putting on her 'fat' jeans before they'd left, but that would have been like opening the floodgates.

And—her blood froze—what if the 'fat' ones were too tight?

Oh, those wonderful days at the start of the year when she'd quietly shed eleven pounds in six weeks! Being a long-term veteran of extreme eating plans, she knew a lot of that had been water. But she'd been in the groove, as if a switch had been flicked and she was in not-eating mode. Everything had stayed good until the evening of 13 February when the kids were in bed. Suddenly some sort of euphoria flooded through her, an ecstatic relief: it was reward time.

'Ed? Honey? Valentine's Day tomorrow. Did you get me chocolate to show you love me?'

'Yeah,' Ed said warily. 'You said it was okay.'

Poor Ed. He had no understanding of the civil war that raged inside her. Again and again she issued blanket bans on any sugar in the house. Sometimes she'd make Ed round everything up and throw it all out—it was too painful to do it herself. But maybe a day or a week later, she'd be pleading with him to give her whatever he'd saved because he'd learnt by now always to save something.

One time, when Ed was out, she'd gone into Vinnie's room and raided his stash. Her behaviour had horrified her: she was behaving like a drug addict, powerless to stop.

But she'd green-lit a Valentine's Day blow-out. Ed had been instructed to buy a big box of fancy chocolates, which she intended to devour without guilt. The plan had been to get right back up on the starvation horse on 15 February, but she'd found she couldn't.

The last eight weeks had been a series of lost battles. Every day had started full of resolve, but at some stage she'd have a narky customer *or* a moment of happiness that deserved to be celebrated and she'd eat something nice. Then she'd write the day off as a failure, deciding she might as well go wild and start again tomorrow.

But she *had* to be thin for the Easter weekend with Ed's family—there would be swimming, fancy dinners, lots of socializing. However, control eluded her and it was only five days ago that she'd finally managed a single sugar-free twenty-four hours.

It was too late. All the weight she'd lost in those quiet, cold January days she'd put back on. She was now almost a stone heavier than she'd been on that February night. She was horribly ashamed of herself. She'd have given her left leg to get out of this weekend—an illness, a migraine, anything would do.

There had even been a brief, insane moment when she wondered how a person broke their own ankle—it lasted an instant, barely a flash—but the flood of relief at the thought of hiding at home while everyone else went to Kerry was glorious.

'Time to go downstairs,' Ed said.

'I just need to . . .' She jiggled a mascara wand on her lashes.

'Honey, no need for any of that *grooming*.' Ed was in high spirits. 'This weekend is family. Relaxed.'

'I need to distract attention from my size.'

'Don't say that. You're beautiful.'

'You need your eyes examined.'

'And you need your head examined. Seeing as you're getting gussied up, should I make an effort?'

She laughed. Ed always looked messy, from his tangled curls to his five-year-old running shoes. 'You've found your look, you're working it, you're grand.'

Out in the corridor, she said, 'We'll take the stairs.' It would make no difference to her size, she knew that, but surely every little helps.

'No!' Vinnie and Tom clamoured. 'We want to go in the elevator.'

'Mum,' Tom was suddenly anxious, 'what if they put tomato on my burger?'

'We'll tell them not to, honeybun. We'll tell them two times.'

'Three times?'

'Three times.' And now fresh shame was in the mix. She worried about the lads being infected by her torment around food. Tom was finicky and small for his age, while Vinnie was far too fond of his grub and starting to look it.

In the restaurant, lots of Caseys were already milling around the long table. Cara found herself doing the Scan, where she automatically checked out the weight of every woman there. She wished she didn't.

Jessie looked the same as always. The thing about Jessie was, she was tall, and weight was always easier for tall people. Even so, you could tell she never gave her size a moment's notice.

And there was Saoirse. Seventeen years of age, the lucky girl had the same body-type as her mum: healthy and sporty but a long way from being skin and bone.

Paige, Liam's ex-wife, now *she*'d been skin and bone. Not scrawny, nothing as tacky as that, but fine-boned and elegantly narrow. The first time Cara had seen her tiny ribcage, prominent clavicles and pretty little face, she'd felt queasy with jealousy. But that had passed quickly. Despite her Very Important Job, repositioning the Irish arm of ParcelFast, Paige was touchingly open about her social anxiety. 'I'm no good at this,' she'd once confessed to Cara, at a party Jessie had forced them both to attend.

'But you're the woman who is "aggressively going after the DHL/Fedex market-share",' Cara had quoted at her. '"A force to be reckoned with".'

'I'm just a nerd. I do okay in work situations. But when I have to be me? Not so much.'

It had long been a mystery to Cara how Paige and Liam had lasted any time at all as a couple. Okay, they were both extremely good-looking, but Liam had lived an unconventional life and Paige was entirely by-the-book.

When they'd finally divorced, two years ago, Jessie had tried to keep Paige in the Casey orbit.

But Paige was so keen to consign Liam to her past that she'd found a new job in her native Atlanta shortly after, taking their two daughters with her. Jessie had been up in arms but forced to stand down when she discovered that Liam had agreed to this arrangement, in exchange for a rent-free apartment in Dublin.

Cara missed Paige—they all did, but Cara's sadness had been laced with a hefty dose of anxiety about what kind of woman Liam would produce next. What with Liam being so sexy, his new girl was bound to be a prestige version and prestige always meant thin. But Nell had surprised everyone. She was fresh and fun, and in no way glamorous. Nor was she a wisp: her hips and chest were curvy and she was almost as tall as Liam. Mind you, she also had a flat stomach, toned biceps and not a hint of cellulite . . .

'Jesus, Cara, your *hair*!' Jessie said. 'It's so sexy! You look great. And *don't* say that your dress hides a multitude. Just for once?'

'Ha-ha-ha. But this dress *does* hide a multitude.'

Saoirse had been listening to this exchange. Earnestly she said, 'I think you're beautiful.'

Cara tended to be intimidated by teenage girls—so shiny and Insta-ready. But Saoirse was sweet, with an innocence that made Cara suspect she was probably sniggered about by the more sophisticated girls in her class.

'Cara, you have dimples!' Saoirse declared. 'Who doesn't want dimples?'

'I'd prefer hip bones.' They shared a laugh.

'Wait till the menopause kicks in for me,' Jessie said. 'I'll be ginormous.'

Cara rolled her eyes. 'The menopause will be far too scared of you. You'll sail through it.' She sat and immediately Tom attached himself to her.

'Tom!' Jessie said. 'Hello, honey. You look so grown-up in your new glasses. What's that you're reading?'

'Harry Potter.'

'But you're only eight! You're so clever.'

'I'm bookish,' Tom said. 'That's just another word for "bad at hurling", but it's okay.'

'You're adorable,' Jessie said.

'That's one more word for "bad at hurling", isn't it?'

Jessie had moved her attention to Vinnie. 'How's Vinnie?' she asked. On the far side of the table, he was having a fork-jabbing competition with TJ. 'Vinnie? What's going on?'

'Vinnie!' Cara called. 'Jessie's talking to you.'

Surprised, Vinnie looked up. 'Hi, Auntie Jessie.'

'How are you, sweetie?'

'I have attention deficit, but it's not bad enough to be a disorder. And I set fire to a wooden crate in the field near the school.'

'Just testing his boundaries,' Tom said.

'That's all. And I won't do it again.'

Menus appeared on the table. Could she skip the starter? No, that would cause a medium-sized outcry. Okay, she'd have a Caesar salad—dressing on the side, skip the croutons. Basically that was only lettuce.

For the main course, maybe the fish. Protein was good. No potatoes, though. Potatoes were very bad. But she needed carbs: if she let herself get too hungry, there was a danger she'd binge later. Oh, God, here came baskets of bread. Bread was always a mistake: it lit a fire in her, making her crave *all the food* and stripping her of any power to resist.

'Look at you.' Jessie scanned the length of the table, all the kids from seven-year-old Dilly to seventeen-year-old Saoirse. 'Everyone's getting so grown-up!'

'We need more babies,' Johnny said. 'Fresh blood.'

'Don't look at me,' Cara said. 'I'm done.'

'And Nell won't, because of the state of the planet.' Liam flashed a smile at his wife. 'It'll be up to the next generation. How about it, Saoirse?'

'Stop!' Saoirse squealed. 'Anyway, Ferdia's older than me. Let him have the next Casey baby.'

'No!' Jessie actually went pale. 'No way. He's got his studies and—no. Just no.'

Pity the misfortunate woman that Ferdia brought home to meet his mammy, Cara thought.

Where was he, anyway?

'Missed the train.' Jessie sighed. 'The clown.' She rolled her eyes but her heart wasn't in it. She tried so hard to pretend that Ferdia wasn't her favourite child. 'While I think of it,' she said, 'is anyone free tomorrow afternoon around four thirty to collect Ferdia and Barty from Killarney station?'

'I'll do it,' Nell said, super-fast.

'Or I can,' Ed said.

'No, please, let me.' Nell was insistent and Cara understood. She was embarrassed by the money being spent on her this weekend and was attempting a—frankly, impossible—rebalancing of the scales.

Cara had been the same back in the day.

Jessie and Johnny had become an item around the same time as she'd met Ed. Very quickly, Jessie had begun inviting Ed and Cara to come along on their family holidays. But when they'd admitted that the costs were out of their reach, Jessie offered to subsidize them. They'd refused. The whole idea made them uneasy. Jessie didn't give up. Over and over she explained that as an only child she'd be getting more out of these family holidays than Ed and Cara. Jessie's generosity was sincerely meant but it didn't stop Cara doing whatever she could to show her gratitude.

Seven months earlier, an opportunity had presented itself. Johnny had made a chance remark about keeping track of their online purchasing. 'It's the returns,' he'd said. 'So much of Jessie's stuff goes back, but I keep forgetting to check if we were refunded.'

'Just set up a spreadsheet,' Cara had said. 'Easy. I can do it for you.'

'But wouldn't you need access to our emails?'

Johnny had misunderstood. Cara's offer was merely to set up a spreadsheet, not to track their online shopping.

'You'd need to come to the house to see them?' Johnny asked. 'Or could you access them remotely? How often could you do it?'

'Er, once a month?' She'd decided to go with this unexpected acceleration. 'But don't you mind me seeing all your financial stuff?'

'Course not! Jessie, come here! Cara's going to monitor—that's a lovely word, "monitor", very reassuring—our online buying. Making sure we get our money back for any returns.'

Jessie wasn't quite as delighted. 'Cara, don't judge me. I'm trigger-happy, especially late at night if I've been on the sauce, but most of the stuff goes back. I know the couriers cost money, but if I was to get in my car and drive to the shops, the cost to my time and the gas, well, it's probably better—'

'Stop. I won't do it if it makes you uncomfortable.'

Jessie had chewed her lip. 'Ah, it needs to be done.'

'It does.' Johnny was adamant.

'And you're family, Cara.'

After a couple of months when Cara had traced over a thousand euro in misdirected refunds, Jessie was fully on board. So much so that Johnny asked if she'd take on more work. 'Could you do monthly accounts for us? Just a breakdown of what we spend the money on. That way, we'll get a handle on where it all goes.'

The thought of discovering how much they earned and what they spent it on made Cara feel panicky. But how could she refuse?

'Ed says you do it for the four of you,' Johnny said. 'He says you're great.'

'I'm *not* great.' But she and Ed operated so close to the bone that rigid financial planning was vital. Conversely, Jessie and Johnny had *no* budgeting system.

'If the bank rings me,' Jessie had said. 'I know I've got to rein it in for a while.'

Jesus.

'Is that bad?' Jessie had added. 'It's just that I'm looking at figures all the time at work so I haven't got the energy for it at home.'

'And I'm useless,' Johnny had said.

Cara seriously doubted that.

'It's true,' Jessie said. 'All he's good for is talking. Buttering people up. Giving them guff.'

'Making deals,' Cara had tried to protest.

'Making people like me,' Johnny said. 'That's the sum total of what I do. Please, Cara.'

She had guilted herself into agreeing to a trial period of four months. But, as she said later to Ed, 'It feels far too personal. It's like watching them having sex.'

Ed snorted with laughter. 'Then just stop doing it, honey.'

'But they're so good to us. I'd been hoping for a chance to do something. Just . . . not this.'

Immediately Cara had seen that Johnny and Jessie spent more than they earned. Maybe they didn't even realize—but, thanks to their five credit cards and generous overdraft, all the plates kept spinning. When she'd completed the first month's figures, she'd advised that a cap on their outgoings was necessary. They nodded in solemn agreement—then completely disregarded what she'd said.

On the second month, she'd made another attempt, which they ignored just as they'd ignored the first.

On the third month, Jessie had jumped in: 'No need, Cara, we get it. Thing is, we had a few one-offs, which is why we looked overspent. But they're done now so the overspending will sort itself out.'

'Okay.' Cara was breathless with hope. 'So you'd like me to stop doing this?'

'Oh, God, no! The info could be very useful, if ever we need to see where the money is going. If you're okay to keep doing it, we'd like you to.'

Clearly Jessie thought that appearing to take responsibility was the same thing as actually doing so.

After wrestling with worry, Cara reminded herself that Jessie owned a successful business. The board she was accountable to consisted of just her and Johnny. Any time she liked, she could increase her own or Johnny's salary.

Or—Cara was hazy on this sort of thing—take money from the company's 'reserves'? Or get a personal loan based on the assets of the business? Either way, this was her chance to repay their generosity.

Six

Cara's dinner had been downright Winning at Life: no bread, no potatoes, no dessert.

Afterwards the five youngest kids began clamouring for 'Auntie Nell' to play football with them. 'Sure!' Nell said. 'Let me change into shorts.'

'And the rest of us will sit on the patio,' Jessie declared. 'Drink loads and pretend to watch them.'

But Cara was afraid of wine—not just the calories but how it weakened her resolve. However, *not* drinking simply wasn't an option—not around Jessie. 'It's nearly dark,' she said, but everyone was already making their way, with unseemly haste, to the patio.

'It's not,' Jessie said.

'Am I allowed a *drink*-drink?' Saoirse had tagged along.

'You're only seventeen,' Johnny said.

'You're not my father.'

'Jessie!' Johnny tried to hide behind his wife. 'Saoirse's Luke Skywalkering me again!'

Cara watched the three of them fall about laughing. It would be a different story if Ferdia were here. When he said stuff like that to Johnny he meant it.

'We know she drinks anyway,' Johnny said to Jessie. 'It's better if it's out in the open. Grab those chairs. Cara, what are you having?'

'Fizzy water.'

Jessie gasped.

Cara couldn't help laughing at Jessie's shock. 'I might as well have ordered stagnant rainwater served in a dirty bucket.'

'You'll have gin,' Jessie said. 'A large one. Medicinal. You're obviously not thinking straight.'

Nell, now wearing shorts, was back. Like the Pied Piper, she'd accumulated several more children, in addition to the Casey bunch. The game was on and all the kids—some of them young teenage boys—were giving it socks. Nell was a vision, racing and tackling, her pink hair flying.

No fake tan on her legs, Cara noticed, which meant her skin had a slight touch of the corned beef about it. And still she looked beautiful.

Jessie noticed Cara's gaze. 'Amazing, isn't she?' Jessie always brimmed with admiration for Nell. 'She's so natural.'

'"Pure"—that's what Liam says she is,' Saoirse chipped in.

'What?' Liam heard his name.

'Liam, Liam,' Saoirse begged. 'Tell us about the first time you saw Nell. I *loooooove* that story.'

'Ah, go on, Liam,' Jessie pressed. 'Tell us again.'

'Okay,' he said. 'I'll tell it.'

Seven

. . . Well, the rose-tinted version.

On a sunny evening last May, Liam was wandering the aisles in the Tesco near his apartment in Dublin's much sought-after Grand Canal Basin. A nameless restlessness bothered him, an uncomfortable, unidentifiable need.

A carton of vegan yoghurt caught his attention. This was good stuff, right? After skimming the ingredients list, he tossed the carton into his basket: he was willing to be convinced. A bottle of green juice, featuring spirulina, also made the cut. Maybe he could clean-eat his way to contentment. Briefly, hope spiked, then plummeted back to scratchy, bad-tempered yearning.

Nothing else on the shelves seemed promising so, more out of habit than anything else, he threw a six-pack of beer into his basket. Could it be the relentless humidity that was getting to him? Not very likely, but maybe if he took a shower, his second of the day, the restlessness would wash away. Better buy shower gel, in that case.

There was that feeling again, of freefalling.

It sucked, this single-life shit. For the last ten years Paige had taken care of all of his day-to-day stuff and now, whenever he bumped up against her absence, it was as if he'd stumbled. Maybe he could . . . Cycle down the coast? Text someone? Go home and sleep? Either way, being here wasn't fixing anything. He might as well just pay up and leave. Then he saw the girl.

She was tall, with a tumble of thick fair hair. Even before she took the strange step of opening one of the big glass freezers, moving forward, practically inside it, then simply standing there, letting the door bounce gently off her back, he was drawn to her. Leaning into the chilled air, she gathered her heavy fair hair onto the top of her head, revealing a neck that startled him with its perfection. He felt like he was the first person ever to have seen that part of her.

He stared and stared. Then, galvanized into action, he stepped over to the freezer, grabbed the door handle and pulled, sending a bloom of chilly air towards him. 'Excuse me,' he said.

She turned around. Her hair tumbled from the crown of her head to frame a face that was unexpectedly innocent. 'Oh!' Then she laughed. 'Just escaping the killer heat there for a few happy seconds.'

Oh, yeah. The heat. The whole country was buckling because it was twenty-five degrees. It was cute but a bit . . . pathetic? They should try cycling from Dublin to Istanbul at the height of summer.

And what was with her laughing? He could have wanted to buy whatever was in this freezer. Now that he looked, it was frozen chicken and, no, he wouldn't touch that processed crap, but she wasn't to know.

'Chicken nuggets and cold,' she said. 'A new spin on Netflix and chill.'

Her blithe good humour surprised him.

'Sorry.' She finally moved out of his way. 'You need to get in here?'

'No,' he said. 'No . . .' Well, who knew? *This* was what he'd been jonesing for. But even then, he was wondering how quickly he'd get bored of her. 'This might sound weird. But will you have a drink with me?'

'When?' She sounded startled.

'Now. Right now.'

'Right now, no. I've no money.'

'But I'll pay. I've money.' In his eagerness, he tripped over his words. Actually, strictly speaking, he didn't have *much* money. He kept forgetting.

She frowned. 'I could pay you back. When I get paid. But that mightn't be for a while.'

'You don't have to do that. I don't care.'

'But I do.'

Unsettled by her vehemence, he said, 'Okay. Grand. You can pay me back.'

Throngs were gathered outside the nearest pub, enjoying the freakishly hot May sunshine. The girl—Nell—asked to sit in the shade. 'I'll get burnt to a crisp without sunblock.'

'Put some on?'

'No, like, I don't *own* any. I'll get some when I'm paid.'

'Wow. Lot of stuff is going to happen when you're paid.'

'It'll be quite a day.' Her eyes sparkled.

'So? To drink?'

'Pint of Kopparbergs.'

'Ah.' He'd no problem with women drinking pints. He just wasn't used to it. 'Grand.' When he returned with the drinks, he asked, 'How come you're so skint?'

'Sticky income. High rent. The usual.' She flashed him a grin. Her two front teeth overlapped each other slightly. It gave her an odd pout that he found vulnerable and sexy.

'But don't you have cards?' he asked. 'While you're waiting to be paid?'

'I only use cash. Keeps me accountable.'

What did that even mean? 'What about the Bank of Mum and Dad?'

She laughed. 'My dad's a painter and decorator. My mum is a cook in a nursing home. They're nearly as skint as I am.'

'So this job of yours . . . ?'

'Set designer. For theatre, movies sometimes, TV, you know?' She paused. 'It's what I studied in college, but it's hard to get a . . . so I—I guess I intern.'

'They don't pay you?'

'Not always, not for—no, not for when I'm learning. But this is what I want to do with my life, my career. I love it, so I'm okay with taking the financial hit. At least for now. I was meant to have made it by thirty and I'll be thirty in November, you know . . .'

He nodded. Oh, he *knew.*

'But it's okay, I have my side-hustle!' She was upbeat again. 'I do house-painting and decorating. Except a lot of people don't trust a woman to do a good job.'

'That's crazy!' He threw a lot of outraged energy into his words. Hey, he could talk the woke talk, when required.

'But when they beat me down on price, they suddenly find they're good with a woman doing their decor.' Another of those crooked grins.

'So you hang wallpaper and go up ladders and hammer stuff?'

'Nails? Yep. And I'm handy with a staple-gun. *Love* me a chainsaw.'

Should he be impressed? Like, he *was*. But would saying so sound patronizing?

'My dad's been doing it for forty years,' she said. 'I learnt from the best.' Then, 'What about you? You look . . . You're someone, aren't you?'

'Hey, everyone's someone.' That was what he always said. Humble Liam.

'You're a bit famous?'

'Well . . .' He let the moment linger so the facts could assemble in her head.

She stared at him with narrowed eyes, until the silence became embarrassing. It shouldn't hurt. She was more than a decade younger than him, a different generation.

'I was a professional runner for a long time. Competed mostly in the States. Then I ran an ultra-marathon in the Sahara.' He really needed her to remember him.

'Oh, *yeaaaah*.' He watched as the memories dropped into place. 'You gave all your sponsorship cash to the Dublin Rape Crisis Centre. You're that guy, right? Wow. Hey, I'm sorry. For not recognizing you straight away.'

She was so sweet. The anxiety that had kept his chest in a chokehold for the longest time loosened.

'That was *such* a cool thing,' she said. 'Three years ago?'

'Five.' It was actually seven, but he needed to hold on to it, to keep him relevant.

'And you still run?'

'My knees blew out. The Sahara was my last big run. I went for broke, tried to make it count.'

'And you did! Raising all the money for such a good cause! But it must have hurt, your body stopping you doing what you love?'

'Mm.' Everything had been easy for him until then. He'd trained hard, met the right sponsors, enjoyed moderate success. 'In the early days, everything just got better and better. Then it sort of . . . plateaued, and it all started to fall away. I stopped winning, a sponsor dropped me, then another, until I was left with nothing. Being part of a slow ending is so fucking . . . *painful*.' It was a well-rehearsed speech. 'You know, it would have been easier if someone had just come in and said, "That's it, Liam. This is as good as it gets. You can stop right now or you can live through the next three and a half years of ever-decreasing returns and destroy your soul in the process." '

'But we don't get those choices, right? Things end,' she said. 'It always hurts. And now? You have a new passion?'

'I cycle. It's an obsession, almost. I'm part of a club. Last summer I cycled to Istanbul.'

'Class! And how do you, like, fund yourself? Did you have cash left from running?'

'Long gone. To be honest, there was never that much in the first place. No, I—I, ah, around the time I stopped winning races, I got married. She, Paige, has a—like, she gets paid a ton of money.' He managed a small smile. 'We've two kids. I wasn't qualified to do anything else, so I accidentally became a house-husband.'

'Re-*spect*!' She high-fived him.

He decided not to mention the nanny and the housekeeper who'd done all of the actual work. 'Not respect. Everyone judges me, my brothers, my parents. They say I stick at nothing.'

'You stuck at your running career for, what, eleven, twelve years? That's staying power. Now you cycle. Sounds like you're committed to that. You're married, you're sticking at—'

He shook his head. 'We split up last year. We're divorced. She's gone back to the States with the kids. So here I am at forty, all washed up, managing a bike shop. I've sustained nothing.'

'Not how it works.' She seemed very surprised. 'You lived one life for a while, another life before that. Now you're living out your passion for cycling. And at some stage you'll evolve to the next thing.'

This little speech had the effect of an epiphany. He and his brothers had had it drummed into them by their blowhard dad that they needed to dig into a straight-arrow career path. According to Canice Casey, you picked your gig early, you got onto the bottom rung of the ladder and gradually you climbed. Anything that deviated from that model counted as a failure.

Although Liam quietly despised that sort of thinking, it was difficult to shake off.

But this girl—woman, whatever she was—was offering a different way of looking at the world. A way that endorsed his choices.

'Another drink?' he asked. 'Please?'

'Seriously, no. I'm late on this month's rent. And I need to keep money for food.'

How could things be that bad? It sounded . . . *Dickensian.*

She saw his astonishment and laughed. 'That's twenty-first-century capitalism for you. People with degrees in the most developed countries on earth wish they could get work stacking shelves. But you're forty, a different generation, you're not going to get it.'

No, no, no, he couldn't have her thinking that. Quickly, he said, 'No, totally, I get it. Life is tough for twenty- and thirty-somethings. Like having to move back in with their parents?' Well, in *theory* iniquities happened, but he didn't believe in it on a big scale. Most people were grand. 'So what can be done?'

'I don't want to lecture you.'

'I'm interested.' Sort of.

'Okay, one of the things that perpetuates capitalism is built-in obsolescence.' She paused and asked solemnly, 'You know what that is?'

That tiny little twist of earnestness did for him.

'Everything we buy is built to break. So we buy new stuff. Or fashion changes and we think we have to buy the new thing even though the old thing still works. So if stuff breaks, I fix it.'

He'd never met a woman like her. He'd never met *anyone* like her. Was it his age? Or his circumstances, which, he admitted, weren't typical?

What pleased him profoundly was how different she was from Paige. They were literal opposites: Paige was the ultimate capitalist. Her sole purpose in life was to get people to spend more money, something she was so good at they'd made her CFO of a corporation.

'I don't buy new clothes—'

'Wait—what, you don't buy *clothes*?'

She giggled at his shock. 'I *do* buy clothes, just not new ones.'

'So you go where? To charity shops? Even for underwear?'

She coloured.

'Sorry.' He'd been inappropriate. 'I shouldn't have . . .'

He'd expected a smile to say he was forgiven. Even—maybe—a flirty remark along the lines that it was too soon for him to be talking about her knickers. But she had kept her head down and her mouth closed.

Eight

Nell, trailed by a clamour of kids, burst into the group of couches.

'We're just talking about you!' Saoirse said. 'About the night you and Liam met.'

'Oh, yeah.' Nell flashed a quick grin. 'That was *so* not what I'd been expecting.'

Saoirse focused on Ed, as if she'd only just considered that her uncle had once been young and single. 'What about you? How did you meet Cara? Tell us.'

'Yeah!' Liam insisted loudly. 'I told *my* stuff.'

'Do it!'

Cara and Ed shared a look: they'd go with the comedy version.

'I'll tell it,' Cara said. 'I met him in a bar.' Pause. 'I was drunk.' Longer pause. 'I slept with him on the first night.'

Solemnly, Ed said, '*Everything* that girls are told not to do.'

'Double standards,' Saoirse stuttered. 'Girls get slut-shamed but no one judges men.'

'But, hey, I married her.' Ed was laughing now. 'Slutty though she was.'

'Still together thirteen years later.'

Even now Cara's blood ran cold at the possibility that they might have missed each other.

She wasn't meant to go out that night. 'I'm too fat,' she'd called, as her flatmate Gabby fluttered around, getting ready.

'You're not fat. You're just not as thin as you were.'

'Can I wear your denim dress?' Erin, her other flatmate, asked.

'Wear what you like.' Cara was stretched along the couch, her feet comfortably up on the arm-rest. 'I'm going nowhere.'

But Gabby and Erin had kept at her. 'Life is for living! You'll never meet someone if you stay at home eating chips.'

'Who says I want to meet someone?'

'We all want to meet someone. Just stop picking bad boys.'

'I don't do it on purpose.' The bad boys she dated came in so many different guises that it had taken her years to identify that she actually had a type. Even when she tried going out with guys who seemed nice, sooner or later they always revealed their true nature.

'Oh, all right, I'll come. I'll be the sensible fat friend.'

In retrospect, she'd been far from fat. But until shortly before that night she'd been a lot thinner. It had been *glorious* but she'd slipped and slid, had a succession of breakouts and now her weight was on the increase again.

Until she was thin once more she deserved nothing, and this gave her a certain freedom. No one would take her seriously—certainly not a man—so the pressure was off. She was cool with being the chubby sidekick.

Their destination was a super-bar in the centre of Dublin. It was thronged with people, the roof lifting with pulsing music. *I'm getting too old for this.* The trio were swept and jostled by the constantly moving crowds until—hallelujah—a small, high table freed up and Cara pounced.

'Good job,' Gabby said. 'We've a base now. We'll be grand. Jesus, look at your man! Over there.' She flicked her eyes towards a huddle of four or five lads. 'Him.' One was conspicuously hot. 'How do I get to meet him?'

'Just go over and say hello,' Cara said.

'I'm not drunk enough. And by the time I am, he might be gone.'

'Hold my beer.' Cara was suddenly energized.

'Wait! What—what are you . . .'

Cara pushed her way through the people, scanned the five men and identified the one who looked least likely to mock her. 'Hey,' she said. 'My friend likes your friend.'

'It's him, isn't it?' The man nodded at the hot one. 'Kyle. It's always Kyle.'

'Yep. My friend is over there. We've a table.'

'A table? Right! We're in.'

Quickly, the five of them up-sticked over to Gabby and Erin. Introductions were made, drinks were bought. Kyle eventually wandered off, but Gabby didn't seem to mind. A couple of hours passed, and the next thing Cara knew, they were all leaving together, en route to a house party in Stoneybatter.

The small two-storey was crammed with people. Cara had just got a drink when a girl rushed into the kitchen and said, 'Is there someone here called Cara? You're needed upstairs.'

A girl had locked herself in the only bathroom, then passed out. A throng of desperate people were outside on the landing, banging on the door.

'Cara, thank God! This is tonight's designated sensible friend,' Gabby announced to the gathered crowd. 'Help us—she can't stay in there! We're all bursting.'

'And we need to know she's okay,' a male voice said.

It was the nice man who hadn't mocked her—Ed.

'What about the people who live here?' he asked.

But no one seemed to know who or where they were.

Cara said, 'I wonder if the bathroom window's big enough for someone to climb through?'

'We could see . . .'

The two of them went down the stairs and around to the back of the house. The small frosted bathroom window was illuminated—and slightly ajar.

'You'd fit through that,' Nice Ed said.

'I wouldn't—I've been on the pies. But you'd fit, skinny boy.'

'So? You want me to shin up a drainpipe?'

'We're not in an Enid Blyton book. Maybe there's a ladder.'

There *was* a ladder, in a miniature shed in the miniature garden. Together they carried it and leant it against the wall. 'Look.' Ed paused. 'I'm afraid of heights.'

'And I'm so hefty I'll break the rungs.'

'No, you're not.' Then, 'But, it's okay. I'll do it.'

He climbed up while she held the ladder steady. 'I've got you,' she called. 'You're safe.'

There were an anxious few moments as he knelt on the windowsill and clambered into the bathroom. The door was opened and the unconscious occupant was helped out. Then came the sound of sirens. Blue lights flashed in the night air and Cara exclaimed, 'Oh, my God, Nice Ed, it's the police!'

One of the neighbours had seen a person on the ladder and concluded that next door was being broken into.

Already many of the guests had melted away into the night.

The police called an ambulance and by the time the girl was ferried off, almost nobody was left, except Cara and Ed.

'Now what?' he asked.

'Now what, what?'

'You could come home with me?'

She looked at him. All of a sudden she was sober. 'Sorry.' She felt awkward. 'You're nice. I like bad boys. I should have outgrown it because I'm thirty now, but it hasn't happened.'

'You don't know the first thing about me,' he said. 'I'm actually a headcase. I get my kicks parading around my bedroom in a gimp mask and wrestling jocks.'

She laughed at that. 'Do you even know what a gimp mask is?'

'Okay.' He paused, seeming reluctant to give up. 'It was great meeting you, Cara.'

'You could come home with me?' She didn't know why. It was just that he was so nice.

In her bedroom she'd said, 'Nothing is going to happen. Like I said, you're not my type and I'm too sober.'

'Sure.' He shrugged super-casually and said, 'We can just hang out.' They both laughed at the cliché. 'Is it okay if I lie on your bed? On top of the covers? I'll take my boots off but it doesn't mean anything sinister.'

'Okay. I'll do it too.'

They lay on their backs, several inches of empty space between them.

'So,' he said, 'you were very proactive tonight. Ladders and that. How come?'

'Maybe because of my job—I work in hospitality. Reservations manager at the Spring Street Hotel. I'm always having to sort out dramas.' Almost sheepishly, she added, 'I won an award last year.'

'For what?'

'I don't know if it's something to be proud of it. For achieving 101 per cent occupancy.'

'Isn't that technically impossible?'

'Everyone thinks you check in at three and check out at twelve. But lots of people check in at, say, midnight, or leave at six a.m. If you keep an eye on who's coming and going, you can turn the same room over more than once in twenty-four hours.'

'So the hotel is over-booked?'

'Management policy in my place. In lots of hotels.'

'What if people arrive at the right time to check in and there's literally no room for them?'

'Promise them an upgrade, send them away with a voucher for a free lunch and ask them to come back in an hour.'

'And if they're pissed-off?'

'They're right to be. I'm very nice to them. Except,' she added quickly, 'I'm not faking it. Just because I'm good at what I do doesn't mean I'm cool with it.'

'That must be hard, working in a way you disapprove of. Cognitive dissonance.'

'Oh, my God, Nice Ed, you don't know the half of it! Anyway, soon some whizz will write a piece of software to do it all automatically and my moment of glory will come to an end.'

'So why do you keep doing it?'

'Holding all that information in my head, shifting things around, finding efficient solutions? I guess I enjoy it. What do you . . . Have you a job?'

'Botanist.'

'A tree-hugger?'

'A scientist.'

'Really? Wow.' He seemed too sincere, too normal, to be a scientist. Mind you, how many scientists did she know? 'Hey, we should get some sleep.'

An awkward pause followed. They were lying on the bed, fully clothed. What was the protocol here?

'You're interfering with my night-time routine,' she said. 'I listen to a guided meditation. To build self-esteem.'

'Work away.'

'Maybe not tonight.'

Another awkward pause followed, and this one lasted.

Into the silence he said, 'I'm not skinny.'

'Exsqueeze me?' She turned her face to his.

'Earlier you called me skinny. But I'm just lean. Muscle, plenty of it.'

That made her smile.

'I had to do a medical for my job. They measured me with a machine. I'm thirty-one per cent muscle. That's quite a lot.'

A ball of warmth radiated from her stomach. He was so cute.

'I could take off my shirt and show you?'

Suddenly the air between them had become thick and charged. 'Okay,' she managed to say. 'Okay, go on, then.'

In the morning, she said, 'You're still here!'

Oddly, he seemed better-looking now than he had last night, an entire reversal of her usual experience. His messy hair, his smoky-grey eyes, his unexpectedly sexy mouth, things she hadn't at first noticed because she'd been blinded by his aura of niceness.

'I wondered if you'd be a curtain wiper,' Cara said. 'It's a name me and my friends have for, you know, a man who tiptoes out in the middle of the night, with his jocks in his pocket and, as a final insult, wipes his lad on the curtains. They're my usual.'

'I could do it now?'

That was funny—and suddenly she didn't want to go through it all again: falling for a man, feeling hope bloom, only for it to turn sour and sad.

'What?' He was watching her face.

'I have form. I keep picking bad boys. But I'm burnt out. So do me a favour, do one good act in your terrible life and leave me alone.'

'I'm one of the good guys. You said it yourself! You kept calling me Nice Ed.'

'But I don't fancy nice guys. And I fancy you. So please hop it.'

'I'm on good terms with all my ex-girlfriends,' he offered. 'Not that there are that many,' he added quickly. 'Just a normal amount. And only ever one at a time. I've never cheated on anyone. I'm a—'

'Please leave.'

'Oh. Okay.'

Paradoxically it was his obedience that persuaded her to take a chance on him. 'All right, you can stay if you answer my questions. What's your worst trait as a boyfriend?'

He gave it serious thought. 'Probably money. My job, it's a niche thing. I'll never be a high earner, and I'm good with that. I love what I do. But my last girlfriend, Maxie, it made her angry that I wasn't more ambitious.'

'What else?'

'I don't care about clothes. Sometimes I wear stuff my brothers are throwing out. I've had one or two complaints on that score.'

'You're a botanist, you said? Does that mean you love the outdoors?'

'Yes! I love hiking and camping and . . . No? You hate it?'

'*Hate* it.'

'I love the indoors too. I love a lot of things.'

'So you mentioned you've brothers?'

'I've two. They're both . . . you know . . . The eldest, Johnny—'

'How much older?'

'Three years. Three and a bit. A successful salesman who never stops talking. One hilarious story after another.'

'Oh, I know the type! Says your name six times a sentence? Accumulates people, knows bars that never close—if you're on an evening out with him, you'll have the best night of your life and you'll need a week in hospital to recover?'

Ed lay back on the pillow and laughed loudly. He sounded delighted but also, Cara thought, relieved.

'And is he one of those—how do I put it delicately?—gnarly-looking, butty Irish men who still manage to get the girls?'

'Nah-ah . . . Everyone says he's a "total ride".'

'Photo?'

Ed flicked until he found one.

Cara stared. Johnny had expensively cut chestnut-brown hair, lush eyelashes, a scattering of freckles and a great big smile. He could have been an estate agent, or a junior politician. 'Like a more groomed—*much* more groomed, in fairness—better-fed version of you.' She let that settle, then gave a sidelong smile. 'Which must mean you're a total ride too.'

'But with Johnny you notice it. You're blinded by it. *And* your ears are bleeding from the funny stories. He's a one-man weapon of mass destruction, and even when he's giving you alcohol poisoning, you still love him.'

This guy is hilarious, Cara thought. He's *lovely*. In that moment, she felt pure happiness.

'And your other brother?'

'Liam. Liam Casey. The runner.'

Oh, my good God.

Even people who had no interest whatsoever in athletics knew about Liam Casey. No one cared that he was only averagely talented and rarely won any of his international races. With his dishevelled dark-blond hair and his sly-eyed, saucy smile, he'd become a household name in Ireland. If Johnny was 'a total ride', he had *nothing* on sexy, swaggery Liam.

Cripes, no wonder Ed felt like Mr Unimportant, sandwiched between a charm monster and a sex god.

'So you get on with your brothers? You like them?'

'Most of the time. Liam is, well, you know . . . Here's this guy and he's an athlete, he's movie-star handsome and it's hard for him not to be affected by that. He kinda thinks life is always going to be good to him, but there's nothing wrong with that. Then Johnny's my big brother. He's got the chat and the charm and he's decent. Maybe not always, because nobody is all the time, but, growing up, he was my hero. He sort of still is.'

‘Right.’

‘They take the piss out of me, the two of them. Because I know the Latin name for plants—like I *have* to for my job—they call me Ordinarius Hominis. It’s Latin for—’

‘“Ordinary man”, yep, I guessed.’

But they were wrong, she was beginning to realize. Ed wasn’t ordinary. Unassuming, maybe, but he was far from ordinary.

Nine

Nell was woken by a ringing phone.

'Good morning, Nell,' Dilly said. 'It's Easter Friday and time for breakfast. TJ, Bridey and I will pick you up in five. Liam can come too.'

'What?' Liam asked sleepily.

'Dilly and her crew are on their way.'

'Grand.' He sat up and rubbed his eyes, while she hurtled towards the shower, then threw on her boiler suit.

Downstairs, the breakfast room was huge and geared up for big groups. Many tables were set to seat twenty or more, all covered with blinding white cloths.

Jessie, Johnny and Saoirse were at a twelve-seater.

'Ed, Cara and the boys are on their way,' Jessie said. 'So, you can order from the menu,' she said to Nell, 'or you can help yourself from the buffet.'

'She *knows*,' TJ said.

Gently, Liam said, 'It's her first time here.'

'Where was she all the other years?' Dilly was confused.

'You'll understand when you're older.'

'Come on, we'll show you how the buffet works,' Bridey said.

Gratefully, Nell stood up. Her in-laws seemed sound, but they were much older than her and lived very different lives. The only ones she felt properly comfortable with were the kids.

'I want to hold her hand!' Dilly complained.

'I wasn't holding her hand, I was *leading* her,' Bridey countered. 'Anyway, she has two hands.'

'Tray.' TJ handed one to Nell.

'*I* wanted to give her her tray,' Dilly said.

'You snooze, you lose.'

My God, all this food. Nell had seen breakfast buffets before but never a wonderland like this.

'That's the fruit,' TJ said. 'We don't bother with that. *Obviously*. There's cheese and ham—that's for the Germans.'

'Smoked salmon and capers here,' Bridey said. 'No. Clue. Why. All along there is the disgusting stuff, sausages, black pudding, horrific. You can skip it—'

'—because these are the best things.' TJ led her to a waffle machine. 'Waffles and pancakes. You can have Nutella or maple syrup—'

'Or both!' Dilly said.

'Then you come back for Coco Pops. But best of all . . .' They pulled Nell to a counter, which sported a mesmerizing array of mini-pastries. The smell alone was heady stuff.

'Excuse me.' A woman tapped her on the shoulder.

Nell, released from the pastry spell, turned around. 'Yes?'

'The toaster is broken, you need to fix it.'

'I can . . . Well, I can take a look . . .'

'But don't you work here?' The woman gestured at Nell's boiler suit.

'No. But I can still take a look.'

'Oh! I'm so sorry.' The woman backed away and collided with a man who was holding the fullest plate of fried food Nell had ever seen. 'I thought you were a mechanic.'

The three girls set up a clamour. 'What did the lady want?'

'For me to fix the toaster.'

'Because you wear man's clothes?' TJ exclaimed. 'That's why I do too. So people know you can do stuff.'

Bridey abandoned her tray, keen to be the first back to the table with the story. Dilly and TJ were hot on her heels, so Nell decided to go too. By then Ed, Cara, Vinnie and Tom had arrived, and the story of Nell's mistaken identity made everyone laugh and laugh.

'So she said, "I thought you were a mechanic"!'

'Then the lady banged into a man and his rashers went all over the floor.'

'He was pretending he wasn't cross, but he was *raging*!'

'And a bit of his black pudding plopped into the big bowl of yoghurt.'

'It was *so* funny.'

Liam was the only one who didn't seem delighted.

Johnny kept making the girls repeat lines. 'TJ, say again, "The toaster is broken. You need to fix it."'

TJ obliged, then Johnny said, 'Now you, Nell.'

'So I said, all doubtful, like, "*Weeell*, I can take a look."'

'The funny thing is,' Jessie said, 'Nell probably *could* have fixed the toaster.'

'Ah, no, electrics aren't my thing.'

'But you'd have *tried*,' Ed said, and that triggered another outbreak of laughter.

'Okay,' Bridey said. 'We need to eat. C'mon, kiddos, c'mon, Nell.'

Fifteen minutes later, Jessie said, 'Killjoy Central here, but our jaunting car awaits.'

'Pray for us,' Johnny said. 'I envy you. All you lot are doing is climbing a mountain.'

'Your packed lunches will be at the front desk,' Jessie said. 'And, Nell, you won't forget to pick up Ferdia and Barty from the station?'

'Course not.'

'You'll be back in time from your climb?' She directed this at Ed.

'Yeah. It's only Torc we're doing. Four hours tops.'

Off they went. Ed unfolded a map—Nell was starting to understand that Ed was a great man for maps, probably because of his outdoorsy job—and consulted Liam on a route.

'These all done?' A waiter began taking away abandoned crockery. He indicated several small plates bearing half-eaten Danish pastries. 'This?'

That was the thing about buffets: people got overexcited and took too much food. It was only human. But when Nell thought about Kassandra and Perla, the waste felt painful.

Nell had met them at a bus stop, in the cold of mid-January. A dark little girl, crying quiet, oddly dignified tears, stood with her mother.

'Are you cold?' Already Nell was unwinding her scarf.

'She's hungry,' her mother Perla said. 'It was fish for dinner tonight. It makes her sick.'

'Can't you have something else?' Nell asked Kassandra.

No, she couldn't. Nell extracted their story. They were asylum-seekers. War had ousted them from Syria, and they'd come to Ireland, hoping for refugee status. But until that was—or wasn't—granted, they had a non-person status. They shared a hostel with other broken, displaced people, from the worst parts of the world. There was no privacy. A single bathroom did for seventeen people. Visitors weren't permitted. Meals were provided by a central kitchen. The quality was poor and choice was non-existent.

When Nell enquired delicately about money, she discovered that Perla got thirty-nine euro a week from the government and Kassandra got thirty.

'Out of this we must buy clothing, medicine, schoolbooks for Kassandra, everything,' Perla said. 'I want to work, but I am forbidden.'

Nell gave her the nineteen euro in her pocket, got Perla's number and arrived home to Liam in tears. Their situation seemed overwhelmingly bad. Nell had no idea how she could help, but she knew she had to try. The world would only improve if everyone made an effort.

Since then, they'd stayed in touch. Nell had little to offer in the way of material things but she did her best to be a friend.

Ten

The Dublin train chugged the last few yards into Killarney station.

'Wake up.' Ferdia nudged Barty. 'We're here.'

Ferdia, a lanky beanpole with a docker beanie pulled low over his hair, stood up, and gave his bag in the overhead shelf a whack so that it rolled off, landing neatly in his arms.

'Do mine as well, fam.' Barty was a shorter, more compact version of Ferdia. Even his hat and loose stevedore-style jeans were almost identical to Ferdia's.

Ferdia passed the bag to Barty, then asked, 'You and me? Are we good?'

Barty had been pissed-off with Ferdia for making them miss yesterday's train—all because Ferdia had wanted to be at a protest. Barty was perpetually skint and really enjoyed his once-yearly weekend in the fancy hotel. 'Ah, yeah.' He shrugged. 'Watch me pack four days' eating and drinking into three.'

Tons of people were getting off. The Good Friday crowds were out in force.

'Mum said Nell was coming to pick us up,' Ferdia said.

'Liam's new wife? What's she like?'

'Dunno. I've barely met her.' Ferdia spotted a woman in overalls. 'That's her.'

'Your woman with the hair? *Wow.* Nothing like Paige, right? Like, wow!'

'And shut up now. Nell! Hey.' Ferdia grabbed her shoulders and gave an awkward half-hug. 'Barty, meet Nell. My aunt. Sort of?' he asked Nell.

'I guess. By marriage.'

'If Johnny was my dad. Which he's not.' He flashed a nervous smile. 'So, Nell, this is Barty, my cousin. He's my dad—you know, my dead dad's sister's son. Keeva's son.'

'Got it.'

'You're quick.' Barty gazed in open admiration.

'Over here.' Nell strode to the car. The boys threw their bags into the trunk, Barty jumped into the passenger seat and Nell reversed out in a smooth curve.

Don't say anything, Ferdia thought. But—of *course*—Barty piped up, 'You drive like a boss.'

Cringe. Nell was old. And married to his step-uncle. No way should Barty be . . . whatever he was doing. Hitting on her?

'Should be a good weekend.' Barty was being such a dick. A *jaunty* dick. 'Looking forward to it.'

'I'm not,' Ferdia said. 'But Mum would tear me a new one if I bailed.'

'I get it,' Nell said. 'You're a grown-up, you don't want to do kids' stuff.'

Wait! What, was she . . . *patronizing* him? Stung, he needed a moment. 'It's nothing to do with going on an Easter-egg hunt. I don't want to be here because I don't approve.'

Nell said nothing, so he told her anyway. 'All that money. It's wrong. Every one of us has a roof over our head.'

'*Ferd*,' Barty muttered.

'Yet we're spending money—okay, not me, I admit—to stay under another roof while there's a housing crisis in this country.'

'Mmm.' Her eyes met his in the rear-view.

'You don't agree?'

'Ferdia, here's the sitch: when your sister-in-law takes you away for an all-expenses-paid weekend, her son throws shade and wants you to pile on?' She gave a little laugh. 'Awkward.'

'So? With four nights' bed and breakfast, and as much chocolate as you can eat, she bought your complicity. *Okaaaay*.'

Their eyes met once again, hers blank, his fierce, and the rest of the short journey passed in silence.

Ferdia's hopes were to avoid his family for as long as possible. But Jessie and Johnny were milling about in the lobby with the four kids, obviously just back from an outing.

'Perfect timing,' Saoirse called.

Jessie lit up. 'Bunny, you're here!' She grabbed him in a hug.

'Mum, don't call me that.' He was embarrassed that Nell was hearing this.

'You'll always be my bunny. Bunny number one.' She smiled at his jacket, his hat, his heavy boots. 'You look like you're off to the waterfront to unload cargo from a ship.

'And so do you, love.' Jessie had moved on to Barty. 'Thank you for coming. We're all so happy you're here.' Next she hugged Nell. 'Thank you for picking them up.'

Dilly flung herself at Ferdia and he lifted her into his arms. 'Hello, missus!'

'We went on a jaunting car! Daddy hated it!'

'Daddy did hate it,' Johnny said.

'He said it was the worst day of his life.' TJ leant against Ferdia.

'It was cold,' Bridey said. 'And *soooooo* boring.'

'Any safety lapses to report?' Ferdia asked.

'No seatbelts in the jaunting car. But,' Bridey conceded, 'we weren't going fast enough to do any real damage.'

'That's what I like about you, Bridey, you're fair. She calls it as she sees it but gives credit when it's due.'

Bridey pinkened. 'Thanks.'

'Nice work, "missing" yesterday's train,' Johnny said. 'You were spared the day from Hell.'

'Ah, stop.' Jessie was laughing. 'It wasn't so bad—and what's that they say about life? We only regret the things we don't do.'

Ferdia noticed Nell hovering awkwardly on the edge of the group, excluded from their well-worn familiarity. *Just leave*, he thought. *What are you waiting for?*

Jessie clasped Nell around her waist. 'Look how handsome Ferdia is. Once he fills out, he'll be lethal. And isn't his little beard lovely?'

'Mum.' Ferdia didn't know who was more embarrassed, him or Nell.

'Speaking of which, Mr Lethal,' Saoirse said, 'your girlfriend is here.'

Sammie was here? His heart leapt. Had she decided they weren't breaking up after all? But how did she get here before he had?

'The fake-ass one from last year,' Saoirse said. 'With the bougie accent.'

Ferdia looked at Barty and together they said, 'Phoebe?'

Phoebe had been both the high and low spots of last Easter. She'd been in the thick of a big family group. A few years older than the other kids with her, she was obviously at the hotel under sufferance, just like Ferdia.

At the family dinner on the first evening, she was at a similarly long, rowdy table. She looked up, did a second take, and held Ferdia's stare long enough to make her intentions clear. An hour later, when he was taking Dilly to the movie at the kids' club, Phoebe was removing a small boy, who was wailing his head off. Another long, loaded look was shared.

Ferdia and Sammie were on yet another of their breaks so, heartsore and defiant, he'd decided he might as well salve his wounds with this girl. Her name had been easy to find out—you had only to listen to what her sisters were calling her. And, yeah, her accent, as she answered them, was slightly affected. But she was *cute*, with long russet-coloured hair, bold brown eyes and, as Barty *kept* saying, 'A rocking bod.'

After bribing TJ to ask one of the younger members of Phoebe's group their surname, Ferdia found her on Instagram. But the account was private. Nor could he find her on Snapchat, not without her username.

He requested a follow on Instagram, but despite the electricity that snapped between them, nothing happened.

'Maybe she'll show up later at the boat-house.'

It was traditionally the place where teenagers congregated for furtive late-night drinking sessions. Ferdia and Barty had emptied their mini-bar of alcohol and taken it to the lake. Though they'd stayed there until 2 a.m., smoking joints and talking shite, she didn't appear.

The next day Ferdia was glued to his phone, moving around to make sure he had a signal. But even though Phoebe smouldered at him in real life, across the lobby and again in the swimming pool, there was no response to his follow request.

It took until Easter Saturday night, before it clicked. 'She hasn't got a phone!'

'You be high.'

'Serious. I've never seen her looking at her phone. She hasn't got one.'

Barty was astounded. 'What are they? Amish?'

'Doing exams soon.'

In the weeks before the Leaving Cert, parents frequently deprived their children of their phones to keep their minds focused.

'That's why she hasn't shown up at the boat-house. She's under curfew.'

'So how are you going to meet her?' Barty asked. 'Send a raven? Get Saoirse to befriend her? Some girly thing? They could talk about periods and stuff.'

'Me?' Saoirse's voice wobbled. 'You ignore me all weekend to stalk that bougie ho—'

'Don't call her a ho.'

'– and now you want me to be your pimp?' She sounded like she might cry. 'Dream on, assholes.'

After an uncomfortable silence, Ferdia said, 'Saoirsh. Sorry. I, ah, yeah, eye off the ball. Forgot about you. A bit. Sorry.'

'You think *I* want to be here? Watching *Frozen* twenty times? Sharing a room with Bridey? Do you know? I haven't had one drink since we got here and I'm *sixteen*.'

'Our bad.' Barty and Ferdia were full of remorse. 'Totally, like.'

Eleven

A bit shook, Nell let herself into her room. Liam was stretched out on the bed, listening to something on his phone.

'They were actually on the train?' He took off his headphones. 'Thank Christ. I think poor Jessie would have driven back to Dublin and physically bundled Ferdia into the car if he hadn't come.'

'He's here now.' She unlaced her Converse and kicked them off. 'Listen, what's Ferdia's deal? He was very judgey. About us being here when there's a housing crisis. I was *dying*.'

'What d'he say?'

She stopped. Bad idea, bitching, especially about family. 'No, forget it. It was just a surprise. He's been grand the other times I've met him.'

Although when had that been? Jessie's New Year's Eve piss-up? The St Patrick's Day party? Where there had been so many rowdy people that she and Ferdia had barely said hello.

'He's an eejit,' Liam declared. 'Spoilt little fucker. And Barty's worse. I think Barty's an actual card-carrying cretin.'

'Liam.' She gave a guilty laugh. 'You can't say that word.'

'But he is. And a total mini-Ferdia. Every time Ferdia gets new ink or a new anything, Barty copies him. Check out the rings they both wear.'

Her phone buzzed. 'Oh! Email,' she said. 'Oh! Liam, it's . . .' Quickly, she scanned it and turned a wide-eyed face to him. 'Liam, I got it! The gig! The show at the Playhouse.'

'Oh? The one about time?'

'*Timer*. Yeah.'

'Wow.' He seemed stunned. 'That's—that's amazing. How much money?'

'Feck-all. But I don't care. This is my first time being head designer. They trust me, Liam! They liked my ideas! We must celebrate. How long before dinner?'

'About an hour.'

'Just long enough.' Looking him dead in the eye, she unzipped her boiler-suit a couple of inches.

His whole demeanour changed, becoming still and alert. 'Like that, is it?'

'*Totally* like that.'

With supple grace, he unfolded himself from the bed, crossed the room and wrapped his hands around her waist. Softly he said, 'Hello.'

'Hel*lo*.'

He cupped his hands around her face. 'You are so, so beautiful.' Her hands fumbled open his jeans and they steered their way to the bed . . .

Their doorbell buzzed frantically, accompanied by open-handed slaps on the wood. 'Open up, open up!' girls' voices commanded.

'What the hell?'

'Ignore them,' Nell begged.

'We know you're in there!' The ringing and slapping continued.

Wide-eyed, they stared at each other, as the mood trickled away.

'You'll want to see this!' someone—probably TJ—yelled.

Admitting defeat, Nell leant her forehead against Liam's. 'Later? You decent?'

'Just about.'

As soon as she opened the door, the ball of energy that was Dilly, TJ and Bridey hurtled towards her. 'Nell, come quickly! You too, Liam, if you want. We're spying on Ferdia's new girlfriend. The one from last year. She's out on her balcony!'

'Wait for me.' Liam tugged his T-shirt down over his jeans.

Bridey looked scandalized. 'Were you two . . . ? That's disgusting! Wash your hands.'

'There's no time!' Dilly was about to explode with impatience.

'Where are we going?' Nell asked.

'Mum's room,' Bridey said. 'Ferdia came up to borrow a charger—'

'—because,' TJ interjected, 'he'd forget his arse if it wasn't stapled to him.'

'His mind is on higher things!' Dilly was shrill. 'That boy is a genius. Saoirse came too.' They'd arrived at Jessie's suite. 'Then she saw the bougie ho on her balcony.'

Saoirse greeted them at the door. 'She's still out there!'

Nell hurried in after the three kids and Liam.

'So this is some girl from last year?' Liam lunged for Jessie and Johnny's balcony.

'Hold on!' Ferdia grabbed him. 'Be cool about this. You and me,' Ferdia took Liam by the shoulders, 'we step onto the balcony, real casual, like. Then look over at the rooms at right-angles to ours. One floor below. Act, like, *relaxed*.'

'But Nell's the one we went to get!'

Ferdia turned, in annoyance. 'Why don't we *all* go out for a gawk?'

Three young women, in bathrobes and sunglasses, were lounging on a balcony. One was painting her toenails and the other two were on their screens. Short comments were being exchanged.

'Which one?' Liam asked.

'The middle one.'

Even from a distance, Phoebe was the obvious alpha. Nell focused on her some more and, as if suddenly aware of the scrutiny, the girl looked up.

She lowered her sunglasses, saw Ferdia, stared long and hard, then abruptly flicked her sunglasses back into place and turned away.

Blushing furiously, Ferdia retreated into the room. 'Thanks a million, Nell. That was fucking embarrassing. You couldn't have been more obvious if you'd tried.'

'Hey!' Liam said.

Ferdia glared at Liam, then at Nell, then at Jessie. 'Fuck this shit,' he declared, and stalked from the suite, banging the door behind him.

Nell was mortified. 'I'm so sorry.'

'No, no, you did nothing wrong,' said Jessie.

'We should just . . .' Liam said, leading Nell to the door. 'We'll see you at dinner.'

'Thirty minutes.' Jessie's voice was shaky.

Out in the corridor, Nell said, 'Liam, baby, I'm really sorry.'

'Not your fault that Ferdia's a spoilt prick.'

Johnny fumed quietly. Fecking Ferdia. At the hotel for less than an hour and already he'd upset Jessie and Dilly. And Nell. He'd *better* turn up to dinner.

And what was he up to with this balcony girl? He already had a girlfriend! Everyone liked Sammie. She *looked* unapproachable, with her heavy boots and shorn hair, but she was very pleasant.

Herself and Ferdia were probably on another of their breaks. The pair of them carried on like Burton and Taylor: big emotional shouting matches down in Ferdia's flat that could be heard clearly up in the house, followed a few days later by a loved-up reunion. It had been entertaining for several months, but now even Johnny was worn out by it.

Several subdued minutes later, Jessie said, 'Okay, gang, we'll go down now.'

'There's something I need to do,' Johnny said. 'I'll be with you in a minute.'

Jessie was too downcast to ask what the 'something' was. Which was just as well, because he wanted a quick look at the comments beneath the profile on Jessie. Simply keeping an eye on how bad they were.

Red Blooded Male
'JESSIE PARNELLS A BALLBREAKING MANH8R'
Bring Back Hanging
'Over-priced shite for the sheeple in Dublin 4.'
Justice For Men
'Whippet thin? Shes bleeden huge.'
Fat Attack
'All the same, I would.'
Justice for Men
'Youd get up on a cracked plate shes a MINGER a right auld DOG'
Dublin Massive
'how she getting them chefs to Dublin? servicing them?'
Fat Attack
'I'd take a servicing from her.'
Justice for Men
'Cracked plate my friend. For his sake I hope that husband of hers is getting it somewhere else.'
Red Blooded Male
'COURSE HE IS ONLY HAVE 2 LOOK AT THE FLASH FUCK 2 NO HES GOT A FEW BIRDS STASHED AWAY PROBABLY WORKING FOR HIM BE A FUCKING FOOL NOT 2'
Death to Feminazis
'Rumours he's a bit of a shagger. Don't fucking blame him. She'd have your balls on a plate, that one.'
Mighty White
'She promotes Islam'
Fat Attack
'Didn't no that'

Mighty White
'Selling halal food. And there filthy spices. If they couldnt bye there filthy food in Ireland, they'd hafta fuck off back home to towel-headStan.'
Paddy Flys Away
'I met her once. She was over-nice. Fake.'

Johnny exhaled. Just the usual bile. He'd told Jessie never to read these and she said she didn't, but who knew?

Ferdia had stomped back to his room and raged at Barty for several minutes about Nell making a show of him.

'But you know your family,' Barty had said. 'They'd have kept going out and staring like mentallers until Phoebe noticed.'

'I just feel mortified that she saw me standing there, with tons of other people, like a stalker weirdo.'

'Did plenty of staring of her own last year. And, hey, least now she knows you're here. Has she a phone this time?'

'She does. I saw it.' He drummed his fingers against his lips. His embarrassed fury was dissolving.

'I sorta feel bad now about blowing up at Nell. She wasn't deliberately . . . I don't think she was trying to mess things up.'

'Yeh, look. You were a bit rough on her in the car too. You're all riled up about the housing stuff, but it's not her fault.'

Nell had got him at a bad time. It really bothered him that his mum was spending all this money when kids were literally sleeping on floors.

'Who knows?' Barty said. 'Maybe Nell doesn't even want to be here.'

'Maybe. I could, I dunno . . . say sorry to her?'

Ferdia never apologized to adults—well he never apologized to Jessie or Johnny. They already controlled so much that he couldn't surrender any more of himself. But Nell wasn't really an adult. Or maybe she wasn't really a member of the family. 'What if she tells me to piss off?'

'She won't. She's lovely.'

'Ha-ha-ha. You fool. Just because you fancy her. Okay. It's time. Let's go.'

In the restaurant, the others were already there. Before he lost his nerve, Ferdia went directly to Nell. 'May I speak with you? I apologize. For swearing. And blaming you. I was just embarrassed.'

She smiled. 'That's okay, Ferdia.'

His relief felt like sunlight. 'And for being narky in the car. Sorry about that too.'

'It never happened.'

'So we're good?'

'We're good.'

Turning to sit down, his phone vibrated in his pocket. He took a look. It was a follow request from Phoebe.

'Bart!' He showed him the screen. 'This thing is *on.*'

Twelve

'Down for the weekend?' Dominique, the massage therapist, led Jessie through the dimly lit corridors.

'With my family. They're hiking around Lough Dan today.'

'And you're having a bit of me-time. Very wise.' She led Jessie into a fragrant room. 'Take a seat. Have you any special concerns?'

'I have horrible feet.'

'I'm sure they're grand. I mean, how would you like to feel after the massage? Detoxed? Relaxed?'

'Relaxed. I guess.' But if she relaxed, who would take care of everything? After Rory had died, when she'd gone for bereavement therapy, the woman had said, 'You think you've to keep the planet turning.' But she'd always been that way. It was impossible to delegate because she felt she could do everything better and faster than anyone else.

The massage was under way. 'You really are quite tense.'

Which is why I'm getting a massage.

'The knots in your neck . . .' Dominique made it sound as if Jessie had tied them deliberately.

Or maybe she was being touchy and unreasonable? She'd a lot on her mind. That article had unsettled her. The implication that she'd been sleeping with Johnny when she'd still been with Rory: why did almost every interview bring it up?

She *could* issue a statement saying she'd never cheated on Rory, but she was entitled to a private life. And, anyway, it was ancient history now. Besides, the people who mattered most to her in this—Rory's parents, Michael and Ellen, and his two sisters, Keeva and Izzy—would never believe her.

As soon as something had started with Johnny, she should have told them. But she'd persuaded herself that nothing was really going on. It was only when she got pregnant with Bridey that she'd had to 'fess up—but by then it was too late.

That was thirteen years ago. She could see now that she must have been jelly-brained with love to think the Kinsellas would be happy for them. She'd hurt them badly and she was far from proud of it. Mercifully, the estrangement didn't extend to Ferdia and Saoirse, who had a close, loving relationship with their Kinsella grandparents, aunties and cousins. Even so, back when the kids were still young enough to need dropping off and picking up, Ellen and Michael quietly, without announcement, always enlisted another adult as a go-between, so that whenever Jessie knocked on the Kinsella door, it was invariably opened by a neighbour or an in-law. Michael and Ellen had gone to a good deal of trouble to avoid seeing her or Johnny.

These days, Ferdia and Saoirse were old enough to make their own way. Jessie thought if she ever did bump into any Kinsellas now that they'd be civil to each other. In the aftermath of that massive row, someone she suspected was her ex-sister-in-law, Izzy, had left a few savage online reviews of PiG. But that had stopped a long time ago. Other than Rory, the Kinsella she'd missed most was Izzy. She'd been her best friend, her soulmate almost. She'd loved Keeva too—both of Rory's sisters had been her bridesmaids because she had no sisters of her own—but Izzy was the special one.

Even now, remembering the confrontation with Izzy, as she took in Jessie's swollen stomach, was like a knife in the guts. 'You're pregnant?' she'd whispered. 'It's Johnny's?' She'd cried her eyes out. 'Rory is gone. You've taken everything and we have nothing.' That terrible day had ended with Izzy yelling, 'You never really loved Rory.'

Which was nuts. She'd been *mad* about tender-hearted Rory.

Okay, Johnny had managed to give the impression that if she was interested, then so was he . . . It was quite a skill, promising something without ever actually committing. And, yes, it had given her a flutter. Was that so bad? Throughout school and university she'd been a freckly nerd—no one had fancied her! And Johnny had been so sexy, so in demand . . . To have *two* men, both after her, had been exciting . . .

Maybe the only reason that Johnny was interested was because his best friend had her. But still. The important thing was she hadn't encouraged it. It was Rory who'd persuaded Johnny to come and work for Parnell International Grocers, insisting he'd be a great asset.

If she were to live her life again, she'd still choose Rory all those years ago. He'd been much more her type—he'd been *reliable*. While Johnny had always seemed just . . . well . . . ever so slightly slippery . . .

But Rory had died, which had hardly been a reliable thing to do. And, despite everything, she'd ended up with maybe-ever-so-slightly-slippery Johnny, so who knew anything?

Thirteen

'The legs are walked off us,' Bridey complained. 'There should be a law against making children exercise too much.'

Silently Nell agreed. It had been a lovely day: the lake had sparkled, the packed lunch from the hotel had included mini bottles of wine, but the temperature had dropped, she'd spent the last hour carrying Dilly on her shoulders and she was tired.

'We're nearly back at the cars,' Johnny said.

'If we were working in a movie, we'd have been allowed a break *hours* ago,' Bridey persisted.

'Oh, shut up!' TJ burst out. 'You're only twelve but you talk like an old woman!'

'They'd have had twins of each of you to do half the walk,' Nell said.

'They would!' Tom was very charmed by this.

'You'd be sitting in your trailer now and your twin would be doing this last bit.'

'There's the parking lot!'

'Finally.'

A squabble—yet another—broke out over who got to sit beside Nell in Johnny's people-carrier. Refereeing their on-going bickering was hard work.

Johnny's people-carrier swung into the hotel parking lot and countless Caseys tumbled out.

'Let's wait for Vinnie and Tom.'

Seconds later, Ed's car arrived. Car doors opened and slammed shut.

'Uncle Liam,' Bridey said, 'let's FaceTime Violet and Lenore! We can pretend they're here.'

'Okay.' Liam cut his eyes at Nell.

This was her cue to leg it.

She'd wanted a relationship with his daughters, but he'd quashed that hope. 'It's too hard for them. They're upset enough by the divorce . . .'

She'd met the girls in person just once, on a speedy visit to Atlanta last October, for Liam to tell them he was getting married again.

'They should at least clap eyes on me,' Nell had said.

'It won't be pleasant . . .'

It wasn't. Ten-year-old Violet had reacted with fury and seven-year-old Lenore was confused and tearful. Nell sensed they all just needed to get to know each other but Liam was having none of it.

'Nell? Where're you going?' Bridey sounded confused. 'You're their stepmum!'

'It's okay,' Liam said. 'Nell doesn't need to be here.'

'But—'

Unexpectedly, Cara spoke up. 'There's so many of us, we'd only get in the way.' She took Nell's arm. 'See you guys in a while.'

Nell let herself be pulled towards the lobby. 'Thanks.'

'No bother.' Cara gave a quick smile and relief stole through Nell.

'Liam tries to protect them,' Nell explained. 'His girls, I mean. It's hard for them that he got married again. He thinks it's better if they don't see me.'

'Okay.'

'He's got to do what's best for them. But I'm being selfish. I feel bad because I'm not going to have kids. I really love them, but the planet, you know?'

'Well, fair play to you.'

As they waited for the elevator, Cara said, 'Fancy restaurant tonight. Time to break out the Gucci.'

'*What?* Oh! You're joking! Jesus, my heart!'

'Sorry!' Cara said, and they laughed.

'You *will* get used to this,' Cara said. 'In time. It took me *aaaa*ges but, yeah, what clothes to wear, everything.'

'So what *should* I wear tonight?'

'A dress. Have you one?'

'I borrowed two. My friend Wanda, we used to share a house, she works in costume design.' She paused. 'Listen, can I show them to you? Have you a minute?'

Cara followed Nell into the room. One glance at the beaded black gown was enough. 'Too formal.'

'So there's this.' Nell produced an off-the-shoulder sheath with a zip that ran from the back of the neck to the hem.

'That's *beautiful*,' Cara breathed. 'Put it on.'

Nell hastened to the bathroom, wriggled into it and returned, plucking at the fabric, weirded out by something so tight.

Cara looked stunned. 'Nell! You utter *goddess*. And that aubergine colour goes so perfectly with your hair . . .'

'There's a "but".' Nell was anxious. 'Not suitable for a family resort?'

'That. You're *waaaay* too hot. Anything more casual?'

'Yeah, but . . .'

Nell's brand of casual wasn't cutting it. As well as the request to fix the toaster, her boiler suits were generating *looks*. Children flocked to her, attracted by her pink hair but confused by her masculine clothes.

'I've this?' Nell produced a dark-blue cotton box-shaped shift. It was a couple of sizes too big, but it had cost only four euro in Oxfam.

'Put it on.' Then, as Nell appeared in it, 'Oh, wow. So *cool*. That's the one. Shoes?' She dismissed the borrowed high heels and fell on Nell's red Converse. 'These! You look amazing. Okay, see you at dinner!'

The lock clicked—Liam was back.

'How are they?' Nell asked.

He was always upset after talking to his kids. 'Okay. I think. Hard to tell, really.'

'Liam, will it ever be okay for me to try to get to know them?'

'How do I know? But did you want to corrupt their happy memories of past Easters, in the thick of their cousins, by hogging FaceTime today?'

'I just meant—sorry. Sorry.' She kept getting things wrong. It was so important that the Caseys liked her but she'd already had that blow-up with Ferdia. He'd apologized, he'd acted normal on the walk today, but it was a reminder that she didn't know these people, or how to behave with them.

'Listen, get ready,' Liam said. 'It's nearly time to eat.'

'I'm ready.'

Liam stared. 'That's what you're wearing? That—what is it, anyway?—giant shirt?'

It hurt. It hurt, it hurt, it hurt.

'It's got a hospital vibe. You look like a nurse.'

'And not a sexy one, right?' She flashed her teeth. 'But, wait, it gets worse, you haven't seen the back.' She pirouetted, displaying the line of buttons that went the entire length. 'It's more like those gowns for when you're having an operation where your bum is hanging out.'

It worked. He laughed.

At first glance you wouldn't think Liam had a taste for expensive threads: his look was low-key and muted. But when you drilled down, you discovered that his knackered-looking black joggers had cashmere in the mix and his anonymous tops were pure merino wool.

It was time to remind him who he'd married. 'Liam, I love beautiful things—I'd love a truckload of new clothes. Getting them second-hand, it's all a bit shit. I know it's a pain, me and my principles. Seriously, I get on my *own* nerves, but I'm not doing it to be sneery.'

'Yeah, I know, baby. I'm sorry.'

In the eleven months she'd known him, he'd never been this uptight. Up to now, almost none of their time had been spent with his brothers. Even their wedding had been family-free. Usually Liam was fun and wildly spontaneous. Their life was a million miles from five-star hotels, and they jumped on any opportunity for adventure. There had been an impetuous weekend in Tallinn. Another in Madrid, where they'd spent two days in the Prado. On 23 December, Liam had chanced on rock-bottom flights to Namibia, leaving the following morning. A frantic afternoon was spent racing around, borrowing camping gear and booking a jeep. By Christmas night they'd been drinking duty-free gin and gazing awestruck at the constellations of stars in the empty desert sky.

In the formal dining room, Jessie rushed at Nell. 'Your dress!'

God, had she messed up big-time?

'Acne?' Jessie said. 'No, don't tell me. Filippa K? One of the Swedish designers? I *adore* that oversized look.'

'Oxfam,' Liam said. 'Probably an ex-hospital gown. If this dress could talk, well, the haemorrhoid operations we'd be hearing about.'

Jessie tuned him out. 'You're stunning.' She spoke directly to Nell. 'You make everything your own. I wish I had your confidence.'

'Bougie ho alert,' Saoirse muttered.

Alpha Phoebe swished past in a Zadig & Voltaire dress with fraying seams and a fashionably torn hem. Nell *coveted* that brand. In her dream scenario, their entire collection somehow ended up in her local charity shop. She slid a look at Liam, who nodded meaningfully at Phoebe. Should she take it to heart? No. Instead she hit him a covert whack and took her seat at the table.

'Now, about tomorrow,' Jessie said. 'I know I'm a control freak and that you all call me Herr Kommandant, but the Easter-egg hunt means a lot to me. Please, could everyone be there? It would make me very happy.'

Ed, Cara, Liam, Nell, even Saoirse and Barty were in agreement.

'Ferdia?' Jessie tried to catch his eye. 'Please.'

'Yeah. Yep.' His laugh was slightly weary.

Ferdia's phone lit up—the message he'd been hoping for. 'Bart,' he muttered. 'Sorry, like, but I'll be needing the room tonight. I don't know how long for . . .'

'Phoebe? Grand. I'll just hang out by the lake, in the cold, in the dark, on my own.'

'Sorry her sister is so young . . .'

Barty shrugged. 'Not my type.'

Hopefully, Ferdia asked, 'Is *anyone* here your type?' If he could hook Barty up, he wouldn't feel so bad.

'I'd take Nell, if you were offering. She's hot.'

Ferdia shrank back. 'Bart . . . She's so not. And she's married to my uncle.'

'Step-uncle.'

'The important part is that she's married.'

'Relax, Ferd.' Barty grinned. 'I'm just fucking with you.'

But what was this . . . almost . . . *conspiracy* that Nell was amazing? He'd overheard his mum and Cara talking earlier about a visible razor nick on Nell's knee. 'If that happened to me,' Cara was saying, 'I'd have to get into the car and drive all the way back to Dublin.'

'She's so capable,' Jessie this time, 'with that job of hers. But so beautiful and wild. And her clothes! Fabulous! I never know what to expect.'

Jessie's non-stop love for Nell's clothes was weird. Was it patronizing, trying to avoid the truth that Nell looked poor? Or was it out of fear? Middle-class Jessie had no frame of reference for someone like Nell, so if she kept insisting how cool Nell was, no one would guess she was actually confused by her?

Fourteen

Phoebe showed up around midnight. Ferdia had been right about last year: her parents had taken her phone because she'd been repeating her Leaving Cert. Now she was first-year UCD, studying law and business.

'I'm in Trinity,' he said. 'Third-year economics and sociology.'

'Trinity. Wow. You in rooms?'

'Got my own place.'

She looked sceptical. It was rare for a third-level student in Dublin to live away from home. 'Where exactly is your own place?'

'Foxrock.'

'And your family live where?'

'Foxrock.'

'So you *do* live at home!'

Her triumph made him laugh. 'It's a mews *near* my folks but it's totally my apartment.' No need to mention that it had been Nana Parnell's granny flat until she'd died and the décor was still old-lady chic. Or that it was at the bottom of the garden, close enough to the main house so that when he and Sammie were yelling at each other, Bridey often appeared, requesting that he stop with his 'anti-social behaviour'.

Phoebe picked up his right hand. 'What's with all the rings, Ferdia Kinsella?'

'There's only four. You make me sound like Lil Yachty.'

'Tell me about this.' She was focused on the hammered silver wrap on his thumb. 'What do these numbers mean?'

'Map coordinates for the place in Kildare my dad came from.'

'Nice. And this one? Looks like something that fell off a tractor!'

'Close.' It was a chunky aluminium nut that TJ and Bridey had found under Jessie's car. Having tried to scratch an inscription into it with a sewing needle, they'd presented it to Ferdia in a formal ceremony, asking that he commit to always being their brother. But he wasn't telling Phoebe that. She'd probably scoff.

'Don't you care about all these tats on your hands?' she asked. 'Like, when you're interviewing for a job?'

'I wouldn't want to work for a place that judged me on them.'

'Principles? You're hilaire. So, you planning on setting up on your own? Making a fortune like your mum?'

Ferdia laughed, a little hopelessly. 'No.'

'You're studying what? Economics and sociology? Economics I get, but sociology? *Why?*'

Because he'd envisaged himself as a high-up in an aid agency, striding around a hot, dusty city of tents, getting doctors to attend to sick children, signing off on orders for emergency supplies to be dispensed to fresh influxes of refugees. However, his ten weeks last summer of volunteering in the Philippines had been a tedious, dispiriting affair, spent counting things and ticking them off endless lists: anything from containers of bleach to packages of protein powder. He hadn't met a single one of the people he was allegedly helping and not once had there been the chance for any heroics. Now he had no real idea of how to steer his future but he couldn't admit that to her.

'What's *your* plan?' he asked.

'Finance law. Big multinational, beast it for a few years, make a fortune, then see what I want to do with the rest of my life.'

'Where? The States?'

'No! The States is over. China. It's the future.'

'You speak Mandarin? Fair play.'

'My Mandarin,' she said archly, 'is non-existent. They'll all speak English. They'll have to.'

'But . . . China *is* the future so *we*'ll have to fit in with them.'

A long pause. 'Say what?'

'How power works. Those who have it set the agenda—what we should look like, how we should speak. The way we should live.'

'We have the power.'

'But you just said that China is—' He stopped. She didn't understand, maybe didn't want to.

And he didn't want an argument. 'So.' He made himself smile. 'Much as I've enjoyed this chat about our careers, there's something I'd rather do with you.'

'Is that so?'

'It *is* so. Maybe you could—I dunno?—take off your dress?'

'Maybe I could.'

Quickly, she slithered out of her silky frock. Her underwear was both cute and sexy.

'Wow. Clearly I'm hanging around with the wrong girls.'

'I could have told you that.' She gave him one of those long stares she specialized in. 'You are *so* not my type . . . But you are *hot*.'

Her glossy confidence was off-putting, almost enough to derail him. It was only because this thing had gone on for a year that he felt obliged to see it through.

But when they got down to it, he couldn't. He wanted Sammie: he missed her voice, her smell, the way she kicked off her boots. He even missed her no-nonsense knickers and unmatched bra.

'Phoebe, hey.' He pulled away. 'I can't do this. Sorry. You're beautiful but I'm going through a rough break-up.'

'What?' She was astonished. 'I don't do this often. You're *lucky*.'

'I know. This is all on me.'

'You *dick*,' she hissed, pulling her dress back on. He didn't blame her for being angry: he'd led her on and messed with her feelings. 'Just so you know,' she said, 'a thumb ring is totally gay!'

She slammed the door behind her, leaving him flattened by unavoidable reality. Sammie wasn't here. He and Sammie would never make things work.

Since they'd both started third year, they'd been falling out of love, gradually, slowly—then all at once. Tempestuous was their thing, had been right from the start, nearly three years ago. Over and over they'd broken up, then got back together. But something had changed. The break-ups were becoming sort of . . . tedious, their reunions no longer felt pure, and the gaps between their spells of civility were becoming shorter. It was time to face it: even though he still loved her, they'd run out of road.

Adulthood, for all its opportunities, meant the simultaneous accumulation of loss. Momentarily the emptiness was unbearable.

Fifteen

'Come on, Ed.' Giggling, Cara took his hand and hurried him in the direction of their room.

Right, he thought. That's the way the night is going.

He tried to gauge how much she'd had to drink. Obviously *some*, because she was initiating sex, which never happened sober. But if she was more than slightly unwound, things felt off. For him, sex was an opportunity—one of the few in their busy lives—for intimacy. There was urgent physical desire, too, but the chance to be really close to her? He needed it.

Without any alcohol, it was impossible for her to relax. But too much took her away from herself.

Trying to catch her when she was still present, but comfortable in her body, was a tricky balancing act.

They slipped into the bedroom. The boys were asleep in the adjoining room. Quietly, Cara closed the interconnecting doors, then stepped forward and shoved Ed onto the bed. 'Clothes. Off.'

Immediately he got up again, slid his arms around her and gently lowered her to the sheets. 'Okay?' he asked.

'Yeah. Grand.' She reached for his jeans.

He stilled her hand and slowly pulled open the knot on her dress. 'Okay?' he repeated.

'Don't look at me,' she said.

He closed his eyes and she laughed. 'You can look at my face. Just not the rest of me.'

Using the flat of his hands, he stroked her soft skin, going for her forearms, her calves, parts of her body that wouldn't have her squirming with apologetic distress.

Before long, she was once again trying to pull the clothes from his body, wanting to speed the whole thing up. It was kinder to just let her direct it, so he obliged, whipping everything off. Her relief was immediate. Her breathing slowed and her muscles relaxed beneath his hands.

'You're so sexy,' he said.

'Oh, God, *don't*.'

'But you are.' This exchange was well-worn.

From their very first night, Cara had never been anything other than apologetic about her body. He'd been naïve enough to think she'd eventually change. He loved her completely. It was unimaginable that he'd ever have this intense a connection with another person but his love wasn't enough to erase her discomfort. It was a painful truth. 'We don't have to do this,' he said.

'We *do*. I want to. Ed, I fancy you. I just don't fancy myself.'

'I'm sorry you feel this way. I'm sorry it's so hard for you.'

It would be over soon and then she'd be okay and restored to normal and glad it was done for another while. Ed had a hard, lean body, with a muscled stomach and sinewy thighs. She wanted this, she wanted him, but it needed to be quick. It was like feeling really hungry but being repulsed by food. She had to eat as fast as possible until the need stopped and the relief arrived.

Now Ed was kissing her thighs. Being in her own body was almost unbearable. She'd reached the limit of her endurance, so she whispered, 'Now.'

It was just her bad luck to fall for a man who longed to kiss the backs of her knees, who wanted to rub fragrant oil between his hands and slide them along her knotted back, kneading her tender spots with his thumbs. Sometimes she joked that she was the bloke in their sex life; she suspected Ed didn't find it that funny.

But he loved her. This was a rock-solid certainty, something that sustained her when life was choppy. Their sex life wasn't ideal but he put up with it.

Of the three Casey brothers, she was lucky he was the one she'd fallen in love with.

Johnny: she could imagine him insisting on sex three times a day. Well, maybe not that much, but a *lot*.

Or Liam, with his famous past: he'd surely have encountered all kinds of kinky stuff—oranges and being strangled with tights, that sort of lark. The very idea made her shudder.

Sixteen

Three years ago, it had been Jessie who'd persuaded Cara to try for the job at the Ardglass.

'They wouldn't employ me,' Cara had said. 'I'd never be able for the grooming.' The reception women there always had their hair in smooth chignons. Never a hanging thread or an unravelling button.

'Ah, go on, Cara, chance it. Seriously, you're great. I'd employ you.'

Even the interview had been on brand: comfortable armchairs, beside a warm fire, with coffee in a silver pot, just as if they were guests.

'Think of this as a chat,' Patience, the hotel's assistant manager, a long, slender Kenyan woman, said.

'So that we can get to know you.' This from round, smiley, baldy Henry from HR.

'You've worked in the hotel business for seventeen years,' Raoul, the Moroccan reception manager, said. 'Why haven't you moved into management?'

Because I took maternity leave. Twice. Once was forgivable—just—but after the second break I was regarded as a liability.

'I like working with people.' That, actually, was true.

'You have two boys? Aged five and seven. So they can mostly take care of themselves?' Again from Raoul.

'And my husband does a lot.' *Except between June and September when he's away Monday to Friday, but that isn't his fault.*

'So, what are your interests?' HR Henry asked.

Cara paused. The thing was that between her job, the dog and Vinnie and Tom—policing their screen time, helping with homework, feeding them again and again and again—she had almost no free time, and with the small amount she got, her very favourite thing was to lie in the bath, drinking red wine, playing music from the mid-nineties.

But she was fairly sure a job interview was not the place to share this.

'I don't have anything special,' she said. 'Like CrossFit or—or . . . embroidery. But we grow vegetables in our little garden, carrots, tomatoes, potatoes . . .'

The trio looked suitably impressed and Cara couldn't help adding, 'The "harvest" is pathetic, TBH. We get probably one meal a year from it. Doesn't stop us swaggering around for half an hour, convinced we're self-sufficient. It's a good feeling while it lasts.'

Patience and Henry seemed entertained.

'What I really love,' she said, 'and I'm not just saying it, is anything to do with hotels. Documentaries, podcasts, anything! I'm *obsessed*. To be honest, my perfect job would be an undercover hotel inspector.'

'Oh, my God!' Henry almost groaned, and both he and Cara began laughing.

'And music's important to me,' she said. 'Prince, En Vogue, people I loved when I was a teenager. Then I like Drake, Beyoncé, the Killers . . . Just pop, nothing too obscure, I'm not a muso, just . . . normal stuff. My nephew Ferdia keeps me current.'

'What else can you tell us?'

'I've two best friends, Gabby and Erin. Seeing them makes me happy. Quick drink, night out, whatever.'

Especially a night out. They were rare, these days, but when they happened, the trio tended to revert to their twenties and get very drunk. If the night didn't end with one of them removing her too-high shoes and hailing a taxi in her bare feet, they wondered where they'd gone wrong. The last time, Erin had said, 'No more tequila for us. It's obviously not strong enough.'

'But my sons, my husband, the dog,' Cara said hastily, 'they're the most important things in my life.'

'Exercise?' Raoul asked.

'Ah, you know.' Might as well be honest. 'I'm always "just getting back on the horse". Recommitting to Zumba, or yoga or whatever. I go a bit mad and do, like, five classes in the first week and then hit a wall. But I walk Baxter! Only round the block, but I do it twice a day.'

'It all adds up.' Henry's eyes were twinkling.

'That's what I tell myself.' She twinkled back at him. He was nice.

'TV?' Patience asked. 'Boxsets?'

'God, *yes*. I'm literally at my happiest, lying on my couch, watching *Peaky Blinders* with my husband.' Briefly she'd forgotten that this was a job interview.

'Obnoxious people?' Henry asked. 'In this line of work you must meet more than your share? How do you feel?'

'If they've a reason and I sort out their issue, I feel good.'

'And those who don't have a reason?'

'I'm even nicer to them. They hate it.' *Noooo!*

But the three of them laughed, she'd got the job, and two years later, she was promoted to head receptionist.

Seventeen

The sun was bright in the sky on Easter Sunday morning. Looking out of her bedroom window, Nell noticed several men, hotel employees, parading almost ceremoniously along the central path of the hotel grounds. Each carried a large wicker basket. At what looked like an agreed point, they separated and fanned out across the grass, and as Nell watched, they began scooping little oval objects from the baskets and strewing them under hedges and among the flowerbeds.

'Liam!' Nell nearly burst with excitement. 'It's the men, the Easter-egg men! Come look!'

'You're so cute.'

'But look! It's magical.'

'I've seen it before.'

'So *jaaaa*ded.' She laughed, then noticed the time. 'Liam, get up! We've to go down now.'

'You go, babes. I feel, you know, I'm missing my girls . . .'

'But,' Nell said gently, 'Jessie will go bananas.'

'I'll text her, she'll understand. Anyway, all of that stuff last night was just because she wants Ferdia there.'

'You don't mind if I go?'

'No. But leave some of the chocolate for the rest of them.'

That wasn't funny, but he was upset, so she let it go. 'Back in a while.'

When the elevator doors opened onto the lobby, the racket from dozens of overexcited children hit her. Two unruly lines, one for the sevens-and-under, the other for over-sevens, snaked back from the doors that led to the grounds. Staff members distributed plastic buckets.

At the front of the smallies' line, Jessie stood with Dilly. They were both ramrod straight, as if marshalling their energy for the task ahead. In the other line she spotted Cara and Ed with their boys. There was Johnny with TJ. Further back were Saoirse, Barty and Bridey. No sign of Ferdia.

When she tried to push her way up to Jessie and Dilly, an apologetic staff member stopped her. 'Like a tinderbox here,' he said. 'Some of them have been waiting more than an hour. Any line-jumping could trigger a riot.'

Nell laughed. 'Grand.' This was funny.

'Soon as the doors open, you can follow them out,' the man said. 'You'll catch up with your family in no time.'

Nell took her spot at the back of the line. A few rows ahead of her, a little boy was balanced on his dad's shoulders, reminding her of a TV image she'd glimpsed on Friday: Syrian refugees standing helplessly in a deluge, a small boy on his dad's shoulders, wearing a plastic bag tied over his ears as pathetic protection from the rain. A knot of painful feelings surged in her: sorrow, frustration at her helplessness—

'Hey,' a voice said.

It was Ferdia. 'Oh. Hey, you made it.'

'More than my life's worth to miss it.'

Rare irritation spiked, erasing the cautiously positive opinion she'd had of him since Friday night's apology. Him and his pathetic little war with Jessie. Would it kill him to be nice?

'One minute to go!' a man, who seemed to be master of ceremonies, called, and fresh energy snaked down the lines.

The kids took up a chant: 'We want eggs! We want eggs!'

A nearby woman muttered, 'I'll give them eggs. Little brats.'

What if this were a *real* food line? Nell thought. Because right now, at this very moment, in countless parts of the world, hungry people were lining up for food. Like Kassandra.

A whistle blew. 'Seven-and-unders, go!' Glass doors opened and the children surged forward, running as if their lives depended on it, Nell and Ferdia bringing up the rear.

'First World children racing for chocolate they don't need.'

For a moment Nell thought she'd spoken the words in her head out loud, then realized they'd come from Ferdia. He was the worst kind of hypocrite, playing at class outrage, while his mum paid his fees and living expenses. All around her, crazed kids were pouncing on hidden eggs and flinging them, rattling, into the bottom of their buckets.

'Now the over-sevens!' A whistle blew.

Within a second, Nell felt the whoosh of bigger children passing by and, momentarily, deep fear stirred. *I'm hunting for food for my family but losing to a faster, stronger adversary.*

'They'll get so much today they'll be sick.' Ferdia was still at her side.

'Happy Easter!' Jessie popped up, all sparkling eyes. Then, with a little frown, 'Where's Liam?'

'Upset,' Nell said. 'Because of Violet and Lenore.'

'Oh.' Nell watched Jessie process her stuff from irritation to reluctant sympathy. 'Oh. Okay. Well, at least you're here.'

Eighteen

Cara was feeling good. Great, even. This weekend had gone far better than she'd anticipated. On Friday she'd climbed to the top of Torc with Ed, their two boys and Liam and Nell. On Saturday, they'd done a full circuit of Lake Dan, which Ed said was eleven K and Liam said was fourteen K and she'd decided to believe Liam. Both days, as soon as she'd opened the packed lunch from the hotel, she'd immediately handed her cereal bar to Ed. She hadn't even given herself time to grieve: it was gone as soon as she saw it.

This morning, even though she was hurting from the two previous days' exercise, she'd shown up for a 7 a.m. yoga class in the fitness studio. Considering it was Easter Sunday, the turnout was high. It was no real surprise to see Jessie – who was dismayed. 'Cara, don't put your mat behind mine. I've the worst feet in the world—seriously, you'll be traumatized if you see them. Take your mat to the other side of the room. We never saw each other, okay?'

That had suited Cara well: the class was tough and she had to spend an embarrassing amount of time recovering in Child's Pose.

But all weekend she'd eaten with excellent moderation. No starvation, because that usually led to a binge, just plenty of healthy protein, lots of vegetables, no pasta, no potatoes, no bread, other than the sandwiches in the packed lunches. Most uplifting of all, despite being knee-deep in Easter eggs, she'd stayed away completely from chocolate.

It was now Sunday afternoon and the end was in sight. She'd be going home tomorrow, unscathed.

As the light glinted silver off the water of the lake, lots of the Caseys were lolling around on the hotel lawn.

'There's real heat in that sun,' Jessie remarked.

'Vinnie, Tom,' Cara called. 'Where're your sun hats?'

'Up in the room.'

'I'll just run up and get them.'

Cara took the stairs, raced into the boys' room, grabbed their hats, turned towards the door . . . then noticed the two buckets of Creme Eggs standing on the dressing table.

I'll just take a look.

Stealthily she crossed the room. *I'll just stand here for a moment and look in at them.*

Keeping well clear, she stretched and silently regarded the Creme Eggs with the same painful mix of love and longing that she used to give her boys when they were sleeping babies.

I'll just eat one.

No, she wouldn't. She was stronger than this. But she should leave now.

One, though. Just one. What harm would one do?

There was no such thing as one.

But the gorgeous feel of it in her hand, the hefty little weight as it lay in her palm, the roughness of the tinfoil against the tips of her fingers. Suddenly she was shaking. Saliva flooded her mouth and she was ripping off the wrapper and, oh, the crunch of the first bite—the *sound* was exciting, the sweetness coating her tongue, the sticky filling on her lips, one more bite, and then it was gone and, without thinking, she was reaching for another, then another, and what did it matter, because they were only small and there were so many in the bucket and she should take some from the other bucket to even things up and her heart was beating very fast and she couldn't stop but she could replace them, she could just drive to the nearest Spar, they were always open, even on Easter Sunday, and now she was looking at a proper Easter egg, a big Wispa one. Dozens more were downstairs for whoever wanted them, it would be no trouble to replace, so she'd just eat it, eat it and enjoy it, because the damage was done, sheep as for a lamb, and then she'd stop. Pulling the cardboard, ripping at the foil, breaking the egg—hearing the crack gave her a thrill that was almost sexual. She was snapping pieces off and swallowing almost without chewing. But she began to feel sick. What she was putting in her mouth no longer tasted like pieces of Heaven but she kept eating until it was gone.

Then it was over—and sanity returned.

Oh, *God.* How had that happened? All those calories. Even as she was calculating the total, she was trying to blind herself to how much she'd eaten.

Friday hadn't been spent climbing Torc for the endorphins or the bonding time with Nell, it had been done to burn fat. Same for Saturday's trek around the lake. Everyone else had been loving life, living in the moment with the sunshine and the fresh air but she was only doing it because she wanted to be thin.

Her fat cells were filling up and expanding. Already her jeans felt tighter.

But it wasn't too late . . .

She grabbed a bottle of water, swigged it all, then went to the bathroom, upended a tooth mug, filled it with tap water and gulped it down. Tasted disgusting, but that was good. Four more glasses, then she crouched over the toilet. Fingers down her throat and she gagged, gagged again, nothing happened and then a torrent, mostly water, but some chocolate.

Eyes streaming, nose running, she drank three more glasses of water and repeated the horrible exercise, with slightly better results.

It was exhausting, it was disgusting and yet, seeing all that chocolate reappear, it felt rewarding.

She cleaned up the bathroom, redid her make-up, gathered all the discarded packaging and bundled it into her bag.

On the way to the Spar, she felt light-headed, almost elated. She probably shouldn't be driving.

She stuffed the evidence into the garbage can outside the shop, then looked at the pile of Creme Eggs on the counter. Would ten be enough? No. She hadn't kept count but she reckoned fifteen might do.

'Kids,' she said sheepishly, to the startled assistant.

So this was very, very bad. But she'd got away with it and it would not happen again.

Nineteen

Johnny's phone rang. *Who* was calling him at ten past ten on Easter Monday? Celeste *Appleton*. What the hell was *she* ringi—Oh. Right. He might have an idea . . . Summoning inhuman quantities of energy, he hollered, 'Celeste!'

'Johnny!'

'Well, this is a surprise!'

'Are you still in bed?'

'Ha-ha.' Christ, trust her to mention bed only ten seconds in.

'Application here for a summer internship from a Ferdia Kinsella. I thought, *That name rings a bell.* Is that Johnny Casey's stepson? I wondered. So? Is he?'

Heartily, Johnny said. 'I believe he is!'

'I *seeeeeeeee*.' He visualized her twirling a pen in her shiny, slippery hair, being pouty-mouthed and suggestive.

'Over two hundred applicants for the spot. Why should I give it to young Mr Kinsella?'

'His résumé is good. And he's a hard worker.' He wasn't. He was a lazy little prick, but he could hardly tell her that. Not with Jessie earwigging.

'All the résumés on my desk are good, Johnny.' There was a laugh in her voice. 'And I'm sure they're all hard workers. What else can you give me?'

There was a blockage in his throat. 'What would you like?'

'You can take me for lunch.'

Thank Christ it was only lunch she'd suggested. 'I will, of course! Soup and a sandwich at a pub of your choosing!'

'You can feck off with soup and pubs. You'll have to do better than that.'

'Seriously?'

'Always. Get back to me in the next few days.'

If he didn't, Ferdia would have to look elsewhere for his summer job. 'Will do. Lovely talking to you, Celeste. Now get out and enjoy some of that bank-holiday sunshine.'

She laughed. 'You know me, Johnny. Hardest-working woman in Ireland.'

As soon as he hung up, Jessie said, 'What?'

'Celeste Appleton. Social Research Institute. Ferdia applied there for a summer job.'

'Small world.'

Not really. He'd suggested it to Ferdia. He might even have said something braggy like, 'Old friend of mine runs the place.' With the unspoken addendum, *She never really got over me.*

'Is she going to give it to him?' Jessie asked.

'If I have lunch with her.'

'Is that right?' Jessie said thoughtfully. 'So, have lunch with her. Get him the job. But make sure you behave yourself.'

'Course I'll behave myself,' he blustered.

Back in the day, Johnny had been a great man for casual sex. Jessie hated being reminded of it.

'You and the kids start loading up the car,' Jessie said to Johnny. 'I'll check us all out.' And pay the doubtless colossal bill.

At the desk, as page after page was being printed out, Jessie was all smiles, yes, wonderful weekend, yes, they'd be back again next year, no, wouldn't miss it for the world, oh, hurry up, for the love of God, put me out of my misery and just show me the final figure.

'There we go, Ms Parnell.' The smiley clerk passed over the sheaf of paper.

Jessie jumped right to the bottom of the last page. Shite. She'd been braced for a certain sum, but even with the early-booking discount, it was more than expected—it always was.

'Everything okay?' The clerk was solicitous.

'Fine, yes, just, ah . . .' But a scan through the list established that nothing unexpected had sneaked in—for example, that she hadn't accidentally *bought* the fecking jaunting car, instead of just hiring it for four hours. But all those accommodation costs and several dinners for fourteen, room service, massages, packed lunches for the hillwalkers, mini-bar refills, casual lattes in the lobby: they tended to add up.

Christ, though, she was glad that Johnny wasn't witness to this.

It was weird with him. He was her husband and they were meant to share everything. To be fair, they *did*: one joint bank account, joint credit cards and a joint mortgage. Most importantly, as soon as they'd got married, she'd given him a raise so that he was paid what she was. They already had several issues on their plates—Ferdia hating Johnny, the Kinsellas feeling betrayed: they didn't need to make things worse by emasculating Johnny into the bargain.

But despite their 'equality', there were times when she definitely felt more equal than him.

She spent too much money. And he didn't like it. He worried. But she felt it was hers to spend. The company was her creation. She and she alone had founded it, she came up with the best ideas and she worked like a dog. She didn't like feeling constrained and she didn't like having to massage the truth.

It had been true what they'd said in that article: if she'd sold up in 2008, she'd have more money than she knew what to do with. She hated being reminded of the opportunity she'd missed, convinced—wrongly—that if she held on for another nine months, the price would just keep rising.

But you couldn't think that way. Her life was great and they had enough money. As long as she kept working hard and business stayed buoyant and—

'Everything all right?' Johnny was suddenly at her shoulder, making her jump.

'All fine.' She summoned a bright smile and slid the enveloped bill into her bag.

'Christ. You're doing the scary smile. That bad, was it?'

'Bad enough.'

'I could look at it online. Find out just how bad.'

'Ah, don't, Johnny.' She followed him to the car. 'Promise me you won't.'

He smiled. 'I promise.'

'Johnny, I don't spend much money on clothes or shoes.'

'*What?*'

'Johnny, I don't. You should see some of the prices on Net-a-Porter.'

'Yeah, it's *Net-a-Porter*, a luxury goods site.'

'So I buy my clothes from Zara. Look, family is my thing.'

It wasn't even her family: they were *his* brothers. But she had no brothers or sisters of her own and she was nothing if not resourceful.

'Who's driving?' he asked.

'You.' She'd a million emails to answer.

Climbing into the car, she was deep in thought. Maybe she needed to make changes to her spending, but it was hard to know what to do. Should you live each second to the full, grabbing every opportunity and making as many precious memories as possible? Or should you carefully salt resources away, having a comfortable buffer zone in place, in the event that disaster struck?

It was impossible to decide, because you never knew what was coming down the tracks.

Five Months Earlier

MAY

Dilly's First Communion

Twenty

Cara hunted through the jumble of cosmetics on her dressing table. She'd pressed so much iridescent shimmer onto her cheekbones that more eyebrow definition was needed to balance it. And one more circle of glittery brown eyeliner wouldn't hurt.

The lip gloss, though . . . She looked as if she'd fallen face down into a field of cherry jam, so sticky she could barely open her mouth. How had they *lived* like this in the nineties?

Her hair was loose apart from the two—frankly, *amazing*—horns on the top of her head, courtesy of Hannah. She'd twisted a thick lock of Cara's hair around a cone of styrofoam, pinned it in place with a gazillion clips—'A nuclear missile won't shift them'—then sprayed each finished horn a sinister shade of dark red.

Unexpectedly, the clothes had been the easy part. The long slip dress, in slithery black satin, left over from her youth, had been lurking at the back of her wardrobe. Astonishingly—and admittedly with the assistance of Spanx—it still fitted. The red top, embossed with silver stars, she'd found on eBay. And Erin had loaned her the super-high leopard-print platform sandals.

Platforms were great. So easy to walk in, and looking taller also made her look slimmer and perhaps she should wear them more oft—

'Hey!' Ed was out on the landing, staring in. 'You look—'

'What?' Suddenly she was anxious. 'Stupid?'

'God, *no*. You look . . .' he studied her '. . . *hawt*.' Moving towards her he said, his voice slightly hoarse, 'Do you *have* to go out?'

'Ha-ha.' The very thought of missing this.

He slid his arm around her waist. 'Are they *your* eyelashes?'

'No . . . God, Ed, you haven't a clue.' She regarded him fondly.

'If I kiss you, will we get stuck together?'

'Yep.'

'For ever?'

'Yep. Have you got my drink?'

He produced her metal coffee mug. 'A hundred mls of vodka in there, four measures. And as much Red Bull as would fit. Honey, you're sure about this? Can't you just go to a pub first?'

'We're reliving our youth.' His concern tickled her. 'We were grand then. We'll be grand now. What'll you do tonight?'

'Put that pair to bed. Watch Kevin McCloud. Maybe smoke the world's weakest spliff.'

'Ed . . .'

'No spliff?'

'Not with the kids here. Even if they're asleep. Sorry.'

'No. You're right.'

Her mobile beeped at the same time as a car outside. 'That'll be my taxi. Bye, honey. Don't wait up.'

Crowds of Spice-Girl-alikes were milling around the gate. It took a while to spot Gabby and Erin in among them. Then, there they were, Gabby in denim cut-offs, a denim shirt over a silver corset and a long, flammable-looking blonde ponytail, Erin in red patent knee boots, a black latex dress and an orangey-red wig.

Cara launched herself at them.

'You look so young!' Gabby squealed. 'It's 1998 all over again.'

'You look *amazing*.'

'No, *you* look amazing.'

'You look *more* amazing.'

'We *all* look amazing.' Erin plucked at her dress. 'But I am *melting* in this. Latex is a young woman's game.' She produced a small Evian bottle. 'Have you got your drink?'

'Are we just going to do it, standing here in the street?' Cara asked.

'Sure!' Erin took a defiant swallow and nodded at a hovering security guard. 'Respectable mother of three, thank you for asking.'

'Really?' Gabby seemed uncertain. But after the first couple of swigs, she said, 'Sneaky drinking is like riding a bike. It's all coming back to me.'

'It *should* come back to you,' Erin said. 'As drinkers go, you were the worst.'

'Excuse me, *you* were the worst.'

'Sometimes I was the worst,' Cara said.

'You were never the worst drinker,' Erin said.

'But she had terrible form with men. Remember, Cara, you were seeing that fool—'

'Which one?'

'The . . . What was he? . . . The magician?'

'*Kian!*' Cara snapped her fingers.

'Him. But there was another fool . . . He had a job . . . Bryan with a Y.'

'Kian the magician showed up one night. Booty call. You didn't want him to come in. *Then* Bryan with a Y arrived.'

'Oh, I remember . . .'

'You introduced them to each other, said they had lots in common, that they were both dickheads, then kicked them out. You were boss! Girl power that night, all right!'

Twenty-One

. . . a ceramic bust of Lenin, a clock with Cyrillic numbers, a collection of military medals, another bust of Lenin . . . Jessie kept on scrolling through Etsy. She was drawn to the Soviet field telephones, with their old-fashioned black handsets, but she had to try to put herself in Jin Woo Park's mindset. *I am a Korean chef who lives in Geneva and collects Soviet memorabilia. What do I like?*

On she scrolled. More military medals, another field telephone—then a vintage rubber chemical-protection suit in a dodgy shade of green. Jessie's heart jumped. This! It was attractively weird and, if nothing else, would get Jin Woo Park's attention. She put it into her basket, then narrowed her search to 'Soviet Memorabilia Cookery'. A paraffin camping stove, stamped with 'USSR', popped up. That also went into the basket, along with some ancient-looking serving spoons and a stack of recipe cards in Cyrillic.

Right, that was plenty. She hurried through checkout and the appallingly high delivery charges. She wanted these ASAP.

Jin Woo Park was one of four chefs she was currently researching in the hope of luring them to PiG's cookery school. He collected Soviet memorabilia, which wasn't too out there. Certainly not as bad as the one who collected human teeth. You had to aim for these chefs when they were at a certain level: not so successful that they had their own range of sauces in Waitrose, but they couldn't be so 'up-and-coming' that no one else had heard of them. If you shelled out five hundred euro to spend a day cooking with a famous chef, you wanted to boast about it—and how could you boast about a chef who was a complete unknown?

Jin Woo Park, chef and proprietor of Kalgukso, which offered Swiss/Korean cuisine, was in the sweet spot. He'd been passed over by the Michelin-star people in the latest round, to much grumbling on foodie boards, so he'd be feeling raw and amenable to flattery.

Those who couldn't understand how Jessie persuaded such a chef to come to Ireland were missing the basics. The chefs came because Jessie put the work in. She researched and researched until they felt like her best friends—like, look at her now. It was almost midnight, and she'd been on her iPad for two hours, doing a deep dive on him.

Most nights, she went to bed around ten o'clock, intending to read a prize-winning book for half an hour, then get eight hours of restorative sleep. Instead, she went straight online, looking up amazing resorts or cheerily buying stuff. Or furtively opening the Mail Online—reading it made her feel almost queasy but she was irresistibly drawn to the comments beneath each story. Seeing the criticisms of Hollywood actresses—too thin, not thin enough, saggy neck, too much lip-filler—took some of the sting out of the hatred that came her way.

Tonight, though, she'd been focused on carefully assembling a gift box that would show Jin Woo Park she truly 'got' him. Jin Woo's Swiss wife, Océane, was a long-limbed blonde at least a head taller than him. No kids, which was a shame because the quickest way to snag someone's heart was to be nice to their children. But she'd work with what she had: she'd love-bomb Océane.

Océane's Instagram was public, in English, and she posted *a lot.* Mostly pre-workout selfies or very expensive shoes. So Jessie would send her a pair of fabulous shoes. But she needed to know her size. If handbags had been Océane's thing, it would have been a lot easier. Taking a chance, she commented on a pair of Océane's Louboutins. 'OMG. So beautiful. You have teeny-tiny feet, are you a thirty-six?' She threw in four heart-eyed emojis and sent it.

Océane had twenty thousand followers—she might not even see Jessie's post. Or she might think Jessie was a foot-fetishist and block her.

But almost immediately, Océane replied, 'I wish lol. I'm thirty-nine.'

What a result! Immediately Jessie jumped on Net-a-Porter and set about matching Océane's taste with the shoes on offer. Océane liked mainstream luxury brands—Manolo, Jimmy Choo or Louboutin. Nothing too edgy. This season's must-have was the Balenciaga 'Knife' – slides with exquisitely pointy toes. They were available in blue or white, and even though Jessie personally preferred the blue, the white seemed more . . . *Swiss.* Well, if Océane didn't like them, she could always exchange them. Buying these beautiful shoes for another woman was excruciating. But it had to be done.

Now, the letter. Though it was always personalized, she had a template: a warm, chatty acknowledgement that the chef was very, very busy.

But a weekend in Ireland wouldn't be all work.

Basically, her letter could be distilled down to 'Come to Dublin. Lash out your greatest hits at a couple of classes, then Johnny and his mates will take you on a never-ending pub crawl. You'll return to Geneva with at least twenty almost unbelievable anecdotes. Yes, you really *were* stopped by the police, in a car going the wrong way up a one-way street. When one of them recognized you as the Korean/Swiss chef from television, they cancelled the ticket and asked for your kimchi recipe. All expenses will be covered, and you will be remunerated handsomely for your time.'

Most restaurants, even the world-renowned, struggled to break even, so chefs tended to find a lump sum of five thousand euro, for two days' easy work, a very attractive prospect.

Once the contract was signed, Jessie gradually layered up the work. Pinging off emails saying, 'Turns out you're a bit of a rock star here in Ireland! Our most popular TV chat show is desperate to have you. More fun than it sounds, the green-room antics are the stuff of legend!'

The more publicity generated by the visit, the more PiG benefited. Long after the chef had departed, PiG's cookery school would be offering courses 'inspired' by the chef's unique cuisine and—

Johnny hurtled into the bedroom, clearly agitated. 'Jessie, what are you *at*? Our PayPal is going mental!'

'Luring Jin Woo Park.'

'Using Net-a-Porter?'

'Shoes for his wife.'

'Five hundred euros' worth?'

'That's what she likes.' Jessie said what she always said. 'You have to spend money to make money.'

Some of Jessie's fishing expeditions came to nothing. They dropped like pebbles into the bottom of a still, dark lake. But she didn't give up easily, treading the fine line between charming persistence and harassment.

'Can I come to bed?' Johnny asked.

'I'm writing to Jin.'

'Saying what?'

'The usual . . . Understand how busy your schedule is, but you'd love Ireland, people so friendly—'

'—hardly racist at all. What are you sending him?'

'Bottle of Midleton, Seavite products for his wife. He collects Soviet memorabilia, so a load of mad stuff is making its way here from Ukraine. Go on, yes, come to bed.'

'Thank Christ,' he said. He tore off his T-shirt, stepped out of his sweatpants, then his jocks.

She looked at him over the top of her reading glasses, realizing that here was a chance to accomplish another thing on her to-do list. '*Jooooohnny?*'

'Yeah?' He looked up sharply.

She removed her glasses and moved her iPad to the floor. 'If you were quick about it . . .'

'I can be quick!'

'No foreplay. Just the main event. Don't worry about me, I'm grand.'

'Is this one of those maintenance rides?'

'It's a ride, Johnny. Don't over-think it.'

Eagerly, he disappeared into the bathroom, looking for a condom. At nearly fifty she was unlikely to get pregnant, but Johnny was taking no chances.

'Johnny,' she called, 'what about a photo of the entire family, all of us holding little Swiss and Korean flags?'

'Yes. No. I don't know.'

'I'll order them anyway.'

'You're way too click-happy.'

Sometimes, Jessie thought, his cautious bean-counting was very dispiriting.

Honestly, though, when she'd first met Johnny, back in the days when he'd been one half of the Rory–Johnny double act, he'd seemed like a *lunatic* risk-taker. But that was a long time ago—an entire lifetime—and now that he was no longer defined in opposition to his best friend, he seemed almost too careful.

Mind you, Rory had been even more cautious.

She'd been seeing Rory when the idea for PiG came to her. They were serious about each other, and she'd sensed they would probably get married. Even so, she'd been nervous about sharing her big, wonderful vision: if he jumped all over it and urged her to include him as partner, would she think less of him for coat-tailing? Instead, he gave careful, measured encouragement. There was no breathless plea to become part of her venture, no reckless offer to put up his flat as extra collateral.

She'd had a bit of a tearful rant at him—she couldn't help it, she'd wanted more support.

Gently he'd said, 'It's your idea. It's brilliant. You deserve any reward. I'll help in every way I can. And if it doesn't work out, I'll take care of you.'

'And if it *does* work out?' She'd been suddenly uplifted by confidence. 'I'll take care of you!'

Twenty-Two

'Too low,' Nell called, from the aisle of the empty theatre. 'If the actor misses her mark by a few centimetres, she'll be brained by a giant clock landing on her head. Take it up a bit.'

High above, on the ceiling walkway, Lorelei shouted down, 'How much?'

'I'll know when I see it. Wind it back up, go on, wind—right, stop! There, yeah! Shout me down the measurements.'

Nell stepped back to check that all thirteen of the MDF clocks still hung in aesthetically pleasing proportion to each other. Moving one had a knock-on effect on everything else.

'Is it okay?' Lorelei sounded impatient, which made Nell glance at her phone.

'Jesus, is that really the time?'

'Ten past twelve? Yeah.'

They'd been working since eight that morning, which made it—Nell counted—sixteen hours. But she'd been totally immersed. This was a small project with a tiny budget but it was hers. Okay, she was doing all the literal construction but she was the actual designer. *And* she was getting paid—if she didn't blow the entire budget on the props, that was.

Even after all these years, this work still seemed magical.

Neither of her parents had known the first thing about art, but as a kid she'd been the only pupil in her class of twelve-year-olds who hadn't sniggered her way through a visit to the museum of modern art.

Off her own bat, she'd begun taking out library books about Damien Hirst, Picasso and Frida Kahlo. Articles about architecture, couture or furniture design caught her interest—and all of this caused ripples at home.

Petey and Angie were proud but slightly baffled.

At the age of fourteen, Nell had found her true calling. Her mum had got a part in the Raheny Players' production of *Tenko*. Nell's dad, a joiner, was enlisted to build the set with Nell's brother, Brendan.

One Saturday morning when Brendan was too 'sick' to get out of bed, Nell was roped in to paint the jungle setting. She was vocally indignant—she had better things to be doing on the weekend.

But she was immediately intrigued by how the panels of 'bamboo' and 'palms' slid on and off stage on silent castors, how the scene could be changed in seconds from a forest to a concentration camp. 'Did *you* invent this?' she quizzed her dad.

'We built it. Stephanie designed it.'

'Right. I want to be a Stephanie.'

'Grand so.' Petey had a twinkle in his eye. 'You can be a Stephanie.'

They'd always encouraged her to be her own person. 'We might as well give you confidence,' was her dad's good-humoured refrain. 'We've nothing else to give you.'

Once again, Liam checked the time. Twelve thirty. She'd been at work for a very long time. He wasn't worried: he just really wanted to see her. Today was their six-month wedding anniversary. Barely a year ago, they hadn't even met.

That very first night, Liam had said, 'Come home with me.' He still wasn't sure about her, but he was curious.

'No.'

That wasn't the answer he was used to getting.

'*Haukart*,' she said.

'Excuse me?'

'Couple of years ago I was in Iceland. They have a dish called Hákarl, pronounced "*Haukart*". It's shark pickled in urine. Tastes disgusting. I knew it wouldn't be for me, but I still wanted to know what it was like . . .'

Her voice trailed off and he felt shame rise in his face. 'I'm a person,' she said. 'Not some novelty.'

'But—'

'Don't.' She put a warning hand on his arm.

He was confused. He'd thought millennials were down with hook-up culture. 'Have you a boyfriend?'

She seemed amused. 'No.'

'Bad break-up?'

'Please. Stop.'

'There *was* a bad break-up!'

'There was a guy . . .' She shrugged. 'I got breadcrumbed for months. He'd give me a little attention, just enough to seem like he cared. Then . . . nothing. Then a booty call. So I blocked him.'

'Harsh.'

'I'm gonna be thirty this year. Time to get serious about life. I've given up on Tinder.'

'Why's that?' Because he found it *very* handy.

'It turns people into disposable collateral.' Her earnestness was touching. 'Something about meeting a person on screen makes them too easy to ghost. It's like your phone conjured them up, so your phone can vanish them too.'

'Have you ever had a *real* boyfriend?'

'Totally.' She looked offended. 'For seven years, from age nineteen to twenty-six. We outgrew each other. Was still hard, though. Seven years is a long time. Even though the final year or two were kind of shitty. I was afraid I'd never meet anyone else,' she said. 'And I haven't.'

'Apart from Breadcrumb Guy.'

'Oh, him!' She made a dismissive flutter. 'He was an asshole. And I was a bigger one for pretending he wasn't. There've been lots of assholes! So, I'm going now.' She stood up.

'Can I have your number?' Hurriedly he got to his feet. 'I promise I'm not an asshole.'

She looked him in the eye. 'You're hot, you're rich, you're bored, you're *totally* an asshole.' But she laughed and gave him her number anyway.

He went home and slept for eleven hours, the first time in two years he'd managed more than five uninterrupted hours. When he woke, he wondered what had changed. Then he remembered. *Haukart.* Fermented shark, whatever she was.

That same morning, Nell woke up in her small, overheated room in Shankill, a suburb perched on the edge of Dublin. The room got unbearably stuffy in warm weather but remained Baltic during the winter. She'd been woken by the ping of a text: **Morning ☺ You busy today? Come to the coast with me? Friends. You are NOT fermented shark.**

Deep in thought, Nell opened her window to let in some air. Last night, her assessment of Liam had been 'interesting but not for me'. He was too clueless about her life. But he was . . . stimulating. She'd quizzed him about the end of his running career and he'd been unexpectedly articulate. 'After I stopped winning,' he'd said, 'disappearing into a marriage was a great place to hide from my failure. Paige had status and money. I wanted someone to take care of me.'

His honesty was intriguing. Attractive.

'We had Violet, and that was a distraction. Then we had Lenore. Same. We were moving around a lot, a year in Vancouver, two in Auckland. Took a few years to notice how worthless I felt.'

'Oh, yeah—performative masculinity. Men are told they must be hunter-gatherers. If you're not one, you feel like a failure.'

'It has a name? Wow. Okay! When we lived in Chicago I went to drama school. But Paige's job moved us again, this time to Dublin, so I never graduated. Moving back to Ireland as a house-husband, that was the death knell. The shame was too much. I could do that shit in another country, but not here. The last two years of our marriage were . . .'

She waited, reluctant to provide the words.

'I wouldn't wish it on anyone,' he eventually said. 'In the end I just wanted it to be over. Paige despised me and I resented her. We went to counselling, which made it worse. Found out we'd got each other wrong from the get-go. She thought I was dynamic. I thought she was strong. We were both wrong.'

'It sounds painful. Really.'

After a silence, he said, 'I was shitty to her.'

'What way shitty? Cheating?'

'Hey, cheating isn't the worst thing you can do.' At Nell's sceptical look, he said, 'I sneered at her job, her dedication, her money. She believed in me for years and in return I was a tool. She hates me now. She's right to.'

Nell looked again at her phone. No, she shouldn't meet this guy. She typed a reply, then clicked back, deleting it all. Bad idea to commit to anything until she'd had coffee.

In the kitchen, used saucepans were piled along the worktops and the garbage can was overflowing. Six people lived in this three-bedroomed house and it was too small for them.

Molly Ringwald was mewing angrily, obviously hungry. 'Sorry, Mol.' She poured kibble into a bowl, then filled the kettle.

Wondering where to start with the clean-up operation, she thought, for the first time ever, *How much longer do I have to live like this?*

In wandered Garr, who lived in the adjoining sitting room. Frosted-glass doors were all that separated his space from the kitchen.

'Morning,' he said sleepily.

'Sorry, did I wake you?'

'You're okay. Kettle on?'

'Yep. But help me clean this pit. Garr, I met this guy last night . . . Not Tinder. Real life. But it's not that sort of thing.'

'What sort of thing is it?'

'He's . . . a babe. I guess. There *might* be something, but I've wasted enough time on mexperiments.'

'Whats?'

'You know, "men experiments". Sleeping with guys just because maybe. Also, he's forty, divorced, kids, baggage. I think he might be a terrible person, but he's honest about it, so maybe that means he isn't.'

'When someone tells you who they are, believe them.'

She smiled. '*Not* what I want to hear. So he wants to hang out today. And I think I want to.'

'So do it. Life's all about adventures.'

'Let's put it out to the universe. If someone in this house can loan me thirty euro, I'll go.'

'Wanda got paid yesterday. The universe says yes.'

Nell cycled home through the busy city. Thursday was always a big party night and tonight was even livelier than usual because of the Spice Girls' gig.

In their underground car park, she slung her bike on the rack. When she'd seen Liam's fancy apartment for the first time, she couldn't have imagined that within weeks she'd be living there. It seemed like an absolute palace—still did: electronic keys, fancy lighting systems and *three* bedrooms, Liam's and one each for Violet and Lenore whenever they came to stay. Which seemed to be never.

That first day they'd gone to the beach as 'just friends' but things had changed quickly.

It wasn't just his sly, sexy face or his ripped body, it was his optimism that dazzled her. People her own age had no hope in the future, but Liam came from a different world—or maybe a different time—where positive expectations were still allowed.

He, likewise, was charmed by her frugal lifestyle, her devotion to her job and the childlike joy she gleaned from small things. Her principles fascinated him—how she felt guilty about 'stealing the chilled air from Tesco', or her refusal to use Airbnb because 'Nobody can afford to rent a flat any longer and Airbnb is a big reason why.'

By the end of the first week, he was saying stuff like 'I wasn't expecting this. But you've really . . . affected me.'

She was more cautious: on paper, they made an unlikely couple. She couldn't shake the suspicion that she was simply a novelty of which he'd eventually tire.

When he asked her to move in with him, she laughed uncomfortably. 'Molly Ringwald would have to come too.' Molly Ringwald was her big, furry, ginger cat.

'Molly Ringwald is welcome. Look, you're spending nearly every night with me anyway.'

But she caved only when a friend of Garr's was evicted and in urgent need of a room. 'Okay. But don't corrupt me and Molly! It'll be very hard to go back to a single bed in an overcrowded house.'

But what finally convinced her they were for real was how he adapted to her life. Last summer they'd spent two weeks travelling the Wild Atlantic Way on Ireland's rickety bus service, staying in hostels or bed-and-breakfasts—*never* Airbnbs.

Sometimes they camped on the soft dunes by the sea.

One evening, sitting on a sandy beach, as the setting sun flooded the sky with radiant peach light, he said, 'I feel so alive. Every cell of me. Like I've been asleep my whole life and you've woken me up.'

Still, she hadn't expected what had happened in October, less than five months after their first meeting.

It was a Saturday morning, in bed. She'd opened her eyes, to find him propped on his elbow, looking down on her. 'What's our deal?' he asked, as if they were continuing a conversation they'd already been having. 'You and me? Where is this going?'

'Does it have to go anywhere?'

He paused. 'Let's get married.'

'You loon! You're barely divorced.'

'I've been divorced more than a year. And the marriage was over long before.'

The truth was, she didn't need convincing. Life was so unpredictable, you had so little control, you might as well take your autonomy where you could. '*If* I say yes,' she'd said, 'and it's an "if", Liam, there's to be no big ceremony. No dress, none of that. I'm not a white-dress kind of person and I couldn't handle the waste of money.'

'Got it.' Thoughtfully, he said, 'Something to think about. We'd only need two weeks' notice to get married in Iceland. Hotel in the Snæfellsnes Peninsula—we could do our vows in an outdoor hot tub, with the Northern Lights in the background.'

'You've already looked it up?'

'. . . I've already booked it.'

She raced up the stairs, so anxious to see him that she didn't bother with the elevator.

'Sorry, sorry, sorry, sorry, sorry!'

'It's okay.' He was fiddling on the computer with what looked like his cycling stats. If he was engaged in his stuff, she felt less guilty about hers.

'Just lost track of time. Happy six-month anniversary!'

Liam kissed her. 'And they said it wouldn't last.' He was joking, but there had been a lot of surprise.

'It's very soon,' her mum had said.

'I'm tired of waiting for my life to start,' Nell had said. 'I'm sure about this.'

'Yeh, but is *he*?' Petey asked. 'I mean, I like the chap—'

'He's more sure than *I* am!'

'We're open-minded people.' Petey sounded anxious, because they weren't really: they were kind but traditional. 'Marriage is a big deal, though.'

'We can always get divorced.' She was half joking.

Petey took a breath. 'I suppose you can.'

'You were both younger than me when you got married.'

'But we felt older. I'd a job, your mother had a job and I know you have a job, love, but we had jobs we got paid for, and I'm not having a pop, I'm just saying.'

'But that's the thing, Dad. I don't know what's going to happen tomorrow, never mind in ten years' time. I can only live life with the stuff I know, and I know that I want to marry him.'

'Tell us why you love him,' Angie said.

'He's done so much living, travelling. He's had a career, a marriage. Fatherhood, twice. He's interesting and knows stuff. Also,' she added, 'he's a complete fox.'

'Holy Mother,' Petey half moaned.

'He treats me like a—a *queen*, I've never had that before.' Seeing herself through his eyes, she felt free-spirited and bohemian. A sea goddess in touch with nature, instead of someone living a shabby struggle of a life. 'He's literally beyond my wildest dreams.'

'Ah, here, that's jayzis codswallop!'

'Dad, listen to me. *Beyond* my wildest dreams. He's great in ways that I couldn't even have imagined.'

'Have you any worries about him?' Angie asked.

'That's shut her up,' Petey observed.

'He barely sees his two little girls. That must be tough but he keeps it inside.' She pressed her hand against her mouth. 'Sometimes he gets narky about me not buying clothes. He likes nice things. But that's it.'

After a pause, Petey said, 'Okay. Well, it's your life. And I *like* the chap—'

'He likes the chap,' Angie said.

'I like the chap too,' Nell said.

'We all like the chap,' Angie agreed. 'We're trying our best here, Nell.'

'So be happy for me.'

Petey and Angie looked at each other and came to some mutual agreement. 'Right so,' Petey said. 'We *are* happy for you, God's honest. So how much money do I need to ask the Credit Union for?'

'None. We're getting married, but we're not wasting money on a wedding.'

'What do you mean? I don't get to walk my only daughter down the aisle? Ah, here!'

'We're getting married abroad. You're welcome to come.'

'Where? It better be somewhere sunny. Iceland? In November? Ah, *goodnight*! You can expect a phone call from Nana McDermott. She won't be happy!'

Sure enough, the following day Nell's nana rang her, raging about the foolishness of not only marrying in haste but marrying in Iceland.

'But I love him so much, Nana,' Nell had said. 'Doesn't that count for anything?'

'I never had you down for an eejit, Nell. But there we are.'

As they were drifting off to sleep, Liam said, 'It's Dilly's first communion on Saturday. We need to give her two hundred euro.'

'Is that the going rate for communions these days?' It couldn't possibly be!

'I'm her godfather.'

After a spell of silence, Nell said, 'Dilly doesn't need that kind of money . . .'

'Oh, Christ, you're planning something, aren't you? You *are*.'

'You know Perla and Kassandra? The Syrian woman and her little girl? Okay, you know *about* them. Instead of us giving the cash to Dilly, how about we ask her to give it to Kassandra? Sort of like sponsorship.'

'I don't know if Jessie will go for that . . . What if it upsets Dilly, and Jessie and Johnny are raging with us?'

'We could okay it with them first. I could get some photos, maybe a letter from Kassandra to Dilly . . .' Nell's head raced with ideas.

Cautiously Liam said, 'Ask Jessie. See what she says.'

Twenty-Three

Ed and Tom were talking softly. Tom must have woken early and climbed into bed with them.

'Lots of cultures have coming-of-age ceremonies,' Ed was saying. They seemed to be discussing Dilly's forthcoming first communion.

'Eight is too young,' Tom said. '*I*'m eight and I still don't know about God. When I grow up I might be a Jedi or a scientist or a—a *postman*. But now I'm only a kid so how should I know?'

She should be hung-over and exhausted from last night but all she felt was happy. It had been like being young again, but without the side-order of crushing insecurity and crippling fear of the future that had been her constant companion when she was twenty-one.

Her red horns were still on her head—Hannah had been right: they hadn't budged. Better get rid of them before she went to work.

'In modern Western society—and that's us, buddy—childhood is extended far longer than the norm. A hundred years ago, you'd already be out at work.'

'Down pit.'

'Down pit, indeed.'

It was lovely to hear their quiet chat. Today was going to be a good day, she was certain of it.

'But you're actually correct,' Ed said to Tom. 'The Catholic Church doesn't think eight is the age of reason, but maybe it's a good idea to give kids a sense of belonging to their Church.'

'Is it mind control?'

'One way of looking at it.'

Ed was so reasonable, Cara thought. Fair-minded and scientific in his approach to everything. 'But for many eight-year-olds, being celebrated forges strong connections with their community.'

'Nah. Kids only like it because they get so much money. That's all Vinnie wanted.'

Under the covers, Cara smiled. Tom was right. Vinnie had had the time of his life on his first-communion day, strutting around in a white suit and shaking all the neighbours down for outrageous sums of cash. If he'd felt 'a sense of belonging' to his Church, Cara couldn't say she'd noticed.

'What's a pit?' Tom asked.

'A coal mine.'

'*Is* it? We always say it, but I didn't know what it meant.'

Cara's phone beeped. A text from her mum: **Coffee before you start work?**

It would be so nice to stay here with Ed and Tom. But in two weeks Ed would be starting his summer work, away from Monday to Friday, and all invitations would have to be declined. Now was the time to make the most of it.

She swept aside the duvet. 'Ed, you're on breakfast and walking Baxter. I'm meeting Mum before work.' She got to her feet, then halted. 'Oh. Stood up too quickly.'

When the dizziness and black dots dispersed, she clicked out, **Big Hat of Coffee, 9.00**

On the landing she knocked on Vinnie's door. 'Up! Dad's doing breakfast. No Sugar Puffs, no Coco Pops, no Froot Loops.'

She hurried into the bathroom before Vinnie started complaining. 'You heard that, Ed?' she called.

'Yep. Got it.'

With the shower running, she got on the scales. She hadn't put on any weight since yesterday. But she hadn't lost any either. And she probably should have . . . Either way, there was going to be none of that nonsense today.

Clean sheet. Fresh start. She promised herself.

Pushing open the door into Big Hat of Coffee, she spotted Dorothy at a window table. Since their retirement, Dorothy and Angus went on as many sailing holidays as they could afford. As a result, Dorothy dressed as if she might be called upon to navigate a catamaran to Greece at a moment's notice. Today, under a yellow anorak, she wore a white fleece, navy chinos and deck shoes. Her silver-grey hair curled softly around her face and her skin had the healthy glow of the outdoorsy type.

'I got you a latte, but held off on the muffin, not because I'm stingy but I didn't know if you're on or off the sugar at the moment.'

'Off. So, how're things? How's Dad?'

'Grand.'

Angus, a mild man, was always 'grand'.

'Vanessa might be getting a new car,' Dorothy said. 'An electric one.' Vanessa was Cara's younger sister. She lived in Stuttgart. 'Not a Tesla. A cheap one. But I've my doubts about electric cars. Would they not be very slow? Like golf buggies? That whiny noise, would you be able? But,' she adopted a sanctimonious tone, '"the environment", she says.'

Cara couldn't help smiling. 'She has a point, though. And your favourite son-in-law Ed would agree.'

Dorothy's expression softened. 'How is he?'

Cara took a breath. Talking about Ed gave her the same feeling as unwrapping a beautiful piece of jewellery from its cushioned box and admiring its beauty. She'd always known she was nothing special. Nor did she want to be. Those poor souls who went on reality shows, yelling that they *believed* in themselves, well, she worried for them. Unexceptional as she was, she'd had hopes for her life: meeting a man—*the* man—was one of them. She wasn't going to settle for just anyone.

Happy marriages existed: her mum and dad were ordinary people, but each thought the other was extraordinary.

It. Happened.

Now, the older she got the more she saw how clueless her younger self had been: she and Ed, their happiness was down to nothing more than sheer dumb luck.

'Ed?' she said. 'Ed is great.'

'I'd a Skype with Champ,' Dorothy said. 'Was it Sunday?' Champ, the youngest of Dorothy's children, was living in Hong Kong. 'He's getting itchy feet again. Might as well just sign up for Elon Musk's Mars project.' Then, grimly, 'That'll give him adventure where he'll feel it. How are the Lovable Eccentrics? Has Vinnie set anything else on fire? No?' Dorothy's face fell. 'But clearly he has spirit.'

'He certainly has.'

'And while he was doing it, at least he wasn't on his screen.'

'You're right, Mum. A nice outdoor activity, setting fires.'

'So.' Dorothy's tone was meaningfully prim. 'Will you and Ed send him to a *child psychologist*?'

'Ah, no. He's just a kid, experimenting. They try to pathologize everything these days.'

'If I knew what "pathologize" meant, I'd probably agree with you. And how's Tom? Reading *War and Peace* yet? I don't know where he gets that intellectual streak from. It's certainly not from our side. So, any news at all?'

'Dilly's first communion tomorrow.'

This perked Dorothy up. She loved stories of Jessie's extravagance. ('*There*'s a woman who knows how to do life,' she frequently said.) 'Well? Flying the Pope in to do the honours?'

'Low-key. A buffet and an inland beach. No, don't ask me, I've no idea either.'

'I'd better give Dilly some cash.' Dorothy whipped out her wallet, then looked uncertain. 'Is twenty enough?'

'Twenty's loads.'

'Is Jessie making you go to the church bit?'

Cara shook her head. 'We're "welcome" to attend, but it's not mandatory.'

'Unlike the buffet and the—what did you call it? Inland beach? Ah, but she's great.' Dorothy could never disapprove of Jessie for long.

Cara's phone rang. She looked at the caller.

'Work?'

She turned it face downwards on the table. 'Yes.'

'Answer it, love! It might be something exciting. A paparazzi man might have made it into the penthouse!'

'More like someone didn't get their gluten-free toast.'

The phone rang again and, with a sigh, Cara picked up.

'Madelyn's sick,' Raoul said. 'Can you get here early?'

'Okay. Be with you in ten.' She hung up. 'Sorry, Mum, I've got to go.' She said goodbye and hurried towards Fitzwilliam Square. She was almost past the Spar when she realized she hadn't had any breakfast. Inside, there were cereal bars, apples, healthy-*ish* options. She bought two bars of chocolate and ate them furtively and very quickly. With the wrappers stowed in a nearby garbage can, she was almost able to convince herself it hadn't happened at all.

Twenty-Four

Tejumola shifted her noise-cancelling headphones off her ears and looked up from behind her monitor, 'I just pinged you the sales figures, Jessie.' Tejumola was PiG's chief financial officer. Well, she was their *only* financial officer. PiG had a mere seven staff at their 'headquarters' in the far-too-ordinary suburb of Stillorgan. Seven was all there was room for and glamorous it wasn't. Tejumola was small, serious, and no craic whatsoever, but that suited Jessie. When it came to finance she needed someone she could depend on.

She focused hard on the weekly sales figures from her eight stores. She took it very personally. If sales had dipped, she felt a protective sorrow, the same way she'd feel if TJ hadn't been invited to a birthday party for being 'weird'. But if one branch's takings were unusually high, she lit up with a warm glow, as if they'd won a medal for Irish dancing.

Kilkenny's take was down. Not drastically, but it was still a worry. She never forgot that she had fifty-six employees. Fifty-six people and their families for whom she was directly responsible.

Running a business was a big burden. At this stage, though, she'd never be able to work under another person. No choice but to carry on. As for Kilkenny, maybe she'd drive down this afternoon and show them some love. Good for morale . . . and, oh, Christ, Rionna had that look on her face.

'Just in,' she said. '*Perfect Living* want a spread of you and your gorgeous family in your beautiful home.'

Jessie turned an exaggeratedly miserable face to Rionna. 'Oh, *God!* My beautiful home is a total shithole.' Between the constant traffic from five children and two dogs, the bicycles, skateboards and dozens of shoes lining the scuffed hall, the kettle bells strewn on the living-room floor where her personal trainer put her through her paces three mornings a week, the house was a monument to wear and tear. 'I'd have to get the place painted.'

'You'd have to get the place *cleaned*.' Rionna was always the voice of reason. 'One of those crack-squad teams.'

'There are specialist companies that clean up crime scenes . . .'

Rionna laughed. 'They get rid of all traces of blood and gore. Grand so. I'll find you one.'

'I'd have to get the dogs groomed, wrestle the kids into clothes the magazine wants to promote . . .'

There wasn't a hope of cajoling Ferdia. Quite apart from his habitual hostility, his third-year exams were starting a week next Wednesday and it would be a mistake to eat into his study time.

But most important of all was TJ. Her decision to dress as a boy would be highlighted by a photo spread. Jessie felt fierce protectiveness and almost unbearable love for TJ. At nine years of age, she understood herself enough to express her wants: she knew she was a girl but she wasn't sure she liked it.

She wasn't sure if she'd like being a boy either. But she was already aware of the limitations of being female and didn't want them. Instead of being called Therese, she wanted to go by her initials TJ (the J referring to her middle name, Jennifer). Jessie and Johnny immediately enforced this. When TJ said she wanted to have her hair cut off, Johnny promptly took her to the barber.

Right now TJ didn't know what was going on for her and Jessie reassured her that it was okay not to know. But commentators and strangers hiding behind social media could be horribly cruel. It cut Jessie like a knife. (Johnny thought she didn't read the comments under any articles about her, but of course she did.)

'I say you should do it.' Mason, their intern, a twenty-two-year-old business-studies graduate, called across the office. Smart and social-media savvy, the rest of the—significantly older—staff tended to treat him as the oracle. He would go far. Not with PiG, sadly: his placement was only for eight months. Much as they'd love him to stay, Mason was bound for bigger and better. 'I can give you demographics, percentiles, readership reach . . .'

'No, no, you're grand,' Jessie said hastily.

'Anyone interested in my opinion?' Johnny didn't even look up from his screen. 'Considering I'll be wrestled into some paterfamilias sweater and slacks and made to smile like a gobshite for eight hours?'

'Nope,' Jessie said. 'Listen, Rionna. I'm going to pass.'

'But—'

'No. It's okay for me to do publicity but it's not okay to involve the kids.'

'Right. Gotcha.'

The office lapsed into silence. All that could be heard was the clicking of keyboards and the occasional sigh.

The decision to turn down the photoshoot sat well with Jessie. Last month's article in the *Independent*, when her old boss had been quoted as saying that not everyone always liked her, well, it had hurt. All Jessie had ever wanted, as a kid, was to be one of the gang. But she missed cues, misunderstood phrases and seemed to be the last to know about trends. It was as if she'd missed bits in life's script—the 'How To Be Cool' page, perhaps.

Her mother had been forty-two when she'd had Jessie, her father fifty-one. As their only child, she wondered if she'd inadvertently absorbed too many of their mannerisms. Maybe that was why adults tended to like her—teachers and other parents. Which, of course, was the last thing she needed.

As a lonely teenager, she had jumped on motivational quotes. Be yourself, she was advised. But that didn't work, and the problem was, she didn't know how to be anyone else.

In college, the role she carved out for herself was Miss Dependable. In shared houses, she did the cleaning and organized the bill-paying. Though her pristine Nissan Micra was scoffed at, no one turned down a lift. As for men, not one fancied her. She would get wild crushes on tormented boys who smoked hash and loved Jeff Buckley. If they noticed her at all, it was only to scoff.

Then she'd got a job. She still wasn't sure what had happened with Rory and Johnny but it was the first time in her life that sexy, good-looking men had taken an interest. The ones who usually glommed on were a lot older than her and tended towards prissiness or pomposity. They liked Jessie's reliable, respectable ways. More than once, she'd been praised for not being 'a ladette'.

Jessie suspected that these judgemental men didn't even fancy her—she'd never sensed passion from a single one. They were convinced they saw insecurity in her, which would make her malleable. Grateful, even.

They were wrong.

She was afraid she'd be on her own for ever—like, of *course*—but she'd never have settled for one of those patronizing, almost paternal men, with their odd hobbies. One had bred and shown Burmese cats. Another played the flute in an amateur orchestra.

Sometimes she found it hard to believe that she had her current life, where she was loved and—sometimes—liked. Her blood ran cold at how easily it could have stayed baffling and out-of-reach.

What beggared belief was that nowadays she was sometimes described as 'beautiful'. But that was all down to money. Without her highlights, her contact lenses, her Botox—yes, of *course* she had Botox, fillers too—without her personal trainer, her veneered teeth and her twelve-week blow-dries, she'd look like a capable, unlovable nobody, who existed only to 'help out'.

Twenty-Five

'Great,' Jessie said, staring at her screen.

Several heads snapped up.

'No, it's a good "great".' Jessie laughed. 'Not a sarcastic one. For once! All the tickets for Hagen Klein's weekend have sold! Seven weeks before he comes.'

This was good news on several levels. Jessie's chefs—she aimed to book four a year—were now the lifeblood of PiG. The profits the ticket sales generated were gratefully received. But the bump the shops got from each chef's visit was the real bonus.

Truth was, left to their own devices, the shops would barely break even. But every time a visiting chef demonstrated one or two of their signature dishes on a daytime television chat show, hundreds of new customers arrived into the stores, looking for the amchur powder or juniper molasses or whatever high-priced item it was that the maestro had used.

Jessie had been anxious about Hagen Klein—also known as the Chainsaw Chef. His Tromsø restaurant, Maskinvare, offered amazing food, sometimes cooked with power tools, but he was odd, unpredictable and he split demographics: his *über*-fans tended to be too young to afford tickets. But those who usually shelled out for PiG's cookery school liked their bad boys sanitized.

'The business is too dependent on chefs.' Mason interrupted Jessie's train of thought.

That was maybe the third time he'd uttered such a heresy and it wounded Jessie.

'All that work you and Johnny do just to get one to commit,' he said. 'It's not a productive use of your time. And what if a chef pulls out at the last minute?'

'We've insurance for that.' Jessie flicked a nervous look at Johnny. 'Don't we?'

'I'll check.' He looked a bit sweaty.

'You might want to drill down into the small print,' Mason said. 'We really need to have that conversation about your online store.'

PiG already had an online site, but in the last few weeks Mason had been pushing them to vastly expand its reach, to 'entirely reconfigure the PiG brand'.

Ordinarily, Jessie considered Mason a little genius, but on this subject he was wrong. Entirely wrong. What made the bricks-and-mortar stores so special was the wealth of knowledge each staff member had to offer. Every one of them cooked with the same products they sold. They had insider tips and hard-earned advice, which an impersonal website could never replicate.

'Jesus!' Rionna said. 'It's twenty past twelve. The table's booked for half past. Come on.'

They were meeting Erno Danchev-Dubois, a self-described food-trend consultant, in the nearby Radisson. The hotel was where they had all their meetings. The office was far too small.

'Am I to come?' Mason asked.

'If you promise to say nothing more about a new website.'

Mason smoothed down his already immaculate clothing and Jessie couldn't help smiling fondly on him. 'Look at you.'

In his rolled-up chinos, checked waistcoat, white T-shirt and red bow tie, he was a sight to behold. He carried a fogeyish floppy leather briefcase and wore no socks under his black-and-white brogues. Even with his mid-century black-framed spectacles, the smiley little face underneath the neat quiff looked about fifteen.

Nerd Hipster, apparently. Erno was bound to adore him.

Erno was a rare beast. Food-trend consultants existed by accident rather than design. They had usually been educated in several countries, spoke at least four languages, knew everyone—and had fallen on hard times. PiG had four such individuals on a retainer to predict what trend or foodstuff might take off in Ireland next. But it was an inexact science and mistakes were made, sometimes drastically.

As they piled into the car, Jessie said, 'Take Erno's guff today with a pinch of salt. He gave us a bum steer on the Bhutanese thing.'

'But he was spot-on about Columbian street food,' Johnny said.

'Which is why we haven't cut him loose.'

Erno had both a gin and tonic and a glass of wine before him. He leapt up, clicked his heels together, bowed and pressed his lips against first Jessie's and then Rionna's hand. Jessie was suddenly reminded of what Ferdia had said the one time he'd met Erno: that he seemed like a bad actor. ('Next time you see him, he'll be playing Mother Goose in the panto at the Gaiety.')

As she watched, Erno kissed Johnny on the cheek, once, twice, three times. Then Mason. That triple-kiss was new. Christ . . .

Taking charge—because no one else would—she gave the menu a glance. 'No starter for me. If I eat too much in the middle of the day, I fall asleep.'

'Me too,' Rionna said, on cue.

Rionna was great. Rionna was so bloody great. Jessie would be lost without Rionna.

'And me,' Johnny said.

Johnny was great too.

'Sure.' Mason smiled.

Mason didn't care about food. Mason was young.

Erno was the only one who looked sorrowful. But Jessie was having serious doubts about Erno.

After the usual chit-chat—talk of ambassadors, *fincas*, the new Aman hotel in Kyoto—they finally got down to business over dessert.

Brazil was Erno's prediction for the Next Big Thing.

'Again?' Jessie caught the waiter's eye and decided to signal for the bill. Bit abrupt, maybe, but she wasn't wasting any more time with this nonsense. 'Do you not remember? About three years ago? *Feijoadas* left, right and centre? More cassava than you could shake a stick at?'

Erno was discombobulated. 'Of course . . . Well . . . Bhutan is about to explode.'

'It certainly exploded our bottom line for last year's second quarter.' Jessie managed to smile. 'Listen, Erno, we can't stay for coffee. Lovely to see you. We'll be in touch.'

As they made their way to the car park, Jessie was deep in thought. Erno had gone off the boil and it was a worry.

'Poor fecker,' Johnny said.

'Wonder what's up—burn-out?'

'Too fond of the drink?'

'I suppose it's an occupational hazard.'

They had three other analysts but they'd worked with Erno the longest.

'Have you stuff to do back in the office?' Johnny asked. 'Why don't we knock off for the afternoon? It's been a hard week.' Johnny had been at a trade fair in Munich. He'd done three eighteen-hour days.

'I was thinking I might jump in the car and drive to Kilkenny, show them some love.'

'Jessie. One afternoon. I feel like I never see you.'

'You work with me and live with me. How much more of me do you want to see?'

'I'd just like to hang out with you for a couple of hours. Kilkenny can wait. It's only a blip.'

'You're making me sound like one of those high-powered weirdos who never switches off.'

'All I want is some alone time with my wife. What's so wrong with that?'

'Look, I'll be home by nine. Make sure the dogs get walked.'

Twenty-Six

'Dad! Get up, you lazy feck.'

Groggily, Johnny awoke. Nine-year-old TJ was peering down on him. 'You've to drive me to ju-jitsu,' she said. 'Here's a coffee. Drink it fast. Be ready in five.'

'Why can't your mother?'

'She's making the kinetic sand.'

The what?

But TJ was gone.

It was Dilly's first-communion day. With the amount of fuss being generated, Johnny couldn't imagine what her wedding day would be like. Down in the sunny, sky-lit kitchen, it was all go. The entire household was milling about and Jessie was head to head over a clipboard with McGurk. Johnny bristled. McGurk gave him the creeps. Usually he worked weekdays but Jessie must have press-ganged him into today.

'Good morning, Mr Casey.'

He'd told McGurk a thousand times to drop the 'Mr' lark, but McGurk persisted, as if it gave him pleasure to be irritating. There was the bang of an ex-seminarian about him. Johnny could see him in Rome debating points of theology with other cold, pointy-nosed young men.

McGurk had 'a story'. Like, of *course* he did—Jessie collected people with 'a story'. He'd been head of housekeeping in a luxury Swiss hotel but he'd had a breakdown. He was looking for a position with less pressure, but he remained 'a dedicated neat freak with a fetish for ironing'. Nothing wrong with that. McGurk's problem was that he wasn't an ounce of craic. He remained immune to Johnny's chat and charm. Unfailingly polite, he still managed to let Johnny know he loathed him.

Johnny had wanted to hire another cheery, chatty Filipina, like lovely Beth, the previous incumbent. But Jessie had set her heart on McGurk. 'It'll be good for the girls to see a man in a servile position.'

'I'm under the cosh,' Johnny had said, 'and they see me every day of their lives.'

To add to Johnny's irritation Ferdia, lanky and dishevelled, was lounging against a counter, eating Sugar Puffs from a big Pyrex bowl. He really did treat this place like a free hotel, Johnny observed. Living it up in his little cottage at the bottom of the garden, as if it were a suburban Chateau Marmont, then popping in and out of here to eat their food and collect his laundry.

'We'll set up the trestle table here.' McGurk was pointing with his pen.

'Not by the kitchen?' Jessie sounded surprised.

'No. Positioning it here will keep the flow going.'

Jessie nodded meekly. Well! That didn't happen often.

Somehow Johnny caught Ferdia's eye and Ferdia said, 'So terrified of her own ordinariness she has to surround herself with weirdos.'

Johnny chuckled, then abruptly remembered who he was talking to and snapped, 'Don't say that about your mother.'

'Speaking of weirdos,' Ferdia said, 'I wonder what Nell will be wearing today.'

He was a fine one to talk, Johnny thought, him and his Girl Power T-shirt.

'Something wonderful,' Jessie said. 'Unique. Individual.'

'Whatnow? *No.*' Ferdia addressed Jessie as if she were a simpleton. 'Her clothes are just plain mad.'

'Because all her stuff is from charity shops. She doesn't buy new clothes because of the planet. Or is it something to do with not "feeding capitalism"? Whatever it is, she still looks amazing.'

TJ jingled car keys at Johnny. 'Come on, you useless arse.' She headed for the door, Camilla and Bubs scampering after her. 'Someone hold the dogs!' she yelled. 'They're trying to get out.'

Saoirse grabbed them by their collars as they strained to escape the house.

Outside, a DHL van had pulled up. 'Howya, Johnny,' Steve, the delivery man, called.

See, *Steve* called him Johnny. Why couldn't McGurk?

'Howya, Steve,' TJ said.

'Howya, TJ.'

Although should Johnny be worried that the entire family seemed to be on first-name terms with their DHL man?

'Delivery for Jessie.'

'I'll take it.'

Johnny looked at the sender—Net-a-Porter! What the feck? Then he remembered the shoes she'd ordered for Jin Woo Park's wife.

'Who's coming today?' Ferdia asked Jessie.

'Ed and Cara, Liam and Nell. Some of the neighbours and a few friends. Twenty-five. Maybe thirty.'

'Unbelievable,' he muttered.

'Ah, don't be cross.' She wrapped her arms around his waist. 'You're only annoyed because we'll be out in the garden, disturbing you in your little flat.'

'You're a hypocrite.' He disengaged himself. 'When did you last go to Mass?'

'You pick your battles.' Jessie was breezy. 'Everyone else in her class is doing it.'

'Don't tell me you're going to take her around the neighbours and shake them down for cash?'

'That's the custom. We did it for you.'

'We weren't so rich then.'

We aren't so rich now . . .

For a moment, a teeny-tiny moment, she'd pretend the shoes were for her. She'd carefully open the lovely Balenciaga box, peep inside and *pretend.*

And, oh, God, look at them! The leather, the lustrous soft white leather. They were so *beautiful.*

Slipping them on for a second would do no harm, as long as she stayed on the carpet. She gazed in the mirror, at the perfect little heel, the fashion-forward pointy toe. The longer she looked, the more she wanted them.

Why can't I have something nice?

She worked *hard.* Yesterday she'd done a fifteen-hour day—she'd gone to Kilkenny and taken the staff out for morale-boosting drinks and pizzas. It was gone eleven when she'd got home.

These shoes were a size too big for her. But because they were slides, she *could* get away with it . . .

With sudden resolve, she made her decision. Feck it, she was keeping them!

'Mum!' Saoirse called up the stairs. 'Cara's here.'

Instantly Jessie was awash with guilt. Cara had come to do their monthly accounts: she was sure to find out about Jessie appropriating Océane's shoes.

Maybe she could just lie about it . . . Mostly she didn't mind Cara knowing what she bought. What she couldn't handle was poor Cara's pep-talks, as she tried to help Jessie and Johnny live within their means.

But they *did* live within their means. Apart from the one-off expenditures that distorted the bottom line—of which today was a prime example. It wasn't every year that a child made their first communion; this party for Dilly was atypical. So, yes, her dress had cost a fortune and a fair bit was being lashed out on this afternoon's catering—it was such a relief not to have to pretend to cook for it—but this sort of outlay wouldn't happen every month.

All Jessie really wanted from Cara was information. So that if the time ever came to cut back, she and Johnny could consult Cara's neat spreadsheets and see instantly what might go.

But, right now, there was no need.

Twenty-Seven

'We'll be gone for about three hours,' Jessie said, as the kids streamed towards the people-carrier. 'You'll have peace and quiet. McGurk is setting up stuff in the kitchen, just ignore him, he likes it better that way.' Then, thoughtfully, 'People *really* aren't his thing, are they?'

'Come *on*,' Johnny yelled.

'It'll only take me a couple of hours,' Cara said.

'But you'll be back later?' Jessie asked. 'For the party?'

'Course. Oh, my God, *gorgeous* shoes, Jessie.'

'Oh! Oh, thanks. The sale. Net-a-Porter.'

A sale in May? Really? Well, whatever, Cara would find out soon enough. It was beyond weird having access to so many of the Caseys' secrets, but they seemed cool about it, so she should be too.

'Don't let the dogs into the house,' was Jessie's parting shot. 'They'll eat the party food and Camilla is too old—she'll puke everywhere.'

The front door slammed. Cara sat at the computer in the living room, put in her earbuds and logged into the Caseys' current account. There were probably better things to be doing this morning, but what the hell? This wasn't so bad, and it gave her a satisfying sense of payback.

Most of Johnny and Jessie's outgoings were on their debit cards. There was so much, though. Pages and pages. In the main, boring basics—gas, groceries, phone bills—but with regular splurges that wildly inflated the overall outgoings.

It was fascinating, having a spyhole into the finances of a much richer family than her little foursome. You could just tell that Johnny or Jessie never anxiously watched the meter in the gas station, carefully timing it to stop at twenty euro because that was all they could afford. But she didn't judge them. If they had it, why shouldn't they spend it?

If she had unlimited money, she'd check into one of those Swiss places that were a cross between a hotel and a hospital and undergo luxury starvation. She'd be so busy being de-cellulited and un-wrinkled that she wouldn't even notice the hunger. Returning to real life would be tricky, though. Maybe she'd hire a person to walk twenty paces ahead of her, sweeping away any chocolate in her path, like a sobriety coach, except for food and—*What on earth?*

Ferdia, dishevelled in sweatpants and a washed-out T-shirt, loomed over her. She yanked out her earbuds.

'Christ!' He was saying. 'Oh, it's you, Cara!'

She laughed, from shock. 'Sorry. We scared each other.'

'I thought I had the place to myself. Creepy-ass McGurk is gone out, collecting tablecloths or something.'

'And you thought the coast was clear? What are you up to? Stealing bottles of wine?' She was very fond of him.

'Wi-Fi,' Ferdia said. 'Too weak down in my granny flat.'

'And instead you find your auntie lurking here.'

'Yeah, but my favourite auntie.' He threw himself into the chair next to her. 'What are you listening to?'

'*A Star Is Born*. Don't judge me.'

'Never. You didn't go to the church?'

'Short of time. You?'

'Supposed to be studying. Twelve days till the exams start.'

'Good luck with them. So? Plans for the summer? One long four-month party?'

His teeth flashed a grin. 'With Jessie Parnell as my ma? Not a chance.'

Cara realized, with a slight jolt, that Ferdia was no longer a gawky, gangly boy, but an actual man.

It seemed like it had happened overnight. With his dark eyes, messy black hair and inkings up and down his arms, he had the look of a sexy messiah.

She opened her mouth to tell him laughingly, then stopped. Jessie went on so much about how good-looking he was that she felt sorry for him.

'Two days after the exams,' Ferdia said, 'I start interning in the Social Research Institute. Apart from my forcible expatriation to a villa in Tuscany for a week in August, along with every other member of my extended family, it'll be nose to the grindstone all summer.'

Still focused on his looks, Cara realized that he was very like the picture of Rory that hung on the living-room wall.

A noise in the hallway alerted them.

'McGurk is back,' Ferdia said. 'See you later.'

'Okay, darlin'.'

Through the sliver between the door and its frame, she caught a glimpse of McGurk's skinny figure carrying trays into the kitchen. Desserts. She had a sixth sense for sugar.

The front door shut, and moments later came the sound of McGurk's car driving away again.

As if the point of a knife was being held to her jugular, she was up and moving towards the kitchen.

Her heart banged hard at the array of beauty before her: macaroons in bright pops of orange, lilac and lime; dense, dark, swoonily moist opera cakes; raspberry tarts glistening with a luscious pale pink glaze; adorably solid little cheesecakes; platters of marshmallow and pineapple kebabs—they must be getting a chocolate fountain . . .

Her heart pounded, adrenalin pulsed through her and the top of her head felt open to the air.

The opera cakes were the ones she wanted, and nobody would mind if she had one. But if she had any at all, she wouldn't stop until she'd eaten at least ten.

For the others to discover she'd devoured half a tray of cakes would be too shaming. She'd have to dispose of an entire tray of twenty.

She *could* do it. They'd just think McGurk had accidentally left a tray behind in the patisserie.

Or she could try to blame the dogs. Camilla was old and slow but Bubs was a scrappy little fighter who'd have no trouble getting on the table.

The deal-breaker was the bathroom. Going upstairs to Johnny and Jessie's family bathroom would feel too much of a violation of their trust.

Her hand gripped the door frame, a sheen of sweat coated her forehead and she only realized how tightly she was clenching her back teeth, when something inside her mouth slipped and snapped. In her head, the noise sounded like a mini-explosion, and something small and sharp was rattling about in her mouth.

Shocked, confused, she spat the object into her hand—it was a chunk of tooth. Using her tongue to explore, it dragged against the jagged edge of a molar. She tasted blood.

Horror shrank her skin. Teeth were vital. On a primal level, teeth represented survival. Why had this happened? She had an electric toothbrush. She had check-ups.

But it couldn't be . . . She'd only been throwing up for about a month. That wasn't long enough to erode a tooth to breaking point.

. . . Was it?

Unwelcome memories of vomiting three and four times a day assailed her. Yesterday, despite all her early hope, had veered out of her control.

She had to admit that she'd packed an awful lot into a very short time.

Twenty-Eight

Liam stood in Johnny's crowded back garden, watching Nell skilfully organize a noisy gang of besotted kids into some game of her own invention. It was only a year since he'd first seen her in that supermarket but sometimes a year seemed a very long time. Sometimes even a week did. Because within days of meeting her, he'd been poleaxed with love.

All of a sudden he'd understood where he and Paige had gone wrong. Marrying her had been a decision motivated by emptiness and fear: his career was over and a huge part of his identity had abruptly disappeared. *He* had almost disappeared. Paige had offered a structure, a shape, a new way to be.

But his feelings for Nell were entirely different. Her spontaneity and joy were contagious and he loved this new version of himself.

Nevertheless, he knew his form, and weeks were spent braced for the disenchantment to kick in. Eventually, cautiously, he'd come to accept that it might never happen.

'Hi, Liam.'

It was Cara, pretty and dimpled.

'Oh, hey.' Everyone always said how 'totally lovely' Cara was, but something about her made him uneasy.

Nell flew past, trailed by a long line of children. They watched her go.

'She's magical with kids,' Cara said.

'Yep.' Liam smiled. 'Almost a shame she doesn't want any.'

'She does, though?' Cara looked puzzled. 'But there are already too many of us on the planet?'

'Same thing.'

'Is it?'

Luckily, this was the moment when that not-so-little thug Vinnie shoved one of the other kids and Cara left to intercede.

It was a relief. Encounters with Cara unsettled him, as if she could see right into his heart, cataloguing every dark thought he'd ever entertained.

One of his most uncomfortable truths was that Nell's decision to be child-free was the final sign that they were perfect for each other. He didn't want any more children. He'd failed at fatherhood. When Paige had been pregnant with Violet, he'd been so buzzed. But his crazy elation at Violet's birth had quickly evaporated in the face of her unknowable needs and incessant howling.

According to Paige, he did everything wrong: fed her too quickly; changed her nappies too clumsily. When he tried to calm her cries, she always wailed louder. Violet didn't like him, he told Paige—who said that now *he* was being a baby.

When Lenore was born, he'd hoped that she'd like him better than her sister did, but the same pattern was repeated.

He didn't know where he'd gone wrong but they'd always been Paige's girls. Now more than ever.

The truth was, he didn't miss them.

Two buddies in his cycling club were in similar situations: divorced, living apart from their kids and doing okay. Sometimes, when they were a bit drunk, they talked about the shame they were supposed to feel.

'I feel bad for not feeling bad,' Dan had said, which was exactly how Liam felt.

Dutifully, once a week, he FaceTimed the girls—and those Sundays always came around so fast. He had so little to say and they had even less to say to him. ('TBH,' he'd told Dan, 'if they decided they weren't bothered about speaking to me, it'd be a relief.'

'I hear ya.')

'Useless heap of junk!' someone—TJ—yelled. The bat she'd been playing with had broken. 'Grown-up needed over here!' Her eyes slid right past Liam. 'Ed,' she called. 'Can you help me?'

Ed had been earnestly counselling Vinnie-the-thug. Ambling over to TJ, he got down to her level.

'Let's take a look. Ah, right.' He pointed at the handle. 'See here, TJ . . .'

Ed had a way with children. It was all to do with how he managed his energy, Liam saw. He slowed it right down to the speed of the child. There he was, patiently explaining what had gone wrong. If it had been Liam, he'd have grabbed the bat, seen it wasn't fixable, then impatiently urged TJ to play another game, while he shifted his attention back to something that interested him.

'Can you fix it?' TJ beseeched Ed.

'I'll give it my best shot.'

Maybe, Liam thought, because he'd been the baby in his own family, he'd never learnt how to behave with younger kids. Or maybe he was too selfish. Maybe some people just weren't cut out to be fathers . . .

For much of the afternoon Nell was watchful, waiting for an opportunity for her 'chat' with Dilly.

Eventually it arrived when Dilly flung herself on her, looking for a hug.

'Hey?' Nell asked. 'Can we have a conversation?'

Dilly squinted suspiciously. 'A good one or a bad one?'

'Aaaah . . .' She didn't want to traumatize Dilly and get into Jessie's bad books. 'An interesting one.'

'*Oooo*kay.'

They sat, cross-legged, on the grass. Liam joined them.

'Liam is your godfather.' Nell got out the envelope. 'I'm Liam's wife and this is from both of us. So. I haven't known you very long but I think you're aces.'

'I think *you*'re aces!'

'Can we tell you about a little girl called Kassandra? She's eight years of age, the same as you. If you open the envelope, you'll find a picture of her.'

Confused, but obedient, Dilly studied the photo. Uncertainly she said, 'Her hair is cool.'

'She comes from a country called Syria, where a war is going on.'

Dilly's face formed into an expression of slightly theatrical fear.

'It's okay,' Liam said, quickly. 'She's safe here in Ireland.'

'But!' Nell was not to be derailed. 'She had to leave all her stuff behind in Syria. Her toys and her clothes and, well, everything.'

'Can't she buy new ones?'

'Her mum has no money. And her dad is dead.'

Dilly flicked a fearful glance at Liam. She seemed genuinely moved.

'She doesn't live in her own house. She doesn't have her own room. All their meals come from a big kitchen that feeds lots of people.'

'So her mum doesn't have to cook!'

Riiiight . . . Dead Dad was good, had impact. Mass catering not so good. Nell had better reframe this. 'But sometimes she gets given . . .' What food did Dilly hate? '. . . shepherd's pie.'

'Ewww!'

'And if she doesn't eat it, no one makes her another dinner.' *Like they would do for you.* 'So Kassandra has to stay hungry until the next morning.'

'Oooh . . .'

Dilly was too privileged to understand hunger, but she knew the concept to be a tragic one.

'So today Uncle Liam and I can give you two hundred euro. Or we can give Kassandra that money. It can be a gift from you to her.'

'Could she buy a house?'

'No, honey. But she could buy two bags of Haribo and two Twirls every week for the next year.'

'That's *all*?'

'But that's lots! That would make her very happy.'

'Well, *sure*. Maybe we could have a play-date.'

And maybe not. Jessie had been charmed by the idea of Dilly's communion money helping another kid. But even the nicest-seeming people were weird about hanging out with asylum-seekers. 'In the envelope is a letter from her, telling you about her life. You could read it if you like.'

'Okay. I will. Ferdia!' Her half-brother was passing. 'Ferdia, can I show you my exciting thing?'

''Kay.' He knelt while Dilly filled him in.

'So there's this little girl from . . . What country, Nell?'

'Syria.'

Tripping over her words, Dilly explained everything.

'Whose idea was this?' Ferdia sounded concerned. Slightly angry, almost.

'Mine,' Liam said. 'Mine and Nell's. Both of us.' There was a belligerent edge to his voice.

'*Really?*'

'It's a cool idea.' Anxiety had risen in Nell. Things had been going so well. This fool had better not derail it. 'Dilly is happy for it, because she's a generous, thoughtful person.'

'Okay.' The fire in Ferdia's eyes had died down. 'Yeah, well . . .' As if realizing he couldn't fault the plan in any way, he said, his tone reluctant, 'So that's . . . yeah, great. Fair play, Dilly.'

'Chocolate fountain!' Dilly cried, clambering to her feet and racing across the garden. Ferdia followed.

'*What* is his problem?' Nell demanded.

'Over-indulged brat.'

'It's like he thinks he's the only woke one round here.'

Quietly Liam said, '"Could she buy a house?"'

Instantly Nell's mood lifted. 'I know! I thought I was going to lose it when she said that.'

'We did a good thing.'

She clasped his hand. Gratitude washed through her, so much that she felt almost high. 'Thank you for this.'

Twenty-Nine

Daddy, when is the chocolate fountain starting?

Johnny, get Liam a beer.

Dad, Camilla needs to do a poo.

Johnny, get Raphaela some rosé.

Buddy, where's your jacks?

Johnny, give your phone to Bridey.

Dad, Camilla's done a poo in the doll's house.

The afternoon had passed in constant motion, attending to the needs of others, until, in an unexpected lull, nobody was looking for anything and Johnny was almost felled by sudden exhaustion.

He made his way to the garden table and gratefully lowered himself to the bench. He felt about a hundred and twenty.

It never stopped. It. Just. Never. *Stopped.*

Shrieking kids were running around the grass that he'd never got the chance to cut. Adults were swigging energetically, crossing to and from the kitchen—probably for more alcohol, God, you could never really get enough on an afternoon like this—and darting around the garden, irritably admonishing their charges for bad behaviour.

He took a long swallow from his beer bottle.

It had been a hard week. The trade fair in Frankfurt, those days were so long. Four meetings an hour, twelve hours a day. For three days. Pitch after pitch from one food supplier after another. Having to make decisions on the spot. Should he order four crates? Or seven thousand? By the end of the first morning his brain had turned to noodles.

But this week hadn't been exceptional: every week was hard.

There went Jessie again, striding with purpose. There was something about her that was giving him that fearful feeling . . . Through exhausted eyes he watched her. It was the shoes. White pointy things that he'd never seen before. Momentarily, he was impressed by how she avoided sinking into the grass in the skinny heels—pure strength of will.

Then the fearful feeling returned. There was some story attached to those shoes. Not a good one. He could check but, right now, he didn't want to know.

All he wanted was a peaceful day, maybe a rainy Sunday afternoon on the couch, watching a black-and-white film, the kids and Jessie slumped sleepily beside him, ice-cream cartons and spoons on the table. There was a yearning in him, for—yeah—a holiday. Not one of their usual action-packed ones, but an actual rest, of sleeping and silence. Jessie often talked dreamily about a restorative break at a spa. It wouldn't be for him—he was scared to have a massage in case he got an erection—but there were men's retreats, surely . . .

Except he suspected that that would probably involve chopping down trees to build his own shelter, which sounded even more stressful.

Oh Christ, here came Jessie, looking like she had a job for him. If Camilla had done another poo, he was just going to get into his car and drive to Rosslare, board the ferry to France, disembark at Cherbourg and keep going across Europe until he ran out of land, then maybe just drive into the sea.

'Johnny, don't go mad, but the box of Soviet stuff for Jin Woo Park? When it comes I want to deliver it in person.'

'To Geneva? No!'

'Ryanair flights are barely more than the cost of FedExing the box.' She stopped. 'Bad time? You're wrecked, babes. Sorry, sweetie. Enjoy your beer.'

That was the thing about Jessie. She always knew when to pull back . . . Hold on, what's happening here?

Ferdia, his face in a too-familiar thundery expression, was striding across the grass—Jesus Christ, he was the *spit* of Rory. How had he not seen this before? Or maybe it was a new development. Either way, it was impossible to move past the Kinsellas. If Ferdia and Saoirse weren't visiting their grandparents in Errislannan, newspaper articles were rehashing the bad blood. Ferdia had just had some sort of a scuffle with Liam, by the look of things.

Liam's phone rang and he looked at it, almost in outrage. 'It's work.' He pressed Accept. 'Chelsea?'

Nell listened to him getting an earful from his manager. 'Busy. Never got the chance.' Then, 'Hey. You do the rosters. Put more of us on. Responsibility?

Call me "acting manager" all you like, but I'm not getting paid what you're getting.' More listening. 'I'll do it tomorrow.' A sigh. 'Monday, then.' He ended the call.

'She's raging I didn't bank yesterday's takings. But if she only has three of us on, what does she expect?'

'Mmm. Totally.' Actually, Nell worried that Liam's attitude to the woman who managed the six PlanetCycle shops was too belligerent.

'Maybe it's time I moved on. I'm getting all the grief of a manager without any of the money.'

'Liam, don't do anything mad.'

'No. But. The sports-massage thing. I've been thinking about it long enough. Maybe I should just go for it.'

'Could you work and study at the same time?' They were lucky that Paige let them live rent-free, but they still needed money for food, a phone, the essentials.

'Ah, yeah, I'll be grand.'

'All okay?' Jessie was suddenly at their side. 'Dilly went for it?'

'Yes! Thank you!' Nell was jubilant.

'*Soooo.*' There was a sly little twinkle in Jessie's eye. 'Wanted to run something by the pair of you. Tuscany, all of us, August? You know about it, Nell?'

'Mmm, sort of.' A villa had been booked and everyone was invited.

'I was thinking,' Jessie said, 'about Violet and Lenore.' She raised a hand. 'Liam! Hear me out!' Speaking quickly, she said, 'There's room for them, they've been before, they loved it, their cousins miss them, *I* miss them, we all miss them, I bet they miss us, Paige can come if she likes—'

'No,' Liam said. 'Not Paige.'

'Okay. But let's invite the girls. How would you feel about it, Nell?'

'Oh, my God, I'd totally *love* it.' A relaxed week in the sunshine would be a great way to get to know the girls. Unlike that one grim, tense dinner in an air-conditioned bunker in Atlanta where the only sound was of expensive cutlery clinking off expensive plates mixed with Lenore's quiet sobs.

'Liam?'

'Yeah,' he said. 'Maybe. We'd have to do something with flights. Would they fly from Atlanta to Ireland first? Or would they go straight to Rome? But we can work it out. I'll talk to Paige.'

'Or I can talk to Paige?'

'Jessie,' Liam said gently, 'she's *my* ex-wife. Let *me* talk to her.'

'Okay! You'll do it? Thanks!' Delighted, Jessie swung away.

'That would be amazing!' Nell sparkled at Liam.

'Whatever makes my angel happy.'

From across the garden, Johnny studied Liam. There was a gleam about him that snagged the eye, as if he'd been dipped in a glossy topcoat. He looked way too glamorous for this suburban garden. Nell, by the same token, didn't. But she was endearing, immensely likeable, taking such joy in living. All the kids were besotted—just look at her there, twirling in a circle with Tom, her pink hair flying. Would *Nell* let him have a quiet life? he wondered.

She was certainly a lot more easy-going than Jessie could ever be. And from one or two things he'd gathered, herself and Liam were a great pair for the alfresco riding—beaches and forests and whatnot.

But you couldn't be thinking like that about your brother's wife.

Johnny's smartwatch beeped, triggering his heart to pound pure adrenalin for a half-second. It was as if Jessie had seen into his thoughts and was on to him. But it was just a new email. Listlessly, he scanned it. If he'd had any energy, he'd have felt despair, but all he could produce was dull acceptance: at least the decision had been taken out of his hands.

Jessie's fiftieth birthday was coming up in July. She didn't want a big party, like she'd had for her fortieth. After that night, she'd admitted tearfully to Johnny, 'I wasn't sure if anyone there even liked me. I felt like I used to as a teenager.' She wanted to spend this milestone birthday with close friends and family, maybe twelve or fourteen people. Hefty hints had been dropped about a murder-mystery weekend. Jessie *loved* period crime dramas—the clothes, the backstories, the scandal in people's pasts.

Johnny had contacted a world-renowned hotel in Scotland, legendary for these events, but the prices were horrifying, almost a thousand pounds a head. Another strike against it was the logistics of flying a dozen people to another country. But a three-hour drive away in County Antrim, a much smaller country house offered something similar. It looked okay, nice even—a Regency-style building. The only worry was the price: disconcertingly reasonable.

ShitAdvisor was no help: the thirty-seven reviews were either five-star or one-star, almost nothing in between. And, of course, the five-star raves, which enthused about the delicious food, the warm hospitality and the great costumes, could be fake. Even though the birthday was hurtling towards Johnny at increasing speed, he'd been umming and aahing between the two places. It was only yesterday that he'd enquired about availability in the Scottish hotel—and now they were telling him they were fully booked. However, reasonably priced Gulban Manor in County Antrim had plenty of room. So, Gulban Manor it was!

Liam grabbed Jessie as she scooted past. 'I messaged Paige. She likes the idea. The girls are already booked into summer camps but she's gonna see about moving stuff around.' He smiled. 'You know Paige. She'll make it happen.'

'Thank you, Liam, thank you.' Jessie was almost more grateful than Nell, which was saying something. 'If you need help with the flights . . .'

'Jessie, you're way too generous.' There was a warning note in his voice. 'But my stuff with Paige and the girls is my stuff. Let me do this. Okay?'

'Okay.'

Thirty

By 7 p.m., the neighbours had drifted home. All who remained were the Casey brothers and their families: the adults gathered around the table in the garden, the younger kids watching YouTube in the living room.

For the thousandth time that day Cara touched her broken tooth with her tongue. Immediately all the conversation around her receded.

A tooth—a big one, a molar—had simply snapped in two. Could it *really* be connected to her throwing up? Worrying about her weight had been a constant, nearly all her life. As a skinny, knock-kneed eight-year-old, she knew that too much bread and butter would make her fat—and fat was the worst thing any girl could be.

Where had she even got the idea from?

Not from her mum and dad: they weren't like that.

The girls at school? Well, everyone was always saying they were too fat and wanted to be much skinnier, but had anyone taken it to the extremes that she had? During her final two years at school, her first thought on awakening was always, Today I won't eat. Despite her poor mum begging her to have breakfast, she often survived on water until late afternoon, when she'd cave, and speedily shove food into herself, consuming far more calories than if she'd stuck to regular meals. Her self-loathing was monumental, and although she understood in her head that anorexics lived lives of misery, in her heart she envied their discipline.

Through her college years in Dublin, she'd always felt too big, but the life she was living—little money, eating cheap carbs, drinking pints—gave her no choice.

Things only really went to hell when, aged twenty-two, she went to Manchester to do her hotel training—homesickness, combined with constant access to food, sent her weight soaring. Desperate, she ordered pills to speed up her metabolism, but they made her so jittery she had to stop. A brief spell with laxatives followed, but what they did to her body scared her. And then she'd found vomiting.

After she'd gone back to Dublin, she'd moved on to other, healthier types of weight control. Bootcamp workouts had featured for a while.

When she was twenty-nine she'd done a liquid diet for ten weeks and was the thinnest she'd ever been as an adult. She'd felt *amazing*. But it hadn't lasted: as soon as she'd resumed normal food, the weight piled back on. The shame had been intense, she'd felt a type of grief to have lost that skinny self. Ever since, she'd been trying to find her way home to that paradise size.

Apart from a short relapse after each of her pregnancies, she'd thought she had the vomiting under control.

Why couldn't she eat normally? Why did she have to know the calorific value in literally everything? Why was she always either on the way up or the way down, desperately clawing for control?

Or she could try looking at it another way: why couldn't she accept herself, whatever her size?

There were lots of overweight people who were fine with what they were. Why couldn't she be one of them?

Cara tuned back into the conversation around the table. Johnny was saying, 'This fiftieth-wedding-anniversary thing, how much are we dreading it?'

Next month, the senior Caseys, Canice and Rose, were holding a weekend of festivities to mark their golden wedding. They lived on the other side of the country in the small County Mayo town of Beltibbet. Attendance at the celebration was obligatory.

'Is their present sorted?' Liam asked. 'Jessie, you're doing it, right?'

'Not that it matters,' Johnny said. 'We could give them actual Fort Knox and they still wouldn't be impressed.'

'Fuck them,' Liam said.

'Ah, Liam!'

'Seriously, though, why did they even bother having kids? All they ever cared about was each other.' Liam had made a good point.

In Beltibbet, Canice was the town solicitor, a justice of the peace and a local bigshot. Every one of his children was a bitter disappointment to him, something he liked to hold forth on: 'Three sons and all I wanted was for just one to follow me into the family business. Keep the name alive. But Johnny is too thick, Ed is in love with a shrub, and Liam was a dead loss from day one, thinking he'd be Roger Bannister when it was clear to all and sundry that he was Forrest Gump. "That boy sure is a running fool"!'

It was always dressed up in laughter and ha-ha-has, but Cara knew that Canice's sons didn't find it remotely amusing.

And Rose was as bad as Canice. She was a 'beauty'—certainly she was where the three Casey men had got their good looks. She was also 'fragile' and very 'proper'. The Casey family home, a detached two-storey with a half-acre of garden, standing apart from the rest of the great unwashed, was a haven of gracious living, with bone-china milk jugs and Waterford crystal sherry glasses. At eighty-one, Rose still got her nails and hair done twice a week. She'd never worked outside the home—or ever really worked *inside* it either, from what Ed had told Cara. Throughout his childhood there had been a succession of flustered, overstretched women from the town, Mrs Dooley and Mrs Gibbons and Mrs Loftus, who did the laundry, the cooking and the polishing of the silver.

No one knew where Rose had got her notions—she was from the nearby town of Ballina.

'They weren't great parents.' Ed was matter-of-fact.

'But was it our fault?' Johnny asked Ed, like he always did. 'Didn't it bother you?'

'It would have been better if they'd been kinder. But when I was about thirteen, I got it. I'd never be good enough for them. So it just stopped . . . mattering.'

'Liam?' Johnny asked.

'Like I said, fuck them.' Liam swigged from his beer bottle, then gave a short laugh. 'Look, they were never physically cruel—'

'You're setting the bar pretty low there, Liam!'

'Seriously, Johnny, calm the head,' Liam said. 'We all turned out okay.'

The varying reactions from the three brothers were interesting, Cara decided. Liam behaved as if he didn't care. Maybe he got enough love and validation from the other parts of his life . . . But she sensed anger low down in him.

Ed was genuinely at peace about it. 'They did the best they could.' He seemed such a mild, unremarkable man, but underneath was a steady self-belief.

Johnny was the one who kept coming back to pick over the pieces. He still held out hope that this could be fixed. Still bound to Canice and Rose by strong, complicated ties.

Thirty-One

Around 8 p.m., Ferdia finished a game of Fortnite and slunk up to the house. The fridge, rammed with beer, rattled as he opened it. He shouldn't have a drink, he should really be studying, but he was so fucking low. Sammie had got a year's placement in MIT. In six weeks, she was leaving Ireland. They'd talked it out, their most mature discussion ever. No shouting, no accusations, just a sad admission that they would never survive a year apart.

If he could just hold her for five minutes, he'd feel better, but that was off the cards this weekend. Since her move to the States had been confirmed, she'd become far more serious about her work.

Ferdia, though, was struggling. Too much of his time was spent wondering if his degree would be worth anything.

If only the exams were over. Living under their impending shadow was a killer—all he wanted was to get drunk and switch his head off for a while. Surreptitiously, he slid two more bottles from the fridge. He'd slope off quietly to the bottom of the garden, lie on his bed and smoke some weed . . .

'Hey!'

Fuck. His mother had spotted him.

'You can drink whatever you want in company, like a civilized person. But you're not sneaking off to get scuttered on your own. Come over here and join us.'

Ferdia hesitated—then gave in. At least that guaranteed a steady supply of alcohol.

Ed, Liam and Nell budged up to make room on the bench.

He swigged steadily from his beer, tuning out their boring bullshit talk. God, how had his life come to this? A Saturday night, trapped with this bunch . . .

'And they came from Syria?' Johnny was quizzing Nell. 'Just the mother and daughter? What happened to the dad?'

'He was killed.'

They must be talking about Dilly's asylum-seeker.

'Honestly?' Jessie said. 'Christ, that's horrific. We don't know how lucky we are. We should organize a play-date with Dilly and the little girl—is it Kassandra? And what's the mother like? Can she . . . you know, speak English?'

'Perfect English,' Nell said. 'But she's very quiet. Understandably. She's been through an awful lot.'

'. . . Has she?'

Scornfully, Ferdia watched his mother wrestle with her desire to know the gory details against the need to be respectful.

'Maybe she'd like to come over for dinner, some night.'

Ferdia snorted.

'What?' Jessie asked.

'You're so . . . *bougie*. Inviting people for dinner, so you can show off and say you're "friends" with an asylum-seeker.'

'Ferdia,' Johnny growled. 'Shut it.'

The scuffle was interrupted by a buzzing noise from Johnny's wrist. His smartwatch. Jesus, he was tragic.

An expression flickered across his face that made Jessie ask, 'What now?'

'Marek and Natusia have given notice. They're going back to Poland.'

'That's a shame. They were lovely. No trouble.'

'What's up?' Cara asked.

'Ah, nothing,' Johnny said. 'Just my flat in Baggot Street, the one I lived in before me and Jessie, the tenants are leaving.'

'You'll have no trouble renting it again,' Nell said. 'People are desperate.'

'I should redecorate it. Now's a good time.'

Nell jumped in. 'I'll do it.'

'Absolutely not. You're a set designer. Not a decorator.'

But Nell wasn't letting this go. 'A lot of the time, painting and decorating is exactly what I do.'

'We'll pay you, then.'

She coloured. 'Please, no. It's on me. You and Jessie give Liam and me so much. It's the least I can do.'

Jessie said, 'The only way you're doing it is if you let us pay you.'

Nell fixed Jessie with a bold stare. 'We'll see,' she said, and gave a small smile.

'You know, you should Airbnb it,' Liam said.

It had been only a matter of time before someone suggested this, but it was no surprise to Ferdia that the person was Mr Arsey McArse of Arse Town, Liam.

'You'd make much more money that way,' Mr Arsey McArse of Arse Town continued. 'Perfect location. City centre, you'd be full seven nights a week.'

Nell looked stricken.

'Ah, no.' Johnny shrugged off the suggestion. 'It'd take loads of micro-managing. Organizing cleaning and keys, and if a pipe burst or something . . .'

'I can take care of all that,' Cara said.

Surprised, everyone turned to her. 'In work, I've access to great house-keepers, Dublin's finest plumbers, electricians. The Ardglass is five minutes' walk from your flat. If anything went wrong, they'd be there in no time.'

'But you've a job and two kids.'

'I wouldn't have to do anything, except delegate. They'd have to be paid, though, the cleaners and such.'

She looked at Johnny, who nodded vigorously, 'Course! Of course they would.'

'But me?' Cara said. 'All I'd need is a key.'

'What about the host malarkey?' Johnny asked. 'Airbnb reviews are always going on about great hosts who leave them freshly baked apple tarts and baskets of logs for the fire.'

'No way,' Ed said. 'I stay in Airbnbs all summer long, and I've *never* been handed an apple tart.'

'No to apple tarts,' Cara said. 'But let me talk to a couple of the house-keepers about running it between them. I'm sure it'll work.'

A stunned silence followed. Had they actually found a solution to a mini-crisis that was an improvement on the original situation?

'Well!' Jessie was radiant with pleasure. 'Fair play,' she said to Ed and Liam. 'Both of you marrying such resourceful women.'

While Cara laughed off the compliment, Nell looked literally sick.

'It'd be very handy if you were having an affair,' Jessie said suddenly.

'What would?' Cara sounded mystified.

'Having the key to Johnny's flat. Knowing the schedule. You could time your meet-ups for when no one was staying there.'

Cara rolled her eyes. 'Yeah, I'm definitely affair material.'

'You're too hard on yourself,' Jessie said. She looked at Ferdia. 'Isn't she?'

Ferdia squirmed. But he didn't want Cara to be embarrassed.

'Do you mind?' Ed said. 'I *am* here.'

Everyone laughed, except—Ferdia noticed—Nell.

She muttered something about going to the bathroom and left the table. Seconds later, so did Liam.

Ferdia decided to follow and found them in the kitchen.

'. . . no one can get a place to rent in Dublin,' Nell was saying. 'All because landlords are Airbnbing flats to tourists.'

'Why shouldn't Johnny get the most he can from his investment?' Liam's face was close to Nell's.

'Johnny isn't hurting for cash. But thousands of people in our city can't afford a flat.'

'So he should just give money away because of the greater good?'

'Actually, *yes*.'

'That's bullshit.'

'He's hardly going to be destitute,' Nell called after him, as he strode off towards the front door. Then she noticed Ferdia. 'What do *you* want?'

In the face of her righteous ire, Ferdia suddenly felt afraid. 'Just to say that Airbnb is only one reason why no one can rent a place. We need much more social housing and an end to—'

'I *know*. But it doesn't help either, does it?'

Chastened, he slunk away.

Thirty-Two

Jessie yawned as her elbow almost slid off the table.

'Go to bed, babes,' Johnny said. 'I'll look after things.'

But Cara and Ed were still there and some weird shit was going on out in the hall with Nell and Liam.

'Ah, no, we'll head off,' Ed said, decent as always.

'Okay. Sorry. Just wrecked.' She said her goodbyes and trailed up the stairs. Unexpectedly, she felt sober, sad and unable to stop thinking about what it had been like after Rory had died so suddenly, all those years ago.

The first year afterwards was a blur. She'd taken almost no time off work. Not because of her, very real, need to keep earning but because—and it took her a long time to understand this—she didn't believe that Rory was actually dead.

The kids were far better than her at expressing themselves. Two nights out of three, Ferdia woke with nightmares. Saoirse, barely two years old, far too young to understand concepts such as 'alive' or 'dead', yelled the house down whenever she was away from Jessie. She read that children who lost a parent at an early age, even if, like Saoirse, they were too young to remember them, would always feel a loss, even if they couldn't consciously attribute it. They were more likely than others to experience depression in later life.

She worried all the time about the kids, and any energy left over, she gave to her job. She wasn't as effective as she'd once been—her concentration was terrible, her ability to grasp facts slippery—but it mattered as much to her as it ever had.

Her head knew Rory was dead but her true self had no clue.

One of the few feelings she remembered from those first twelve or eighteen months was embarrassment, at once again being a bit of an oddball. By falling in love with Rory, him falling in love with her, and going on to have a little boy and a little girl, she'd felt that she finally fitted in. No more pompous boyfriends with strange hobbies. No more being sniggered at by other women, either. Courtesy, once again, of Rory were the first real girlfriends she'd had in years—his sisters, Izzy and Keeva. But suddenly she was a young widow, enraged by the logistical challenges of life without Rory. Getting Ferdia to school and Saoirse to daycare, making time to collect them—well, she and Rory had had a system. Now that she was doing it all on her own, she was furious.

'I have to do everything!' she complained to her grief counsellor.

'What else are you feeling?'

'Worry. For Ferdia and Saoirse.'

'What about you?'

'I'm pissed off that I'm working full-time and I'm basically a single mother.'

'Anything else?'

'There *is* nothing else.'

The few tears she cried during that first year were of frustration or exhaustion, never grief.

Eventually she got a nanny, choosing a man, so the kids would have a consistent male presence in their lives. It wasn't enough to quiet her crushing guilt at her failure to be both a mother and a father to them, so she overcompensated, organizing far-too-frequent treats, always striving to be 'fun', but feeling like she was single-handedly pushing a giant stone up a steep hill.

During those months it seemed as if the weather was always misty and grey.

One ordinary afternoon, during the second year of Rory's absence, she was in her car. She automatically reached across to hold Rory's hand—they'd always been great hand-holders. When it wasn't there waiting for hers, the full impact of his forever absence hit her. *He's gone. He's dead. And I won't get to squeeze his hand later today. Or tomorrow. Or ever again.*

The shock felt like a physical blow and shunted her abruptly into a new phase of life without him. He was dead and she was ruined. She would never fall in love again. She had her children, her business and her friends, and they would have to be enough.

Trying pre-emptively to ward off disaster, she worked harder than she had when Rory was alive, travelling incessantly to and from PiG shops around the country. Now and again, a frantic feeling seized her with sudden force. It would come on without warning, a type of panic, a sense that there was something she'd left undone, which would have catastrophic consequences if it wasn't addressed. While she tried to identify this urgent task, the juddering agitation tried to burst from her body, struggling against skin, too violent to be contained. At the height of the fear, a voice in her would howl, Oh, my God, Rory is *dead.*

Those were the only times she'd understand the truth and it was terrifying.

Even so, she rarely cried. She numb-walked through her life, now and again jolting against the appalling reality in a horribly bruising way.

'Am I doing it wrong?' she'd asked Johnny. 'Being a widow?'

'You're doing it the only way you know how,' he'd answered.

Because that was the thing about Johnny: no matter what she needed or wanted, he was always there.

Thirty-Three

'I'm sorry,' Liam said, for the hundredth time. 'You won't stay in Airbnbs because you have a moral objection. Because I love you, I won't use them either when I'm with you. I didn't actually lie. I just kept something to myself.'

'But you said you agreed with me!'

'Yeah, because I'd just met you. At the start of a thing, you'd agree with whatever the other person says.' He hadn't done anything that every person on earth hadn't done at one stage or another. All the same . . . 'I've disappointed you.' He looked sick. 'I hate that. But—I'm sorry to break it to you, Nell—I'm only human.'

She swallowed. It would have been far nicer to hold on to her starry-eyed version of the two of them, but maybe she had to grow up a little. 'Okay. Is that the worst thing I'm going to discover about you?'

'Definitely.'

She sighed. 'Tell me about this week in Italy.'

'Jessie's rented a villa—I was there three years ago. It's just outside a Tuscan village that's so perfect it's *ridiculous*. The villa has a swimming pool and its own olive grove, where you can literally eat the olives from the trees. There's a pool table, an actual wood-fired pizza oven, and an old chapel in the garden. Best bit? Lots of hills all around—the cycling is amazing.'

'Is it anywhere near Florence?' Her knowledge of Italy was sketchy.

'Yeah. About an hour's drive. I can show you on the map.'

Suddenly excitement was fizzing in Nell's veins. 'Liam, could we go to the Uffizi? The art gallery? It's got Caravaggio's *Medusa*, Botticelli's *Primavera*—paintings I've wanted to see since forever.'

'Sure! Whatever makes my baby happy.'

'Would Jessie be pissed if we went off for the day?'

'You kidding? Jessie loves an outing.'

'Oh, *wow*.' Joy spread through her, right into her fingertips. 'Liam, Liam.' Her words were tripping over each other. 'How about I get tickets for us *all*?

To say thanks to Jessie and Johnny. And Violet and Lenore can come too. How great would that be?'

'Paige might die of the shock.' His laugh was wry. 'The girls getting some culture while they're with me.'

Monday morning, 6.47 a.m. and it was already mayhem. Johnny was leaving for Amsterdam, for meetings with Indonesian food wholesalers, and he couldn't find his charger.

'Mum, where's the milk?' Saoirse yelled from the kitchen.

'In the fridge,' she yelled back.

'It's all gone.'

How?

'Jessie, I'm going to miss my flight.'

'Look in your case.'

'I've looked.'

'Look again.'

'Mum,' Bridey this time, 'Camilla's frothing at the mouth!'

'Again? Take her out the back!'

Jessie dived towards Johnny's bag, unzipped an inside pocket and handed him his charger. 'There.' Thundering down the stairs and into the kitchen, she wrenched open the fridge, took out one of the two cartons resting in the door and slammed it onto the counter.

'It wasn't there a minute ago,' Saoirse said faintly.

Where the hell were the school lunchboxes? Not in the dishwasher, not on top of the freezer. Tearing open drawers, she eventually found them in a cupboard with the frying pans. *Why?* Quickly buttering bread for the sandwiches, she rummaged in the fridge. 'Where's the sliced cheese?'

'Vinnie ate it all on Saturday,' Bridey said.

'Mum! Grozdana is here.'

Already? Grozdana was her personal trainer.

Jessie stuck her head into the hall. 'Grozdana, hi, five minutes!'

With fumbling hands she made four peanut-butter sandwiches. Johnny came to kiss her goodbye and she jutted the side of her face at him. 'Your ear,' he murmured. 'Always my favourite part of a woman.'

'I'll kiss you properly when you come home. Which is when?'

'Tomorrow night.'

'Bunnies!' she commanded. 'Be nice to Dad, he's away for two days.'

'*You* be nice to him,' Bridey said.

'I'm making your effing lunches!'

'Bye,' Johnny said.

She flung the sandwiches into the lunchboxes, along with apples and protein bars, then hurtled upstairs to change into her gym stuff. First World problems, that's all this was. And to think she had someone to do her cleaning, laundry and afternoon childcare. How hard would life be if she hadn't?

Pulling on her leggings, she looked at her phone. A text had arrived late last night, from Nell: **So excited for Italy. Can I take you guys to the Uffizi? On me? Just let me know numbers x**

Jessie felt weak. An art gallery. Christ, no, they were *not* an art-gallery family. She despised her little tribe—especially herself—for being so uncouth. But after that terrible Sunday afternoon in the National Gallery a couple of years ago, when the kids had been almost murderous with resentment and she'd been bored to the point of panic, they'd steered clear of art. 'Johnny,' she'd said quietly. 'I'm hating every second of this.'

'Thank God,' he'd replied.

'Johnny. I think we might be . . . a family of peasants.' Looking for a more positive reframing, she'd said, 'Maybe we're a *sporty* family.'

But they weren't that either. They didn't play golf or tennis or any other middle-class sport. The kids played games at school but only because they had to. None of them displayed an actual aptitude.

So what did Jessie, Johnny and their family actually *stand* for?

Neither she nor Johnny was interested in the novels that people discussed earnestly. Although she dutifully bought them, cookbooks were the only books she enjoyed. Johnny loved Lee Child and got the new one every year, for his summer holidays—and that was him for books.

They weren't theatregoers either. All that clattering around on wooden floors and speaking far too loudly—she squirmed with embarrassment for the actors and longed to leave in the interval.

Other than that, though, what did they do?

Get-togethers. Jessie had seized that word. They were a sociable family. She was a sociable person. Tentatively she tested that idea. Yes, it was true. And, no, there was no shame in it. She'd reply to Nell after Grozdana.

But what if Nell booked the tickets in the meantime? *Then* they'd *have* to go.

God, no, that would be the very worst. She couldn't run that risk.

Thanks, Nell, you're a pet, but we're a crowd of philistines here. Work away without us xxx

Four Months Earlier

JUNE

Nana and Granddad Casey's
fiftieth wedding anniversary in Mayo

Thirty-Four

She squeezed Ed's hand. He turned, they smiled at each other in the sparkle-lit night, then went back to watching the stage. It wasn't his birthday for another three weeks but this gig was her gift to him. Fleet Foxes had a special place in both their hearts and the gods were conspiring to make tonight perfect. The rain had held off—having an outdoor gig in Ireland was always like playing Russian roulette—and the weather was properly warm.

Unlike other gigs, no one was dancing into her and slopping their beer everywhere. She already knew all the songs inside-out, but hearing them live was different, enhanced. When they played 'The Shrine', an image of eagles flying past white-tipped mountains against a too-blue sky flashed in her head. What was that from? A movie she'd seen as a young kid? Something about the height of the mountains, the feelings of awe and fear they generated, felt very young.

In the break before the next song, she pulled Ed's head close to her mouth. 'That made me feel nostalgic for a life I didn't live. High in the mountains. Maybe in Nepal.'

'It reminded me of *Cannery Row*. Even though I haven't read it.'

Solemnly, she nodded. 'I get you,' she said.

'I know you do.' His teeth flashed in the darkness.

The mood here tonight was perfect. Everyone seemed happy, and no one was messy drunk and shouting rowdy requests at the band . . .

Another song began. She tried to hold onto the poetry of the lyrics, but the next sentence came, equally enthralling, until all she had was the feeling, and none of the meaning. But the meaning *was* the feeling. How profound was *that*?

'Y'okay?' Ed asked.

'I feel a bit stoned,' she called, over the noise of the band. 'Just from the music.'

His sidelong smile, the way his eyes crinkled, the bat of his lashes tipped her into a momentary wonder.

'What?' he asked.

'You're mine.'

'Of course I am.'

'Good. Thank you, Ed. Good.'

They held the gaze a moment longer, then both dissolved into laughter.

'Two glasses of wine,' he said.

'Cheap date. Always was.'

Song after song played, an unending chain of beauties, each better than the one before. But suddenly it was over, the band were thanking Dublin, then leaving the stage. In alarm, she said to Ed, 'They haven't played "Mykonos".'

She and Ed had discovered the first album in their early days of falling in love. Nearly every track was great, but 'Mykonos' was special.

'Encore,' he said. 'They'll do it then.'

'You promise?' she asked.

'I can't.' Ever literal. 'But I'm ninety-nine per cent certain. Oh, they're back. Here we go . . .'

When the guitar chords of 'Mykonos' started, she turned to Ed. 'You were right!'

He was already reaching for her. She pressed her back against his chest and he held her tightly.

After the second encore, even when the lights went up and people began drifting to the exits, she didn't want to leave. 'Are they really gone?'

'Really gone this time, honey.'

'Oh, Ed,' she said. 'That was just . . . I don't have the words . . . like *amazing*.'

'It was. Totally. Thank you for this.'

'You had a good time? Because you deserve the best time. It was like a spiritual experience. Wasn't it?'

He laughed. 'I don't know what they're like. But if it felt like one, then *ipso facto*, it was.'

'It felt like one.' She was definite about this. '*Ipso facto* indeed!' Then she began to laugh. 'The state of me. "Woman Explodes From Her Own Intensity".'

'Be as intense as you like. So what now? We go for a drink?'

She shook her head. 'Just want to go home and listen to the first album again. I want to listen to nothing else for the rest of my life.' Then, 'Oh, Ed, sorry! It's your night. This is your date. You get to decide.'

'We're on a *date*?'

'. . . Yes. Even though it's a cringe concept, yep, we're on a date.'

He laughed. 'In that case, I just want to go home with you.'

'You sound very sure of that.'

'I am.' Holding her hand, tightly, he moved them towards the Luas.

The house was empty. The boys and Baxter were on a reluctant sleep-over with Cara's parents.

'Tonight was *everything*,' Cara said, dreamily, wandering after Ed as he unplugged stuff and turned off the lights. 'The weather—can you believe the *weather*? The crowd were so mellow. No one off their face or pushing or . . .' She yawned. 'It was totally . . .'

She climbed the stairs, Ed following.

Absently, she unwound the bobble around her ponytail and threw it over her shoulder at him.

'Oh, yeah?' he said.

Oh. *Yeah.*

In the bedroom, she put on the music. With careless distraction, she removed her clothes as Ed rolled a spliff. Tonight, she was comfortable in her own skin. He lit the spliff, she lay back against the pillows and he put it to her mouth.

As she inhaled, the very last of her tension drained away. Then they kissed.

Every touch felt different, better. Moving with Ed, the feel of her skin against his, was delicious. The judgey voices in her head were dialled right down to silence.

Afterwards, they lay entwined, listening to the music. Through the open window, the cool night air moved over their bodies.

Cara was falling asleep when 'Mykonos' came on. 'I've just realized. This. It's about addiction? His brother is an addict?'

'What it sounds like.'

'And he's telling him to go to rehab? "You go today"? It must be so tough to do that.'

'Brutal.'

'So what's the "ancient gate" he's waiting at?'

Ed laughed sleepily. 'Some old three-bar to keep the donkey from escaping?'

'It's a *choice*, right? Between getting clean or not?'

'Well, if you knew, why're you asking me?'

'Because . . . I like asking you things . . . Are you asleep? That's okay. I'm asleep too . . .'

Thirty-Five

'. . . throat or jaw pain.' Johnny read on, with interest: 'Feeling sick, sweaty, light-headed or short of breath.'

An article titled *How To Tell If A Heart Attack Is Imminent* had popped up in his feed. 'I'm only forty-eight!' he told his iPad.

So much for targeted advertising!

But he'd read on and was now anxiously rubbing his ribcage.

'Sudden sweats'. A sheen of perspiration was suddenly beading his forehead. According to this, you mightn't even get a pain in your chest if you were mid-heart attack. You might just feel 'uncomfortable'.

No, hold on, you've got me all wrong. I run fifteen K a week.

He didn't, though. In *theory* he ran five K three mornings a week, but between the school run and the work travel and the sheer, unrelenting knackeredness, he managed maybe one run a fortnight.

But he often walked the dogs. That counted for something.

'Coughing or wheezing'. Instantly he coughed. Ah, he was definitely having a heart attack!

The following article covered signs that indicated a person had a blood clot. 'Coughing for no reason'—he'd just done that! 'A racing heart'. Well, it was racing *now*.

He needed Jessie. She'd talk sense into him.

Well, maybe not. But she'd mock him back into his right mind.

Jessie, however, was on a day trip to Geneva, armed with gifts for Jin Woo Park and Océane, giddily hopeful that the chef was about to sign on the dotted line.

Even thinking about how much all this was costing was enough to start Johnny's heart racing again. But when she was in chef-stalking mode, there was no talking to her.

It wasn't just that. Even though he and Jessie were equal shareholders in the business—it was her wedding present to him—he never felt he had the right to criticize. How could he ask her to tone down her spending either on the business or in real life? Ultimately she had earned the money.

. . . Maybe he'd have a little snooze for himself. It was a Sunday afternoon, the rain was pelting down outside, and for once he had nothing urgent to do—

'Oh, *Joooooohnnneee*?' Saoirse sidled into the room.

Noooo! She was about to ask for something. Something *awkward* . . .

'I need a favour.'

A sweat broke out on his face. *Now, which one was that? Heart attack or a blood clot?* Or just the realization that his rare peaceful afternoon was being stolen from him.

'Ferdia and me are going to Errislannan.' She meant Rory's family. 'To Granny Ellen's. It's their wedding anniversary. There's going to be cake and that.'

A lift, that was what she was about to ask for. She'd point out at the rain and appeal to his kinder instincts.

'It takes an hour and fifty minutes by public transport. Or twenty-five minutes by car. Google Weather says the rain's not going to stop. Would you give us a lift?'

'Ah, Saoirse! Can't you drive? Or Ferdia?'

'We're not insured on your shit-bucket.'

'The Beast?' But, no, Jessie had driven to the airport in the people-carrier. Johnny admitted defeat. 'Okay. Come on.'

As Johnny drove through the rain, he was reminded of the first time he'd visited Errislannan. It had been a Friday evening, a few months after he, Jessie and Rory had started working together. They'd had a particularly gruelling week.

'Pub?' Johnny had suggested. 'Pints?'

Jessie had shaken her head. 'Going home to bed.' Then, 'You know what? I want my mammy to make my dinner and put her hand on my forehead and tell me I'm great. But I'm too destroyed for the four-hour journey to the backarse of Connemara.'

'I'd like that too,' Johnny said. 'But without the mammy.'

'Come down home with me!' Rory said. 'We'll be there in forty minutes. Mammy Kinsella will feed us and praise us.'

'She's had no notice.' Johnny was thinking about how his mum Rose would react to unexpected visitors.

'And we've no things,' Jessie said.

'What do you need? Pyjamas? Face-cream? My sisters will sort you out. And Ellen Kinsella doesn't need any notice. She'd love the challenge.'

'Seriously?' Johnny was tempted.

'Course! C'mon, the lurcher had pups last night—you can't miss that.'

'We'd have to bring something,' Jessie said urgently. 'A tin of biscuits, a bottle of Baileys.'

'We can get them in the Spar on the way to Busáras.'

Jessie and Johnny looked at each other. 'Will we?' she asked.

'Feck it, why not?'

'Hurry it up, so,' Rory said. 'We'll get the eighteen ten bus.'

Errislannan was a hamlet a few miles outside Celbridge, where the Kinsellas' low bungalow, a jumble of small, cosy rooms, was attached to three acres of land. The senior Kinsellas were both schoolteachers. As a sideline, Michael bred lurchers and Ellen kept hens.

From the word go, for Johnny, it was like stepping into a fairy-tale family.

Ellen, short and bright-eyed, welcomed them with energetic warmth. 'Johnny Casey, we've heard so much about you.'

'Sorry for arriving in on top of you with such short notice.'

'Haven't you lovely manners?' Ellen said admiringly. 'And Jessie! *Cailín áileann! Tar isteach.* Michael Kinsella, come out here.'

Michael, an older but otherwise identical version of Rory, came from the kitchen. With a gentle smile, he pressed hands. His kindness triggered quiet panic in Johnny. Someday he might have to return the favour and invite Rory to Beltibbet, to his awful parents. They treated Johnny like a useless embarrassment and upped the ante for any of his friends.

'Into the good room with you,' Ellen said. 'I'll shout when the dinner is up.'

Michael opened the door into a well-preserved-looking sitting room, with brown velvet couches and a smoked-glass coffee table. A heavy crystal tumbler was placed in Johnny's hand, then Michael was pouring hefty measures of Johnnie Walker for the four of them.

'*Sláinte.*' He took a sip. 'Ah, here's Izzy.'

'Hi!' Izzy, tall and lanky, with a thin, mobile face and dark curly hair, stuck her head around the door. She focused on Johnny. 'Hel-lo, you're a bit of a lash. But mind you don't get lumbago from that couch.' Then, turning to them all, 'They could slap a protection order on this place. It's a museum piece.' She stuck out her hand. 'You must be Jessie?'

Jessie took the offered hand, her face glowing. She looked like she'd just fallen in love.

'Come on for the dinner,' Ellen called.

In the small, steamy kitchen, mismatched chairs were clustered tightly around the table. Ellen was flinging thick slices of roast lamb onto plates.

'Milk, MiWadi or stout?' Michael asked Johnny.

'Milk!' Johnny was delighted. Rose had never countenanced milk at the dinner table: she said it was 'a bog-trotters' drink'.

Then Keeva showed up. She looked like her mother, short, fair-haired and gimlet-eyed. 'I'm the eldest, a nurse and getting married next year to a fella I've been going with since I was eighteen. I'm the boring one.' But she laughed when she said it. 'Izzy here, she's the youngest. A right bright spark, a graduate fast track.'

'I've my own car,' Izzy said. 'I'd have driven the three of you down if I'd known.' She gave Johnny a long, hard look. 'Especially you.'

'She has no confidence, though,' Michael said sadly.

Everyone laughed.

Ellen, bright-eyed and interested, wanted to discuss world events. 'That's an awful business in Rwanda. It escalated very fast . . . Didn't it?'

Johnny hadn't much of a clue, but he nodded anyway.

'Ah, now!' Ellen complained, to the table. 'What's the point of having children educated to third level, if they won't talk about important matters of the day?'

After Ellen had eventually stopped pressing lamb and roast potatoes on them, she produced a rhubarb tart from the Aga, with custard made on the hob by Michael.

Then came tea and biscuits.

When the conveyor-belt of food finally came to a halt, Johnny said, 'I'll do the washing up.' Right then he'd have walked through fire for this family.

'We've a dishwasher, you eejit,' Izzy said.

More laughter.

They played rummy and beggar-my-neighbour in the back living room (the 'not good one', Izzy said), until nine o'clock, when the evening news was put on and it was time for more tea and biscuits.

Jessie slept in Izzy's bed, and Izzy and Keeva shared Keeva's.

Rory slept on the divan in the back living room. Johnny got Rory's bed. He slept deeply and dreamlessly on the soft, often-washed cotton sheets and awoke to the sound of rashers and sausages spitting on a pan.

'Come over and see the pups,' Michael said, when breakfast ended.

In the porch there was a jumble of wellington boots. 'Have a rummage around,' Michael said. 'Find a pair that fits.'

Outside, the day was bright and blowy and the air was thick with the smell of fresh earth. The pups were in an outhouse in the next field. Tiny little things, still blind, trying to suckle. 'Only born on Thursday night.' Michael smiled, looking daft with love.

'Is there something wrong with that one?' Johnny moved forward to take a better look at the puppy on the margin.

'Yes. He's the—'

'—runt.' Johnny's heart twisted. 'Will he be okay?'

'Indeed he will,' Michael said. 'We'll make sure of it.'

Thirty-Six

Extract from Irish Times *theatre page.* Timer*, The Helix, 13 June to 11 July*

> Undoubtedly, the star of the show is Nell McDermott's set. An immersive, imaginative, almost phantasmagorical experience results from an ingenious partnership of props and lighting (courtesy of Garr McGrath).
>
> Thirteen giant clocks, from sundials to mobile phones, form the centrepiece but the audience are kept aware of the restless activity of time, thanks to unceasing ambient motion on stage: autumn trees shedding their leaves morphing into snowfall, which eventually becomes flurries of cherry-blossom petals as the lighting moves from russet through silver into pink.
>
> Using mirrors, McDermott pulls off ingenious tricks with perspective, where water appears to flow backwards and rain falls upwards. What makes these feats more remarkable is that they are undoubtedly managed on a shoestring.
>
> McDermott's undeniable talent and commitment to resourceful work bode well for her future, perhaps in collaboration with Garr McGrath.

It was 7.32 a.m. and Nell was late. Her dad was waiting outside Johnny's Baggot Street flat, surrounded by decorating equipment.

'Sorry, sorry, sorry!' She cycled towards him at speed and hopped off just at the last minute.

'Ah, you're okay,' he said. 'You'd a big night last night. Will the van be all right there?'

'Did you pay and display?'

'I've a yoke on me phone. An *app*. I've to do it again in three hours.'

'I'll see you right. It's enough you're giving your labour for free.' She put the key into the lock of the red door. 'Here, I'll take the ladder. In you go there, Dad. Pull everything into the hall.'

When all of Petey's paraphernalia was hauled across the threshold, she shut the door to the busy street. Immediately everything quietened down.

Nell lifted her bike. 'We're going to the first floor.'

'Careful on the stairs. They're shocking steep, but.'

In two journeys, they hefted the ladder, their rollers and bags of equipment up the treacherous stairs to Johnny's flat. The tenants had vacated it just the day before.

'A cosy little spot.' Petey stood in the living room and looked around. 'Even though we're right on Baggot Street. The fecking angles of the walls, but.' Petey did a walk-through of the kitchen, bedroom and bathroom. 'These old buildings are all on the slide. If you'd a' been asking me to paper this place, I'd be on me way home now.'

'Just painting,' Nell said. 'Freshen the whole place up.'

'We'll do a good job for Johnny,' Petey said. 'I like the chap. Are you still upset about the Airbnb business?'

'Yeah, but it's not Johnny's fault.'

'It's the way of the world, Nell, the way of the world.'

Maybe. But if Liam had never suggested it to Johnny, some lucky local people would be moving in, delighted with their new pad.

That evening at Dilly's first communion, confusion had been the first thing she'd felt when Liam had opened his mouth—why would he suggest something they were both so opposed to? But then to discover that, actually, he *wasn't* opposed to it had led to further puzzlement. Then anger.

He'd apologized and apologized until her shock went away.

But he wasn't exactly the man she'd thought he was and that scared her. Because they were *married*.

When she'd been persuading her dad to help with the decorating, a short, angry rant had burst from her. About a week ago, she'd blurted it out to Garr: 'You're a man, what do you think? Am I overreacting?'

'Did he literally lie? Or just nod along with you?'

'I can't remember. Maybe just the nodding along.'

'You set sorta high standards.'

'*I* should change?'

'No, but . . . So, I'm not married,' he'd said tentatively, 'but they say marriage needs work.'

What did that even mean?

'I guess you have to forgive someone for being an asshole sometimes,' he said. 'Instead of just dumping them.'

'Working on your marriage' had always sounded dull and noble—and vague to the point of being meaningless.

Now she saw that this mysterious 'work' meant discovering an unattractive streak in your special person and accepting that you couldn't change them.

'No one's perfect,' Garr said, and Nell gratefully grasped onto that.

Liam had doctored his value system to present himself in the best light in their early days. But one flaw didn't turn him into a terrible person.

'Right!' Her dad swept his hand around. 'We'll start here in the living room, sugar-soap the whole apartment, give us a nice clean canvas.'

'So, Dad.' Nell couldn't dampen down her fizzing excitement one moment longer. 'What did you think of my play last night?' Petey and Angie had been to the opening night.

'Didn't understand one blind word of it. Time can't go backwards! They're just misleading people.'

'It's a metaphor.'

'So your mother kept telling me, if I only knew what one of those is. But!' He held up a hand to forestall any objections. 'You did a good job, Nell. Everything flush, although I'd need to get up closer to see the edges. I was proud of you. Tell me, did you use a mitre box to do those curves on the clocks?'

'Joking me! Got me a circular saw.'

'Ah, here, that's cheating . . . And what's up?'

Nell's phone had beeped with a text, which was taking all her attention.

'What is it?' Petey asked. From the expression on her face, he couldn't decide if it was good news or bad.

'A screen shot. From Garr. Oh, Dad! It's a review in the *Irish Times*. Of the play. And they're nice about my set!'

'Show us.'

Petey read it. Then he read it again. 'In the *Irish Times*? The paper? The *paper*-paper, I mean, not just this online bit? That's . . .' He paused. 'D'you know something? This might be the proudest moment of my *life*. It's a pity none of the neighbours ever read the *Irish Times*. Muck savages, the lot of them. Ring your mother.'

'Can I ring my husband first?'

'That's right, you've a husband. I keep forgetting. Because you didn't let me walk you up the aisle, the memories never got a chance to *embed* . . . You ring Liam and I'm going down to buy twenty copies of the paper. The *paper*-paper.'

Liam didn't pick up, so she rang her mum, who was tearfully proud.

When Petey returned with a thick bundle under his arm, he grabbed the phone. 'Didn't I teach her well, Angie?' After he'd got her to agree that it was all thanks to his excellent joinery tuition, he passed the phone back to Nell.

When she eventually hung up, she'd had three missed calls. All from the same number, one she didn't recognize, but the congratulations in the air made her reckless.

'This is Nell McDermott.'

'Nell. Right. Iseult Figgis from Ship of Fools here.'

Oh. Nell was struck mute. Ship of Fools was one of the most successful theatre production companies in Ireland.

'We're putting together a production of *Trainspotting* for the Dublin Theatre Festival in September. We'd like you to pitch for the design.'

Adrenalin coursed through Nell, turning her mouth woolly.

'Can you come and see us? Now? I know it's early.'

'Sure,' she choked out. 'Of course.'

'We're in Dawson Street.'

'I know. I'll be with you in ten. Unless you need my portfolio? No?' Nell ended the call and, clutching her phone to her chest, 'Da-ad?'

'You're leaving me here on my own to paint this flat?'

'Ship of Fools want to see me now. They're a production company—like, Dad, they're *the* production company, they're doing *Trainspotting*.'

'That Scottish yoke? The disgusting one? I'll never be right again after I saw that bit about the—'

'I've to go. Dad, this is a *big* deal.'

'Fair play. G'wan then. I'll carry on here.'

Nell hopped onto her bike and cycled five minutes across town. Ship of Fools was housed in a suite of offices six floors above ground. Exiting the elevator into the lobby, seeing the walls hung with posters from past productions, Nell thought she might pass out. They even had a Nespresso machine!

Iseult herself was there to meet her, and took her into an office to meet Prentiss Siffton, the other powerhouse in the company. Both were probably in their mid-to-late forties and dressed in running shoes, jeans and T-shirts. They looked casual but expensive. Neither was exactly friendly.

Business people, Nell realized. That's why she felt so uncomfortable with them.

'We saw *Timer* last night.'

'You did a good job.'

Instantly Nell melted. 'Coming from you, that's . . . I don't know what to say.'

'Do you enjoy the work?' Prentiss asked.

'I *love* it. It's all I've ever wanted to do. Since I was fourteen.'

His smile was slightly warmer.

'We'd like you to pitch for *Trainspotting*,' Iseult chimed in. 'We'll email you the script. Only thing is, we'd need to see your ideas by Monday.'

Nell's euphoria dropped like a stone off a cliff. Of *course* there was a catch. 'But . . . today's Thursday. That's not enough time to come up with anything decent.'

After a hesitation, Iseult said, 'We'd pretty much decided who we were going with, until we saw *Timer*. Work needs to start ASAP—it's a big one. This is a huge chance for you, but you need to hit the ground running.'

Could she do it? She was supposed to be going to Mayo tomorrow for the weekend—Liam's parents' fiftieth wedding anniversary. Could she skip it? How would Liam react? Maybe he'd be okay about it. Yes, he'd probably understand.

Then there was this dinner tonight at Jessie and Johnny's with Perla and Kassandra. She *had* to be there: she was the common link.

'So, the budget is forty thousand euros.'

Oh, *God*, that was approximately twenty times as much as she'd had for *Timer*. She could do so much with it . . . 'When on Monday do you need to see my pitch?'

'We can push it until one p.m.,' Iseult said.

'Okay. Right, email me the script now and I'll—'

'Don't you want to know how much you'd be paid?' Prentiss gave a slightly patronizing smile.

Nell literally couldn't think of a thing to say. She'd assumed her wage was included in the design budget. That there was *extra* money was a surprise.

The figure spoken was higher than anything Nell had ever been paid before.

'Acceptable?' Iseult smirked. She knew how it was for Nell, for most of Ireland's theatre workers: they usually got paid so little that this would seem like riches.

Acceptable? Of course it's acceptable! But for me, it's not about the money, it's about the work. Nell wished she'd said that, but she always thought of great responses far too late. *Just one thing. I do my best work with Garr McGrath. Have you hired a lighting director? Because I'll only take the job if I can work with him.*

Molly Ringwald slunk out to greet her. 'Molly, I have great news!'

'I'm here too,' Liam called.

'Why aren't you at work?'

'Why aren't you painting Johnny's flat?'

'Did you get my message?' she blurted, words tripping over each other. 'There was a review, a good one, in the *Irish Times* and Ship of Fools rang me—'

'What? Slow down. Why aren't you painting Johnny's flat?'

'Dad's there. There was a good review of my set in the paper.'

'Will Johnny's flat be finished by Tuesday? Because that's what you promised him.'

'Probably.' Then, 'Yes, it will.' She'd ask Brendan to help out.

Her fingers fumbled as she found the review. 'Here.'

In silence, he read it. 'Wow,' he eventually said. 'That's . . . wow. Well done.'

'There's more. Ship of Fools rang. They want me to pitch for a production.'

'Ship of Fools?'

'I went to see them in their office.'

'Ship of Fools?' he repeated. 'Where did they get your number?'

'I don't know. But they want to see ideas for a September production.'

'That's amazing.' He sounded stunned.

'There's just one problem. I've to have it done by Monday.'

'So? You'll have to work down in Mayo?'

'Liam, I can't come.'

He stared. He looked . . . shocked? Angry? 'You're kidding. You are? Right?' He was definitely angry.

'Liam . . .'

'It's my parents' fiftieth wedding anniversary. And you want to skip it because of some work that isn't even definite. This has been planned for months.'

'I might never get an opportunity like this again.'

'My parents will definitely never have a fiftieth wedding anniversary again.'

He was right. And yet . . . 'If I told them how important this is.'

'They wouldn't get it. You'd upset them. Nell, you're part of a family now. Sometimes we have to do stuff we don't want to do.'

He was right: she was being unreasonable. Selfish, even.

But if she worked every free second? Got by on minimal sleep? Turned up at the beginning of things and sloped off when people started to get drunk? She'd bring a box of materials with her . . . 'I'll have to work down there.'

'There's stuff you *must* show up for, like tomorrow night's drinks, the party on Saturday and the lunch on Sunday. And, look, don't let Johnny down on the painting. So what's for dinner tonight?'

'We're out. Humanitarian play-date.'

He looked blank.

'You know. Taking Perla and Kassandra to Jessie and Johnny's for dinner.'

'So you're okay to do that, but not my parents' fiftieth. Noted.'

'That's different. Perla doesn't even know where Jessie lives.'

He turned away, radiating rancour.

'. . . Liam, why aren't you at work?'

'I'll go in a while.'

'You're already late. What's going on?'

He shrugged. 'Chelsea takes the piss and I deserve some respect. She needs to learn what happens if I'm not there—things fall apart.'

Another blow struck in the on-going battle of wills between Chelsea and Liam. Liam was resentful that he ran the Capel Street shop, while earning nothing like as much as Chelsea, who had the actual title 'Manager'. Nell feared that Liam would get the push for being too much trouble. But he always assured her that Chelsea needed him too much.

She couldn't worry about that now, though. Speed-reading the script, it was immediately clear that it was a complex proposition, with a lot of location changes. A device was needed to pull it all together, something clever like a rotating stage. Anxiety gnawed at her. It was hard to know in what direction she should push her design. Should she replicate what she'd done with *Timer*? Tricks with lighting and mirrors? Or did she challenge herself to try something she'd never tried before?

One voice was telling her that this was no time for risks. Another warned that she needed to show her range. Garr would know: he'd always been her best sounding board. She felt weirdly uncomfortable about Liam overhearing their conversation but she picked up her phone and defiantly talked within earshot.

Garr was certain. 'They want you because they saw your work on *Timer*. Don't try new stuff just for the sake of it.'

'Okay.' She was calmed. 'That sits right with me. Thanks.'

She hung up, and Liam asked, 'What did he say?'

'Stick with what I'm good at.'

'Really? You want to get typecast already?'

All of Nell's certainty vanished. Maybe it would be better to press ahead with the rotating stage. That was different.

Ambitious, though. She could easily cock it up.

'Hey, I think I'll go for a bike ride this evening,' he said.

'But we're going to—'

'Yeah. But we'll be away all weekend and I won't get the chance again until next week. I need to do it, babe, for my head.' This was the first time Nell had seen Liam actually sulking. But she couldn't—or didn't want to—waste scarce time and energy playing his new game. 'Okay, Liam. Enjoy your cycle.'

Thirty-Seven

Cara peeled off the latex gloves, threw them into the garbage can, then faced herself in the small mirror. Watery grey-black blobs pooled beneath her eyes. Maybe she needed to buy waterproof mascara. But doing that would mean admitting this had become an actual part of her life. With a cotton swab, she wiped away the stains, then repaired the patches in her foundation with dabs of concealer. A swig of mouthwash, which she swilled energetically: her worst fear was of someone smelling her.

Her chignon had come slightly asunder, so she added a few more clips and a blast of spray. Stashing her little bag in the cupboard, she took a final look, checking that her uniform was clean and neat, then stepped out into the narrow corridor in the hotel basement.

As always, there was no one to see her. Walking with purpose and faking a vague smile, she made her way back upstairs to the front desk. She'd been gone thirteen minutes.

'You missed it,' Madelyn said. 'Mr Falconer is here.'

What? Where? He wasn't due for another hour.

'His meeting finished early. But it's okay, Vihaan took him up.'

That wasn't meant to happen. She would never abandon her post at a busy time. There was always a chance that a guest would arrive early, everyone knew that, but the urge had been too strong so she'd taken a risk.

Here was Vihaan now, with Ling. 'Where were you?'

'Upset tummy.'

'Again?' Madelyn said. 'Oh.'

She, Vihaan and Ling regarded Cara. They seemed suspicious, or perhaps they were just worried.

'Sorry,' Cara said. 'Just . . . So how was he?' She knew Mr Falconer of old.

'Complaining about the weather. It's too sunny. He doesn't come to Ireland for the sun.' Some people would find fault with anything. Trying to box away her guilt, Cara got on with her morning.

Gabby had left her a voice-note. 'Cara, meet me for a quick coffee at lunchtime! I hate my children. I need to rant.'

Her heart lifted in anticipation—then her mood veered off in a different direction. She adored Gabby, but . . . today there was something else she needed to do.

Again? So soon?

She'd done it already today.

And she needed to do it again.

It was only ten past twelve but Tesco in Baggot Street was overrun with office workers, lining up to pay for their lunch. She jigged her knee, finding the waiting almost unendurable. It was always like this: the closer she got to eating, the more the need intensified. And *thank* you, God, a till had freed up. She scooted forward with her basket—self-service tills were the best things ever, because no one could judge. Beeping speedily, she slid a doughnut, a giant cookie, then bar after bar of chocolate past the scanner. She hadn't paid much attention to what she'd flung into her basket: quantity mattered more than quality. And her two-litre bottle of water, of course: she couldn't forget that.

Twenty-nine euro, though.

That was . . . a lot.

What the hell? She'd stop soon.

The day was warm and sunny and she sat on 'her' bench in Fitzwilliam Square—it was perfect: only a four-minute walk from the Ardglass but not on a direct cut-through route. It was unlikely she'd be spotted by any of her co-workers. The doughnut first—the ecstatic *relief* of those initial few mouthfuls—next the giant cookie, then the chocolate. It all happened extremely quickly. She was tearing the wrappers off, having the next bar lined up, even while she efficiently and methodically slid the current one into her mouth. It wasn't about the taste, it was about the feeling, chasing the calm, then the high. A Wispa disappeared in three bites, a bar of Whole Nut in four. But in between, remembering to drink her water.

The few people who passed paid her no attention. Hiding in plain sight, she looked just like anyone else, having her lunch.

With almost everything eaten, she felt good. Only a Starbar was left, she always kept one to finish with. It felt like a punctuation mark. Standing up, gathering all the bags and wrappers, still eating, she began walking quickly. Without breaking stride, she dropped the bag into 'her' garbage can and now came the fear. The fat and sugar molecules were already migrating through her stomach walls, turning into sheets of yellow blubber on her thighs and belly and arms. It needed to be got rid of. Now.

In through the discreet staff entrance of the Ardglass, down the back stairs and, oh, no, there was Antonio, one of the sous-chefs. 'Hey, Cara.' He greeted her with a dazzling smile.

Please, no. They'd had lovely chats a few times in the past about Lucca, where he was from. He'd be expecting her to stop and talk. 'Hi, Antonio, great to see you.' She slid past him. 'Hope you're well.'

His surprised hurt followed her and the guilt was hard. But she. Could. Not. Stop.

Wrenching open the door of the little bathroom, she suddenly felt exhausted at the mini-ordeal ahead. Her stomach muscles were sore, her throat already felt raw.

This is the last time.

She didn't know where the resolve had come from but she was certain. No more. It was crazy. She loved Ed, the boys, her job, her life. Doing this was *insane.*

Thirty-Eight

June already. How did that happen? Jessie slung some Middle Eastern food onto the dining table. *Next month I'll be fifty and, seriously, what's the age when a person finally feels safe and secure? Because I really thought it would have happened by now.*

She surveyed the dining table: fried halloumi, *baba ganoush*, hummus, olives, pitta bread . . .

She'd done a lot with her life. She *had*. Five children, a happy marriage—it *was* happy, wasn't it? Running a profitable company, employing more than fifty people, her life was a success.

She'd forgotten water glasses. Turning back towards the kitchen, she wondered if anyone really liked her. She was dogged by a recurring sense that everyone just put up with her—Christ! She'd almost toppled over!

It was these bloody shoes: Océane Park's slides. They were *lethal* but she wore them every chance she got, to reduce the cost-per-wear.

Poor impulse control: that was another thing she despised about herself. She should never have tried on Océane's present. As soon as she'd slip-slapped down the stairs in them, the soles were too scratched to be gifted or returned. She'd been secretly delighted—for about half an hour. Then the guilt had arrived: there wasn't the money for a spontaneous self-gift of expensive shoes.

For all her giddy insistence that there was enough money swilling around, she knew, oh, she *knew* that her spending verged on out-of-control. No need for her to see Cara's accounts, because, lodged deep in her soul, was an internal calculator. Most of the time she stayed resolutely deaf to its incessant clicking, but now and again, often just before she fell asleep at night, it suddenly became like a fruit machine that had hit the jackpot.

Neon price tags would start flashing—the staff party, the school fees, the overtipping, the crazy-dear jacket for Saoirse because she was a good girl, the first-aid course for Bridey because she wouldn't shut up about it, the smartwatch for poor Johnny because she worried that he felt neglected . . .

Carrying four glasses, she shuffled back into the dining room—she couldn't chance any striding movements in these lethal fecking shoes. Christ, she'd ordered a lot of food!

Johnny came in and stopped short. 'Jessie. There's enough here to feed half of Aleppo.'

'And more in the kitchen. A Syrian speciality made with lamb, cherries and pomegranate molasses.' She'd made the lamb dish herself, the only one of the entire meal, because she hadn't been able to buy it anywhere in Dublin. 'Me and my bougie notions, Ferdia says. Apparently I can't talk to someone for more than a minute without inviting them over.'

'He's a cheeky feck, but maybe this time he has a point.'

Kassandra had already had a couple of play-dates with Dilly—she was just a regular kid. Perla, understandably, was different. At the play-date handovers, her facial muscles barely moved. There was an awful deadness to her. Driven by a helpless need to nurture, Jessie had blurted out a dinner invite, without thinking through the implications. What were she and Johnny, in their safe, comfortable lives, going to say to a woman who had seen horrors they couldn't even imagine? She'd begged Nell and Liam to come as moral support.

When she'd mentioned it to Ferdia, he'd said, 'She's not just some freak show.'

'I never said she was.' Christ, she couldn't open her mouth to him.

'Oh, look, we're white and middle-class, let's gather round and poke a stick at an asylum-seeker.'

'I'm poking a stick at no one, Ferdia. I'm just giving the woman her dinner. But you're studying sociology. You've a social conscience.' Allegedly. She never saw much evidence of it. 'I thought you might be interested.'

'Johnny,' she said now, 'did you find any Syrian music?'

'Found. Downloaded. Ready to go.'

'Do you think it'll be okay if we drink? Like you, me, Liam and Nell?'

'She doesn't drink?' Johnny asked. 'Right! Of course. Maybe we shouldn't either. Do us no harm to give it a miss. Or is that being condescending? I'm way out of my comfort zone here.'

'Johnny, babes . . . I'm kinda dreading this.'

He laughed out loud. 'Oh, Jessie, you and your randos. Come here.' He gathered her in a hug and she let him.

'Do you think she smokes weed?' Jessie asked, leaning against him. 'Could we get some from Ferdia?'

'Are you serious?'

'Jesus, I dunno. I just want her to have a nice time . . .'

The doorbell rang. Dilly and TJ thundered down the stairs, claimed Kassandra and ferried her off. It was all so easy for kids. Nell, who'd mysteriously come without Liam, had to put up quite a fight not to be dragged along with them.

Perla presented a small box of strange East European chocolates. They'd clearly been bought from a cut-price outlet like Dealz and it broke Jessie's heart. 'Come in, come in, come in.' She led the way into the living room and sat Perla down.

She was a small-framed, serious-eyed woman in loose, drab clothing and Jessie had to resist the urge to put a blanket across her knees.

Out of nowhere, Ferdia appeared. Well, that was nice. Jessie did the introductions, then asked Perla what she'd like to drink. 'We have water, apple juice, Diet Coke . . .'

'White wine, please,' she said.

'Oh! . . . Sure! What do you like? Dry? Sweet?'

'Do you have a Sauvignon blanc?'

'Indeed we do!' Johnny was almost bellowing with relief.

Perla accepted the glass, took a sip, closed her eyes and sighed. 'Wine, I've missed you.' After another mouthful of wine, bigger this time, she looked around at the startled faces and said, 'I know you have questions. Please ask them.'

Jessie, Johnny and Ferdia were silenced with embarrassment.

'Okay.' Perla took another gulp. 'I'll start. Why am I drinking?'

'Sorry for presuming,' Jessie said. 'We thought Muslims weren't allowed.'

'I'm not a Muslim. Although lots of them drink.'

'Are you a Christian?' Jessie thought there might be a Christian community in Syria.

'I'm not an anything.'

'Okay.' Jessie was meek.

'Secular.' Perla gave a smile. 'People like to label us. Asylum-seekers, I mean.' She was halfway through the glass of wine, and a more relaxed, sparkly woman was emerging. 'I just thought I was middle-class.'

'R-really?'

'I know.' Another smile, more twinkly this time. 'You think we all lived in stone huts and I had to wear the burqa. But I am a doctor.'

A doctor!

'My husband worked in IT. We had a beautiful air-conditioned apartment in Damascus, two cars, a holiday home. On weekends we went to the mall and bought stuff we didn't need. There were lots like us.'

Right. Well. That was them told, thought Jessie. 'How come your English is so good?'

'Lessons as a child.' Perla shrugged and smiled. 'And I've been living in Ireland for five years.'

'So what happened?' Ferdia asked. 'That you ended up here?'

'The war. When the fighting in Damascus got too dangerous, we moved to Palmyra, a smaller city. Temporarily. I got a job. There was no work for my husband, but he took care of Kassandra. And we waited for life to get back to normal.'

'I'm guessing it didn't,' Johnny said.

'One morning we woke up to black flags and bearded men with machine-guns. They came to our home.'

'Jesus,' Ferdia muttered.

'They didn't like me being alone with men in my consulting room.'

Ferdia shook his head. 'So they told you to stop?'

'They told my husband to stop me.'

'Like he was your controller?' Ferdia tightened his lips. 'And did he? Stop you? No. You're brave.'

'We needed the money. I stopped going to my clinic, but people visited me at home. In secret. But somebody informed.'

'And did they . . . hurt you?' Jessie asked.

'Me? No. But my husband . . . They took him to the square and . . . they killed him.' She swallowed. 'Eventually.'

'What happened?' Jessie asked, in a near-whisper.

Perla dropped her eyes.

Ferdia glared at Jessie, who quickly muttered, 'Sorry. Sorry. I'm so sorry.' After a period of respectful silence had elapsed, Jessie said gently, 'We're so sorry for all that you've suffered. Let me get you more wine.'

'Thank you, Jessie.' Perla gave a small smile. 'More wine would be very, very good.'

*

Unexpectedly, they all got quite drunk quite quickly.

'Maybe we should eat now?' Jessie suggested. Before they were entirely incapable . . .

The younger kids joined them for the starters, before losing interest and asking for ice-cream.

'What about the special Syrian lamb?' Jessie demanded of them. 'It's coming now.'

'No,' Bridey said. 'We've had enough. We're kids, we don't need as much food as adults.'

'Kassandra wants ice-cream,' Dilly said.

'Fine.' Jessie was too tipsy to care. 'You know where it lives.'

Jessie, followed by Johnny, went into the kitchen to fetch the lamb dish.

'Fond of the wine, isn't she?' Johnny said, getting another bottle from the fridge.

Jessie rounded on him. 'Wouldn't you be?'

'I wasn't saying . . . I only meant it's good. It's normal. She's *normal*.'

'Sorry. I'm a bit drunk.'

Everyone oohed and aahed at the smell of the lamb but Jessie insisted Perla taste it first.

She took a forkful, chewed, swallowed and paused. 'Who made this?'

'I got the recipe from the internet,' Jessie said. 'Is it all right?'

'It's so *good.*' Alarmingly, Perla began to cry. 'It reminds me of home.'

'Oh, now, now, now.' Jessie clucked around her. 'Ah, I'm crying too.'

'And me,' Nell said.

'And me,' Johnny said.

'I'm sorry,' Perla said. 'I'm just a bit drunk.'

'Cry away,' Jessie urged. 'No one here minds. Cry your heart out. Is it awful being an asylum-seeker?'

'Mum!' Ferdia said. Then, to Perla, 'I apologize on behalf of my mother.'

'No, don't. People tiptoe around my situation and it is good to speak. I am happy that Kassandra and I are alive but, yes, it is awful being an asylum-seeker.'

'Is it true that you have to sleep in a dormitory?' Jessie asked. 'That you get terrible food served in a communal canteen?'

'All true. The food is usually disgusting.' She swigged from her glass and almost smiled. 'There is no privacy, ever. People from eleven different countries live in the dorm with us. We all have different manners, so it's a challenge . . . But what truly kills any joy in life are the countless small indignities.'

'Like what?' Jessie asked tentatively.

'Like . . .' Perla eyed Johnny and Ferdia '. . . I apologize to the men for saying this, I do not mean to embarrass. But not having the money for tampons is particularly depressing.'

Johnny began an intense staring competition with his knees. Ferdia swallowed hard but remained steady.

Jessie looked appalled and said, 'I never even thought of that.'

'No money for soap, no money for paracetamol, no money for new socks for Kassandra when the old ones fall apart. The relentlessness of the struggle makes me want to go to bed and never get up.'

'Why don't you work?' Jessie asked. 'Ireland's crying out for doctors.'

'Mum!' Another explosion from Ferdia. 'Asylum-seekers can't work.'

'But there was a Supreme Court decision. I read about it!' Jessie was sick of being made to feel stupid.

Ferdia interjected, 'They have to pay a thousand euro for a permit—'

'*And* there's a list of sixty jobs they can't take: hospitality, taxi driving, cleaning . . .' Nell said.

'The kind of jobs that people with language difficulties can usually get.'

Ferdia and Nell did a one-two exposition on the sneaky ways the government had effectively blocked asylum-seekers from working.

'God, that's awful. I didn't know . . .' Jessie said. 'I'm sorry for not knowing.' By way of an apology, she filled Perla's glass again.

Thirty-Nine

. . . while maintaining the basic psychoanalytic paradigm, K. Horney draws attention to the fact that the girl grows, knowing that the man for the society has a 'heavy price' in the human and spiritual terms, and thus the cause of masculinity complex in women should look at individual and . . .

Jesus, he'd literally nearly nodded off there. The two weeks Ferdia had been at this job felt more like two years. All he'd done was read long, *teeeeeee*dious reports and reduce them to one-page bullet points for the directors. He was studying sociology because he wanted to make an active difference to people's lives. A trained monkey could do this shit.

But he couldn't walk away. Johnny had as good as got him the internship because, according to the boss-lady Celeste Appleton, she used to be his girlfriend. Earlier this week, Johnny had actually showed up at the office, giving Ferdia a moment of extreme confusion. Taking Celeste for lunch. 'Old friends,' he'd said. Trying to let everyone know that he'd once doinked Celeste, the pathetic old melt.

'Less of the old,' Celeste had said, applying a perfect mouth of red lipstick without a mirror—*that* was kind of cool.

A lot about Celeste was kind of cool. She was hot in a porny, office-ballbreaker kind of way. She stalked around in spiky shoes, silky blouses and narrow skirts, wearing sexy black-framed glasses.

Her hair was beautiful, some sort of shiny dark colour, and she wore it gathered in a heavy bun at the back of her neck.

Sometimes, part way through most of the tedious reports he had to summarize, he fantasized about opening Celeste's hair clip just to watch that hefty weight of hair tumble slowly down her back, like a molasses waterfall.

Thank God it was Friday. Wow. Did he really just think that? How quickly he'd become a serf.

Today they'd let him come in early and work through his lunch hour so he could leave at three to catch the train to Westport, a concession they made probably because of Johnny. It was insane making him go to Mayo for Nana and Granddad Casey's wedding anniversary—they weren't even *his* granny and granddad. But his mum had begged him to come. She was tragic, her need for a fakey happy family. She should give it up, because he would never like Johnny and Johnny would never like him.

Saoirse didn't feel the same, probably because she was too young to remember Dad. She seemed quite happy to be part of a big Casey clan.

Ed was okay, though. Ed was sound.

Liam, on the other hand, was a clown, literally worse than Johnny.

The only reason Ferdia was going to Mayo this weekend was that Barty and Sammie were coming too. Barty was one of the most important people in the world to him. They even looked alike—Barty was a shorter version of Ferdia; people often thought they were brothers. They drove each other mad, but they were literal family.

And Sammie? Sometimes it felt like an odd relief that it was almost over. He was twenty-one now, nearly twenty-two. A man. Which filled him with cold fear. His future was unknown, but whatever it was, he didn't feel equipped for it. Like, what did actual grown-ups *do* with their lives? Some high-achievers in his faculty, still a full year out from graduation, were already assured of positions in big banks or accountancy firms—but to do *what*, exactly? Some sort of murky workings, manipulating capitalism, making even more money for organizations that already had obscene amounts of it while simultaneously accruing a personal fortune.

Even if he'd had the stomach for that sort of work, Ferdia didn't think he was smart enough.

His grades were okay, slightly above average. Jessie said if he made more of an effort, he'd do better. She was wrong. Even if he killed himself working, he'd never be up there with the alphas. Others in his year—a small, earnest group—planned to be social workers. Their dedication was admirable but he wanted to help on a bigger scale. However, last summer's stint counting barrels of cooking oil in the Philippines had shown him the reality of working for a big charity. It had been *ridiculously* boring, and in no way gave him the good feeling he'd been expecting.

Would he be different if his dad hadn't died? Less afraid of the future? Who knew? And what did it matter? All he could do was play the hand he'd been given.

Forty

Jessie barely noticed the sun-drenched greenery of Westmeath as they whipped past in their people-carrier. Everyone in the car was subdued by the misery leaking from Johnny. Canice never missed a chance to tell him he wasn't up to running the family business. Which wasn't true. Johnny just hadn't wanted to be a solicitor, doing wills and conveyancing, in a town so claustrophobic it made him feel as if bricks were being piled on his chest. As for Rose, she seemed incapable of love. Except when it came to clothes: she was a valued customer at Monique's, Beltibbet's fanciest boutique. And it really *was* fancy—Jessie had been staggered by the prices, while recognizing none of the labels. Most of their dresses featured robust internal corsetry. It was a whole other world.

What amazed Jessie was how much pride Canice took in Rose's appearance. He was always given a chair outside the dressing room, and whenever Rose emerged, he made comments and suggestions, genuinely engaged. Jessie had no memory of her own mother ever buying new clothes and it was laughable to think of her dad even noticing. They'd run the general store in their small town in the wilds of Connemara. Because they lived right next door they were always on duty. The shop was open seven days a week but, even so, a knock on their window late at night or very early in the morning was commonplace, people looking to buy emergency matches or milk or a short length of rope. Dilly Parnell had lived in a flowery apron. Jessie supposed she didn't have the need for anything else. Maybe she hadn't had any interest. Both her parents had been humble, quiet people—old-fashioned but very loving.

They'd encouraged Jessie every step of the way and had been fit to burst with pride in her. It was nearly twelve years since her dad, Lionard, had passed—he'd had dementia and just faded away, like a picture left in the sun. His death had felt like a soft landing.

Not so when her mother died. Granny Dilly had come to live in the granny flat in Jessie and Johnny's back garden, a gentle, undemanding presence, loved by the children. Nine years ago, when she'd died, Jessie was devastated. TJ was only six months old but Jessie decided that the only thing that could save her was another baby. Which was how Dilly—named after her granny—had come to be.

Jessie still cried for her parents, but mostly from simple gratitude for her good fortune. They'd been decent, kind people. *Very* different from Canice and Rose.

When Jessie and Johnny had gone to Beltibbet to inform them that they were getting married, polite conversation was made in what Rose called the 'drawing room'. Jessie thought it had gone okay.

It was only as they were leaving that Rose gripped Jessie's wrist, stopping her progress. 'My son is nobody's second choice,' she'd said, in a low, pleasant voice.

Shocked, Jessie acted as if she hadn't heard. In retrospect, that had been the best approach: if she and Rose had had words, they would never have got past it. But Rose's hostility had caught her on the hop. Especially because Rory's parents, Michael and Ellen, had been *lovely*. She began to wonder if Rose's enmity *was* her fault. She *had* been married to Johnny's best friend—perhaps Rose was only being protective of her first-born. But Cara had been welcomed into the Casey family with the same icy hostility. There was no intel on Rose's first encounter with Paige. But Jessie *had* been there when Rose said to Nell, '*Another* daughter-in-law. Lord.'

Christ, she was dreading the next forty-eight hours.

Her suspicion—never far from the surface – that no one really liked her, hit her once more. Her closest women friends—Mary-Laine and Annette—were from the Women In Business network; they tended to exchange wry identification rather than secrets of the heart.

As for Ed and Cara and Liam and Nell, if she didn't offer expensive outings, would she ever even see them? *You have to rent your friends.* Where had that awful thought come from? But it was true, wasn't it? If she didn't shell out loads of cash, she'd be totally alone.

She had to stop thinking this way. But it just showed what proximity to Canice and Rose did to her, to them all.

At least they were staying in a beautiful place. She'd hired three holiday cottages, outside town, within walking distance of Bawn Beach and the bracing Atlantic waves. The leasing agent was a regular at the PiG cookery school. She'd given Jessie a cut-price rate in exchange for two free tickets to Hagen Klein. Jessie, Johnny and the four girls were in one house, Ed, Cara and their boys in another. The third she'd dubbed 'the young persons' house'. Liam and Nell were there, along with Ferdia, Sammie and Barty.

Jessie had played slightly sneaky to guarantee Ferdia's attendance: she'd invited Sammie, who liked the sound of an alcohol-fuelled weekend in the west before she left Ireland. Ferdia had grudgingly said he'd come if Barty was also invited. So there it was.

Rose and Canice did their best to ignore Ferdia—and Saoirse, of course—and Jessie wanted to push back. She loved Johnny but she would not pretend that her marriage to Rory hadn't happened . . .

A series of beeps from her phone distracted her: they had coverage again. But, scanning her emails, there was one from Posie, the manager in Malahide, with the happy news that she was three months pregnant.

Ah, *shite.*

Shite a *thousand* times.

Posie ran that shop brilliantly. All *kinds* of logistical personnel shenanigans would be needed to cover her absence.

Even when it was *highly inconvenient* Jessie prided herself on being good to her staff. Posie's maternity leave would be six long months. Jessie would throw a baby shower and buy a high-spec Bugaboo.

Six months off, though! She'd barely taken a month with each of her own children.

Now she'd take a quick look on Facebook. But that also gave her a shock.

'God.' She swallowed.

'What?' Johnny asked.

'Facebook's suggesting I friend request Izzy Kinsella. Why would they do that? Why now?'

'Their algorithms are mad. Ignore it.'

'But . . . has something happened? Someone I know must have friended her.'

'Their metrics are far more random than that.'

'Sorry, babes.' It didn't matter, and poor Johnny already had enough going on. 'Are you okay?'

'Ah, you know.' He tightened his hands on the wheel and kept driving into the sun.

Forty-One

Liam braked suddenly, sending Nell's pencil skidding across her graph paper. They'd come to a standstill in yet another small town.

'How much longer?' she asked.

'You sound like a kid.'

Sitting helplessly in the car for the last four hours had been torture. Four precious hours that she could have been working, instead of desperately trying to draw in a moving vehicle.

'Are we there yet?' he taunted.

She checked her phone: another seventeen minutes before they arrived at Westport station to pick up Ferdia, Sammie and Barty. After that, another twenty minutes before they reached the holiday home.

Another thirty-seven minutes of achieving nothing.

Even talking about the project would have helped untangle some of the ideas in her head, but Liam was still off with her. It was hard to know whether she should feel guilty or resentful. They'd never had a situation like this before, where he chided her for being selfish. But her work was really important to her and he knew that. Surely he knew what a great opportunity this was. Or maybe she should be kinder. Liam's parents were both total pieces of work. This weekend would be hard for him.

'Text them,' Liam said.

They were parked outside Westport station, waiting for Ferdia and gang. Their train should have arrived about ten minutes earlier, but there was no sign.

'What's his number?'

Liam made a 'Pffft' of irritation. 'I don't have it. Text Jessie.'

She clicked off a text. But after staring at her phone for a long, silent time, she said, 'She's probably out of coverage.'

'So what are we supposed to—'

'I'll go in and have a look round.'

She jumped from the car and headed into the deserted-looking station. A man in a uniform was measuring a bench on the platform. 'It's delayed,' he called. 'The Dublin train. Twenty-five minutes.'

Okay. She could sit on a bench—so long as she didn't get in the way of any measuring—and work while she waited. She'd go and get her stuff.

But back at the car, Liam said, 'We're not hanging around here.'

'Liam, please, I promised Jessie.'

'They say twenty-five minutes, but it could be anything.'

She went back inside to the man. 'When you say twenty-five minutes, do you actually mean twenty-five? Might it be longer?' If he said something twee like, 'The man who made time, made plenty of it', she'd literally cry.

The man straightened up slowly. 'This isn't Switzerland!' He sounded wounded. 'Someone was telling me about a train there that was six minutes late and they gave all the passengers free cake.'

Nell was too anxious for this. 'Thanks.' Outside, she came back to the car and said, 'Your man was a bit vague. But, Liam, we can't just abandon them.'

'They can get a taxi. Or a bus. Or hitch.' He started the engine. 'I'm not hanging around here all evening. Get in.'

Reluctantly, she did so. They'd been driving for several minutes when her phone rang.

'You were looking for Ferd's number?' Jessie said. 'What's up?'

'Their train is delayed. The man wasn't sure how long it would be. So we didn't wait. I'm sorry, Jessie.'

'You're fine. I'll send Johnny in when they arrive.'

Forty-Two

'The sun's too bright,' Tom said. 'It needs a light-shade.'

'We're driving directly west.' Ed explained to the boys how the sun rose and fell and it gave Cara a safe, happy feeling.

Then she got her first whiff of the salty air. 'Vinnie, Tom!' she exclaimed. 'Can you smell the sea?'

'There it is!'

Out past a long stretch of pale sand, the sun had turned the water into liquid silver. Ed, following his satnav, kept driving towards the edge of the land. The road got narrower and quickly became a single-track boreen.

'We're not lost?' Cara asked anxiously.

'Have I ever got you lost?'

He hadn't. 'But where are these houses of Jessie's? We're nearly in the sea.'

'They should be right . . . about . . . here!' Ed turned in off the boreen.

Out of nowhere, an enclave of six perfect-looking houses, made from cream-coloured clapboard, had appeared. These were a far cry from the usual grim bungalows that were Irish holiday homes.

'We're practically on the beach!' Cara laughed with delight. 'Trust Jessie. I mean, how does she even know about this place?'

There were no formal boundaries, but each property was demarcated by bunches of rough sand grass.

'*Ammophila*,' Ed said. 'Coming from Greek words meaning "sand" and "friend". These grasses survive in soil with high salinity—'

'Dad?' Vinnie said.

'Son?'

'Shut it.'

'Yes, son.' Ed chuckled softly.

Jessie and her lot were milling about outside the first house.

'You're in the second house,' Jessie called, waving them along. 'The key is in the door.'

As they jumped from the car the roar of the waves was much louder. Grainy white sand blew up underfoot from the nearby beach and Ed's sand-grass was bending in the breeze. At almost 6 p.m., the sun was still hot.

'What took you so long?' TJ and Dilly came running over to Vinnie and Tom.

'I can't believe you're even later than us!' TJ exclaimed.

'Daddy drove really slowly!' Dilly said. 'He doesn't want to be here.'

'Because Nana and Granddad are nightmares. Are you coming for a swim?'

'Course!' Vinnie said.

'Can we, Mum?' Tom asked.

'Bring your stuff in first and then off you go.' Cara opened the front door of the little house, and the four children swarmed in ahead of her.

Inside, it was airy and light, with hardwood flooring and Hamptons-style furniture, in pale blue and cream. Marine motifs abounded. Behind each house sat a slab of salt-roughened decking, facing directly towards the water.

'My God.' Ed, hefting a suitcase into the double-height hall, stopped abruptly. He dropped the bag. 'This is incredible. Too bad that—'

'What?' she asked. 'You okay, honey?'

'Ah, you know.' He squinted towards the sun. 'This is amazing. But Mum and Dad . . .'

Cara was surprised. He so rarely got rattled.

'I know.' She went to him and hugged him.

'Especially Dad,' he mumbled into her hair. 'Being round him is like being around an unexploded bomb.'

'All be over by Sunday.'

'Say it,' he said.

'I've got you.' She squeezed him tighter. 'You're safe.'

'Thanks.' He pulled away and flashed a smile. 'I can cope now. Right. Bedrooms.'

'Can this be my room?' Vinnie called from somewhere in the house.

'Is it the biggest?' Cara called back. 'Does it have an en suite? Because then the answer is no.'

I need my own bathroom.

With that, her mood dipped. She'd managed to forget about food and all that other stuff. It was no surprise that now she found herself navigating to the kitchen. The fridge was filled with wine, beer and other 'essentials'. 'Ed, look!'

'Jessie's doing, no doubt.'

And here came Jessie now, in a floaty beach dress, carrying a glass of rosé and accompanied by Bridey.

'This *place*!' Cara exclaimed.

'I know, right. This weekend is going to be awful—no offence, Ed, but when Canice and Rose have once again broken our spirit, at least we'll have somewhere nice to lick our wounds.'

'Seriously, though, was it really spendy? I feel guilty.'

'Would you stop? I got it for half-nothing from a customer. Anyway, spending money calms me. I needed to stay somewhere nice for the sake of my sanity, and I'm not booking my crowd into a swanky place, leaving the rest of you in some shithole. We're all in this together.'

'But you got that wine and beer in.' Cara took a wad of notes from her bag and pushed them into Jessie's hand.

'No.'

'Yes!'

'Christ, you're strong-willed when you want to be,' Jessie grumbled. 'Thanks, hon.'

The four younger children stampeded into the kitchen.

'They're in here.' Dilly wrenched open a cupboard door.

'Deadly!' Vinnie had found a stash of biscuits. He tore a packet open and shoved one into his mouth.

'Hey!' Bridey called. 'You can't go for a swim now. You'll get cramp.'

'You'll be fine.' Cara whipped the packet away from him. 'Get your togs and go.'

Returning the biscuits to the press, she couldn't help taking a glance—*tons* of stuff in there: chocolate, Haribo, what looked like cupcakes . . .

'Ice-cream in the freezer,' Jessie said.

'Oh.' *No*.

'Just, we all need every possible prop to get through this weekend. Cara, Ed, take a good long look at me now. This is the last time there'll be a sober sighting of me. I plan to start drinking, get scuttered and stay that way until Sunday afternoon. I'll be in a constant process of topping up.'

'Maybe it won't be so bad,' Ed said.

Jessie gave a hollow laugh. 'Ya think?'

It was harder for Johnny and Jessie, Cara knew. Canice was nasty to all three of his sons but it cut Johnny to his quick.

And while Rose was hostile to her three daughters-in-law, she definitely had it in for Jessie the most.

'Okay,' Jessie said. 'I'll get my swim out of the way, then make a good run at the drinking.' She looked at Ed and Cara. 'You coming?'

'I am not.' Cara made her voice good-humoured but no way *on earth* was she putting on a pair of togs.

'What about you, Ed?' Jessie's phone rang. 'Ferdia? You're actually there? No, Liam couldn't wait, but hang tight, I'll send Johnny in.' She hung up. 'Ferdia. Train was delayed.'

'I'll go,' Ed said. 'It's no bother.'

'Ah, no . . . Are you sure? Just Johnny's not in great form . . .'

'Course.'

Jessie, surrounded by children carrying togs and towels, strode off towards the water's edge, Ed got into the car and drove away, and suddenly Cara was alone in the sunny little house.

She wasn't quite sure what to do. She could unpack but that would only take five minutes. Maybe she should sit on the deck and simply be.

She touched her tongue against the ragged edge of her broken tooth. The day it had happened, she'd been freaked out, convinced she'd managed to rot her entire mouthful of teeth. She couldn't face the judgement of the dentist. But, as it happened, the broken tooth didn't hurt, so everything was grand. A bit weird that a lump of enamel had broken off for no reason, but maybe it was just natural shedding.

Out of nowhere, the idea of ice-cream appeared in her head. The clock was ticking. Ed would be back in about forty minutes and the kids might be even sooner.

She'd intended to have a healthy weekend, but the proximity to food and the freedom of her solitude . . .

Her heart was thumping. Her blood was pumping through her hands and feet, pulsing against her fingertips. Like an automaton, she went to the kitchen and opened the freezer door. There were four tubs of Ben & Jerry's. One of them was Cherry Garcia, her favourite. A horrible combination of soaring relief and bleak misery meant that this was now out of her hands.

Three sharp raps on the front window made her jump.

'Knock, knock!' It was Johnny.

She hadn't been doing anything bad, but she was shaking as she went to the front door.

'God bless all here.' Johnny pretended to remove a cap, mimicking an old-fashioned farmer.

'Hi . . . ah, hello. What's up?'

'Can we talk a bit of business?' He went to the living room. '*Small* bit of business. Tiny. Nearly invisible.' He seemed slightly manic. 'About the Airbnb thing. I know, Cara, you offer to do this out of the goodness of your heart and I pester you on your weekend away.'

'No good deed goes unpunished,' she managed to say.

'That's it. So look, just a simple change: instead of the income going straight into our current account, can it go into a new account? I've already opened it, all the info here.' He slid the pages towards her.

She scanned it. The account was in Johnny's name alone. Every other account, every other bill she'd seen, was jointly shared between Johnny and Jessie.

'Will the mortgage be paid out of this same account?' That made sense, to keep the whole enterprise self-contained.

'Ah, no. Who knows how this Airbnb thing will work out? What if there isn't enough income to cover the mortgage every month?'

The mortgage was tiny. Airbnb in central Dublin was booming.

'Let's try it this way,' he said. 'At least for a while.'

Cara was still grappling to understand: the mortgage on Johnny's apartment was to be paid from the account he shared with his wife, but the income was to go into a new account that was solely in his name? Maybe Johnny picked up on her confusion. 'It's actually for Jessie.'

That made zero sense.

'Just in case,' he said.

Just in case of *what*?

Forty-Three

The house was *ridiculous*. New, really upscale, like in a movie. Everything was blue or creamy-coloured and full-on discreet luxury. What if they spilt something?

The kitchen. Jesus. A high-spec wonderland with an icemaker, a boiling-water tap, a literal Gaggia coffee machine that you'd see in an authentic Italian coffee bar . . .

It was too much.

Liam baggsed the master bedroom, an expanse of white and dove-grey. Nell stood anxiously at the doorway, eyeing the walk-in wardrobe and massive bathroom. 'Shouldn't we give it to Ferdia? Jessie's paying for this, and he's her son?'

'*Him?* He's only a kid!'

'*Oooo*kay.' This room was bigger than the others. She could annex a corner for her work and still leave plenty of space for Liam. 'Is it okay if I use the dressing table to draw at?'

'Sure,' he said.

She hefted in her box of tools and materials and laid out the crude little models she'd hastily fashioned from MDF. This presentation on Monday would be the shoddiest she'd ever done . . .

'You coming for a swim?'

She looked at him steadily. 'Working. Enjoy your swim.'

With an over-elaborate quizzical look, he left and she exhaled. Right, let's do this. She sat cross-legged, focusing on the challenges of the job, but just as her head began to burrow a pathway into them, Jessie arrived, glass of wine in hand. She stood up. 'Jessie. I'm so sorry about Ferdia—'

'Stop. Who wants to be hanging around a station, waiting for an Irish train? Ed has gone for them. All grand.'

'If you're sure? And, really, Jessie . . .' She was incoherent with gratitude and mortification. 'This house. There was no need, we could have slept in a tent.'

'Ha-ha, you young people. No, we need a bolthole. This weekend is going to be brutal.'

'You mean Canice and Rose?'

'Yeah, but especially Rose. She's always making out that I had Johnny on the go at the same time as Rory. Which I totally hadn't!'

'Of course.' It was none of Nell's business.

However, she liked Jessie. She was a bit insane, her and her extravagance, and they didn't have much in common, but she was basically sound.

'No, seriously, Nell. I really totally didn't. I'm a stone-cold Goody-Two-Shoes. Even if I'd fancied Johnny, which I didn't, I'd have been too repressed to do anything about it. But if I said to Rose, "Actually I didn't even notice Johnny when Rory was alive because I was so in love with Rory", she wouldn't like that either. She told me she wasn't happy that Johnny was my second choice.'

Nell nodded as sympathetically as she could. Jessie, caught up in righteous defensiveness, barely noticed. 'You can't fecking win with Rose. Don't even try, Nell, that's my advice to you.'

'Okay.'

'All right! I admit it, I *knew* Johnny had a thing for me. Well, I suspected. But is that so bad, Nell? For my whole life, no one fancied me, only prissy old fools who lived with their mothers and had wacko hobbies, and then two rides come along at once. And I didn't encourage it. Plus! *Plus!* I was sure he only wanted me because I belonged to his buddy, you know?'

'I do.' Nell realized that Jessie was slightly drunk.

'No one believes me, Nell. Maybe Saoirse does. But Ferdia doesn't. Ferdia *really* doesn't, no matter how often I tell him. Izzy—you know, Rory's sister—wrote a thing on TripAdvisor, saying I was a whore. Me! I've only slept with four men in the whole of my life.'

'That's rough.'

'Do you know what age I was when Rory died? Thirty-four! Barely older than you are now. By which I mean, *young*! I really loved Rory, I was devastated. People said I shouldn't have fallen for his best friend. But doesn't that seem the most logical person to fall for? Ferdia and Saoirse knew him—wasn't that better than bringing a stranger into their lives?'

'Of course.'

'But it was very sad, losing the Kinsellas. Took a long time to get over it. Ah, don't mind me, Nell, I'm a bit drunk.' She stared into her now-empty wine glass. 'I've finished my drink. Nature's way of telling me I've overstayed my welcome. Right, I'd better go down and feed the bunnies. See you later.'

For some reason, lately Jessie couldn't stop thinking of those early days with Rory and Johnny.

Within weeks of each other, the three of them had started in sales at Irish Dairy International. Almost the same age, doing the same job, in friendly rivalry with each other, they'd bonded instantly.

The Three Amigos—they'd actually been nicknamed that. From the word go, they'd had *so* much fun.

Johnny was the charmer: chatty, entertaining, generous with compliments and widely regarded as very sexy. For one of his birthdays, the girls in marketing Photoshopped his picture with a star glinting off his smile.

Rory was the steadier of the two, amusing and witty in a quiet way.

The funny thing was that, seeing she'd go on to marry both of them, she hadn't fancied either of them.

She liked fey, creative boys, the more anguished the better. Loving them back to happiness was always her hope but, at best, those types were simply bemused by her. Neither Rory nor Johnny was remotely angst-ridden. Cheerfully they talked about wanting to own their own home, drive a cool car, get promoted—the same life goals Jessie had.

They liked the same music and the same movies—middle-of-the-road stuff. (Despite Jessie's fondness for unsuccessful creatives with dirty hair, her taste was solidly mainstream.) She was never tongue-tied or shy around either of them. They, in turn, treated her like one of the lads. In a lifetime first, she fitted in.

It became their thing to go for drinks on a Friday and dissect their disappointing love lives. Rory and Jessie seemed to specialize in unrequited crushes, while Johnny was a commitment-phobe who accumulated obsessives. It had taken well over a year for Jessie and Rory suddenly to become awkward around each other, while Johnny circled, confused and anxious. For about a month, all three were locked in an uneasy tension until one Friday night it came to a head.

It was late, there were no taxis to be had, so Rory and Johnny said they'd walk Jessie home.

It had happened before, it was no big deal. Except that, walking along, three abreast, with Jessie in the middle, Rory quietly took her hand.

She'd been expecting it. Expecting *something*. And he'd picked that particular night to make his move.

Then, almost laughably, on her other side, Johnny slipped his arm around her waist.

She hadn't reacted to Rory holding her hand and she didn't react to this.

She didn't know how to.

The three of them marched along the rain-glistening pavements, perfectly in step. No one spoke. Sandwiched between both men, in a state of almost feverish confusion, Jessie wanted this never to end. Or perhaps she wanted it to stop immediately. She had no idea.

Did Rory and Johnny each know what the other was doing?

At the time she'd thought they didn't. But in later years she'd decided that maybe they did, that they were locked in some sort of almost-sibling rivalry and she was their battleground. After a lifetime of pining for the wrong men, it was the strangest thing to realize that both of them were the right kind and both were hers for the taking.

Without ever acknowledging Johnny's interest in her, she weighed up the pros and cons of Rory, as if it were a business decision. This was too important a choice to let her inexperienced heart make.

She'd asked herself if she could live with him, if she trusted him with money, to be a good father, to stay faithful. If she could be faithful to him. It was impossible to predict the future, but as risks went, Rory looked like a safe bet.

Other factors helped to cement her decision. She and Rory had both grown up in a small place, without much money but with loving parents. They had the same values—work hard but live decently.

There was also the suspicion that Johnny only wanted her because Rory did. If he got her, he'd probably get bored and start playing games. And that was something she could *not* handle—she was well able to be tough at work, but her heart was tender.

Once she'd decided, she was certain. There was to be no messing with Johnny, no occasional moment when they stared longingly at each other and pretended to be thwarted lovers.

She married Rory and Johnny was their best man.

Forty-Four

What about a set that was partially *suspended*? The main set would be at stage level, but there could be, perhaps, two or three 'rooms' hydraulically lowered and raised, as required. Maybe even one would be enough. She'd have to check the cost but, as an idea, it was ingenious. She'd create so much more space. Other factors played into this, though. Insurance, mostly. Covering themselves against actors falling off and injuring themselves might be prohibitive.

Liam burst into the room, breaking her train of thought. 'Back from my swim,' he said. 'Am*az*ing out there. You'd have loved it.'

'Guess I would.' She angled herself away from him and towards her drawings.

'The sun is *so* hot. Like being in Greece. Except for the water. Baltic!'

He sat at the bottom of the bed, watching over her shoulder as she worked. Now that she had an audience, her brain emptied.

'I should have a shower. Shouldn't I?'

When she remained silent, he said, 'Nell? Hey? Should I have a shower?'

'If you want.'

'Like, I don't *want* but do I want to feel salty all evening? . . . Do I? Nell?'

'. . . Probably not.'

After remaining on the bed for several more minutes, he got up. Her nerves were taut, waiting for the bathroom door to close. But he left it open, then started to sing.

A bomb of rage exploded inside her, she flew across the room and slammed the door shut.

As soon as he came out again, he demanded, mock-wounded, 'Why'd you close the door? Did you not like my singing?' Then he began drying himself vigorously, sending water droplets over her drawings.

'Careful, hon.'

'This *is* a bedroom,' he said mildly.

He even got dressed noisily, chatting away to himself: 'Where's the neck-hole in this T-shirt? Jeans or shorts? Hard to know. It's warm now but could get cold later?'

New footsteps and chatter sounded in the hallway, then Barty, short and smiley, stuck his head around the door. 'Hi, Nell.'

Next, Sammie, a rucksack on her shoulder. 'Hi, Nell, hi, Liam.'

Finally Ferdia, towering over the other two. 'Why didn't you wait for us?' he demanded hotly.

'Because your train was delayed,' Liam said.

'For a few minutes!'

'Nearly an hour.'

'It was my fault,' Nell said. 'I had work to do and . . . Sorry. We should have stayed.'

Ferdia looked from Liam to Nell, then back again. He seemed about to throw another accusation, then his ire visibly drained. 'What's the story with the bedrooms?'

'There's two more,' Liam said. 'Take your pick.'

'Oh. Okay.'

Within moments, Ferdia was back. 'Who said you could have the best room?'

'First come, first served.' Liam was cheery.

'Is that why you didn't wait for us?'

'Come *on*.' Liam laughed. 'Please save us from millennials and their sense of entitlement.' Then he added, 'Present company excepted, maybe.'

'I have a sense of entitlement?'

'. . . *Weeeeeelll* . . .'

Oh, just fuck off.

Ferdia and the others left. 'Okay!' Liam clapped his hands together. 'Time for a beer. Beer, Nell?'

'No, thanks.'

'Ah, go on.'

Finally, she turned her entire body towards him. 'Liam, I'm sorry I can't give you my full attention right now. You know how much this opportunity means to me. Please let me get on with it, just for the next two days.'

'Jesus, I only offered you a beer!' He strode from the room, leaving acrimony in his wake.

*

Sometime later the light was fading and Ferdia loomed in the doorway.

What now?

'You like some food?'

'No. Well, okay—wait, is someone making something?'

'I'm doing a stir-fry. You vegetarian? Okay. I'll bring you some.'

Liam lounged, his legs over the arm of the chair, swigging from a bottle of beer. In the kitchen, Ferdia and his little friends were gathered around a wok. In good form, he idly scrolled through Facebook, half read two articles on cycling, took a look at Twitter . . . and realized that the three kids had moved outside to the deck. He twisted his body to get a better look. Wait a . . . Had they a joint on the go out there? Why would they sneak out on him? Did they . . . They couldn't possibly think he was a disapproving adult?

He swung his feet to the floor and went outside. Barty had a reefer in his hand.

Suddenly Liam was angry. This was bad manners. 'Hey! Why are you sneaking around with your doobie? Not cool.'

Ferdia and Barty exchanged amused glances.

'Yup. It's not cool.' Barty wheezed with mirth and passed the joint to Ferdia.

Liam's stare was cold. The little prick.

'Give him a toke,' Barty said to Ferdia. 'G'wan, give the oul fella a toke.'

At this, Sammie lay back on the deck and laughed and laughed. 'Sorry,' she tried to say to Liam. 'I'm sorry.' She sat up again. 'I'm not laughing at you. I'm just a bit . . .'

Stung and confused, Liam was trying to figure this out. Sammie *was* laughing at him. Barty *did* think he was old. It was total bullshit. Liam knew he was cool—he'd always been cool. 'You keep your little joint, kiddos,' he said. 'Careful you don't get too stoned.'

Tonight was the 'relaxed' part of the anniversary celebrations: a session and a sing-song in Canice Casey's favourite pub. An open bar had been laid on for the townspeople who hadn't made the cut for the lavish dinner on Saturday night.

Nell had had the foresight to borrow appropriate clothes. Tonight was a crisp cotton shirtdress in pale grey. She wound her pink hair into a bun on the crown of her head and shoved her feet into her ancient Birkenstocks.

In the living room, Liam was lounging on an armchair, several empty beer bottles on the floor beside him. Doritos bags littered the table.

Sammie looked up. 'Nell! You look fucking amazing.'

'Thanks, hon. Hey, Liam, we'd better go. You guys coming?'

'Yep,' Ferdia said. 'Free bar, right?'

Liam narrowed his eyes at him. 'Say what?'

'Say what, *what*?' Ferdia replied.

Oh, for God's sake! 'Where are the car keys?' Nell asked.

'What do you need them for?' Liam said.

'To drive the car.'

'It's only a few kilometres.'

'I'll be coming home on my own.'

'Why's that?'

You know why. 'Because as soon as everyone's drunk enough not to notice, I'm sloping back here to work.'

'You won't get parking in town.'

Nell noticed Ferdia watching this exchange. He seemed to be enjoying it and she felt angry. 'And maybe I might,' she said pointedly. 'Let's be positive.'

'There's a spot!' Sammie said to Nell. 'Just there. Your man is coming out.'

'Thank you, you awesome creature.'

'It's a bit narrow,' Liam said. 'Don't scratch my car.'

She took a breath. 'I. Won't.'

She slid the car in and the five of them piled out.

Forty-Five

When Liam pulled the pub door open, a roar of heat and noise hit them. The place was rammed.

Nell spotted Canice standing about halfway down, big, balding, boomy, a pint in his hand. He was loudly holding forth, surrounded by those who probably depended on his patronage for a good portion of their livelihood. Bursts of raucous laughter accompanied his every remark.

Rose, beside him, perched on a high stool, dressed in a spangled cocktail frock, was similarly garlanded with sycophants.

Liam pushed his way through the crowd and Nell followed. 'Congratulations, Rose,' she said politely. 'Congratulations, Canice. Fifty years. That's, ah . . . awesome.'

She wasn't certain if a hug might be in order. But the imperious bow Rose gave disabused her of any such notions.

'Who's this?' her mother-in-law asked, with a cold smile. 'Ferdia? Oh, Jessie's boy. Good Lord, you've got very . . . *hairy*. And here's Barty. Honestly, I feel I see Barty more than I do my own flesh-and-blood. Not that *you*'re my flesh-and-blood, Ferdia.'

Nell hoicked Sammie forward to introduce her, then set her free. Time to end this chat, before Rose got really nasty.

'What'll you have to drink?' Canice bellowed at Liam.

'Pint, thanks,' Liam said.

'Nellie, my girl?'

'Fizzy water.'

'Not drinking? What's up with you?' Canice winked.

'Ugh, I'm not pregnant, if that's what you're getting at.'

His eyes bulged. She'd shocked him. Shocked several people, she realized, to go by the sudden lull.

'Young lady, I *beg* your pardon,' Canice blustered.

She smiled and repeated, 'A fizzy water, please.'

It was produced instantly by a nervous-seeming boy. He reminded her of a bar-keep in a Western, poised to duck down behind the counter just before the shooting started. She took her drink, smiled again at Canice, at Rose, at Liam, then pushed away from the bar, feeling their eyes on her back.

Being stone-cold sober was hard when everyone else was knocking them back—and everyone really *was*. Johnny was in the thick of things, regaling a crowd with funny story after funny story but his energy was fractured, almost glinting from him, like flint sparks. Jessie, her eyes too bright, was flitting around, being everywhere at once.

Cara grabbed Nell's arm and locked her into a strange, dark conversation where she insisted over and over that Nell didn't know how beautiful she was. 'Don't let anyone ever body-shame you, Nell. Do you promise me? Promise me!'

Even Ed, normally calm and upbeat, was sculling pints with a quiet desperation.

It was quite *mad* how scared everyone was of Canice and Rose. Yes, they were terrible people, but Johnny was ancient, heading for *fifty*. Far too old to be scared of his dad!

It was also hard having to yell to be heard and answering the same questions again and again. After an hour of shouty, repetitious shite, she struggled through the crowd to Liam. 'Have you the key?'

'Why'd you say that to my dad?'

'What? Oh? About being pregnant? Because I'm not.'

'You shouldn't have. He's furious.'

He was always furious. 'Key?'

'That little fuck *Ferdia* took it.'

She had to push hard through the dense knots of people until she reached Ferdia and his gang clustered in a corner, down near the back. 'I need the key.'

'Why are you leaving?'

'Work. I've a big-deal presentation on Monday.'

'Woo-hoo for you.'

Steadily she looked at him. 'Key?'

'I was trying to be funny.' He was sheepish and clearly drunk. 'Epic fail.'

'You're funny,' she said, with polite sarcasm. 'Key.'

He handed it over. 'How will we get in?'

'Knock. I'll open the door.'

'What if you're asleep? Oh, but you won't be, right? You have your big-deal presentation on Monday to prepare for.'

She rolled her eyes, fought her way back down the pub, then slipped out into the mild night, exhaling with relief.

Forty-Six

Ferdia opened his eyes into darkness. He felt he'd been asleep for a long time during which the world had altered irreversibly, but it was only 1.43 a.m., less than an hour since he and Sammie had gone to bed. Now he was *wide* awake with so much of the night still to get through.

The reality of losing Sammie had settled in him, like a ball on a lottery wheel coming to a final rest. It was too hard to stay here with these thoughts. Sliding from the bed, he located some sweats and a T-shirt on the floor, grabbed his phone and slipped out onto the deck. Listening to the rush and hush of the waves, he lay on a lounger and his eyes began to adjust to the dark. The white foam of the wave caps became visible and—What the fu–! A noise! Behind him! A rat?

A woman's voice—Nell's—said, 'Who's that? Ferdia? You gave me a fright!'

'You gave *me* a fright!' His heart was pounding hard.

'What are you doing out here?'

'Having a fucking heart attack, thank you very much! Why are *you* here?'

'I'm stuck. On my work thing.' She took the lounger next to him. 'I came out to ring my friend.'

'Work away.'

'Ah, no, I'll wait.'

They sat without speaking, the only sound that of the sea roaring and pulling. When his heartbeat slowed down, he said, 'Nice parents-in-law you've got.'

Her clothes rustled as she shrugged. 'They'll be dead soon.'

He snorted with involuntary laughter. 'Did you really say that?'

'I dunno. Did I? So, what are you doing, sitting out here on your own?'

The darkness made it easier to admit things. 'Sammie's going away on Tuesday. We're officially done, and I feel, you know . . .' He felt rather than saw her nod. 'Aren't you going to hit me up with some patronizing shizz about young love?' he asked.

'I'm only thirty. *I*'m young.'

'To me, you're old.'

Quickly she sat up and swivelled her body so she was on the edge of her lounger, much closer to him. 'Here's some "patronizing shizz" for you, Ferdia: you haven't a clue.'

'That's totally an old-person thing to say.'

After another long silence, he asked, 'So what's this job? What do you do?'

'Set designer. For the theatre.'

Oh. He'd had a vague idea she did some sort of painting and decorating thing. Set designing sounded more interesting. 'You like it?'

'Love it. It's all I ever wanted to do.'

'How does someone even get that sense of purpose? I haven't a clue what to do with my life.'

'You're studying what? Sociology and economics? You must have picked them for a reason. Did you?'

'. . . Yeah.'

'So?'

He was reluctant. There was a chance this story could make him sound sanctimonious and he didn't want her mockery. 'Remember 2008, the financial crash? I was ten. I was going to this private school, and in the first term back after the summer, five kids just disappeared. They'd be there one day and next day they were gone. No one told us why. We never got a chance to say goodbye—they just left like normal one day and never came back. It was weird and kinda . . . awful. Mum's business was in trouble, shops kept being shut down, so I was waiting to be one of the disappeared.'

'Wow.'

'You know who Keeva is? Barty's mum? She's a nurse. I heard her telling Granny Ellen that lots of men were showing up in A and E with botched suicides. They cut their wrists but did it wrong, stuff like that. Then Barty's dad's company went into receivership and it was *really* bad. They'd have been kicked out of their house if Izzy hadn't jumped in to help. Then one of my mates from school, his dad hanged himself because he owed so much money.'

'Jesus,' Nell murmured.

'I used to watch the news, trying to understand why decisions by some people made life so hard for a ton of others. I wanted to "help" so . . . economics and sociology seemed like the right mix. But nearly everyone on my course wants to be either a social worker or to make a fortune working for a multinational. I want to work for a cause, one I believe in. Or at least I did.'

'What d'you mean?'

'Last summer I volunteered for Feed the World and all I saw was the inside of a warehouse. I litch didn't meet one human I was supposed to be helping. And I know that's really uppity, me saying, "I'll decide how I'll do my compassion." I'm just saying.'

'Aaaah, you're after the "warm glow", right? "I'm a good person and I've made life so much better for these lovely poor people." That it?'

To his surprise, he laughed. 'You got me. I totally want my warm glow. Does that make me a terrible person?'

'Feed the World is a huge charity. You've a better chance of getting your glow on if you work for a smaller one. Lot of grass-roots activism, volunteer if they can't pay you.'

'Why didn't I think of this?' Answering his own question, he said, 'In college, it's all been about a career path, getting a place with one of the huge charities.'

'Go local. Try the Refugee Council,' Nell said. 'Helping people like Perla from last night.'

'She was totally great. Like, she's so *normal*? What age is she?'

'Twenty-nine.'

'That's not *so* old. When I saw her first I thought she was, you know, *forty*, but after she had wine and loosened up, yeah, she just seemed regular. It was hard listening to what she and the little girl went through. All because those religious loons hate women.'

'Speaking of hating women . . .'

Her change of tone made him glance up. He could see the flash of her teeth and eyes.

'What's your beef with your mum?'

'*What?*' That was none of her business. How fucking *dare* she? 'You haven't a clue.'

'So explain it.'

He was explaining nothing.

They sat without speaking. He could hear his own breathing, angry and fast. After a long pause he said, 'She shouldn't have got with my dad's best friend.' That would shut her up.

'Is that the part that bothers you? Would you have minded if it was a stranger?'

Spluttering with injustice, he said, 'She was with both of them at the same time.'

'She wasn't.'

'She was. Everybody knows. I heard Izzy and Keeva talking about it, like, *years* ago.'

'She *wasn't*. She really loved your dad. She was devastated when he died. Have you ever talked to her about this? You should. It'll change your mind.'

All of a sudden, in the strangest turn of events, he believed her. Just the smallest shift in attitude changed his mum from a conniving cheat into an ordinary woman whose husband had died far too young.

Now he didn't know *how* to feel.

'Did she know that Johnny fancied her?' Nell asked. 'Yes. Was she flattered? Yes. Does that make her a bad person?'

'It makes her pathetic.'

'How pathetic? She was thirty-four, which sounds ancient to you, but it was no age to her. She was entitled to a life. You're all about rights for women, but you don't cut your own mum any slack.'

Forty-Seven

'Johnny . . . Johnny . . .'

Jessie's voice pulled him up from the depths.

'Babes, it's too bright . . .'

Reality came at him in flashes. *I'm in Mayo. For my parents' wedding anniversary. I've never felt so depressed.*

'Babes.' Jessie plucked at him. 'You need to do the blind.'

He opened his eyes and immediately squinched them closed again. What was happening?

They'd got *so* drunk last night. They'd tumbled into bed without pulling down the blinds and now savage sunlight was glaring in at them.

'Please,' she whimpered. 'Do the blind.'

With one eye open, he stumbled to the window and merciful dimness calmed the room.

'Thanks,' she whispered. 'What time is it?'

'Four seventeen.'

'In the morning?'

'Yeah. Have we paracetamol?'

'Some in my bag. Can I have some too?'

He scrambled through her handbag until he located the tablets and filled a glass from the bathroom tap.

'Bathroom water, mmm.' Her eyes stayed closed as he held the glass to her lips.

I'm a hollow man. A fake. Full to the brim of nothing.

'Christ.' She groaned. 'We've to climb Croagh Patrick in the morning. Today. It's arranged. I've the stuff in for the sandwiches.'

'No.'

'We'll go to sleep for coupla hours. Wake up again, be grand.'

I want to go back to sleep and never wake up.

She gave him a little shake. ''Kay?'

'No.'

That shocked her into opening her eyes. If she mocked him now, there was a real fear that he would actually cry.

She looked into his face. 'What is it, sweetie?'

You only married me because your other husband, a much better man, died. My job consists of being a borderline conman. I'm forty-eight, I still want my dad's approval and he'll never give it.

I try to be a father to Ferdia, but I'm just like my dad. Ferdia hates me and the girls think I'm a joke.

'I'm a hollow man.'

Her eyes flared with alarm. 'That's only the hangover talking. And seeing your ma and pa. You know that.'

She was wrong. 'I'm pointless.'

'No, babes, no . . . that's . . . Look. It's just a hangover. But there's no need to come on the climb. Stay in bed. Sleep.'

I'm a very weak man, with too many failings.

'Jessie, do you love me?'

'Of course I love you, you giant eejit!'

He turned on his side, letting tears leak into his pillow and she spooned herself against his back, holding him so tightly that he eventually felt safe enough to tumble down into sleep.

Whispers and hushed voices and tiptoed footsteps, tapping lightly up and down the hall.

'Daddy. Daddy.' It was Dilly, breathing her sweet breath over him. 'I brought you some flat Coke.'

'Are you really sick?' TJ was behind her. 'Or just hungover?'

'I'm sick,' he croaked.

'Told you,' Dilly hissed at TJ.

'What time is it?'

'Nine o'clock. So, Dad, we're staying here with you today. We've decided that instead of Making Memories, we'll mind you. Bridey and Saoirse are going to Make Memories, if that's okay, so Mum has company. Now sit up and drink your flat Coke.'

'We brought you a straw, even though it's a single-use plastic,' TJ said. 'All they had in the house. It can be your guilty pleasure.'

'Go on the climb,' he said. 'I'll be grand.'

'We want to stay with you. We'll check on you every half-hour. But if you need us, then summon us. We couldn't find a bell—'

'And even if we could have, we thought you had a hangover so a bell would be bad—'

'But you can hit this glass with this fork.' Dilly demonstrated and the glass vibrated and hummed. 'And we'll come.'

'We could read to you,' TJ offered.

'. . . *Dad* . . . what's wrong with your eyes?'

'Hayfever,' he managed.

'Quick,' Dilly instructed TJ. 'Get a tablet from Mum.'

TJ hurried off and Dilly placed her cool, small hand on his forehead. She sucked in her breath and said, 'You're burning up.'

'Am I?'

'*Noooo*. But that's what people say when you're sick.'

Forty-Eight

In the house next door, Ed awoke alone in bed.

'Cara,' he called weakly. 'Cara.'

The house hummed with emptiness.

Slowly turning on his side, his phone said it was 9.07 a.m. Maybe they'd already gone up the mountain.

Would they have done that? Left him all alone?

He felt unusually low. Last night had been one of those rare ones where too much emotion and too much alcohol had turned everything shadowy and toxic. That mood still lingered, this morning.

He needed liquid, but the kitchen was miles away. On the Casey Family WhatsApp, he stabbed out **Bring me pint weak milky tea. 4 sugars. Begging here.**

Minutes elapsed and no one showed.

Berocca: would that cure him? Usually he spurned tablets, but this was an emergency. If he could just get to the bathroom, to Cara's washbag. She always had tablets, a pill for every ill. On rubbery legs, he crouched on the floor, hunting through her toiletries. What had he here? Dioralyte, that would do. And some Nurofen, that was also good. And . . . What was this? A flattened, crumpled piece of waxy cardboard.

Slowly he unfolded it. It was an empty ice-cream carton, a big one.

He went hot and cold. Underneath the carton—Cherry Garcia flavour—was the torn wrapper from a packet of Lindt biscuits.

Fuck. There was no more avoiding this.

Everyone seemed to think that he noticed nothing. With his optimism and gratitude for the small stuff, he was—affectionately—painted as a bit of a joke.

But Ed noticed plenty.

It was in Kerry at Easter that he'd first sensed something was wrong with Cara. On the Sunday night, when the two of them were settling down to sleep, he caught a faint whiff of something sour, a throwback to when the kids were babies. The smell of sick. The logical thing was to ask her, but instinct told him to say nothing. Not yet. From then on, he had been alert.

Immediately it was obvious that she was hiding something. From the very first night they'd met, she'd either been abstaining from sugar or fighting a drawn-out battle. This binary state had become a fixed part of their lives. But lately neither had been happening. No more cheery statements, like, 'Fifteen days without chocolate! Am I skinny yet?' Nor were there any sheepish orders for him to produce whatever emergency chocolate he had stashed about the house, her saying, with desperate hope, 'Look, the weekend is ruined. I might as well eat what I want and get back on the horse on Monday.'

Then came the morning, maybe four weeks ago, when he'd been hunting in the bathroom for a fresh razor, unwilling to believe he'd actually run out. He'd opened the door of a high-up, rarely used cupboard and found himself face to face with a collection of about twenty bars of chocolate. The incongruity of those shiny, colourful wrappers, lurking in the dark space, made him feel as if his world was falling away.

Shortly after that, he'd once again caught a faint whiff of sick from her.

A long time ago, she'd told him about her eighteen months in Manchester, when she used to binge-eat, then make herself vomit. Seized by a tender sorrow for that lost girl, he'd elicited a promise that if she ever felt drawn back to it, she would tell him. But, as far as he knew, it had been consigned to her past.

Until now.

He was a scientist: he dealt in facts. The simplest explanation was the one most likely to be true: Cara was overeating, then making herself sick. Bulimia. He might as well call it by its correct title. She *was* bulimic? She *had* bulimia? Either way, he'd hoped it would go of its own accord, because he didn't know what to do.

He'd come to accept that a thread of darkness ran through Cara, like an underground stream. Once upon a time he'd thought that their love might lift her permanently into the light. But although she frequently seemed content, there were times when she withdrew emotionally, leaving him going through the motions alone, waiting for her return. This was one of them.

In the last few weeks, he'd spent a lot of time online. Cara was right about one thing: overeating was an addiction. So, apparently, was bulimia. A study said that sufferers had similar dopamine abnormalities in their brain to people suffering from cocaine or alcohol addiction. But, as far as Ed could see, food was nothing like as dangerous as alcohol or drugs. Drugs and drink could kill, but food only became an issue at the extremes, if a person was morbidly obese or dangerously thin. Cara was neither.

He'd held out hope that she'd snap out of this as suddenly as she'd started.

But yesterday when he'd come back from fetching Ferdia and his mates, he'd found her in the kitchen hurriedly, furtively, crunching something in her mouth. Her cheeks bulged and her eyes were frantic. She didn't explain what was happening—and he hadn't asked.

Why not?

Because he hadn't wanted to shame her. If she wasn't ready to tell him, was it right to blow her cover? He sensed it would be a bad idea to force it, a little like waking a sleep-walker.

However, finding these wrappers—stashed in a place where she thought he wouldn't look—meant something needed to be done. He was worried for her health, he was worried about what her trouble with food might be doing to Vinnie and Tom, but it was more than that. He and Cara were best friends. Even when she disappeared into herself, he was prepared to wait it out. She knew he would—it gave her solace, she'd once told him.

But by doing whatever she was doing now, she'd removed a part of herself entirely from his reach.

The Berocca forgotten, he climbed back into bed.

Forty-Nine

When Johnny woke again, he felt less apocalyptic. News reached him that the climbers hadn't set off yet. According to TJ, Ed was 'in a bad way': 'Auntie Cara said she'd never seen him so drunk as he was last night. We've all been swimming while you and Uncle Ed were sleeping. But Uncle Ed's getting up now.'

'You know what, bunnies? I'm coming on the climb.'

'No!' Dilly yelped. 'You'll have a relapse if you get up too soon! I'm getting Mum.' She pointed at TJ. 'Don't let him out of that bed!'

But as soon as she'd scampered away, TJ nodded towards the shower. 'Go for it.'

Jessie was waiting when he emerged from the bathroom. 'You sure about this, babes?' She was more solicitous of him than he ever remembered her being.

'The shower helped. Maybe the exercise and the oxygen will too. You only regret the things you don't do. Right?'

She paused. 'I'm a nightmare. How do you put up with me?'

Surprisingly, considering how drunk so many of them had been the previous night, there was a big turnout for the climb. Apart from Nell, who had some deadline, everyone was there—even Ferdia and his cohort.

Perhaps it was the weather. The sky was a perfect blue and the heat of the sun was cut by a balmy breeze.

Assembling in the car park at the foot of the mountain, Johnny had to bend over, his hands on his knees, waiting for the dizziness to pass.

'State of you!' Ferdia mocked. 'D'you need a sick-bag?'

'Call yourself young.' Johnny strove for a cheery voice. 'In my day, we wouldn't have been up until six in the evening.'

'We're making memories.' Sammie was already taking photos.

Christ, not another one. Living's such hard work, these days. Every moment has to be Instagram worthy.

Ed was slowly emerging from the passenger seat of his car; he and Johnny locked eyes and laughed. Lurching across the gravel, they half fell into each other's arms.

'You're so white you're luminous.'

'That's an improvement. I was as green as a mint Aero earlier, according to Vinnie. Should we be doing this?'

'Kill or cure.'

'Right. Up we go.'

Johnny fell into step with Dilly because she was the slowest. He could pretend that he was hanging back to make sure she was safe. TJ walked alongside them. Then a stray-seeming dog came and kept them company. It was a lovely dog, part spaniel, part . . . lurcher, maybe. Friendly, bright-eyed, keen to play.

To his alarm, Johnny felt, once again, tearful. The uncomplicated love of an animal was a beautiful thing. If only he was at home in Dublin with Camilla and Bubs . . .

As if she'd read his mind, TJ said, 'I wish Camilla and Bubs were here.'

'Me too.'

'Will they be okay with McGurk?'

Johnny had his doubts. He had a vision of McGurk with his clipboard, punishing the dogs for some tiny infraction. 'Course!' He was all reassurance. 'McGurk is very reliable.'

'McGurk's a weirdo,' TJ said. 'He doesn't like animals.'

'He doesn't like people either, but he likes being reliable. The dogs will be grand with him.'

'I think I prefer animals to people,' TJ said.

'I think I do too.'

'When I grow up, I might be a farmer. Or a vet.'

'Or a zoo-keeper.' Johnny suddenly realized that that was his unfulfilled life ambition.

'Dad, no! Zoos are bad! It's cruel to keep wild beasts locked up!'

'Unethical!' Bridey cried, from further up the climb, her sharp admonishment floating back on the warm air.

A wave of bleakness broke over Johnny's head. Once again he felt as bare and broken as when he'd woken up. There was nothing good in the world. He wanted to be a zookeeper and for it to be ethical but it was too late.

By some miracle, they all made it to the top. The view from the peak was jaw-dropping. The sky above blazed a vivid azure while, far below them, the numerous islands scattered across Clew Bay popped brilliant green.

The mood was celebratory and Jessie began organizing the picnic. 'Saoirse, Bridey, get out the rosé!'

Sammie was clicking away on her phone, taking selfies with Ferdia. 'It's so beautiful up here', Johnny heard her say. 'Thanks for this, Ferd.' She touched his face tenderly. They stood staring into each other's eyes, for a long moment. She was the one to move away.

Johnny hoped Ferdia didn't fall to bits when she was gone. He was enough fecking trouble already. But he was young, and young men didn't fall to bits. *He*'d never fallen to bits at Ferdia's age. He didn't know *what* it was to have his heart broken. No one had ever come close. Well, not until Rory had taken Jessie. Then he'd known all about it.

'Nell,' a gentle voice whispered. 'Nell.'

A small hand touched her aching back and Nell woke up.

She'd been asleep on the floor of the bedroom.

'You were sleeping,' Dilly said helpfully. 'You must of needed it.'

She must have. She'd woken at around two in the morning, cold with fear that she'd overstretched herself and her talent.

Liam was asleep beside her but she'd prefer to talk to Garr. She went out to the deck to ring him—and stumbled over spoilt-brat Ferdia.

She hadn't gone back to sleep again until early afternoon, when she'd lain down beside her little set and fallen into a dream-free blankness.

'How was your day?' Dilly asked.

Shite, but she couldn't tell that to an eight-year-old. It had become clear that she wasn't an experienced enough designer to pull this off. The gig was already lost.

Even talking to Garr hadn't helped: he'd counselled that it was too late to junk her work and start again. 'On Sunday evening, I'll do an all-nighter with you,' he'd promised. 'You might still pull this off. Keep the faith.'

'Would you like a glass of wine?' Dilly asked.

'Oh. Ah. No, I'll have a coffee.'

'But it's five o'clock, you're allowed.'

'Coffee is grand.' Nell got to her feet and together they wandered into the kitchen.

'I missed you today,' Dilly said.

'Missed you too.'

'But you had to work. Want to blow some bubbles?'

'Sure.'

They sat on the deck, Nell sipping coffee, her eyes and muscles savouring the rest.

Dilly blew bubbles with little success. 'It's too windy. Here, you have a go.'

Nell blew a long, graceful ribbon of bubbles out into the salty air. They bobbed here and there, little iridescent balls, before popping in the sky above them.

'That's *amazing*. Do it again!'

It really was so relaxing, Nell thought, just sitting there, watching the waves, sipping coffee, having her aching back rubbed by Dilly. 'How was *your* day?' she asked.

'Glorious.'

'Glorious?' She was funny.

'Glorious. Except Daddy had too much pink wine and then he was crying because he couldn't be a zookeeper. It was sad.'

A clatter of footsteps heralded the arrival of TJ and Bridey.

'You sneaked off!' TJ accused Dilly. 'We were *all* coming to see Nell!'

'Oh dear,' Dilly said solemnly. 'It must of slipped my mind.'

'Are you going to this party tonight?' TJ asked Nell.

'Yep.'

'We're getting a babysitter,' Bridey said. 'From the town. A raw-boned chit of a girl, her whey-white skin sprinkled with cinnamon freckles.'

'She's so embarrassing,' TJ said. 'The crap she talks. Nell, why can't you be our babysitter?'

There was a commotion behind them as Jessie appeared. She looked a little wild-eyed. 'Bunnies, hop it. I need to speak to Nell.'

'Is she in trouble?' Dilly gasped.

'Please, just go. Back to the house.'

Frightened by Jessie's evident agitation, they scarpered.

'What did you say to Ferdia?' Jessie asked Nell.

Cold dread slid through her.

'About me, Johnny and Rory.'

'Jessie, I didn't mean to interfere—'

'Stop. No. Listen. He came and found me. Just now.' She looked manic. 'Said he was sorry. He was only a kid when Johnny and I . . . Down in Errislannan, he'd hear Izzy and Keeva hinting at stuff. He was too young to understand that they were hurt and just saying things.'

So she hadn't messed up horribly?

'He's been angry with me for years.' Jessie couldn't stop talking. 'It's been hard to live with. I was able to tell him how much I loved Rory. He said he knows that now. I couldn't have imagined . . . Just, thank you, thank you. I'm very . . . you know . . . You're great. We love you. Everyone loves you. Thanks. Right. See you at the dinner from Hell.'

Fifty

'Nervous fecking *wreck*.' Jessie hurtled across the restaurant to Cara. 'That's me. If there's one single thing wrong with the food tonight, I'll get the blame.'

Poor Jessie, Cara thought. Tonight would be grim for them all, but extra so for Jessie: Canice and Rose had commandeered the posh restaurant outside town for their special evening, then demanded Jessie bag them Ireland's most in-demand TV chef to cook for them.

'Something's bound to go wrong,' Jessie said. 'And I'll be keel-hauled. Whatever the hell that is.' She plucked two glasses of champagne from a passing tray. 'Drink up. If we survive this, I'll buy us all new livers. There's Nell, grab her.'

Nell was wearing the sexy, aubergine-coloured body-con dress she'd brought to Kerry, but not worn, a couple of months back.

'You look uh-*maaaay*-zing. And heels! Look at you in heels!'

'I can't walk in them.' Nell laughed. 'Liam says I look like a builder.'

'Don't mind him,' Jessie said. 'Oh, sweet Christ, Rose is in da house. Cluster close to me, daughters-in-law of doom.'

Cara slid a glance across the room. Rose was glammed up in a purple taffeta gown, not that Rose would ever describe the shade with as banal a word as 'purple'. It might be 'mauve' or 'amethyst' or 'grape'—her type seemed to have an entire lexicon to convey the exact hue of their clothing.

'Monique's has pulled out all the stops.' Jessie's face was set in a giant fake smile.

'Enough internal scaffolding in that dress,' Cara said, 'to construct an office block.'

'Smile. She's probably watching.'

Cara took another look and felt physical shock from Rose's piercing stare. 'She *is*. She knows we're talking about her.'

'Smile,' Jessie ordered Nell. 'Whenever you're talking about her, smile like a loon. Like me, look.' She lunged at Nell with a mouthful of flashing-white teeth and Cara fell about laughing. 'Sorry. Mildly hysterical here.'

Oh, thank you, God. Here come the canapés.

She took four, even though decorum decreed she should choose only one. Or, even better, none. But the food would calm her.

'You're fairly new to this game,' Jessie told Nell. 'But the only way to survive Rose is strength in numbers. You must remember it's not personal.'

'It *is* personal,' Cara was compelled to say.

'*Is* it, though?' Jessie said. 'Because she's a bitch to all of us?'

'She's an equal-opportunities bitch.'

'If a mother-in-law bitches in a forest,' Jessie mused, 'but there's no one there to hear her cackle . . . Ah, no, this analogy is going nowhere. Where's that lad with the champagne? But let me tell you, Nell, not all mothers-in-law are like Rose. I had another, one of the nicest women I've ever met—'

'Who are you talking about?' Johnny approached. 'My mother?'

Jessie turned to him. 'Yeah, right!'

Then all of them laughed far too hard.

It was a long night and she ate everything: too many canapés, too much bread, the *amuse-bouche*, the extra potato gratin, her own dessert and now Ed's too. He hadn't wanted it and she couldn't stop herself.

Canice was standing up to make his speech.

'This'll be good,' Cara heard someone say. 'He's funny. A real comedian.'

Canice beamed around the restaurant. 'Look at them all, the great and the good of Beltibbet. Enjoying your dinner, are you? Because if you're not, take it up with Jessie over there. She's the one to blame.'

Cara threw Jessie a sympathetic look.

'I've lived in this town and worked for the people of this town, all my life . . .'

Cara zoned out a bit as Canice made bitchy stabs at various poor bastards who had the misfortune to live in the same place as him, then zoned back in when Canice started talking about his family.

'. . . As you know, I've three sons. Johnny, bit of a fly boy, wants life to be one long party. But, all credit to him, married into money. So what if the wife is a bit of a sergeant major? Can't he muffle the noise by stuffing his ears with fivers!'

He paused to let everyone laugh.

'Shur I'm only joking, Jessie!' He twinkled at them. 'Now Ed. Ed and his beloved trees. Married to the lovely Cara. There she is, eating cake. Don't worry, Cara, plenty more where that came from.'

Another pause to let laughter fill the room.

Cara burnt. She hadn't even been eating, but that cruel old bastard knew exactly how to wound. In addition, she didn't want Ed on alert as to how bad things were with the food. Although only yesterday he'd interrupted her when she was desperately trying to swallow the remains of a packet of biscuits and he hadn't noticed a thing. She was lucky that he was a man with no real interest in day-to-day detail.

Canice had moved on to Liam. 'Liam thought he'd be the next Usain Bolt. Run a race? Shur, that eejit couldn't run a bath! And would he listen when I warned him he'd need a profession to fall back on? Indeed'n he did not! Do you know what he does with his time now? He *cycles.* Where was it you cycled that time, Liam? Istanbul, that's right. Took him thirty-one days.' He paused for a breath. 'You can fly there in four hours.' Howls of laughter erupted. Canice beamed benignly around the room. 'Ah, I'm only having a bit of craic. But seriously, folks.' He reached for his wife's hand. 'Rose, what would I have done without you? Fifty years married. I've been a lucky, lucky man. Ladies and gentlemen, please fill your glasses for Rose Casey!'

People were dabbing tears from their eyes as they stood up. 'To Rose Casey.'

Fifty-One

Nell was sketching at the kitchen table when the knocker began banging madly: the others were back from the dinner.

Laughing and talking loudly, Liam lurched into the hall, followed by Ferdia, Sammie and Barty.

'I didn't expect to see any of you until the sun came up.' Nell was worried by how drunk they seemed. She'd get feck-all done now.

'We got kicked out at midnight.' Ferdia followed her into the kitchen. 'They closed the bar. Can you believe it?'

A bottle of red wine had already appeared on the table and Barty was pouring.

'How're you getting on?' Liam asked. He went in for the snog, but he was so drunk that she slid away easily.

'Grand.' She started gathering up her pencils and sketches.

'Nell?' Barty asked. 'Glass?'

'No, thanks.'

Ferdia, Sammie, Barty and Liam settled themselves around the table and were already drinking enthusiastically.

'Have a glass of wine,' Liam said to Nell.

'I'm good.'

'Ah, go on, you're no craic.' Liam had picked up Dilly's tube of bubbles. He blew out a stream of them. They rose upwards and popped at the ceiling. 'Have a drink.'

'Not tonight.'

'You're no fun.'

'Nope. Night all, see you in the—'

'Is anyone having another drink?' Liam locked eyes with Sammie, sitting beside him.

'Sure.' She shrugged.

'Good girl.'

His tone was a worry, Nell thought. He sounded a bit creepy . . .

Liam picked up the tube of bubbles again. 'Good girl,' he repeated, in that same crooning voice, then gently blew a steady stream of pretty little bubbles into Sammie's pretty little face.

Frozen to the spot, Nell stared, as the bubbles burst like rainbow-shot exclamation marks against Sammie's eyelashes.

Barty gave a strangled laugh, then abruptly shut up. A shocked silence seized the room.

Sammie swallowed, went pink, then became steadily more and more red.

Liam, grinning, was balanced on the two back legs of his chair.

Shock had wiped Nell blank. What Liam had just done was so . . . *wrong* that she didn't have any response available. Then her hand reached out and whacked the back of his chair so that all four legs clattered down against the floor. Such *rage* was in her.

'What the fuck was that?' Ferdia bit the words out.

'Say what?' Liam tipped his chair back again, looking the picture of innocence.

'Blowing bubbles at my girlfriend?'

'They're *bubbles*!'

'That was a fucking come-on.' Ferdia got up and stood behind Sammie's chair. 'It's—it's *predatory*, what you just did to Sammie. *And* you've insulted your wife.'

'It's just bubbles.' Liam was insistent.

He was nothing like as calm as he was pretending to be: Nell knew him too well.

Liam laughed at Ferdia. 'Look at you, the big man protecting his girl.'

'You're a fucking asshole.'

'No, *you*'re a fucking asshole. Getting all up in my grille about a few fucking bubbles. Calm the fuck down, would you?'

Liam was very, very angry, Nell realized. Had been ever since she'd told him about the call from Ship of Fools. She wanted to leave this room, leave this house, park this fucked-up shit with her husband until some faraway time in a very different future. But Sammie was only a kid.

'Sammie?' She touched her gently. 'Hon, come with me.'

Obediently, Sammie got up and followed her into the hallway.

'Are you okay?'

'Yeah. Like, I'm sorry, Nell, I didn't encoura–'

'Stop. You did nothing wrong.'

The kitchen door opened and Nell tensed. If Liam came out—But, no, it was Ferdia. He made for Sammie, touched her arm and, fluidly, pulled her against him. 'You okay?' he whispered to her. He turned to Nell. 'Are *you* okay?'

Probably not, but this wasn't about her. 'Good. You?'

'Yeah.' He cradled the back of Sammie's head as she pressed her face against his chest. They were young and beautiful and clearly loved each other. Watching them, Nell felt bereft.

Fifty-Two

'I love dogs,' Johnny slurred, slightly. 'Dogs are just pure . . . goodness. I'm serious, Jessie, I'm going to be a dog-minder.'

'Okay, Johnny, but now go to sleep.' She was sitting up in bed beside him, trying to read tomorrow's papers on her iPad.

'You think I'm drunk. I'm not drunk,' he stated bleakly.

Maybe he wasn't. Neither was she, despite all the drinking they'd done at that terrible dinner.

'I'll be fifty next year. Fifty years old.' He was lying flat on his back, addressing his remarks to the bedroom ceiling. 'And I've done nothing of worth.'

'That's crap.' She didn't look up from her screen. 'What about our girls?'

'They think I'm a joke. And they're right. There's nothing to me, Jessie. Surface all the way down, that's me. Surface all the way down. No wisdom, no substance, that's why I wanted *you*, Jessie. You were so *sure* of everything, but I can't keep mooching off you. I've got to find my own worth.'

'Babes, stop. It's just being around your parents—'

'Rory, he was another one. He had *worth* as a person, like. Me and him were a great team. I had the—the *charm*,' he almost spat the word, 'but Rory was the substance.'

'Johnny, you'll feel differently in the morning.'

'I've felt like this for a while now. I'm hollow. There's nothing to me. Jessie, do you love me?'

'Of *course* I love you. Sweetie, what is it?'

'Are we real? Or are we just colleagues who got married? To halve the hotel costs when we're travelling for work?'

'Johnny!' This was so unlike him that she struggled for the right words. 'Has something happened? To upset you?'

'Ah, no, don't mind me. I'll go to sleep now. Turn off the light.'

'It's off.'

'But it's bright. Is it the sun? Even the sun is laughing at me.'

Within seconds he was snoring heavily.

She carried on reading, now and again giving him curious, anxious looks. Poor Johnny. Having Canice Casey as a father would dent the most robust of personalities. Was it any wonder that Johnny had become so attached to Rory's dad, Michael Kinsella? He'd been such a lovely man: calm, wise, kind . . .

Well, until Johnny and Jessie had fallen for each other and all of that calm, wise kindness had been turned off like a tap.

Sometimes she wondered if Johnny still missed him. On weekends like this, she was sure that he did. But Johnny had been presented with a choice: Jessie or the Kinsellas. He'd picked Jessie. Occasionally Jessie marvelled that they'd ended up together at all. After Rory's death, she had seen Johnny non-stop, but she'd never considered him as a man: she'd been allotted one love and he'd died. Her work was what had kept her going.

At the time the pressure to keep expanding was relentless. Her big focus was Limerick but premises there were few and far between. Naturally enough, the day a suitable site came free, she'd been up several times in the night with Saoirse. She didn't trust herself to drive.

'Wait until tomorrow,' Rionna had advised.

But it was Spring 2007, boom time, and premises went *fast.*

Johnny, as he often did, offered to drive her.

It was early evening when they arrived in Limerick. The site looked good. The next step was for the architect to take a look. But Clellia couldn't come until the next day.

'Johnny?' Jessie asked. 'I don't know if I could handle a seven-hour round trip home and back for tomorrow morning. If I can get the nanny to stay over with the kids, could you stay the night?'

They'd gone for a sandwich, Jessie peppering Johnny with questions. 'You don't think the economy is top-heavy?' And 'You don't think I'm opening shops too quickly?' And 'You don't think people have stopped cooking?'

When they went to the hotel—one of a chain, clean and cheap—Johnny saw her into her room to check that no one was under the bed or in the bathroom.

'I'm pitiful, I know,' she said, as she always did.

'You're not.' He looked into the bathroom. 'All clear. Night. See you for breakfast.'

'Night.' As he shut the door behind him, she called out, 'Johnny?'

He reappeared.

'You don't think the site is too big?'

Wearily he shook his head, and she remembered that he was only her employee, a person with no vested interest. She was asking too much of him. 'Sorry. I'm treating you the way I treated Rory.'

'Not quite.'

'What—Oh. Right.' Her skin felt hot. 'Ah, stop. You were only interested when I belonged to your friend. Now I'm available you wouldn't want me.'

After a silence, he said, 'I do want you.'

I do want you.

Hold on. Hold. *On.*

'Oh, fuck.' He'd rubbed his eyes. 'I shouldn't have said—'

'But you should, you should, Johnny. And it's said now.' Sudden sensations were flowing through her—she visualized them later as snakes of electricity, as if a giant lever had been flipped over and she had been shocked back into life.

'Listen.' She clambered off the bed. 'Wait, will you?' She didn't know what she was thinking. She *wasn't* thinking, that was it. She was motivated by instinct, emotion, anything but thoughts. 'Stay the night.' She'd reached him. 'Here. With me.'

'Aaaah . . . *no.*'

She gave the door a gentle push, cocking her head to listen, as it softly clicked shut. Then she placed her hand on his jaw, rasping her thumb along his stubble. He was *such* a ride.

His face was a mix of desire and confusion. 'Jesus, Jessie, I don't know . . .'

'We're still alive,' she said.

'People will judge us.'

Feck that. She'd always played by the rules and Rory had died. Anything could be taken from you in the blink of an eye. 'Who'll judge?'

'Everyone.'

'Right now, I don't care.'

'Right now,' and he seemed like a broken man, 'neither do I.'

The surprise reveal of his body as she slowly undid his buttons, savouring every second, stroking her hands in wonder along his honed pecs, down his sides to his hip bones. Casting the cotton shirt back off his shoulders, she reached for his belt buckle and then his zip.

He'd stood like a shop dummy as if all of this was happening to another man, then abruptly reached for her, pulling her hard against him, his hands pressing on her back. The first touch of his tongue against hers felt so heady she thought she might faint. His lips butterflied along her skin, moving from her mouth to her neck, as shivers shook her body. Down her back, a rope of energy uncoiled as his hands opened her dress, helping her to step out of it.

This was the first time in more than two years that her skin had had any sensation, instead of feeling coated in a thick, rubbery lagging jacket.

Lying on the cool white sheet, his skin touching hers, thigh to thigh, stomach to stomach, calves intertwined, felt almost unbearably pleasurable. It was everything she'd never let herself think about—slow, tender, intense. Then passionate, vigorous, loud.

There was so much that was unexpected: his dedicated patience as he took her in his mouth, and stayed, until she burst into incredible sensation; the revelation of his upper-body strength. 'How did I not *know* that you've these guns?' she demanded, in happy outrage.

She wouldn't compare. She'd loved Rory. She still did. She'd fancied Rory. She'd been really happy with him.

Johnny was different. That was all she could admit.

And maybe more adventurous in bed. She'd let herself admit that too.

Definitely more adventurous.

But that was all she let herself think about as she finally drifted into sleep.

As the early-morning light stole into the bedroom, she woke to find him watching her. 'He*lllooo*.' She stretched like a happy cat and slid herself up against him.

He looked woebegone.

In a cartoony sympathetic voice, she asked, 'Johnny not happy?'

'You're my best friend's widow. I've a duty to mind you.'

'We're not in a Victorian novel, Johnny. I can mind myself. But think about it, we could have so much . . .' What? Fun? Pleasure? Sex! That was the word. 'Johnny, you and me, we could have so much sex, so much lovely sex.'

'This doesn't feel right, Jessie. It's not noble.'

'We could have lots of non-noble sex?' she said gaily.

'No.'

'Okay.'

'We keep things strictly professional.'

'Okay.'

'I'm going to my room now. See you for breakfast.'

In a haze of bliss, she watched him leave. Things would never be professional again. She knew it. He knew it.

He just needed to make his peace with it.

She hadn't planned to get pregnant.

She hadn't planned not to get pregnant either.

She'd behaved as if there were no consequences to what they were doing. Almost as if it wasn't really happening.

Looking back, she found it hard to believe she'd been so . . . *stupid*? Irresponsible? But those descriptions weren't accurate.

Dishonest: that was the word. She'd been lying to herself: she wasn't sleeping with Johnny so why would she be on the pill?

Clearly he wasn't sleeping with her either, so there was no need for condoms.

They were both adamant that their thing was temporary and top-secret. She was deluded enough to believe that no one knew.

But they knew in the office, they knew in the shops, they knew at the industry conferences. Not one person dared ask about it, but everybody knew.

Jessie's periods stopped and she felt nauseous most days. She thought nothing of it until the night Johnny eyed her suddenly enormous breasts and asked haltingly, 'Jessie . . . could you be, you know—pregnant?'

She considered it calmly. 'I think, mmm. Yes. I could b— Yep, I am. I think.'

Eleven weeks, the scan showed.

'You really didn't know?' the nurse asked. 'But you've missed three periods.'

For the first time in a long time, Jessie burst into a bout of noisy crying. 'I don't understand. I'm a sensible person. I'm really copped-on.'

The nurse flicked a suspicious look at Johnny, then asked, 'Is there some situation here?'

Jessie blurted, 'My husband died two and a half years ago. Him there, Johnny, the father, was his best friend. I'm sleeping with him.'

'Right. Well, that's—'

'Have you seen this ever happen before?' Jessie asked. 'Someone being pregnant and not telling themselves.'

'I've seen women who didn't know they were pregnant until they went into labour. The human mind is capable of a lot.'

'But me, this sort of behaviour, where I've checked out of reality, it's . . . new to me.'

After the appointment, she said to Johnny, 'I'm going to see the Kinsellas. To tell them I'm pregnant.'

They were always going to find it hard if Jessie met another man—*any* other man.

'And about me? I want to stop all this sneaking around. I love you.'

'They'll be very upset.'

'I said I love you.'

'I love you too.' She was distracted. 'Okay, we'll go to see them together.'

Because they'd been worried that their chemistry might be obvious, they'd taken to visiting the Kinsellas separately in the months since their fling had started.

'We're having this baby. We need to be brave.'

It had been terrible, worse than either of them had anticipated.

'I didn't think I'd feel so ashamed,' she said to Johnny, on the way home.

'I know. And sad.'

'Maybe it'll be okay in a few months.'

'Maybe.'

But the upshot was that she was now officially with Johnny. Sleep-walking her way into a pregnancy had forced the situation. What was also official was that they and the Kinsellas were estranged. And that was hard.

Back in the present, she looked at Johnny lying beside her. Even in sleep, he appeared anxious.

Maybe they needed some together time. But the mad thing was, they were together for almost every second of every day. How much more togetherness did they need?

She and Johnny were doing all their stuff side by side—the work and the kids and the social life. But were they on parallel paths, never connecting?

Fear corkscrewed in her stomach. These thoughts were scary.

But, look, she told herself, if that's the case, *do* something. Fix it. Organize some alone time, some one-on-one. Be nice to him, ask questions, try to prise him open and find out what's up.

As she returned to her iPad, she still felt unsettled. Something caught her eye on the news page and her heart plummeted: 'Hagen Klein Goes Into Rehab'.

What the hell? Hagen Klein was lined up to do their next cookery school in three weeks' time! And, according to this paper, he'd gone into rehab for amphetamine abuse.

No, no, no! Like, poor Hagen Klein and all, but poor Jessie too!

If he didn't come—and how could he, if he was in rehab in Norway?—their quarterly take would plummet.

Her immediate impulse was to ring Mason, because he knew the answer to everything. But, no! He'd take this as proof that Jessie's way of running PiG was completely wrong. Shifting PiG's current set-up to a company that operated almost entirely online was a natural evolution, according to Mason. He was confident that public goodwill for the shops would translate into online sales.

As far as Jessie was concerned, the two ideas were entirely different. Because what no one knew about Jessie—except Jessie herself—was that she wasn't an entrepreneur. Entrepreneurs were people who noticed gaps in a market: they could suss out weakness, had nerves of steel and negotiated like demons.

Jessie had a reputation as a resourceful business person, but all she was was someone who'd turned her hobby into a living.

In her innermost heart, Jessie suspected that her *only* talent now lay in bagging chefs. If they turned PiG into an online grocery, she would be literally redundant.

Fifty-Three

'Nell? What are you doing out here?'

Blearily, she opened her eyes. Ferdia was staring down at her. A beautiful pink-gold light filled the sky. The sun must be nearly up.

'Sleeping,' she mumbled. 'Trying to.'

'But—Ah, for feck's sake, you let Liam have the room?'

'I was hardly going to share a bed with him.' She'd taken a pillow and a throw and slept outside on one of the loungers. It was surprisingly comfortable.

'You could have had Barty's room!'

'I'm good. Is Sammie okay?'

'Or you could have slept in with her.'

Just go away, Ferdia, I need to sleep.

Later, she was awakened again, this time by Liam. 'Nell? Baby, I'm sorry. Please talk to me.'

Angrily, she sat up. 'What the *hell*, Liam?'

'I just felt . . . left behind. What if you get really successful and you don't want me any more? What if I'm too old and boring and you're really in love with Garr?'

'*Garr?* Cop on! Garr is my best friend! And you know what my work means to me. I thought you'd be happy for me—'

'I'm jealous of your passion. And it was a weird night, Dad being such a spiteful old bastard . . . And there's something else . . . Violet and Lenore aren't coming to Italy. Paige says she can't move the dates of their camp.'

'When did you find out?'

'. . . Like, ten days ago? I'm sorry for not telling you. I was just gutted. All of it together, it made me be a dick. Forgive me, Nell?'

'It's sad about your girls. But, Liam, what you did last night was very wrong. To me and to Sammie.'

'Tell me what to do and I'll do it. Anything so you'll forgive me.'

'Apologize to Sammie. And Ferdia.'

'Ferdia's only a kid . . . I won't apologize to him.'

'He's a grown man. And what about Sammie? That was . . . You *scared* her, Liam.'

'. . . Did I? But . . .'

'If you don't make it right with the two of them . . .'

At that moment Ferdia and Sammie emerged from the house carrying their rucksacks, followed by Barty.

Ferdia asked, 'Nell, can you drive us to the station?'

'Not staying for the lunch?'

'No.'

'Aaah,' Liam intervened. 'Ferdia, Sammie, can I . . . Last night, I'm sorry. I've, you know, *stuff* going on. I was acting out. Involved you two, I shouldn't have. Apologies. Like, sincerely.'

Ferdia and Sammie, hands entangled, flat-eyed Liam.

'No hard feelings?' Liam sounded anxious.

It was Sammie who spoke. 'No hard feelings.' Her voice was free from emotion. 'No hard feelings, right, Ferdia? Right?'

'. . . Okay.'

'So we're good?'

'You also owe your wife an apology,' Ferdia said to Liam.

'That's none of your business.'

Nell could see things escalating again very quickly. 'He's apologized to me, Ferdia.'

'Okay.'

It was hardly a tearful reunion, but it would have to do. As for her own feelings? She didn't think she'd ever been as humiliated, not in any relationship.

Three Months Ago

JULY

Jessie's birthday

Fifty-Four

> Great stay in the heart of Dublin City. Cara was quick to respond to my questions and her associate was welcoming at check-in. The apartment was super-clean and looked freshly decorated. Beautiful, stylish, well equipped, more like a luxury hotel suite. Close to amenities, restaurants, bars and shops.

Johnny read it again, his chest aglow with pride. Five stars, they gave it, for cleanliness. Five stars for location. Five stars for everything! He'd swept the boards with his first Airbnb gig! Mind you, everyone had done a great job in preparing the flat for its new life. Nell's dad and brother had given it a fresh look, not just painting the flat but sanding floorboards, fixing wonky shelves, whatever needed doing.

As for the décor, once again Nell had been a superstar, advising on affordable furniture and doing that mysterious transformative business with cushions and throw blankets, which had always baffled Johnny. It was a guilty relief that, because of the Hagen Klein shitshow, Jessie had been too busy to get involved. Christ alone knew how much they'd have ended up spending.

The day-to-day running of the flat had been delegated to an ex-employee of the Ardglass called Hassan. Cara was responsible for the broad-brush stuff but, as far as Johnny knew, it didn't take too much of her time.

Fired up with delight about his review, he rang her. 'Did you see our first review? Five stars! They had great things to say about you and Hassan!'

'Oh, good.' She sounded distracted.

'And our bookings?' he enthused. 'We're nearly full for the next two months and people are already reserving into October and November.' Liam had been right: even with the occasional empty nights, the Airbnb income was much higher than when Marek and Natusia had been tenants. Admittedly, he hadn't increased their rent in seven years.

'And the income is going into—'

'Yep. New account.'

Cara seemed stressed. Immediately he felt guilty. She had a lot on her plate and he was hardly helping. He'd been the one who'd pushed for her to do their monthly accounts, in the hope that it might focus Jessie's mind on their spending. It had done feck-all to curb Jessie's excesses, but poor Cara was still soldiering away. Probably—and this was where his guilt really kicked in—because she felt she ought to, as payback for all the holidays Jessie insisted on paying for. 'You still okay to keep doing this?' he asked. 'It's grand if you want to stop.'

'It's fine,' she said. 'No bother. But I'd better go.'

'Course. Sorry.' He shouldn't have rung her at work. According to the latest etiquette, he shouldn't have rung her *at all.* Not without having checked in advance that it was okay. God's sake. Soon it would be illegal to say hello to someone without having first sent a telegram to see if now was 'a good time'. 'See you tomorrow night at Gulban Manor.'

He turned his attention to the final details of Jessie's birthday. Her *fiftieth*. He wasn't too far behind and, like, Jesus Christ and all, but how had that *happened*? Assuming they lived their full number of years, they were both over halfway through their lives. Even that wasn't guaranteed: what about Rory, snuffed out at the ridiculously young age of thirty-four?

Lately life, with its unpredictable, precious qualities, had been troubling Johnny. Too much of his time was spent looking either back at the past or anxiously at the future. He'd better stop: he'd be no good to anyone if he went a bit mental. Although, from the sound of things, you got no say in it—mid-life madness was entirely out of a person's control. You just had to roll with it.

Enough of that. So, Jessie's birthday. It wasn't until Tuesday, five days away, which was when themselves and the kids would have a takeaway and a cake with candles. Nice and simple. The heavier guns were being deployed for the weekend at Gulban Manor. A Wonder Woman cake had been ordered—all credit to the baker, she'd captured Jessie's 'take-no-prisoners' energy.

His gift to Jessie had plunged him into a bout of soul-searching. Obviously, it had to be meaningful, but jewellery had never been her thing: she said she had 'man's hands, goofy ears and no neck'. Bracelets were banned because they got on her nerves. ('All that jingling and jangling, I sound like a herd of Hari Krishnas.')

So, following Mary-Laine's directives, he'd bought a Fendi handbag. The one Jessie liked was adorned with furry baubles, which looked like an evil little face. He'd had to check with Mary-Laine that this wasn't a joke. And for all its furry, evil weirdness, the bag had proved spectacularly elusive. One had finally been run to ground in Abu Dhabi only three days ago and—shredding his nerves—had arrived in Ireland that morning.

He wasn't enjoying these feelings half as much as that lovely warm glow of pride, so he looked again at his Airbnb page. Already they were heavily booked—this weekend, all of next week and the following weekend. In fact, for the next three, four . . . *six* weekends! Many of the weekdays too. Oh, yes! As he scanned the calendar, his eye snagged on 6 August. There was something about that date . . . Ah, right. It was Michael Kinsella's birthday. Funny the things you forgot and the things you remembered. Because now he was remembering that long-ago night when he and Rory had borrowed Michael's lightweight Honda and headed for the bright lights of Celbridge. Driving home at 3 a.m., on dark, rural roads, the bike had spluttered to a halt. Rory had alleged that he could fix it, but that it was too dark to see. Johnny had called him a chancer. He still remembered the way they'd laughed, clear and echoey, in the still night air.

'There's a phone box about a mile away,' Rory had said. 'We'll wheel the bike, and ring Dad.'

'At three in the morning?' Johnny had never rung Canice for a lift. He never would. Not only would Canice refuse but he'd use it to mock Johnny for having a substandard bike. For coming running to Daddy. Whatever. But Rory had made the call, and about ten minutes later, misty headlights shone through the darkness. Michael pulled alongside them in a small pick-up truck. He was wearing his slippers and an anorak over his pyjamas.

When he got down from the truck, Johnny instinctively stepped back.

'Pair of eejits,' Michael said, in a gentle, chuckley way. He hoisted the bike into the back and the three of them climbed into the warm cabin. 'I hope you weren't drink-driving the bike,' Michael said, as he drove off.

Rory would never be that reckless. He was always so good, so law-abiding, that if anyone had deserved to live to be a hundred, it was him.

Fifty-Five

'Another?' Garr pointed at Nell's nearly empty glass.

'Can't. Got to go.'

'Where?' Triona asked. 'Your loaded sister-in-law flying you all to Fiji for the weekend?'

'Stop!' Nell scolded, even as everyone laughed. 'It's a thing. For asylum-seekers. A public meeting. Speeches and, I don't really know, fundraising, maybe.'

'Fair play,' Lorelei said. 'I wish I was as sound as you.'

'So no trip to Fiji?' Triona asked.

'Would a fancy villa in Tuscany in August do you?'

There was an odd little silence. 'Tuscany?' Lorelei wrinkled her nose. 'No offence, but won't it be just tons of old people boring on about wine?'

'*Noooo.*' Nell laughed. 'It'll be beautiful and sunny. Near to Florence. Me and Liam have tickets for the Uffizi and we might go to Rome another day and, like, *art*, dude!'

'You and Liam going to the Uffizi,' Wanda cooed. 'I want your life!'

'But she has to spend a week with her in-laws,' Triona said.

'Isn't it freaky that Nell has in-laws?'

'Seriously,' Nell said, 'they're cool.'

'But are they not a bit, like . . . old?'

Nell laughed. 'I'm *married* to an old man! I'm old by association.'

'Jesus *H*!' Wanda said. 'Liam Casey is so *not* old.'

Nell accidentally made eye-contact with Garr, then looked away quickly. She didn't want to talk about Liam and definitely not with Garr there. In many ways, she was closer to Garr than anyone else in the world. He'd never said one less-than-pleasant thing about Liam but she had a niggling suspicion that he wasn't crazy about him. Age difference? Divergent lifestyles? Maybe he just thought she'd got married too soon. Whatever the reason, she suspected that Garr wouldn't be one bit surprised that things had gone weird for Nell and Liam. She did *not* want to go there.

'Seriously,' she said. 'Gotta go.'

'Will you come out with us again soon?' Garr asked.

His voice was soft yet pointed, and she was mortified. 'Yeah, like, *course*. God, I'm sorry. I miss you. I miss you all. The whole thing with Liam, it was intense there for a while, but I'm back to normal now.' She wrapped each of them in a tight hug, spending longest on Garr because he was the one she loved the most. 'Sorry,' she mouthed into his face. 'I'll be a better friend.'

For a moment, she wished she could step back into her old life with them all, where everything had seemed more innocent and *much* more fun.

'There she goes! Worthy Nell!'

She got onto her bike and cycled fast, in the hope that she might leave her shitty feelings behind.

She'd had the loneliest, strangest month of her life.

Once again, she'd discovered what they meant by marriage being work.

After what Liam had done with Sammie, she felt horribly disenchanted. Liam had been feeling insecure, he was heartbroken about the girls not coming to Italy—was that enough to absolve him? She wasn't sure. 'I didn't get married so that you could mess around with another girl,' she'd told him. 'That's what boyfriends were for! And I swear to you that if you ever try a stunt like that again, I'm gone.'

They'd had a long, searching talk, in which he'd abased himself with remorse. Enough time had passed so that she had—mostly—forgiven him. It had changed her, though; she was far less starry-eyed.

Maybe that was how it should be.

But how would she know? She was too ashamed to tell anyone. Her mum would go crazy with worry; Garr would probably tell her to leave Liam. As for Wanda, every time she saw Nell and Liam, she yelled, 'Goals!' The only creature she could talk to was Molly Ringwald.

The bottom line was that she loved Liam less than she used to. Or maybe she'd never loved the real Liam.

None of this was the way that love was depicted in movies. In real life when your person disappoints you, you have to readjust yourself—and not them—so you can keep loving them.

Maybe—and this was another scary thought—Liam was having to do that too.

*

She moved through the busy function room. It was her first time at a public meeting about asylum-seekers, and it was nice to know she wasn't the only one who cared. She recognized a politician from one of the smaller parties, maybe the Social Democrats. And a woman who might be from the Refugee Council of Ireland. Where was Perla? Perhaps she hadn't arrived yet.

As she made her way to the top of the room, her attention was caught by a striking-looking man, half a head taller than everyone else—Was that . . . *Ferdia*?

Jessie must be here. Good on her.

Someone called her name. Barty, who was all smiles.

'Barty. Hey.' They shared an awkward hug.

She and Ferdia nodded at each other and Nell looked around. 'Where's Jessie?'

'Dunno.' Ferdia shrugged. 'What are you doing here?'

'Perla's doing a talk for this. So, you know, supporting her. You?'

'Same.' He coloured slightly. 'Supporting Perla.' Then he blurted, 'You don't mind? She's your friend, really.'

'We're not at school. I mean, more than one person can be friends with her.' Nell had intended to sound jokey but it came out sounding snide.

'Here's the woman herself,' Barty said.

Here, indeed, was Perla, smiling prettily, her hair bouncing over her bare shoulders, wearing a flax-coloured sundress that Nell had previously seen on Saoirse.

'You look nice,' Barty said.

'Recognize my dress?' She turned her sparkling eyes on Ferdia. 'It was your sister's. Jessie insisted I took it.'

Knowing Jessie, Nell thought, she'd probably tried to give Perla every stitch the Caseys possessed.

'I'm sorry.' Ferdia sounded mortified.

'No! I am grateful. You are all very kind to come.'

'Are you nervous?' Nell asked.

'I feel excited.'

Nell had to admit that she was unrecognizable as the woman she'd met that cold, miserable night at the start of the year.

'Perla?' A young man wearing a lanyard had come to take her to the stage. 'We're about to start.'

'Good luck,' they called after her.

'You'll be great!' Barty yelled. 'Break a leg!'

'Bart,' Ferdia hissed. 'Could you just *not*?'

'Calm your keks,' Barty said. 'Nell, sit with us.' Furtively, he widened his eyes at Ferdia and mouthed, *Looper.*

Positioned between Barty and Ferdia, she was suddenly afraid she was going to be felled by an attack of inappropriate, uncontrollable laughter.

'How's things?' Barty asked. 'Haven't seen you since the weekend from Hell in Mayo.'

He was funny, she decided. Zero sensitivity but hilarious. 'That was a bad one,' Nell admitted.

'And now he brings me to this! Sometimes I wonder if he hates me!'

Her smile dimmed. This thing tonight was meaningful. It wasn't right to slate it.

'How's Sammie getting on?' she asked Ferdia.

'They're being *mature*,' Barty said. 'Aren't you, Ferd? They'll always "think fondly" of each other.'

'It's true.' Ferdia surprised her with a smile. 'She said to say hey. So how's your summer going?' That was a sore point. 'Did you get that job?' He'd clearly just remembered. 'Down in Mayo, weren't you doing some project?'

'Yeah. Yep, I was.' She cleared her throat and made herself speak cheerily. 'I didn't get it.'

Ship of Fools had been gentle but, weeks later, it still hurt. 'You overstretched yourself,' Prentiss had said, almost sadly. 'It's a shame, Nell. We wish you the best for the future.'

There was a lame attempt to argue her case, but he was right: she'd tried to do something she wasn't experienced enough to pull off and the person responsible for that, she felt, was Liam. He was the one who'd urged her to take things in a new direction while her own instinct had told her to stick to what she was good at.

In her heart she knew the only person to blame was herself, but the sting of losing the gig was rolled up with her general disillusionment.

So she shook her hair back, all cheery. 'Hey, ya know, just wasn't meant to be.'

'That sucks.' He sounded sincere. 'You really wanted it, right?'

'Yeah . . .' Then she blurted, 'I was devastated. Even now . . .' Her confidence was in bits.

'Give it time.' His voice was halting. 'It sucks. But, dude, you need to get back on the horse.'

'Right.' She hadn't gone near the horse since the rejection. It was as if she'd lost all love for her work.

'Right?' Ferdia repeated.

Actually the smaller productions for September's theatre festival would be looking for people. Maybe she'd send a couple of texts, see what came back. At least Liam would be happy. He hadn't known how to deal with a negative, pessimistic Nell. Especially because he'd enrolled on a massage course and was all gung-ho about it. Which made a change from his usual bitterness about Chelsea's lack of respect.

A squeal of feedback returned her to the room.

Up on the stage, the first speaker started talking about lobbying the government. After a while, someone else focused on fundraising, then a journalist spoke about calling the media out on inaccurate articles.

Eventually it was Perla's turn.

''Bout time,' Barty whispered loudly. 'I was nearly nodding off there.' Then, 'Whoops. Sorry, Ferd!'

Perla described day-to-day life in Direct Provision. She was concise and confident. Increasingly, the woman she'd once been was coming into focus: a middle-class wife and mother and a respected professional.

Nell had always thought of her as physically small but, although she was thin, these days she looked far less diminished. It was her posture: she stood differently now, fully inhabiting her space.

'I am a doctor,' she said. 'I deal with situations scientifically, logically and without too much emotion. But when I talk of Direct Provision, it is all emotion, because there is no logic. I feel wrong to criticize the system, because I am grateful that I am here. But why can I not work and live independently while I'm waiting to find out if I can stay in Ireland?

'All my life I have worked to help people. I want to help people in Ireland. They have been kind to me. The principle of Direct Provision is designed to humiliate. We are treated almost as prisoners.

'People need to live like human beings, to be independent and to work for their livelihoods. You let me move to your country, you keep me physically alive, but you don't let me live a full life. Please try to imagine yourself in my situation and remember that the only difference between you and me is the luck of where we were born.' She stopped, smiled briefly and said, 'Thank you for listening.'

Instantly Ferdia got to his feet, clapping enthusiastically.

Perla bounded over, giddy and energized. 'It was okay?'

'More than okay,' Ferdia said. 'You were great. Really great.'

So . . . ? Ferdia liked Perla? *Liked* liked?

'We going for a drink?' Ferdia asked.

Perla literally turned out the empty pockets of her dress. 'It's not looking good.' She gave a goofy little grin.

'It's on me,' Ferdia declared.

Wow. Seemed he really *did* 'like' her.

And did she like him back? They certainly seemed comfortable with each other.

Nell's worry was Jessie. She was cool—much cooler than Nell had first realized. She was clearly fond of Perla. But she might turn on a hairpin if Ferdia fell for Perla—a woman eight years older than him, who already had a child.

Right now Nell was high in Jessie's estimation, but as the person who'd brought Perla into the Caseys' life, she'd get the blame if things went sideways. Maybe she was jumping the gun here. They might just be friends.

'I've to head off,' Nell said. 'Enjoy your night.'

'See you for Mum's birthday thing,' Ferdia said.

'You're going?' She was surprised.

'. . . Yeah. Like, you're right.' He seemed embarrassed. 'She's not so bad.'

'Oh. That's cool. What character did you get?'

'Quentin Ropane-Redford. Racing-car driver and eligible bachelor.' He rolled his eyes. 'You?'

'Ginerva McQuarrie. An adventuress.'

'What's that? Someone who does extreme sports?'

Nell laughed out loud. 'I think she's a swizzer, a woman who pretends to be rich—'

'"—who schemes to win wealth or status by unscrupulous means",' Ferdia said, reading from his phone. 'Wow. That's a bit . . .'

'*Thank* you, Ferdia, it *is* "a bit" . . .'

'All the women's roles seem decorative or, like, *menial*,' he said. 'Saoirse's a showgirl, Mum's a secretary, you're some grifter. It's so not cool.'

'No.' She kept her face solemn. 'It's not cool, Ferdia, not cool at all.'

Fifty-Six

'It's a fancy-dress party?' Patience asked.

'Worse,' Cara said. She was trying to explain the concept of a murder-mystery weekend to her non-Irish colleagues. 'We've been given identities, like people from Agatha Christie books, you know, vicars, explorers, retired majors. We dress up and stay in character all weekend. A couple of people will be "murdered" and we have to figure out who did it.'

Patience's smooth brow puckered. 'White people are weird,' she eventually said, and went off to her office.

'Who's your character?' Zachery asked. 'Do you know yet?'

'Madame Hestia Nyx, renowned spiritualist.' She'd been terrified that she'd have to squeeze herself into a short dress or a fitted evening gown, so she'd pleaded with Johnny for a role that didn't require figure-hugging clothing. Johnny had protested that the hotel made those decisions but Cara had insisted, 'It can't hurt to ask.'

He'd come back and said, 'Would a spiritualist do you? Sort of like a fortune teller?'

'What does a spiritualist wear?' Ling asked Cara.

'You know, floaty stuff, scarves, jingly bracelets, black kohl. I provide the clothes and the hotel provides the props—I suppose things like a crystal ball. Maybe tarot cards.'

'What's the hotel?' Vihaan asked. They were all very interested in hotels.

'Gulban Manor. In Northern Ireland. Antrim.'

'Never heard of it,' Ling said.

'Well,' Vihaan sighed, 'not everywhere can be the Ardglass.'

In fact, Cara had been able to find out almost nothing about Gulban Manor, save the location, which was two miles from the nearest village. The website gave no information on room amenities—specifically mini-bars—except to say, 'Gulban Manor offers a variety of accommodation, from generously sized family rooms to fun, themed spaces.' That meant she'd have to sneak chocolate into her luggage, just in case the urge to overeat came on her. And, with a sinking heart, she realized that it probably would.

Despite her incessant resolutions to stop, she didn't seem to be able to. It was scaring her now. Every day—at least twice or three times, sometimes even more—the longing overtook her. Being out of her routine seemed to make her more susceptible.

Her ribs ached, her throat felt raw, and all of a sudden, her broken tooth had begun to throb.

Fond as she was of Jessie and Johnny, she was worn out by these elaborate weekends. After those horrible few days in Mayo, only a month ago, couldn't Johnny have done something simpler? Her time with Ed and the kids was limited and precious. Johnny had decreed that this party was a no-kids thing, which meant that the lads would barely see Ed for two weeks in a row.

As for finding a decent gift for Jessie! Usually she gave spa vouchers for the Ardglass, because she got a 50 per cent discount. *And* because everyone was in love with that spa. But she needed to up her game for a fiftieth. The Ardglass gave an annual two-night stay to many of their employees, which could be bartered with staff in other hotels around the world. By doing a deal with the woman who managed a small gem of a hotel in Finland, she'd got a two-night stay for Jessie and Johnny, in a suite overlooking Helsinki harbour. And Tiina and Kaarle would have a dreamy weekend in the Ardglass at a time of their choosing. Lucky feckers.

Peak time for a complaint was twenty or thirty minutes after a guest had arrived in their room. That was when the relief of finally being in their own private space wore off. Suddenly they found themselves back in their body, redirecting all their habitual dissatisfactions at their new surroundings.

They might decide that actually, 700 square feet was too small and they needed an upgrade. Or, beautiful though the view over the square was, they didn't like the sounds of the traffic.

It was fifteen minutes since Mr O'Doherty had been shown to his suite.

'Five euro says he will want a second bathroom,' Vihaan said.

'No,' Ling said. 'My bet is he will want a higher floor.'

'Five euro?' Vihaan was sharp-eyed with delight.

'Guys,' Cara said, 'we can't bet actual money. This is only okay if we do it for fun.'

'So what's your prediction?' Vihaan asked.

'It won't be straightforward. It'll be something about the décor, that it's too—'

'Beautiful?'

'Which rooms are ready?' Cara picked up the latest list from the housekeeping team. She was already mentally shuffling bookings. Today only two rooms in the whole hotel weren't reserved: the Penthouse Suite and the mezzanine roof-garden. Some of today's expected guests had requested specific rooms, so they couldn't be changed, but there was a certain leeway with the others: so long as they got the grade of room they had booked—or a better one—they tended to be happy. Most of their guests were decent. It was just the occasional arse, like Owen O'Doherty, who took delight in finding fault.

'What's keeping him?' Ling asked.

'He's taking a shower, messing up the bathroom, so Housekeeping will have to do it all again.'

'It's been twenty-nine minutes,' Vihaan said. 'I think you're wrong.'

The phone rang—but it was an outside call, from Gemi, one of the drivers. 'Good morning, Cara. I'm with Mr and Mrs Nilsson. We should be with you in four minutes.'

'. . . Thank you, Gemi.' *Shite.* 'The honeymooners will be here in four!'

'They're early!'

By almost an hour. 'Vihaan, get Madelyn back off break. Ling, get the flowers and the paperwork.'

. . . And what now?

Anto darted into the lobby, exuding panic. 'Incoming,' he said. 'People-carrier. A man, a woman, three kids. The mother is in a sari.'

The Ranganthans? They weren't expected until tomorrow. Unless . . . Oh, God, *no.*

'Second people-carrier behind with the luggage. Tons of it. Like an LV shop on wheels.'

It was then, with impeccable timing, that Owen O'Doherty decided to call. 'This room sucks.'

'I'm sorry to hear that, Mr O'Doherty.' Cara grabbed Vihaan and scrawled on a pad, 'Get Hospitality NOW.' The Ranganthans would need to be fed and watered while their booking mix-up was untangled. 'Mr O'Doherty, is there anything in particular about your room?'

'Try all of it. Too many tassels and flowers and shit. It's fugly and, ya know, *old-timey*.'

Here came Mr Ranganthan, trailing his wife and three children. Still stuck to the phone, Cara widened her eyes and smiled madly at them.

In her ear, Owen O'Doherty barked, 'I want a calm space. Don't you have a Zen sorta room?'

Still smiling like a loon, she said, 'Sadly not, Mr O'Doherty.' She knew what was coming.

'You gotta have a room that's all white.' Right on cue, he said, 'What about your Honeymoon Suite?'

Thinking fast, fast, fast, she went through the permutations: she could upgrade the honeymooners to the Penthouse Suite. They were young and would probably be thrilled. But the Honeymoon Suite was romantic—it even had an outdoor hot-tub on a tiny roof-garden, shielded from the neighbouring buildings by honeysuckle topiary. 'I'm afraid our Honeymoon Suite is booked.' Sudden rage flared. 'By *honeymooners*.'

'Can't you move them? No? What about the penthouse?'

See, that's what he wanted. Not the penthouse *per se*, just to be the most important person staying in the hotel.

And the thing was, she *could* move him there.

But the Ranganthans were here, milling around impatiently in front of the desk, and even though it was her fault that they didn't have a reservation for tonight, she could fit them in, in the penthouse and the connecting room on the lower floor.

If she moved the people who'd been booked into the connecting bedroom to another. She could actually move them into Mr O'Doherty's room. Which meant that the mezzanine was still available.

'We're fully booked tonight,' she said. 'But juggling things around, there is another room I could free up. It's bigger and has a roof-garden. However, the décor is similar to your current room. Very *old-timey*.' She couldn't keep the scorn from her voice. He'd stayed here in the past: he knew what their look was. 'Why don't you view it? If that's to your liking, we can you move there. You'll take a look? Well, that's . . .' in exaggerated fashion, she cooed into the phone '. . . *peeeeeeachy*. Vihaan will be with you shortly.'

'Gimme five. I just took a shower.'

She put the phone down, ready to devote herself to the Ranganthans—and her heart banged hard when she found Patience standing behind her. Had she overheard her sarcasm?

'Mr Ranganthan, Mrs Ranganthan.' She hurried to greet them all. 'Izna, Hiyya and—' What was the youngest one called? 'Karishnya!'

The by-now-familiar routine: latex gloves in the garbage can, cotton swabs, concealer, mouthwash, comb, clips, hairspray, finish. She took a breath, stepped out into the corridor—face to face with Patience. The shock wiped her clean and blank.

'Cara?' Patience asked. 'What's going on?'

'Aaah . . .' She shouldn't have to feel guilty: it wasn't illegal to use a bathroom.

'Come upstairs,' she said. 'Henry's office. We'd like to talk with you.'

'. . . Now?'

'Right now.'

Every explanation deserted Cara. It was as if her brain had shut down. But she'd better come up with something . . .

'Ah.' Henry's round face wore an expression of concern. 'Shut the door and sit down.'

On trembling legs, she took a chair.

'So,' Henry said, 'quite apart from the Ranganthan debacle, we've been concerned. It's been noticed that you're spending a lot of time downstairs. In a bathroom.'

'I . . . em.'

'Time when you should be at the front desk,' Patience clarified. 'Are you ill?'

Before Cara could answer, Henry said, 'Because if you're ill, Cara, ill enough to impact your work, you should see a doctor.'

God, *no*. 'I'm not ill. Not like that.'

'Have you a drinking problem?' Henry asked.

'No!'

'Drugs? Cara. We value you. You're an exceptional member of staff. If you're in some sort of trouble, we want to help.'

'I'm fine.'

'If you won't trust us,' Henry said gently, 'how can we help you?'

'I don't need help. Honestly. It was just . . . I was only . . . But I'll do better.' She would.

'Can you explain what happened over the Ranganthan booking?' Patience asked.

Shame flooded her. 'They emailed that they wanted to come a day earlier. There was availability. I replied and told them so. But I didn't amend the room grid. I'm so sorry.'

'You've never messed up like this before,' Patience said. 'And this is a biggie. Taken in conjunction with your frequent absences downstairs, we're understandably worried.'

'I don't know how I missed it.' Cara felt close to tears. 'But I promise it won't happen again.'

Fifty-Seven

Johnny drove the car through the gates of Gulban Manor and—oh, Jesus *Christ*: this was worse than he had feared. Way, *way* worse. Only now did he see how gullible he'd been—he'd let himself be fooled by the old photo-from-a-flattering-angle trick: basically Gulban Manor had a nice front door.

His heart was pumping out neat adrenalin: based on a photo of that Regency-style door, fourteen people were driving one hundred and fifty kilometres, to celebrate *Jessie's fiftieth birthday*.

'*This?*' Saoirse, seated behind him, sounded surprised.

His panic was so bad, his heart felt trapped in his throat.

In his defence, it really *was* a very handsome door, a leaded fanlight curving elegantly above it, set in a portico of slender columns.

The house itself might once have been a small period gatehouse. Directly on either side of the entrance were graceful sash windows, but from there on, the look was pure seventies suburbia.

For one mad, mindless moment, he sincerely thought about doing a U-turn and driving out of there—heading for *anywhere* and doing it fast. Instead, he meekly parked the car. Sliding his eyes sideways, he saw that Jessie was coolly taking it all in. 'Jessie, babes.' His voice was low and urgent. 'If this is a disaster, I'll make it up to you.'

'It'll be fine.' She sounded uncharacteristically quiet.

God, *no*. She was giving him the I'm-not-angry-I'm-disappointed treatment. Feeling sick, he got out, Jessie, Saoirse and Ferdia trailing after him.

In the photo, the front door had been a clean creamy colour but in real life it looked as if it had been cured in nicotine. The paint was flaking, the knocker was loose . . . and a short, solid man, laden with shopping bags, hurtled past him, shouldering it open.

They landed into a gloomy hallway.

The man, a round-faced, apple-cheeked individual, surveyed Johnny and his crew. 'Are you . . . ?'

'Hoping to check in,' Johnny said faintly.

'Oh. Aye. No bother. I'll just stick these in the freezer.' He indicated the overflowing bags. 'Tomorrow night's canapés. Can't have them going bad. Then we really *would* have a murder on our hands. MICAH!' he yelled up the stairs, making Johnny jump. 'MUIRIA! Come down, the first ones are here!'

He turned back to Johnny. 'Welcome to the Gulban Manor Murder-Mystery Weekend. I'm Clifford McStitt, the proprietor, with my wife Muiria. Here's Micah now.'

A teenage boy descended the stairs, with the same round, apple-cheeked face as Clifford, obviously his son. 'Mammy'll be here in a second,' he said. 'She knows about the bookings.'

And here came Mammy, who looked surprisingly similar to her husband. Her hair was even cut in the same pudding-bowl style. The three McStitts could have been triplets.

'Welcome.' Her smile was warm and Johnny clung to the small bit of hope this gave him. Maybe it wouldn't be a total disaster.

'Johnny Casey. Right. You're booked into our Empress Suite.' She turned a few pages in her notebook. 'For the weekend, you will be Dr Basil Theobald-Montague, once-eminent heart surgeon, now with—'

'—a stain on my reputation. Yes.'

'Your wife, Jessie? You are Rosamund Childers, secretary to MP Timothy Narracott-Blatt and a—'

'Yeah, "thoroughly good sport".'

Muiria was pleased. 'You've read your potted histories? Good. And you've brought suitable clothing? Very good. I'd say you'll enjoy yourselves. People said it was fun the other time.'

The other time? Only once? Christ on a stick, this was a nightmare.

It was crystal clear now that he should have sprung for fourteen flights to that criminally expensive place in Scotland.

Muiria had turned her attention to Ferdia. 'My goodness, you're some hunk, *hai*. My, my goodness. Who does he look like?' she asked Micah.

'Oh, *please*.' Ferdia was mortified.

For a couple of excruciating seconds, Micah and Muiria studied him.

'He has a look of the *Poldark* lad,' Muiria declared.

'Aidan Turner. He does, aye!'

'And you're here on your lonesome?' Muiria asked.

He'd wanted Barty to come but there wasn't enough room.

'We were going to put you in the studio apartment,' Muiria told Ferdia. 'But looking at you now, I think it'll be too small.'

What?

'Are *you* on your own?' she asked Saoirse. 'You are? Micah, take this young lady to the studio apartment and we'll sort Aidan Turner here out with something more suitable. CLIFFORD!' she howled, in the direction of the corridor her husband had disappeared down. 'CLIFFORD!'

Clifford burst through a door at the same time as Johnny heard a car parking outside.

'Take Mr and Mrs Casey to the Empress Suite and look lively. Another lot have just arrived.' To Johnny and Jessie she said, 'When you've settled in, come to the drawing room to get your name badge and props.'

'I'm sorry,' Johnny said to Jessie. 'I've fucked up on an epic scale.'

The Empress Suite wasn't a suite. The only thing that was in any way 'empress-y' about the room was the curvy headboard on the bed. The rest was bog-standard white melamine.

What made it even more horrifying was that this weekend wasn't just family. Rionna was coming with her wife, Kaz.

Also on their way from Dublin, expecting a stylish murder-mystery weekend in a luxury country-house hotel, were two of Jessie's friends and their husbands.

'It's clean,' Jessie said. 'That's something.'

'What if I could get us into the Lough Erne?' Fired by desperate hope, he reached for his iPad and tapped urgently. 'That's five-star! . . . Oh. No Wi-Fi. I'll just go down to—'

'Johnny, stop. We're staying. Let's unpack and then we'll go down.' She opened the wardrobe and said, 'What the hell . . . ?'

The wardrobe was full of clothes, probably Clifford's and Muiria's.

'That's it!' Johnny said. It was definitely the Lough Erne for them.

'Mum, Johnny?' Saoirse's voice came from outside their room.

'Just come in,' Jessie called. Because there was no lock on the door—yet another issue.

'You have to come and look,' Saoirse said. 'I'm crying! It's the funniest thing ever! My "studio apartment" is a kitchen. I'm literally deceased! A kitchen with a washing-machine. A camp bed where the table should be.'

'Come on!' Suddenly energized, Jessie jumped up and grabbed Johnny.

On the way they met Ferdia.

'Hey, are your rooms a bit mad?' he asked. 'Mine has five single beds in it, put together like a Tetris game!'

'Wait till you see where I'm at!' Saoirse said.

Saoirse was right. Her bed was in a pleasant little fitted kitchen, with a microwave, knife block, toaster and such.

'Have you a bathroom?' Johnny asked.

'Out here.' She led them into a hallway where they met Nell and Liam, who were being shown to their room by Clifford. Everyone seemed in high spirits, except for a bristling hostility between Ferdia and Liam.

Johnny had heard about the carry-on with Sammie that awful weekend in Mayo. He hoped there would be no argy-bargy this weekend: things were bad enough.

'You two are in the Swiss Suite.' Clifford opened a door.

Terrified of what he might see, Johnny stuck his head around the door. Christ on a bendy bus . . .

'Give me a look.' Jessie pushed forward. 'Stop, this is too funny!'

It was a small kids' room with a treble bunk bed. A double on the bottom, with steps leading up to a single.

'Swiss!' Jessie declared. 'Why is it Swiss, Clifford?'

'Because of the mezzanine element, *hai*.'

'Mezzani– . . . You mean the top bunk? That's the mezzanine?'

'Aye.'

'It's very cute,' Nell said.

'Bless you.' Johnny could hardly speak.

He hurried to the entrance hall to beg Muiria to give the best rooms—whatever they might transpire to be—to the non-family people in their party.

There were three halfway decent double bedrooms, two with en suites. Jessie's friends, Mary-Laine and Annette, along with their husbands, were to be given those. Rionna and Kaz could have the non-ensuite room: Rionna was sound—she wouldn't be offended.

'Who should I put in the yurt?' Muiria asked.

A *yurt*?

'Nobody.'

'Someone has to.'

'It can't be Mary-Laine, Annette or Rionna.'

'No bother.'

But he was afraid to trust her, so he stood at the front door, intercepting people as they arrived, and shepherding them through check-in.

Here came Rionna and Kaz.

'This is a bit of a shit-show,' he muttered. 'I'm very sorry. I'm deeply, truly sorry.'

Rionna and Kaz laughed it off. 'So long as Jessie has a good time, that's all that matters.'

Jessie's friend Mary-Laine and her husband Martin were similarly relaxed.

Annette and Nigel, though . . . Annette was Jessie's friend and she was okay. But her husband Nigel was as arsy as they come. Too aggressive, always had to win and *delighted* with any chance to make life unpleasant for others.

Here came a gang of people Johnny didn't recognize. These must be the other guests, he realized. Six thirty-somethings, a smiley, rowdy group of friends. Johnny scanned them, looking for the alpha, the person he could join forces with, to keep this thing on track—but they were all betas. So he was completely on his own, carrying this weekend entirely by himself. He'd only been trying to save money. He'd been ultimately thinking of *everyone*'s good. But who was going to cut him any slack?

No one, that was who.

His was a heavy and a lonely burden.

The only ones left to arrive were Ed and Cara and they'd be happy with anything. So when Micah whizzed past and told him to come to the drawing room, he decided it was safe to stand down.

Fifty-Eight

'Nell McDermott?' Micah called. 'You're Ginerva McQuarrie. Socialite and ruthless adventuress.'

Her props were a pair of vintage sunglasses, an onyx cigarette holder, a feather boa and satin elbow gloves, all of decent quality.

'Ferdia Kinsella?' Micah called. 'Quentin Ropane-Redford. Racing-car driver and eligible bachelor.' Ferdia was given a pair of driving gloves, a fake Cartier cigarette lighter, an elaborate-looking watch and goggle-style sunglasses. 'For the weekend, *become* your alter ego.' Micah winked at him. 'And expect the unexpected . . .'

Mary-Laine's husband, Martin—or MP Timothy Narracott-Blatt—was accessorized with a silver-topped cane, a monocle and a top-hat.

'Liam Casey? You're Vicar Daventry.'

Liam received a white dog-collar, a set of buck-teeth and a Bible. 'Feck's sake.' He pawed through his haul. 'Everyone else is playboys and good stuff and I'm a crappy vicar.'

'Hot vicar,' Nell said.

'Oh, yeah?' He shoved in his false teeth and lunged at her. 'Still think so?'

She waved him away. 'I'm going to the room to get changed.'

Johnny intercepted her, with the aspect of chief mourner at a funeral. 'Nell, I apologize. This is a bit of a cluster-fuck.'

'No way,' she said. 'It just isn't very, you know, Johnny-and-Jessie. But it's going to be the best fun. The props are *class*. They got them from a theatre group. It's all cool.'

'You're so nice.'

For a scary moment, it looked like he might kiss her.

'When should we give Jessie her gift?' she asked. 'We got her a powder compact. Vintage. Silver and enamel. Will it be okay?'

'Aaah . . . We'll play all that by ear. I'm sure she'll be happy with it.'

He clearly hadn't a clue and she felt sorry for him. Whatever, it would have to be okay. She'd wasted days on eBay searching for something adequately 'Jessie'.

Micah called, 'Johnny Casey! Dr Basil Theobald-Montague, once-eminent heart surgeon.'

'I'm up,' he said, and skedaddled.

Nell saw that Cara and Ed had finally arrived. They looked upset. 'What's wrong?' she asked.

Cara looked around furtively, until she saw that Johnny was too far away to hear. 'Ed and I, our room is a yurt.'

Ferdia had also come to say hello. 'A yurt? Cool!'

'Except it's not a yurt,' Ed said.

'It's just a tent, like a four-man tent.' Cara's chin wobbled. 'We can't even stand up in it and there's no bathroom. I'm too old for this—'

'Have my room,' Ferdia cut in. 'I've five beds and at least one bathroom.'

'Stop, Ferdia, I couldn't.'

'You could. I don't care. I don't need a bathroom. C'mon, Cara, let's get your stuff and we'll swap now.'

'Thanks, Ferdia,' Ed said. 'That would be great.'

Tears actually spilt from Cara's eyes. She seemed slightly broken. Ferdia led her away, his arm around her shoulders.

As the birthday girl, Jessie was the first Casey to the drawing room, to welcome her guests for the pre-dinner drinks. She'd already passed through about a dozen states of mind since they'd arrived. To begin with, she'd been surprised—surely this wasn't 'the country-house hotel' where her much-anticipated fiftieth-birthday weekend was happening? When she understood that it was, she felt violent disappointment.

It was only when she saw how mortified Johnny was that she felt some sympathy. It was a horrible thing to organize a disastrous weekend, then to have to see it through.

But very quickly, she'd moved on to fury: she'd hinted long and hard about the world-famous place in Perthshire and this was a million miles from it. Johnny was happy to spend lots of money on everyone else. *Her* money. But he wouldn't spend it on her. She could have organized the weekend herself and she'd have made sure they all went to Scotland. But she'd wanted to be 'surprised'.

Well, she was fucking surprised all right.

But her anger would have to be parked for the next two days because it wasn't just about him and her. Other people were tangled up in this shit-show and she was obliged to be mannerly. There were times, though—more and more often lately—when she wondered about Johnny. Anonymous creeps online were always saying he was a cheater. Not just because he was good-looking and charming, but because, as the main breadwinner, she'd emasculated him. What other choice did he have, they reasoned, but to be unfaithful? Was this shitty weekend a passive-aggressive punishment? Was everything finally catching up with them?

Persuading him to sleep with her, that night in Limerick all those years ago, had been pure spontaneity. He'd been there, his hair rumpled, his tie askew. She'd made a jokey remark, he'd said, *I do want you*, and bam! She'd gone from dead to alive, from nothing to everything. Out of nowhere had come that astonishing spurt of lust, that flood of longing. *Oh, my God, I'm a woman and you're a man and let's have sex because I bet sex with you would be pretty amazing.* She'd wanted him and she didn't give a flying fuck about the consequences. Like buying a fabulous coat she didn't need and couldn't afford.

But sleeping with Johnny wasn't like buying a Tory Burch coat. Tory Burch coats could be returned and her money would be refunded.

That first night confirmed that, yep, they were *very* sexually compatible. That, yep, they were mad about each other. That this thing was real, that this thing was *on*.

She and Johnny had hit the ground running. Sex, sex, sex. Work, sex and more sex. Getting pregnant had given her a wobble—just what the hell was she *at*?

The distress of the poor Kinsellas gave her an even bigger wobble. But then it united herself and Johnny more tightly, in an us-against-the-world bond.

She'd thought they were happy, but when you've got kids and you share a frantic work schedule, there's a lot of scaffolding keeping you operational. If things slipped off the tracks, it might take a while for someone to notice.

She had to admit that, despite their relative harmony, Johnny sometimes treated her like a joke: a headstrong nightmare, who needed robust management. When he and the kids sometimes ganged up, calling her Herr Kommandant, she'd assumed it was good-natured, but was she wrong?

Love faded and soured, so she'd heard. Had Johnny's feelings for her curdled because she was too much of a bossy-pants?

Look at how different Ed and Cara were: Ed *adored* Cara. It was so obvious. There were no grand gestures from him, but he behaved as if he were the luckiest man alive. And Cara loved Ed back: that was for sure.

She never really got that from Johnny, that feeling of being cherished. Instead, she had a picture in her head of him slinking around, fearful of more chores and on the constant lookout for sex, like a raccoon around a garbage can.

He *could* be cheating. He actually genuinely could. The possibility made her feel sick. He had no shortage of opportunity—he travelled a lot without her. God knew who he met. People fancied him. She'd seen it in action. Jealousy surged, like hot lava.

Again she thought of him, like a raccoon nosing around a garbage can, wondering if he could persuade her into bed. There was a constant imbalance between the amount of sex she felt he wanted and what they actually managed. The thing was, she liked sex. She liked it a lot. It was just that accessing it felt like having to hack her way through a dense jungle, clearing obstacle after obstacle out of the way. Work and tiredness and children interrupting and last-minute chores all conspired to wreck any opportunities.

Once again she remembered the strange things he'd been saying during the weekend from hell in Mayo. All that stuff about being a hollow man had alarmed her. Back then, she'd decided they were going to have some alone time, right? To get to the bottom of whatever was up with him. But as soon as the decision was made, the Hagen Klein disaster had blown up. Next thing she was on a plane to Lebanon, then to Switzerland, trying desperately to persuade another chef to take Hagen's place at very short notice, all the while running interference from a hundred punters, as pissed off with her as if she'd been personally buying the wraps of crystal meth and standing in Hagen's kitchen forcing them on him.

In the end, Mubariz Khoury from Beirut had jumped in. It had all gone ahead last weekend, without ultimately causing too much damage to the PiG brand.

But the drama had taken up all her time, focus and every scrap of energy. It was only now that she was surfacing from the mire of panicky planning back to the rest of her life—to discover that Johnny was still being weird.

Fifty-Nine

Micah approached, carrying a tray of cocktails. 'Ah, Miss Rosamund Childers, you're looking well tonight.'

As a secretary, Jessie hadn't been given much leeway with her outfit. That was another thing! Johnny should have pushed for something more fun as her alias—a showgirl like Saoirse in a short, shimmery halterneck or a woman of mystery like Nell. Instead, she was done up as Dowdy Central in a wool skirt, lace-up brogues and a twin-set, accessorized with *pince-nez* glasses, fake pearls, a leather-bound notebook and fountain pen to keep details of all MP Timothy's appointments.

'Please take any glass,' Micah said. 'Except the pink one. That is the special drink of Lady Ariadne Cornwallis, Argentine heiress.'

'Right so.' Nothing like signalling ahead that Lady Ariadne Cornwallis, whoever she was, was not long for this world.

Next to arrive was Rionna, as Phyllida Bundle-Bunch, a 'world-renowned' opera singer, dressed in an extravagant taffeta evening gown, an elaborate wig and a giant bejewelled choker. 'Y'okay?' she asked Jessie.

'Faking it to make it. I'm going to enjoy myself if it kills me.'

'Good woman. Here's Hanging Judge Jeffries.'

It was Kaz, in a voluminous black cape and a long, yellowish, itchy-looking judge's wig. 'This is fantastic.' She waved her gavel about, flapping fabric everywhere. 'I feel I could take flight.'

As more people began to flood into the drawing room, it was a relief that they'd made an effort with their costumes. There was a lord in a frock-coat, fob-watch and mutton-chop sideburns; a lady do-gooder in a drop-waisted shift and a cloche hat; a 'mysterious beauty' in a floaty frock and veil.

Nell, as always, was magnificent as some sort of socialite con-woman, in a champagne-coloured figure-hugging satin dress.

A pair of buck-teeth loomed at her. 'Have you opened your heart to Jesus Christ, our Lord and Saviour?'

'Feck off.' Jessie managed to laugh, but truth be told, she'd soured on Liam, since she'd heard about his caper with Sammie.

It had been blind good luck she'd been up so early that Sunday morning last month, had never got to sleep, in fact. When she'd heard noises from outside the 'young persons' house', she'd opened the front door—and there was Barty, flinging rucksacks into Liam's car. She'd called, 'What's happening, Barty?'

He'd been quite happy to spill the beans. No ability to keep his mouth shut, that lad.

'There's an apology going down in there right now.' He'd nodded at the house. 'But Liam is a shithead.' Then, 'Sorry for the language. He's not a shithead.'

But Jessie wondered if Liam actually *was* a shithead. Men acting the arse because their wives' careers were going well weren't her favourite people—and especially not tonight.

. . . Oh, God, here came Johnny, looking stressed, holding a porn-star moustache to his face.

'I can't get my moustache to stick. Could you . . .'

. . . Jessie pivoted towards Annette and her horrible husband Nigel, presenting Johnny with her shoulder.

'For the weekend, *become* your alter ego,' Micah called, for the millionth time. 'Expect the unexpected—no! The pink drink is for Lady Ariadne!'

'Holy *shit*!' Kaz exclaimed.

'Wow,' Rionna agreed.

Jessie turned around to see Ferdia, tall and lean, in a white dinner jacket, a black bow tie and black dress pants. For once his dark hair was slicked back tidily. He looked groomed and glamorous, and her chest bloomed with love. *You'd be so proud of him*, she told Rory.

'I'd turn for him,' Rionna said.

'So would I,' Kaz chimed in. 'Hey! You there, boy! Over here.'

Rionna and Kaz took ownership, pulling at his jacket and touching his crisp white shirt. 'Look at you, Ferdia. All grown-up.'

'And hot.'

'Ah, stop.' His cheekbones reddened. 'They're only clothes.'

'Aha!' Micah called. 'I hear the dinner gong!'

'I heard nothing,' Jessie said. 'Am I going deaf?'

'I think the gong is imaginary,' Rionna said. 'Like the luxury accommodation, the three-hundred-thread-count bed linen, the—'

'Sorry,' Johnny said. 'I'm so sorry about all of this.'

So you fucking should be, you mean-spirited, stingy bastard.

Startling everyone, a woman burst in. 'Lady Ariadne Cornwallis,' she announced herself. 'Argentine heiress!'

It was Muiria in a black dress, a wig of long, dark curls and a slash of Frosty Shimmer lipstick.

'Oh, Jesus Christ!' Rionna turned away quickly, her shoulders shaking.

'Lady Ariadne,' Micah said. 'Here is your special cocktail.'

'Indeed! My special cocktail!' Lady Ariadne made quite a show of drinking her special drink and replacing the glass on the tray. 'Thank you, young Micah.'

'How was it?' Kaz asked eagerly.

'Taste slightly different from usual?' Rionna's voice held a hint of malicious glee.

'A touch of almond?' Jessie said.

'Why almond?' Kaz asked.

'That well-known poison, cyanide, is almond-flavoured.'

'Please stop!' Johnny said.

Nervously, Micah said, 'Let us process through to the dining room.'

Surprisingly, the dining table looked the part. An elaborate chandelier hung over a long, white-clothed table, the light winking off silver candlesticks and crystal glasses.

'Sit where you like,' Micah called.

In high spirits, everyone found a place and introduced themselves to their neighbours, under their new name. Jessie was glad that their crowd were bonding with 'The Other Six': it made things less awkward.

Clifford arrived with a trayful of small plates. He and Micah placed mozzarella salads in front of everyone.

However, Annette's husband Nigel, at the end of the table, was given nothing and not a single item remained on Clifford's tray. No one could begin eating until Nigel got his starter—and that didn't look like it was about to happen any time soon. All three of the McStitts were in the room and Jessie knew in her bones that no one would bound through the doors with a spare mozzarella salad and save the day. Tense expectation hung in the air. People were hungry: they wanted the night to get under way, the wine to be poured, a murder or two to take place . . .

Behind her, Clifford and Micah were murmuring: '. . . sixteen, seventeen, eighteen, nineteen, twenty.'

'We're missing one.'

'But how? You said *twenty*, I plated *twenty*.'

'It's Mammy!' Micah said. 'She shouldn't have got one.'

'Bang on!' Clifford picked up Lady Ariadne/Muiria's starter, gave her a glare and placed it before Nigel. '*Bon appétit*,' he declared to the room.

But now Lady Ariadne had no food. 'Please start,' she said.

'Aren't you eating, ah, Lady Ariadne?' Ferdia asked.

She looked longingly at his plate. 'Ah, no, I'll get something in the kitchen later. I mean, I'm . . . I never eat!'

While Micah poured wine, Lady Ariadne engaged all of them in meaningful conversation. 'Who are you, sir?' she asked Ed.

'Stampy Mallowan.'

'So, you are a ruthless American industrialist?'

'Stampy', accessorized with a cigar and a gaudy, yellow tweed waistcoat with matching bow tie, said, 'Ah, yes!'

'Are you married, Mr Mallowan?'

'I believe I'm not. But I am in the company of,' he consulted his piece of paper, ' "Jolly Vandermeyer, a picaresque showgirl".'

'That's me,' Saoirse said.

'But you were once married?' Lady Ariadne pressed Stampy Mallowan.

'Was I?' Ed consulted his page. 'So I was. But my first wife died in "mysterious circumstances".'

'This is a hoot,' Rionna said.

'Take it seriously,' Johnny begged.

Lady Ariadne pressed on with her interrogations and, even though it was stilted, a picture began to take shape. 'We have met once before, Lord Fidelis . . .'

'Miss Elspeth Pyne-Montant, I believe you knew my late husband . . .'

'Were we not at a weekend shooting party at the estate in Monserrat, Dr Theobald-Montague?'

Eventually it was clear that everyone had previously crossed paths with Lady Ariadne.

The main course arrived and was 'perfectly edible', to quote Rionna.

Just after it was cleared away, Micah and Lady Ariadne exchanged a nod, then she made a choking noise, grabbed her throat and fell, face down, onto the table.

'Game on!' someone said.

'I will fetch the doctor!' Micah cried.

'I'm a sports masseur!' Liam yelled.

'Hold on,' Johnny said. 'I believe *I*'m a doctor!' Now even *Johnny* was sabotaging things.

'Don't you have a stain on your reputation?' Ferdia asked, and laughter rose to the ceiling.

'Aye!' Micah said, in evident relief. 'You have been struck off.' He darted from the room.

'Are you really a sports masseur?' Mary-Laine's husband, Martin, called to Liam.

'Yeah.'

'He isn't!' Was that really Saoirse who'd shouted that? Civilization was breaking down here.

'*I did something to my calf when I was running.*'

'*Come over and show me.*'

Moments later a man in a black coat, black hat and carrying a doctor's bag hurried into the room. It was Clifford. He performed a cursory examination on Muiria, before declaring, 'Lady Ariadne Cornwallis is dead! Poisoned! And you are all suspects!'

'Does that mean we're not getting any dessert?' Jessie heard Annette ask quietly, and she was afraid she was going to start laughing and not be able to stop.

'Do the decent thing,' the doctor commanded. 'Avert your gaze while young Micah and I remove the poor lady's corpse.'

But this was too good to miss.

'Avert it!' he said. 'I must insist, *hai*.'

But no averting took place and a very much alive-looking Lady Ariadne was hustled from the room.

Dr Clifford returned. 'While we wait for the detective, dessert will be served for those with the stomach to eat it.'

Which was all of them.

Sixty

'Like, *obviously* that young fella Micah did it!' Phyllida Bundle-Bunch cried.

'Yeah, he was the one with the tray of drinks.'

'But young Micah,' Clifford, now dressed up as 'Inspector Pine', tried to be heard above the racket, 'I said, YOUNG Micah had never met Lady Ariadne previously.'

'But he had the tray of—'

'*. . . it was a sudden twisty feeling, then a dart of terrible pain.*' Martin had rolled up his trouser leg and was demonstrating his wounded calf to Liam.

'*I see . . . yeah. So does it hurt if I do . . .* this?!' Liam poked his finger into the fleshy bit of Martin's calf and Martin howled with pain.

'Any one of you could have slipped poison into her glass!' Inspector Pine yelled.

'But no one had more opportunity than Micah there.'

'Christ in the Prada shop!' Mary-Laine's eyes were far too bright in her hot face. 'Is he still going on about the pain in his leg? He should try pushing out a TEN-POUND BABY!'

Cara felt as if she were watching this whole scene—the over-lit room, the red-faced people, the ridiculous costumes—from a distance.

'*Pulled muscle . . .*' she heard Liam saying.

'It wasn't me,' Micah said.

'It *wasn't* him.' Inspector Pine was adamant. 'It is one of you here in this room!'

'Maybe it was me?' Jessie said. 'I *have* been feeling murderous.' She flicked her eyes until they landed on Johnny. Cara watched as he quailed.

'*Can you work on it?*' Martin asked. '*I can pay you.*'

'*No charge for a friend of Johnny's.*'

'*I'm not actually a friend of Johnny's.*'

'We must work together to solve this dastardly crime!' Inspector Pine yelled plaintively. 'You must all split into teams of two. I SAID, YOU must—'

'*I've never really liked Johnny. My wife is friends with Jessie. That's how we're here. So you'd better charge me.*'

It was like picking up signals from several radios, Cara felt. There was too much noise and talk.

'—in order to help me to reveal the identity of the murderer.'

'*Okay. Fifty euro?*'

'*Hold on there, Tonto. That's a bit steep.*'

'Where's the wine?' Jessie said.

'You can buy more.' Inspector Pine sounded panicked.

'You mean the all-inclusive stuff is gone?' Johnny asked.

'For tonight. You'll get more tomorrow night. Now, to solve the murder mystery—'

'*Well, how much do you* want *to pay?*'

'*I won't know until you've finished. If you fix me, I'll pay you forty.*'

'Can we see the wine list?' Johnny asked.

'There's no wine list.' Poor Inspector Pine was unravelling. 'But you can have the dinner wine for fifteen pounds a bottle. Deal?'

'*You know what? Fuck you.*'

'*What?*'

'*Yeah. Fuck you. I offer you my expertise, free gratis for nothing, and you insult my brother, then haggle over a service I offered for nothing—*'

'Good. Grand,' Johnny said. 'Start us off with six of white and six of red and we'll see how it goes.'

'Muiria will see to that. Now, then. About solving this dastardly crime! Madame Hestia Nyx? You are partnered with Major Fortescue.'

'What?' Cara thought she could just choose to be with Ed.

'We're mixing things up.' Micah had spotted Cara's distress. He looked nervous.

Annette's husband Nigel had arrived at her side. He nodded and she responded with an even smaller nod. She'd met him once or twice in the past and she'd found him hard work.

'Here are your clues.' Micah whipped off a sheet of paper, which Nigel intercepted.

'Ginerva McQuarrie?' Inspector Pine called. 'Quentin Ropane-Redford? You'll be working together.'

That was Nell and Ferdia. Dreamily, Cara studied them. In his white dinner jacket and slicked-back hair, Ferdia was so grown-up and good-looking tonight. As for Nell, in her figure-hugging dress and elaborate hair . . . Both tall and young and glamorous. And *similar*, as if they'd been spat off a production line of generic gorgeous young things.

Jessie hates me, Johnny realized. *She wants to murder me, and I deserve it.*

Nell, bless her heart, had taken his arm and said, with sweet sincerity, 'You often have the best time at something like this. When everything is perfect, you might get wowed, but you don't really relax. Here, we're *dead* from laughing and we're *totally* bonded.'

She was a very good-natured person. Nice: that was the word. Although someone had told him that 'nice' was an insult, these days. Still, Nell looked very beautiful this evening. Jessie was always banging on about how gorgeous she was, but until tonight, he hadn't seen it. What was she doing with Liam, who was *not* nice? Not really.

He shouldn't think these damning thoughts. He'd turn into his father.

Johnny had been partnered with one of The Other Six, a 'Hollywood producer', but he had Jessie under constant surveillance. She'd been paired with Liam and, although she was joining in with the general mockery, he knew she had a reservoir of cold rage set aside just for himself, to be delivered at some later, unknown date.

Christ, how hard would it have been to do this properly?

Jessie wasn't generally high maintenance. She didn't expect regular flowers and expensive presents. Yes, she spent a lot of money on holidays, but it was nearly always on group activities.

This was her fiftieth birthday and she had hinted. *Heavily*. She'd basically told him what to do and he hadn't obeyed.

Could he put something else together quickly? It was *way* too late to organize a proper murder-weekend thing—that chalice was poisoned for ever.

How about taking her to Paris? But she'd *know* it was a bodge job. Actually, she didn't even like Paris: she said French women were 'scary bitches'. Wasn't gone on Italian shop assistants either, he remembered. Something about someone being snotty in the Versace shop in Milan.

Where else did people go? Barcelona, everyone loved Barcelona. But it was a gastronomic hotspot and she'd probably start pestering chefs if they were there for more than half an hour . . .

When everyone had been paired up and given cryptic clues to solve, Inspector Pine said, 'One hour. We must find this dastardly murderer before he—or she—strikes again! We meet back here at eleven and we will pool our findings.'

Then he left to do the washing-up.

'High up in Switzerland.' Nigel and Cara were looking at their 'clues'.

'One of the rooms must have a Swiss theme.'

'It's obviously outside.' Nigel was insistent. 'It's got to do with a nearby hill.'

'It's someone's *room*. They've planted incriminating things in people's rooms and we've to find them.'

'No. It must mean a mountain. Come on. Outside.'

Her broken tooth throbbed, her throat was raw, her ribs ached and her job was in jeopardy. 'Seeing as you're so great at this,' she spoke quietly, 'why don't you just do it on your own?' She made for her bedroom, where she had a wheelie-case half full of chocolate under the bed. Everyone would be busy for the next hour: she'd closet herself in the bathroom, where she could release the terrible tension in her chest.

Ferdia and Nell were on the first floor, following a clue about 'the Empress' when Nell's phone beeped. She took a look and exclaimed, 'That's three now!'

'Three whats?'

'I texted people last night, putting feelers out for work on the theatre festival. Two directors got back today. Now it's three.' She'd been half convinced no one would ever want her again.

From nearby came an odd noise: stumbling followed by a hard bump.

'What's that?' she asked. 'Another murder?'

But that first bump was followed by several smaller rhythmic bangs, followed by a cry.

They looked at each other.

Nell blushed. 'Is it . . . It sounds like two people . . .'

Colour crept up Ferdia's face. 'God . . . Should we just leave them to it?'

'Maybe. I don't know. Whose room is that?'

'Cara's.'

Another faint cry reached them.

'I don't think it's shenanigans,' Nell said. 'It sounds . . . different.'

'Should we go in?' If it really was people having a quick ride, he would die. He knocked, and when there was no reply, carefully opened the door.

No one was to be seen, but when they pushed into the bathroom, Cara was on the floor. Her eyes were closed, her body was spasming and her legs were banging a plastic garbage can against the wall.

'Nell!' Ferdia was on his knees beside Cara. 'Help me turn her onto her side.'

Frozen with fear and confusion, Nell then snapped to it.

Kneeling beside Cara's thrashing body, Ferdia trying to contain her, they gently moved her.

'It's a seizure?' Nell asked.

'A boy at school used to get them. Bring some pillows. Protect her head.'

In the room, there were lots of pillows because there were lots of beds. They all managed to be both flat and lumpy, but they'd have to do.

While Ferdia cradled Cara's skull, Nell arranged the pillows around Cara's head and face. 'I'll stay with her,' he said. 'Go and get Ed. Ring an ambulance.'

Nell raced down the stairs, calling, 'Ed, Ed!'

A scatter of gaudily dressed guests, Ed included, flooded into the hall, gleefully energized by the new turn their night had taken.

'Ed, you need—'

'I'm Stampy Mallowan.'

Oh, God, he was jarred.

'Ed, Cara's not well. Someone call an ambulance.'

'Dr Basil Theobald-Montague at your service.' Johnny shouldered his way forward, then bowed with exaggerated courtesy.

'No—'

'Struck off though I am, with my reputation in tatters, I believe I may—'

'Johnny, stop. This is real.' Nell twisted around desperately. 'Clifford! Muiria! Call an ambulance, *please*. Cara is sick.'

Muiria looked terrified. 'Sick?'

'Some sort of seizure.'

That word had the desired effect: Ed scooted up the stairs, Jessie rang 999, and Clifford conducted an urgent, muttered conversation with Muiria.

That mozzarella was out-of-date.

Only by two days.

But you said—

'Muiria.' Jessie thrust her phone at her. 'Talk to them, tell them how to get here.'

Nervously Muiria took the phone. 'The quickest way is to turn off at the—That's it, aye . . . No, keep going. You'll come to a burnt-out tractor. Keep going past a sign for Molly's Hollow. You'll be thinking you've gone too far. You haven't. You'll come to a new bungalow. A man will run out into the road and shout after you. That's Howard, pay no heed, he just likes the lights. We're in there on the left. If you pass the stony goats, you've gone too far . . . Goats. Made from stone. Aye.' She took the phone from her ear. 'They'll be here in fifteen minutes.'

With rustling yellow clothing and crackling radio mics, the paramedics were up the stairs and, within moments, had Cara efficiently strapped onto a stretcher, while everyone watched in silence. She was being taken to a hospital in Belfast and only Ed could go with her.

'We'll follow you,' Johnny promised, as the doors slammed shut and the van drove away.

But the idea of getting a taxi to Belfast made Muiria and Clifford almost shriek with shock. 'The cost. You could be looking at sixty pounds!'

'More, *hai*. And the same back again.' After a long, thick pause, Clifford said, '. . . There aren't any taxis. There's one in the town. But he won't come up here. We had a—a . . .' Nervously Clifford looked at Muiria for the right word.

'Disagreement. One of you could *drive* to the hospital. That lassie there.' She pointed at Nell. 'She drank almost nothing. She must be near sober. Are you?'

Nell nodded.

Jessie seemed hurt. '*Why* are you sober on my birthday?'

'I'm not really a wine person.'

'She drinks cider.' This came from Liam, who sounded slurry and almost accusatory.

'I'll come too,' Ferdia said.

'Johnny will go.' Jessie overruled him. 'Ferd, you're only a kid. Ed needs his brother.'

'Ed needs his *wife*. And I'm not "only a kid". I took care of Cara. I'm going.'

'He's right,' Johnny said. 'Ferdia should go.'

Sixty-One

Dr Colgan marched down the corridor in Belfast's Royal Victoria Hospital and crooked a finger at Ed, who hopped up from the moulded plastic seat. They'd been waiting for almost three hours, three long hours in which their costumes had generated interest from all but the most badly injured of patients in the waiting room.

Full moon tonight?

Break-out from the nut-house?

The nineteenth century called. It wants its clothes back.

'Just the husband,' the doctor said, as Nell half rose from her chair.

Ed followed Dr Colgan into a makeshift room behind a curtain.

This was exactly the sort of room where they broke terrible news. But if Cara was dead wouldn't Nell and Ferdia be here too?

The percentage of deaths from bulimia was 3.9, Ed knew. In other words, very rare. But someone had to be in that number . . .

'Sit down.' The doctor was harried but sympathetic. 'She's stable, she can leave soon, just the paperwork. So, Mr, ah, Casey, did you know your wife was bulimic?'

Ed had thought it would be a relief to have the problem out in the open. Instead he felt overwhelmed. For as long as it had lurked underground, he had hopelessly believed there was a chance it would go away by itself. Now it had to be addressed. 'I guess I did. She had a bout, years ago. I suspected she'd started again. Will she be okay?'

'From her blood work, the state of her teeth, she's packed a lot of purging into a short time, but it's impossible to know exactly how much.'

'Can we ask her?'

'She's likely to lie.'

'Not to me.'

A sympathetic look from the doctor made him twitchy with fear. She knew more than he did about Cara, about what she'd been doing. And Cara *had* been lying to him: lying by omission was still a lie.

'In my experience,' the doctor said, 'Cara will need residential care—'

'Wait—what, a *hospital*? You said she was stable.'

'A treatment centre. For addiction. Yes, it's an addiction. I can give you a leaflet.'

'But . . . How long would she have to go in for?'

'It's generally twenty-eight days.'

'And then she'll be fixed?'

'I can recommend a couple of places in Dublin. I'd ring first thing in the morning, get her on the wait lists.'

'And then she'll be fixed?'

'You can see her now. Fancy-dress party, was it?'

She'd had a sense of bumping and moving at speed. Bright lights were shone into her eyes. She knew Ed was there. Others, too, but Ed was the only one she needed.

Unfamiliar voices were asking and answering short, urgent questions.

'What's going on?' Her voice was hoarse.

Ed's face was very close. 'You had a seizure.'

'Why?'

His face was blank. 'You tell me.'

No. No, no, no, no, no.

It couldn't be. That was too crazy. It must be stress. Or some neurological thing that had only just appeared . . .

This could *not* be her fault.

Then they arrived at a big busy hospital. Ed was no longer with her as she was wheeled into a small, curtained space, to be examined by a succession of people in blue scrubs. 'I'm okay now,' she kept saying anxiously.

'Excellent. I'm just going to . . .'

Then she was hurriedly hooked up to a drip, attached to a heart monitor, and had four vials of blood taken from her veins. 'Really,' she pleaded. 'I'm fine. Can I see my husband?'

'After your CAT scan.'

A CAT scan? Cold horror overtook her. If she'd triggered all this medical expertise and expense from too much chocolate and puking, the guilt would kill her.

And to think she'd done it on Jessie's special birthday.

As she lay on her back in the tight white machine, for a moment she hoped the scan would show that she had a real condition, like epilepsy. Then shame kicked in once more. When she got out of here, she would take a long, hard look at things. Perhaps she could see a hypnotherapist, to help her stop.

The curtain of her cubicle swished aside and in came the doctor, followed by Ed.

She tried to smile.

'No neurological issues,' Dr Colgan said. 'You can leave shortly. How long have you been bulimic?'

Cara flicked a look at Ed. 'I'm not—'

'You've a chronic eating disorder.' The doctor was clearly in no mood for nonsense. 'You can see the results of your blood work. Your electrolytes are acutely out of balance. And your tooth enamel shows signs of recent acid erosion.'

All of her secrets were written in her body.

'How long?' the doctor repeated.

'Three months.'

She shook her head. 'Longer than that.'

'I swear. Only three months.'

'Well, you've certainly packed a lot in. This isn't your first bout?'

This mortification would never end. 'No.'

'I'd recommend in-patient care for at least four weeks.'

What? No. 'I can't. I've a job and two children.'

'I've seen this before. You could die if you don't stop. It's unlikely that you'll stop on your own.'

'I will.' She was scared shitless.

'Bulimia is an addiction.'

That wasn't true. She'd just been eating too much chocolate and now the very idea of it made her feel sick.

The drive back to Gulban Manor was in silence, but as soon as they were in their room of many beds, Ed rounded on her. 'You should have told me.' He was furious. 'What's the use of this—you and me—if you can't tell me about something so, so . . . *important*?'

'It was only for a short time. I was going to stop and—'

'I thought you were going to die,' he said. 'Can you imagine how that feels?'

'I'll stop. I'll do it with your help.'

'You go into a residential place. You do what the doctor said. For a month.'

Her guts seized with fear. Oh, no. No. 'There's no need, Ed. I've scared myself so much that I'll never do it again.'

'She gave me a leaflet. Bulimia's an addiction. You need to go to a place.'

'What about my job?'

'You won't be much use to them if you're dead.'

'Ed, I won't be dead.'

'But, honey, you might.'

The sadness that was hiding beneath his rage was suddenly obvious and her heart turned to jelly. 'Ed, sweetie . . . You got a fright. I got a fright. But I've stopped now. It'll be okay.'

'The doctor knows what she's talking about. I'll ring the places in the morning.'

Ed took professional advice literally. It was something she had always found endearing, but not now.

Sixty-Two

Cara knocked on Jessie's door, and a voice shouted, 'Come in, unless you're Johnny the arsehole Casey!'

Cara tentatively stepped into the room, Ed behind her.

Jessie was in bed, in her pyjamas, Saoirse asleep beside her. The curtains were open, letting in dull morning light.

'Jessie, I'm so sorry for ruining your birthday.'

Breezily, Jessie said, 'You haven't ruined it, you big eejit. Johnny did that, all by himself. But I'm worried about you! Is it true? Bulimia?'

Cara burnt. This must mean that the whole house knew. 'I'll be fine.' She tried to smile. 'It was just a blip.'

'We're going to head off now,' Ed said. 'Cara has an appointment this afternoon at St David's.'

'The nut-house?' Jessie's eyes flared with something. Glee? 'On a Saturday?'

'The psychiatric hospital.' Ed corrected. 'To see if she'd be a good fit.'

'Sure. Sure. Do whatever you need to do.'

Out on the landing, Cara said, 'Where's Johnny, do you think?'

'Probably Saoirse's room, if Saoirse stayed with Jessie.'

Johnny was indeed in the camp bed in the small kitchen. His doctor's accoutrements were flung about the room, the top-hat balanced on the kettle. He radiated exhausted, manic conviviality.

'Sorry for ruining the weekend.'

'Not at all!' He shrugged extravagantly. 'Everything is my fault. Don't even think about it.'

'I need to apologize to Ferdia and Nell too,' Cara said. 'And thank them.'

'This reminds me,' Johnny was talking too loudly, 'of the day after Ed's stag night. I had to apologize to every one of my neighbours. Woudja *stop*! I banged saucepans against their doors all night long. Marching up and down the stairs, singing rebel songs. Drinking rum. Never again, ha-ha-ha, never again.'

Johnny was clearly still a bit drunk and very distressed.

Cara managed a polite ha-ha at his story but everything was dismal.

'Off you go,' he said. 'Good luck at the loony-bin!'

As they made their way to the car, Cara felt the eyes of the house on her. She was a fuck-up, a weak, greedy person, and everyone knew. She'd never, in her entire life, felt as low as she did right now. 'Jessie's thrilled,' she said.

'Oh, honey. Not in a mean way. She's just excited about having an interesting family.'

'Compulsive overeating is a mental illness,' Varina, the admissions officer at the hospital, was clear. 'So is bulimia.'

But Cara knew that the only thing wrong with her was simple greed. She wasn't a mad person and she didn't want to be treated as one. 'I can stop on my own.'

'Have you tried?'

'Yes. Not really. But it's different now. I've scared myself.'

'If nothing changes, nothing changes,' Varina said.

Cara didn't even know what that meant. She just wanted to return to her ordinary life and put all of this behind her. 'I can stop on my own. I'm sorry for the inconvenience I've caused everyone and thank you for your time.'

'But—' Ed was white.

'If you're bothered by the stigma of being in a psychiatric hospital, we could take you as a day patient. It's not ideal, but—'

'I can stop. I've stopped. It's in the past.'

Bouncing the end of a pencil against her desk, Varina appeared deep in thought. 'Maybe you *can* stop on your own. Time will tell. Having a seizure is generally a red flag that bulimia is at an advanced stage . . . However, as your life isn't in immediate danger, you can't be compelled to come in here.'

'But—' Ed said again.

'I'm sorry, Mrs Casey,' Varina said. 'I cannot help you if you don't see the need yourself.'

Out in the corridor, ecstatic that she'd dodged a bullet, Cara whispered happily, 'It'll be okay, honey, I promise.'

Ed regarded her coldly.

'I mean it. Everything is going to be different. I'm glad the seizure happened, well, not glad for upsetting you, but finally I feel free of the food.'

*

Ed saw the traffic light up ahead change to amber and he floored the pedal. By the time he roared the car through, the light had been red for at least two seconds. Irate beeps sounded. *Fuck them.*

'Honey,' Cara said, with soft alarm.

More bullshit up ahead, some fool in the wrong lane, trying to turn right, holding up the whole road. 'Fucking *move*.'

'Ed!'

He ignored her. In his entire life, he'd never been as angry as he was now. Not just with her but with himself. He'd been complicit: throwing out all the chocolate in the house; holding some back for the inevitable emergency; worst of all, for not asking her about the chocolate he'd found that time in the unused bathroom cupboard.

He *really* should have said something when he'd found the empty ice-cream carton in her washbag.

Why hadn't he?

Because she'd have lied.

Lied. To him. Cara, his best friend, his wife. If soul-mates existed, he could have been persuaded to believe that that was what they were.

She had, in fact, already lied to him, by hiding her cravings, her behaviour, her shame and her fear. Perhaps he'd been waiting for things to become so serious that they were undeniable. Which said precisely *what* about him? That he was a coward. Because she could have died last night. She'd become a danger to herself and she still wouldn't admit she had a problem.

Plenty of frustrated rage was reserved for the admissions officer at St David's. Cara was obviously unwell, sick, whatever the correct word was. It was the job of the medical profession to help people like her and they hadn't.

'Should we swing by Mum's and pick up the kiddos and Baxter?' Cara asked.

'No.' If the kids were with them, they'd have to park this. It was too serious to sideline.

'It would be great to have the weekend together, just the four of us.'

'A normal weekend? Where we pretend you didn't have a seizure last night?'

'Hey! Don't yell at me.'

He took a breath and tried to calm his frantic heart. 'Cara, think about this. Last night you. Had. A. Seizure.'

'A "mild" one.'

'You could have died. The boys could be motherless right now. I could be without you. That could still happen.'

'I won't die. I've stopped.'

'You've been offered help. There's a lifeline for you to get better. Cara, please take it.'

'I don't need it.'

'What do you want to do about dinner?' Ed came into their bedroom, where she was scrolling through Facebook.

They were alone in the house. On any other evening, they'd have loved this unexpected freedom, but tonight they were barely speaking.

Ed had never yelled at her before today. In the last thirteen years, she'd seen him angry a literal handful of times and never with her.

'Dinner?' he repeated.

'Oh? I'm allowed a dinner? I thought I had an eating disorder.'

'You have to eat. We could get a Deliveroo?'

'Should a person with an eating disorder be getting a takeaway? Anyway, how could I enjoy it with you watching me eat?'

'How about afterwards you drive down to the garage, buy ten bars of chocolate, eat them in secret then make yourself puke?' he asked, in a hot blurt of rage.

It shocked her into silence.

'I shouldn't have said that,' he said. 'I'm scared. I've been reading about bulimia.'

'Where? Dr Google? You should know better than to believe that stuff.'

'The leaflet Dr Colgan gave me last night says the same things.' He produced it and pressed it on her. 'Can you take a look?'

Irritably, she scanned it.

Secrecy. Escalating behaviour. Lifelong problem. Body dissatisfaction. Severe self-criticism. Eating very large amounts of food, often in an out-of-control way, in a short space of time. Avoiding social activities which involve food. Thinking about food all the time. Abusing laxatives. Over-exercising. A constant sore throat . . .

'I don't abuse laxatives or over-exercise.'

'But you do some of the other stuff.'

She read from the leaflet. 'Avoiding social activities which involve food? I don't think so, Ed.'

'You might not avoid them, but you hate them.'

'So why make me do them? It's your family. My family is different. None of my real friends put me through that sort of misery.'

'I'm sorry—'

'Good. Moving on.' She took a breath and strove to sound reasonable. 'Ed, please, sweetie. Can we forget this happened? It'll never happen again.'

'No.'

This surprised her. 'What's up? You just want to get your own way?'

'It's because I'm worried.'

Abruptly, she said, 'I don't want any dinner. I don't want anything.'

'You're absolutely sure? Well . . . Okay.'

Forty minutes later the doorbell rang. Then came the sounds of Ed talking to a person at the door. Someone called *Thanks*, the front door slammed, then a motorbike started up outside.

He hadn't . . . ?

She thumped down the stairs and into the kitchen. He *had*. The utter bastard had got an Indian delivered just for himself. 'Why didn't you get me something?'

'You said you didn't want any.'

She thumped around the kitchen and made herself a bowl of muesli.

To punish him, she slept in Vinnie's bed.

When she woke on Sunday morning, everything that had happened seemed far less dramatic. Clearly, she'd been really stressed at work and finding it hard to adjust to Ed being away Monday to Friday. Whatever had happened to her in that mad hotel—and it probably hadn't been an actual seizure—was the result of stress. Everyone had overreacted because they were drunk.

She and Ed were not falling apart. Everything just needed to be made normal again.

In their bedroom Ed was asleep. Even in slumber he looked worried.

'Ed?'

He jumped awake, looked frightened, then his face softened into a smile. 'Honey.'

'We should talk.'

'Okay. Right.' He rubbed his eyes.

'I'm afraid, Ed. I don't want to have a label. I don't want to have an "eating disorder".'

'But you *have* a label, you *have* an eating disorder.'

She hadn't been expecting such a spirited comeback. 'I can think myself better. I don't need all this hospital stuff.'

'You do need it.'

Frustration rose. In the past, Ed's willingness to Follow the Instructions had seemed like a cute personality trait. But now he simply seemed wilfully stubborn.

'Seriously, Cara, if you won't get help, I can't stay.'

Incredulously she asked, 'Are you . . . *threatening* me?'

'I guess I am.'

He *couldn't* be serious.

On the pillow beside his head, his phone vibrated. 'I've got to take this.'

Startled, she listened. What could be so important?

'Scott,' Ed said. 'Thanks for calling back.' He listened to whatever this Scott said. 'You can? That's great, man . . . Mostly Louth. I'll email you the brief.' He listened some more. 'For a week anyway. Maybe longer. We can touch base on Friday. I'll have a better idea then . . . Yeah? Great. Thanks, I owe you.'

He hung up, and Cara said, 'What the hell, Ed? Did you just get someone to cover your work?'

'A freelancer. Yep.'

'*Why?* You're staying here to spy on me? Ed, don't be such a—a prick.' She'd never before spoken to him in that way. 'Tomorrow I'm going to work as normal.'

'You need to go into hospital.'

'You just want a skinny wife who doesn't give you any trouble.'

'Why would you say that?' He sounded distraught. 'When have I ever . . . ? Cara, I love you. And you're unhappy. I wish you were happier. Not for me. For you.'

She didn't know how it had happened, but they were on opposite sides of an unsolvable problem.

'Fuck you.' She clambered off the bed. 'Just fuck you, Ed.'

All morning they avoided each other. She ironed her uniforms and the kids' clothes but picked out everything of Ed's and left it, wrinkled, in the basket.

Had Ed gone actually insane? It was impossible to understand why he was making such a thing of this. But his mind worked in straight lines. Everything was black or white: there was no room for nuance.

Is this the hill that we die on? she wondered. Then, *This can't actually be happening.* Hanging her crisply ironed shirts in the wardrobe, she was infused with sudden happiness. In far less than a second, a scenario played out like a movie: tomorrow morning leaving for work fifteen minutes early, stopping off at Tesco in Baggot Street, scooting round the aisles, picking up her favourites, sitting on 'her' bench, visiting 'her' bathroom, then showing up, bright and breezy, to start work at 10 a.m.

It was astonishing—after Friday night, her decision had been final: there would be no more of that behaviour. But the thought had popped back into her head, *ambushed* her, despite her iron resolve. This was Ed's fault. All his talk of eating disorders had half convinced her that she had one. Hand on heart, she had to admit that she could no longer be a hundred per cent certain that she wouldn't buy chocolate tomorrow. How utterly mortifying would it be to pass out, have a seizure, whatever it was, at work? They'd have to sack her. And what were her chances of getting a good reference?

For several minutes, she remained in the bedroom, trying to recapture the rigid resolve of earlier that morning, but it remained out of reach. No matter which way she thought about it, the desire to overeat wouldn't go away.

'Ed?' she yelled down the stairs. 'Ed.'

'Yes?'

In tears of frustrated fury, she said to him, 'Tell me about the day-patient option.'

'. . . Right.' He took a few moments to compose himself. 'Four weeks, Monday to Friday, ten a.m. to four p.m. You'll have one-on-one every day with a counsellor, go to lectures and be under the care of a dietician. You'd get an eating plan. They'd prefer if you were residential so they could monitor your food. But this is better than nothing.'

'Starting when?'

'Tomorrow.'

'Okay. But only because you've forced me. You'd better ring Henry and break the happy news.'

'You ring him. You have to take responsibility for this,' he said.

Despair surged but she picked up her phone and stared at Henry's number. This was so difficult. Then, taking a nervy breath, she hit call.

Sixty-Three

Fifty years of age today. A half-century, surely old enough for all of her struggles and worries to be long behind her? So where was her lovely life? Her happy marriage? Her feelings of contentment? Why was she in bed, alone, the curtains drawn, with no intention of getting up?

After poor Cara had been ferried off in the ambulance on Friday night, Jessie had hoped they could knock the whole sorry shambles on the head and go home early. But Rionna and Kaz were insistent that, no, the murder-mystery weekend could be salvaged. They'd thought they were helping: it just meant that Jessie's agony was prolonged by another thirty-six hours of 'great fun'.

During the excruciatingly long hours of Saturday and Sunday, she didn't address a single word to Johnny. Because she was having such 'fantastic craic' with the others, she reckoned nobody had noticed.

That mattered: she had her pride.

Johnny worried about money, she *knew* that. But it was her fiftieth birthday: that was surely a big deal.

It was disgraceful to be that upset about spending a weekend in a crappy hotel. First World problem if ever she'd heard of one. But this wasn't simply a tantrum. Since forever, Johnny and the kids had behaved as if she was a bit of a tyrant: she gave orders and, after much complaining, they complied.

Until now she'd always felt it was affectionate. Not any more. Now she was wondering if they despised her for real.

It didn't take much to pitch her back into her younger self, always hovering on the outside, wondering if everyone was laughing at her.

Johnny had said some very weird things during that horrific weekend of his parents' wedding anniversary: he'd talked about feeling hollow and worthless. She'd been concerned, but when the Hagen Klein drama had blown up, she hadn't had time to address it. With the benefit of hindsight, it had sounded like the beginnings of a confession.

Over the past four days, she'd been visiting and revisiting the possibility that he was seeing someone else. He really could be and the idea was *horrible.*

She should ask him. But maybe she didn't need to: maybe his behaviour was proof enough.

As soon as they'd got home from Gulban Manor, she'd chucked his razor and toothbrush out of their bathroom and onto the landing. Let him figure out that that meant he should sleep elsewhere.

When Monday morning had rolled around, she drove herself to the office, leaving him to make his own way. The entire day had passed without her speaking to him. Several couriers showed up, bearing orchids or bottles of wine from various business acquaintances. In other circumstances, she'd have loved the whole circus.

Now it was Tuesday morning, her fiftieth birthday, and she couldn't face going to work. This had literally never happened before. Even after Rory had died, she'd shown up every day unless there was an emergency with the kids.

'Mum, are you awake?' Dilly stuck her face up close to Jessie's, then darted off the bed. 'Mum's awake!' she shouted down the stairs.

Oh, here we go.

In they came, her five children, singing 'Happy Birthday', their faces radiant in the light of a cake bearing fifty candles. Bringing up the rear was Raccoon Man, Johnny. The whole scene could have been lifted from a movie about a happy family.

This was Johnny's transparently pathetic attempt to fix things. He'd probably had to bribe the kids to be nice, because, let's be honest here, none of *them* gave a shite about her either.

Except Dilly.

And Saoirse.

And maybe Ferdia.

'Happy birthday, Mum! Blow out the candles.'

As she did, a tear escaped. Trying to be discreet, she wiped it with her knuckle.

Johnny made some gesture to Bridey and she stepped forward. 'Happy fiftieth birthday, Mum. Here's my gift.'

'Thanks, bunny.' She tried to make a big deal of the unwrapping but more tears were threatening.

'Perfume!' Bridey declared, as Jessie opened the box.

Johnny had obviously bought this. Probably on an emergency department-store dash yesterday lunchtime. If he took any interest in her, he'd know that she never wore perfume. It just wasn't her thing. And she was disproportionately upset that Bridey hadn't picked out the present herself. Last year, Bridey had bought her a whistle—'In case of emergency.' *Thought* had gone into that.

She braced herself for the next present, Dilly's this time. Same wrapping paper as Bridey's. Her money was on red satin knickers in the wrong size. And a matching bra from TJ, no doubt.

'Mum, are you *crying*?' Dilly asked, appalled.

'No, bunny. No, I'm just . . .'

'Guys!' Ferdia sounded super-cheery. 'You know what? Let's leave Mum to enjoy her birthday rest. We'll finish this later.'

Confused, everyone except Johnny trooped from the room.

'Jessie. I'm so—'

'I know. You're sorry.'

'I have a gift for you.' He proffered a fancily wrapped box.

She knew about the Fendi bag, like of *course* she did, Mary-Laine's instructions to Johnny had come directly from Jessie. 'I don't want it.'

He swallowed. 'I don't blame you for being angry.'

'I'm not angry. I'm *hurt*.' She burst into a storm of noisy tears. 'No, get away, I don't want your smelly, selfish hands on me.' Her face was drenched from crying. 'It's not just the weekend. What was going on last month in Mayo? What were you trying to tell me?'

'N-nothing.'

'Johnny. Look. I can't stop thinking terrible things. Are you . . . Is something going on? Have you met someone else?'

'No. I swear.'

'So what's up with you?'

'I was trying to save money. I was worried, but I picked the wrong thing to worry about.'

'I work hard, Johnny. Easily as hard as you. But you all think I'm just some bossy gobshite who pays for everything. Nobody cares about me.'

'It's not true.'

'It *is*. Look at how you all treat me. That insane fucking weekend in that insane fucking place! That's what you thought I deserved?'

'I didn't know it would be as mad as it was—'

'You bought all those shit presents from the kids? *They* didn't bother.'

'Ferdia and Saoirse bought theirs.'

'Other mothers get homemade presents. Papier-mâché things that *thought* and *love* have gone into. Instead my children's *dad* has to buy generic "pissed-off wife" presents on a department-store trolley dash.'

'Is there any way I can salvage this? I'll do anything.'

'*You*'re asking *me* to help you fix your fuck-up with me? That says it all. Fuck off, Johnny. Just fuck off. I'm going back to sleep.'

For ages, he hovered.

Curled into a sad, angry ball, she couldn't see him but his nervy breathing was audible. After a while the sound stopped so she concluded he'd left.

Though she craved oblivion, it was impossible to sleep.

Instead, to self-soothe, she went through the permutations of leaving him.

He could live in his Airbnb flat in the city and she'd stay here in the house with the kids. Although right now she didn't want *them* either.

Maybe *she* could live in the flat. With the dogs. Johnny could stay here with the children. That would fucking show him.

Their finances would have to be disentangled, of course. PiG had only two shareholders—herself and Johnny: pulling those separate strands apart might be messy.

But she didn't want to fight over money. For all his faults, Johnny had given a lot to the company and he deserved his stake.

She would *shame* him with her magnanimity. Although continuing to work together in the same space could pose a problem.

What about his brothers and their families? Would they remain close?

She'd like to. With Cara and Nell anyway. And Ed, she liked Ed. Liam, she could take or leave.

Yes, maintaining those relationships would require some manoeuvring, but something would be sorted. Especially because she was going to be irritatingly mature about the whole business.

She noticed that her mood had shifted—planning to leave him was cheering stuff.

What was most heartening was imagining how sorry he'd be that he hadn't treated her better.

They'd *all* be sorry.

Downstairs, Johnny lurked in an agony of uncertainty. Going to work would compound Jessie's conviction that none of them cared. Sitting on the stairs, ear cocked for any movement from above, he rang the florist with whom he'd placed a last-minute order yesterday and begged them to intercept the driver so that the ginormous bouquet could be delivered here instead of the office. Then he rang the expensive restaurant and cancelled the lunch reservation he'd pleaded for yesterday. Objectively speaking, he must have felt this awful at some other point in his life, but he couldn't remember when.

Spurts of panic kept erupting in his stomach—what if she never forgave him? Worse than the fear, though, was witnessing her pain—pain that he'd caused. Soppiness had never been their thing. Instead they demonstrated their love by making fun of each other. They were both resilient but she had always seemed almost un-hurtable—and that had fooled him into complacency.

The long and short was that this was a big, big birthday. Jessie had survived so much. She supported them all. She *deserved* a song and dance.

Tightening their belts was a commendable objective but Jessie's fiftieth birthday was the wrong time to launch it.

He couldn't remember them ever before having a bust-up like this. Countless times when they were tired and had too much on, they'd snapped at each other, even had a bit of a rant, but it had been out of short-lived frustration rather than a deep wound.

When the flowers arrived at the house, he was both grateful and terrified to have a pretext to pester her. He climbed the stairs and knocked lightly on the door.

She lay on her back, her eyes open.

'Hi,' he said. 'How are you now?'

'Thinking about leaving you.'

He had to press his hand against the wall. 'Jessie. Please don't. Let me make this up to you.'

'How d'you think you'd get on without me? You'd be grand, wouldn't you?'

'I wouldn't.' He swallowed hard. 'Jessie, I'd be lost. I'd be heartbroken.'

'You'd miss me bossing you around, running your life, but that's all.'

'Seriously, Jess, that's the last—'

'What's going on, Johnny? You were upset and weird in Mayo. What was up with you?'

'. . . Just Dad and that. And I felt sad and old.'

'Why?'

'Maybe because I am. Old anyway.'

'Look, are you having an affair?'

This was the moment, the chance . . . 'No.'

'Affair' was the wrong word.

'Then what's going on? Is it my fault?'

'Nothing's going on.'

'Johnny, if you want us to stay together, you'd better tell me what's up with you.'

'Okay.' A breath. 'I'm worried about money. We spend so much, and after the Hagen Klein thing—yeah, I know you rescued it, but it could have gone so badly wrong. I think Mason and Rionna are right about the website.'

'Oh.' Her voice was, once more, cold.

'You asked.'

'If I'm emasculating you, you can work for someone else.'

'Who's talking about you emasculating me? Oh, Jess! You promised not to read the comments.'

'Well, I did! I do! So off you go, get another job, I don't care.'

'I don't want another job. I love you, but I'm very bad at showing it. I promise you I'll do a lot better. I'll just stick these flowers in a vase.'

'I can think of somewhere else you can stick them.'

Sixty-Four

'Mum?' Someone was knocking on the bedroom door.

Dozily, Jessie came to. It was gone six o'clock, she must have fallen asleep.

'Mum?' It was Ferdia. He stepped around the door. 'Can I come in?'

'You're already in,' she said. 'Have you my present?'

He seemed startled but handed over a flat, A4-sized parcel: a framed photo of Ferdia and Johnny, their arms around each other, looking like they were the best of friends. 'I'm sorry I've made it so hard, Mum. With Johnny, I mean. He's a good guy, he always was. My behaviour has been heinous.'

'A day late and a dollar short, Ferd. I'm leaving him.'

'Whatnow? Mum . . . Are you serious?'

After a long pause she said, 'Probably not. But thinking about it is making me feel nice.'

'Do we not grow out of that stuff?'

'Doesn't look like it.'

They both laughed.

'Will you come down for dinner?' he asked. 'They're all mortified, the girls. And Johnny, of course,' he added.

'Good enough for them.' But what the hell? She'd got bored holding the grudge.

In the kitchen, at the table, everyone looked sheepish.

'We're crap children,' TJ said.

'We don't really get enough pocket money to buy you something good.' This from Bridey.

'But we love you, Mum,' Dilly said. 'I think you're aces.'

'And I actually bought you something myself.' Saoirse slid a small parcel across the table. 'It's a dream-catcher!'

'Thank you, Saoirsh. Bunnies, it's all grand,' Jessie said. 'I'm sorry I cried earlier.'

'Are you going through the change?' Bridey asked.

'The what?' TJ said.

'It happens to ladies of Mum's age. They dry up and act weird with their loved ones.'

'Dry *up*?' TJ looked confused.

'I am *not* going through the change.' Well, maybe she was. 'I was upset because I felt no one loved me.'

'*What* dries up?'

'Their vagina.'

'Bunnies, not *now*. If you sing "Happy Birthday" again, I'll blow out the candles.'

'That's bad luck!' Dilly seemed spooked. 'Doing it twice.'

'No, it isn't!'

'Isn't it? Oh, grand, so!'

After dinner and the cake, the kids peeled away until only Johnny and Jessie were left at the table.

'I really am sorry,' Johnny repeated. 'I'll never let anything like that happen again.'

'I'm sorry too. I was being a diva. I shouldn't have wanted to go to the expensive hotel in the first place. Who do I think I am? But look. Can I apologize for something else? At your parents' anniversary shit-show, I knew we needed some alone time. Then the Hagen Klein thing blew up. I was firefighting and, yeah, eye off the ball. I'm sorry.'

'I accept your apology.' His smile was fake-grave.

'You still want me to change the business to the website.'

'Well, to think about it . . .'

'It would be so much work. And chaos. We'd have to buy storage facilities, take on packers and couriers, new staff . . . It would cost tons of money. Which we haven't got.'

'That's what banks are for.'

Jessie was afraid of banks. Banks had made her shut down eight of her stores during the crash. Banks wouldn't loan money without taking a good old rummage in the Caseys' personal finances. Banks had the power to withdraw their generous overdraft at a moment's notice. 'They'd want a guarantee and the only thing we really have is the house. If everything goes tits up, we'd have no business . . . and no house.'

'It won't go tits up.'

But it might. 'There are lots of websites, Johnny. What would make ours different?'

'The PiG name, the goodwill.'

He didn't get it. *Nobody* seemed to get it, except her. 'Goodwill counts for nothing on a website. It all comes down to pricing, and we wouldn't have the purchasing power that bigger companies have.'

'We can't stay as we are, though.'

But why not? They worked hard but they had a nice life. What was wrong with staying *exactly* as they were?

Seven Weeks Ago

LATE AUGUST

Tuscany

Sixty-Five

'Oh, my God.' Nell darted towards a low sideboard, its teal blue colour polished to a dull sheen. 'The workmanship!' She ran her fingertips along the shallow carving on the drawers. 'The detail.' She admired the pattern-work of scrolls, so faded they were barely visible. 'That's definitely not Italian Ikea.'

'I think Nell likes the villa,' Ed said, carrying a suitcase up the stairs.

'Nell *loves* the villa,' Nell exclaimed.

After the shock-to-the-system early-morning flight, the car-hire hell and the difficulty of satnavving narky Liam through the snarl of Florentine traffic, Nell's day had dramatically improved as soon as they emerged into the Tuscan countryside. Every five seconds there was something new and beautiful to exclaim about: the sun-baked slopes, the sandstone fortifications perched on a steep hill, the green-and-beige drills of grapes. 'Like, this is totally amazing!'

In the back seat of the car, Saoirse and her new best friend Robyn were being world-weary and unimpressed.

'She's cute,' Robyn dead-panned.

'How come you've never been to Italy before?' Saoirse asked Nell.

'Never got the chance.'

As they turned off the road towards the villa, Nell was newly astonished at the size of the estate.

'Seven acres,' Saoirse said. 'Those are olive trees, grape vines there. That's the vegetable garden.'

'Totally wow.' This from Robyn.

Abruptly Saoirse shut up.

Surrounded by cypress trees, which looked like moss-covered stalagmites, the villa appeared: a solid, handsome house, with sloping roofs of terracotta tiles and distempered walls of pale yellow. Shutters painted ivy-green bracketed each deep-set window and the heavy front door stood invitingly open. 'It's perfect.' Nell could barely breathe. 'Like an eighteenth-century painting.'

'Don't think they had satellite dishes in the eighteenth century,' Liam muttered.

Up the stone steps, Nell passed from blazing sunshine into a cool, dim, tiled hallway and from there into a huge sitting room. Light poured in through six statement windows.

Everything was perfect. On one wall, a fitted wooden bookcase, painted a gorgeous dusty sage, reached the ceiling. The other three walls were distempered in a warm, almond, rustic finish. Two giant L-shaped linen sofas shared space with sturdy little armchairs in a colour Nell decided to call celery. At seemingly random points through the room there were low tables, made from gently distressed oak or finished with a tile mosaic. Proportions, balance, colour: this was a room so right that it thrilled her.

'Nell!' Jessie called. 'What was the rush? Are you okay?'

'We saw you running in!' Dilly was hot on her heels. 'Do you need the loo?'

'I'm fine, sweetie. But, Jessie, this place is amazing! I can't even—I mean, thank you for inviting me.'

'You're more than welcome.' Jessie lit up with pleasure.

'Mum.' Bridey was inside and heading for the stairs. 'I don't want to share with Dilly.'

'Charming,' Dilly said.

'How old is it?' Nell asked Jessie. 'The house?'

'Two hundred and fifty years, something like that.' Then, 'NO!' She raised her hand to Bridey. 'No! It's agreed, you're sharing with her and that's that.'

'Nell,' Liam called, 'am I to bring in our stuff all by myself?'

More and more Caseys were gathering in the hall, dragging bags, bumping against the people ahead of them.

'Liam, let her be!' Jessie said. 'She's in raptures about the house.'

'Raptures!' Dilly cried.

'Saoirse and Robyn, you're over in the barn.' Jessie shooed them away.

'The barn?' they heard Robyn say. '*Seriously?*'

'It's super-cosy.' Saoirse sounded anxious.

'Lil bitch,' Jessie whispered to Nell. 'The barn is the best place. C'mon.' She took Nell by the arm. 'Come and see the kitchen.'

'I'm not Bridey's biggest fan either.' Dilly chatted away to herself. 'But *I* didn't tell *her*.'

'*Regardez*,' Jessie breathed.

The kitchen was a large, light, rectangular room. Dominating the centre was a giant slab of amber-veined marble, over which sheaves of lavender hung from a suspended pot-holder. Decoratively carved cupboards painted a creamy apricot opened noiselessly to reveal bread, pasta, breakfast cereals and condiments.

'Where did all the food come from?'

'And drink.' Jessie pointed out gallons of water, slabs of beer and boxes of wine. 'Pre-stock of groceries.'

It was another world, a rich people's one.

'It'll all be gone by tomorrow,' Jessie said. 'But it's handy not to have to head to the supermarket the minute you arrive.'

Three French windows opened onto a long dining table, which could probably seat twenty, under a pergola woven through with wisteria. Just past it lay a herb garden drenched in sunlight. Jessie smiled, as if she were gazing at a basket of puppies. 'Most days I think I've fallen out of love with cooking.'

'Do you?' Nell was surprised.

'Ah, yeah, you know yourself. Cooking for kids would kill anyone's joy. But this kitchen always rekindles the magic.'

'This sink!' Bridey had come in with Robyn. 'You should pay attention too, Nell. This sink is where you rinse off the dishes. See that giant hose. Use that. You must never prepare food in this sink.'

'Bridey, you're mean.' Dilly sounded like she'd rehearsed this. 'I'm not your biggest fan either, but I didn't want to hurt your feelings.'

'Jessie.' Johnny stuck his head around the door. 'I'm going down to Marcello before he starts work and get some practice in on my espresso drinking.'

She came to kiss him on the mouth. '*Bonne chance, mon brave*. Don't drink too many.' Then, 'Nell, would you like to see your bedroom?'

'Yes, *please*!'

Accompanied by Jessie, Dilly and now Bridey and TJ, Nell was led upstairs.

OMG, the bedroom! The walls and an arched ceiling were stippled a parchment colour. On the floor was wide-planked white oak. Two walls—*two*—had beautiful deep-set windows, which fastened with ornate silver hasps, giving views over the olive grove, then to the hills beyond. The furniture, once a pale blue, but now faded to near-white, was unadorned and impeccable. The bed had a simple fabric headboard, in a muted silvery-grey.

'Oh, wow.' Nell ran her hand along the bed linen. 'Jessie, I love it. It's luxurious but not a bit nouvy.'

'Nouvy?' Jessie asked. 'Short for "nouveau riche"? Bougie, nouvy Jessie!'

'No, I didn't say—'

'Lookit, if the cap fits!'

The more Nell spotted, the more impressed she was. Everything worked. The plug sockets were in exactly the right places. You didn't need a degree in advanced mathematics to figure out the lighting.

But when she saw the attached bathroom, a vision in white and cobalt blue marble, her face changed.

'Feeling guilty?' Jessie asked.

'No.' Then, 'Ah, sorry.'

'Well, this is the best bit. I've been dying to tell you! Little story: we came here five years ago, booked through an agent and, yeah, it wasn't cheap. First three nights we went to the same restaurant in the village, run by Loretta and Marcello. We hit it off, stayed late, having the chats, free limoncello, the usual. I invited them to us on their free night, said I'd cook something Irish. I was drunk, like, you know how it is. Bougie. And nouvy, obviously. No, Nell, I love that word! So they came, we had a great night. I mean, they're lovely people, it's not hard. Turns out that Marcello's brother owns this house. Giacomo's his name. Scary. Different kettle of kippers from Marcello. He's all a bit "Do I amooze you?" But, scary or not, he must have liked us because he said to book direct with him if we ever wanted to come back. Now we get it for a third of the price we paid that first year. Does that make you feel any better?'

'Giacomo fancies Mum,' Dilly said. 'Daddy says.'

'He always calls around when Dad is out.' This from TJ. 'With grappa. He tries to get her liquored up.'

Bridey spoke: 'Dad says that if Mum has intercourse with Giacomo, we'd get the house for free. And he didn't say "intercourse", he said "sex", which is hardly appropriate for us children to hear.'

'Shush now,' Jessie said. 'Daddy's just joking.'

Bridey sighed. 'Daddy would really want to sort out his sense of humour.'

Sixty-Six

'Ferdia?' He heard Jessie's voice outside. 'Are you in here? I just brought Nell to see—'

Ferdia opened his door. Jessie, Nell and Dilly stood outside in the blazing sunshine.

'Oh, bunny, sorry!' Jessie took a step back. 'Sorry. Just, I'm showing Nell around. I thought you'd be at the pool.'

'Come in, you're grand.'

'No, no.' Nell was reluctant. 'We'll come back some other time.'

'It'd be worse to have you poking around if I wasn't here.' He'd been aiming for jokey but instead he sounded narky. 'Seriously, come in.' He made himself smile. 'Welcome to the Old Granary.'

Cautiously they entered.

Nell's face was full of wonder. 'The low ceiling, the exposed beams, the stone floors, two storeys,' she marvelled. 'Very rustic. Hey!' She'd suddenly noticed something. 'Is Barty not here?'

Shit. How many times would he have to answer this? 'Yeah, he didn't come. Busy. You know.'

'I only realized now.' She laughed at herself. 'Shows how awake I was at the airport. That's too bad, Barty's the craic.'

You think?

'So poor Ferdia has no one to play with,' Jessie said.

'What about Seppe and Lorenzo? I can play with them.' Then, to Nell, 'Marcello's sons.'

She nodded, not interested, still all about the décor. 'Look at this beautiful stone archway!'

He'd never noticed it before and this was his fourth visit. The archway opened to the shallow stone steps, leading to his upstairs bedroom.

'Can we . . . ?'

'Work away.'

Tap-tapping up the steps, they crowded into the small, light bedroom.

'Best Wi-Fi in the whole of Santa Laura,' he said.

In the shade of the town square, Johnny was drinking espresso with Marcello. He didn't like espresso and, this late in the day, it made him feel slightly sick.

'You like something else?' Marcello urged.

'Nah. I'm practising. For when I run away and come to live here. The other men won't let me sit with them if I'm drinking a caramel frappuccino.'

'You are a big eejit.' Jessie had taught him that word.

'I'll learn to play draughts. I'll sit under the arches in the company of other men and life will be peaceful.'

'You misunderstand,' Marcello said. 'We work like dogs for four months to earn money for the other eight months of the year.'

'But you live in this beautiful place, you can walk to work and you don't have to go to trade fairs in Frankfurt.'

'We should exchange lives for a time.'

'The stress would kill you.'

'My life is not so easy. Another drink? Please, my friend, have something different.'

'No. Another espresso. I've to build up my endurance.'

'Ferdia,' Saoirse called. 'We're ready.'

'. . . Er. Wow.' It was barely gone 6 p.m. but Saoirse and Robyn were dressed for a nightclub: short shimmery dresses, spindly-heeled sandals and stripes of shiny stuff on their faces.

'Contouring,' Saoirse informed him.

'Will you be okay in those shoes?' he asked Robyn. 'Ten-minute walk uphill to the town and cobbled streets when we get there.'

'I was born in high heels.'

Maybe so, but by the time they arrived in Il Gatto Ubriaco, he had a girl leaning on each arm.

Marcello's kids, Seppe, Lorenzo and Valentina, were at a table overlooking the sun-baked plain below. There were warm hugs and double kisses. Briefly Ferdia forgot about Barty. 'What's everyone drinking?'

'Aperol Spritz.' Valentina indicated the orange drink in front of her.

'2014 called. It wants its statement drink back.' Robyn gave Ferdia a malicious smile.

He slid his eyes away, embarrassed. 'So, six Aperol Spritzes,' he said, and went to the bar.

It was *passeggiata*. Family groups, some of just two or three people, and others much bigger, wandered past the bar. They were mostly Italian, with only the occasional cluster of tourists.

Jessie should have been Italian, Ferdia thought. They were all about family. Hey! There went Cara, Ed, Vinnie and Tom. Ferdia watched Cara. She was holding hands with Tom and Ed and she looked okay, normal. But she'd always looked normal and it had turned out that she had bulimia. It was weird how they were all acting like she hadn't had a seizure and scared them sideways. Was it hard for her here, surrounded by so much great food? Or was she cured now?

'Orders from on high,' Bridey announced. 'We have a reservation at Loretta's restaurant for our dinner. We leave at seven fifteen sharp. Don't be late.'

Nell had a shower, washed her hair, dried it and put on a red cotton dress. Her electronic toothbrush was buzzing its way around her mouth when she heard Liam coming up the stairs. She tensed without knowing why. The toothbrush had been a gift from Liam, given at a time when everything he'd said or done was bundled up in his love for her. Then, it hadn't seemed like an insultingly practical thing to receive: it had been just one more sign of his devotion. The correct way to use it, he had informed her, was to spend thirty seconds on each quadrant of her mouth—instead of roaming randomly like she was doing now.

'Hi. Just changing my shirt.'

She moved into the bathroom, out of his way. It was only a small thing, a very small thing, but she wanted to brush her teeth the way she wanted to brush her teeth.

'. . . a start-up grant from the government.' Seppe was telling Ferdia about the small e-commerce company he'd just started. 'They would like for Arezzo to become a hub for gold—'

'Yawn,' Robyn said loudly.

Ferdia made an apologetic face at Seppe, and Seppe smiled to show he understood.

Seppe had just finished university, and while his career path wasn't what Ferdia was aiming for personally, he was heartened that Seppe saw a future for himself. It was hard to earn a living here in rural Tuscany, far harder than in Ireland.

'What about you?' Valentina asked Ferdia. 'You have one more year in college? And then what?'

'Yeah, well—' He was keen to discuss his recent venture, but Robyn cut in, 'Blah de blah de blah. When are we going to have some fun?'

Saoirse's phone beeped. 'It's Mum. We're late for dinner.'

'We'd better go. Catch up with you later?'

Ferdia, Saoirse and Robyn hurried through the narrow, brick-paved streets, under sandstone archways and past cave-like grocery stores. Dinner was in Loretta and Marcello's place, on the other side of the small town. They passed an old-fashioned apothecary, then a shiny little jewellery shop, its wares aimed firmly at tourists.

'Ohmygod!' Robyn pointed at glass-beaded bracelets. 'They're the cutest! I wanna try.'

'We're late,' Ferdia said. 'The bracelets will still be here tomorrow.'

'I wanna look at them now.'

'Okay. Work away. Saoirse, you know how to get to Loretta's. See you there.'

'You're not waiting with us?' Robyn pouted.

'I don't want to be late.' He strode on.

'What an utter bastard,' Robyn said loudly.

'". . . I fought the LAAAAAAWWWW . . ."' Johnny sang. 'Ha-ha-ha! I sound like an opera singer.'

'A baritone,' Liam said. 'Marcello, are they the deep-voice ones?'

'*Sì*.' Marcello rolled his eyes. '*Cafone*.'

Cheeky Italian prick. *Cafone* meant something like 'ignorant peasant'.

'". . . And the LAAAAAAAAWWWW won!"' Johnny sang on. 'Listen to the reverb on that!'

It was late on Saturday night and they were playing pool in the basement, which had freakishly echoey acoustics.

Liam took a swig from his beer bottle, hit his chest and belched.

'" 'Cause girls like YOOOOOUUU,"' Ferdia cut in.

'"Run around with BOYS like me,"' Seppe and Lorenzo chorused, and the three of them fell around the place laughing.

Call him paranoid, but Liam suspected they were laughing at him. He didn't know what, but there was some subtext here. He was drunk enough and feeling reckless enough to—

Ed stepped in front of him. 'All right?'

Taken by surprise, he said, 'Ah. Yeah.'

'You sure?' Now Johnny had blocked him in.

'I'm grand.'

'Right!' Johnny moved off, then bellowed, '"I FOUGHT THE LAAAAAW."'

Nell woke into darkness, her heart pounding. *Where am I?* She was in bed but not at home. Slightly panicked, she stretched out a leg and discovered she was alone. Where was Liam?

Pawing around, she hit a switch, and suddenly she could see. She was in the beautiful room in the beautiful house in Italy.

There was her phone. It was only 1.23 a.m.—Liam was probably still playing pool.

Then she remembered her dream—it was what had woken her.

God, it had been horrible. In it, she and Liam didn't love each other any more. They'd made an abnormally calm decision to break up.

'We got carried away,' he'd said. 'Getting married, that was mad stuff. You'll have to move out.'

'That's grand. I never liked the flat anyway.'

It had been awful—and it didn't make sense. She loved Liam. *And* she loved the flat. She really needed him to hold her and hug away this shaky fear, but she couldn't go sneaking around the house at this hour of the night, trying to find him. He'd be embarrassed. And so would she.

Would it be okay to send a text?

Baby I had a bad dream. Can you come to bed? I love you xxx

Knowing she'd see him soon dispersed the last few smoky threads of the nightmare.

She waited and waited, until after a long time she felt sleepy again and decided it was safe to go back to sleep.

Sixty-Seven

'What about Mum?' a voice whispered.

'Let her sleep.' Another voice—Ed's.

Cara opened her eyes. Italy. Tuscany. In the world's most comfortable bed, in the world's most perfect bedroom, in the world's most beautiful house. Ed, Vinnie and Tom were up and dressed and peering down at her.

'Hi, Mum,' Tom whispered. 'It's ten past eight. But that's Italian time. It's only ten past seven in Ireland. We're going to pick fruit for breakfast.'

'I'll come.' Cara was suddenly energized. Throwing on a loose dress, she slid her feet into sandals and followed them down the stairs.

Outside it was still cool, and dew sparkled on the leaves. The sun, a long way from its height, cast a pale yellow light. Carrying their wicker trugs, they made their way to the orderly rows of ridges and trees, where colourful butterflies swooped and fluttered.

'What fruit is here?' Tom asked.

'Cherries,' Ed said. 'Peaches, probably. Tomatoes.'

'Tomato isn't a fruit.' Vinnie was always ready with the scorn.

'Actually, it is,' Ed began.

'*Nooooo*, one of Dad's explanations!'

But everyone laughed.

Someone looking on, Cara realized, would think she lived a perfect life.

To be fair, it was all here—the beautiful setting, the good man, the two beloved children, enough food, enough love.

It was just that she couldn't feel it properly.

Since this whole drama had kicked off, it was as if the real Cara wasn't entirely aligned with reality. Her outline kept slipping, like a wonky contact lens that wouldn't sit on the iris. When other people were around, she could do the back-and-forth talk, but lately it felt like muscle memory, rather than genuine engagement. Now and again both her selves overlapped perfectly, clicked into place, and suddenly she was there, in the moment. Intense feelings would surge through her, both good and not-so-good, then her outline would detach again.

She was living her life a short distance from herself.

And what had this to do with eating too much and making herself sick? If what her counsellor Peggy said was true, she'd been doing that to change her mood. Now she had no way to alter her feelings, and she had to make sense of them again.

But, as she kept telling herself, it was early days. It would be a mistake to try to understand everything now. She should just keep treading water, keep living, until things became clearer.

'I want to pick the cherries!' Tom ran towards a ladder under a tree.

'I'll get the peaches,' Vinnie said.

'I'll get tomatoes,' Cara said.

'They're not fruit!' Vinnie insisted.

She laughed. 'They'll do for lunch.'

While Ed instructed the boys on how to know if a fruit was ready to pick, Cara tried to pluck the tomatoes mindfully from their vine, feeling their firm weight in her hand. Something Peggy had said came back to her: 'The purpose of food is to feed your body. Nothing else.'

Unexpectedly she had one of those rare moments of alignment: these plants had come from the earth to keep her alive. Briefly, she knew her place in the cycle of life.

It happened again, when Tom and Vinnie displayed their baskets. The pale pinky-orange fuzz of the peaches, with their distinct, sweet smell, and the shiny purple of the cherries were beautiful.

Maybe everything would be okay.

Back at the house, the French windows were thrown open. Dilly and Nell scurried back and forth, carrying stacks of plates to the long table under the wisteria trellis. Jessie, in a floaty kaftan, was cooking something hot and spitty on the stove, Saoirse and Robyn blitzing smoothies. Johnny and TJ manned the coffee machine while Bridey was busybodying about and Ferdia decanting what looked like home-baked granola into a heavy ceramic bowl. The only person missing was Liam.

'Look at you, my little hunter-gatherers!' Jessie exclaimed, when she saw them. 'You're like an ad for wholesome living. Photo. Where's my phone?'

Examining the contents of the trugs, she lavished praise on Vinnie and Tom. 'You got great stuff. Look at these peaches.' To the room she called, 'I could do fried peaches, with honey. Have we honey? Course we've honey! And pistachios?'

'Bougie!' Bridey yelled.

'I'm with Bridey,' Johnny said. 'Settle the head.'

'I just want Nutella,' Vinnie said. 'I could easily eat that giant jar and not even feel sick.'

Nervous laughter rose and suddenly no one was looking Cara's way. They must be thinking Vinnie had inherited whatever was wrong with her—the overeating part anyway. It was mortifying.

But early days, she reminded herself. Early days.

'So, what can I cook for people?' Jessie asked. 'Cara?'

Immediately everyone cocked an ear.

'Two-egg omelette, please,' she answered politely. 'With tomato.'

'Cheese?'

'No, thanks.'

Jessie was about to start twisting her arm—as a feeder, it was her automatic reflex. Then she remembered. 'Coming up.'

The daily food plan, drawn up by the hospital's dietician, was meant to stop the dips and spikes in Cara's blood-sugar levels that apparently led to binges. Maybe it was working, because she'd had no cravings for sweets or chocolates for the last few weeks. Which was the maddest thing ever because in those months before Gulban Manor it had been literally her every thought: what chocolate she'd buy, when she'd buy it, when she'd eat it. Now she seemed to have freedom.

But who knew that freedom could feel so . . . flat?

Sixty-Eight

Robyn was a mean girl, Jessie observed. Saoirse's gratitude towards her for being her friend was painful to witness. It reminded Jessie of her own teenage years, a time she never wanted to remember.

Robyn was also lazy. She'd scarpered when the breakfast clear-up needed to be done, then appeared poolside in a bikini, where the bottoms were pulled right up her bum.

'What's that about?' Jessie asked Johnny, as they stood by the window, washing the pans. 'Why didn't she just buy a thong?'

'It's the look, I think. They were doing it on *Love Island*.'

'But what if they all fancy her?'

'So what?'

'But what if they all, you know, get turned on?'

'So what?'

'But what if they get erections?'

'*Who?*'

'Well . . . you.'

'Don't. That's horrible.'

Doubtfully, she looked at him. 'I think all men are dirty yokes, raring to go, day or night.'

'I won't get an erection.' He looked towards the pool where Ed was in a splashing war with all the younger kids. 'And neither will Ed.'

'Liam?'

'Time will tell, if he ever appears.'

'Ferdia?'

'Ah, yeah, course. He's that age. Where is he anyway?'

'Knocking something down with Seppe and Lorenzo. A wall, I think.'

'That's all very wholesome.'

'Look at the bunnies,' Jessie said indulgently. 'Little Dilly.' She was the cutest thing, small and sturdy in her mermaid swimsuit with the ruffles on the bum. And Bridey, ever the catastrophist, in a yellow floatsuit.

'What's the deal with Bridey and the flotation tubes?' Johnny asked. 'She can swim.'

'She says you can never be too careful.'

Robyn stood up to rearrange her bikini.

'Why's your woman's bum bothering you?' Johnny asked.

'I just want everything to be nice. Because I'm nouvy, Nell says.' She added, 'I really love Nell.'

As if Jessie had summoned her, Nell popped up into their line of vision wearing a white bikini.

'God!' With a soapy hand, Jessie clutched Johnny's bare arm. 'Look at Nell.'

'*Now* I've an erection. Though it seems like you're the one with a boner for Nell.'

'Johnny, don't say "boner".'

He was squinting at Nell. 'What's different about her?'

'The hair. Not pink any more. Look at it there, a blonde cascade, tumbling down her back. Oh, here we go . . .'

Robyn—maybe threatened by Nell's clean-cut sexiness—stood up again and tucked her bikini bottoms even more tightly between her bum cheeks.

'There's no more room up there! And where does she think she is?' Jessie demanded. 'Nikki Beach? This is a family holiday and there will be no erections! I'm going to patrol the side of the pool with a metal pipe. I'll be the erection police. Any evidence of twitchy mickey, I'll hit it a whack with my pipe.'

Johnny laughed. '"Twitchy mickey". You're the very best.'

'Oh, yeah?'

His smile faded. 'Oh. Yeah.' He slid his arms around her waist and pulled her hard against him.

'Woah. What's with the sudden mood change?'

'My sexy, beautiful wife.'

'Am I, indeed? Hey, Johnny? Is that . . . ?'

'Twitchy mickey? Your fault. Going to whack it with your pipe?'

'. . . I'll deal with it another way. Come on.'

'Seriously?' They'd been so much nicer to each other since the terrible row over her birthday but daytime sex hadn't happened in years.

'They're all in the pool, no one will miss us. Let's go.'

*

'1.23 p.m., lunch. Salad, 1 tbsp dressing, ½ med avocado, 2 med slice sourdough, sml bunch red grapes, sparkling water.' Cara typed it all into her phone to report later to Peggy.

When Cara had first seen her food plan, she'd panicked: there was *so much*. She'd put on tons of weight.

Apparently—so Peggy said—her body was so confused by all the food restricting, then bingeing, she'd been doing that it needed to relearn that a regular, steady supply of nourishment was guaranteed.

In addition, Peggy insisted that many of Cara's binges had been triggered not by cravings but by actual old-fashioned hunger.

Maybe there was something in that. She'd always skipped breakfast to cut her daily calories. But by mid-morning, she'd get such a voracious need for food that she ate much more than the average breakfast.

In their first few sessions together, Cara had found Peggy far too bossy. She reminded her of a primary-school teacher, with her air of absolute conviction that she knew best. Now, though, Cara liked it. It was a comfort to be in the care of a counsellor with such confidence.

Now she needed to input her 'mood after eating'. No need to even think about it: horribly self-conscious. For the first time in for ever, she was in a swimsuit, without a sarong concealing her hips and thighs. It was a sturdy navy one-piece with a built-in stomach-flattener, a million miles from Robyn's day-glo little bikini, but still.

Maybe if only Ed and the boys were here, it would be okay. But with all these people around the pool, especially Robyn . . .

Cara could read her mind: the girl's expression veered between disgust and pity for Cara. She could almost see Robyn deciding that she would never become a dumpy woman with cellulite. And maybe she wouldn't. Not everyone was weak like Cara.

Oh, God, here came Liam, another person who made her feel vulnerable. She suspected his judgement of her thighs was savage. But it gave her a small gleam of pleasure to know that her judgement of him was equally unforgiving. There he was behind his sunglasses, thinking no one could see him checking out Robyn.

Johnny's opinion, she worried about far less. He was all talk and, actually, a very kind perso— Jesus! With an involuntary suck of breath, she almost choked on her own epiglottis. It was Ferdia, shirtless, in a pair of board shorts. She took in his long, lean body, his hair dark against his pale skin. His shoulders and arms were adorned with various tattoos, a fuzzy dark line led from his belly-button down to his waistband and it was just all a bit . . . much.

'Swit-SWOO!' Dilly yelled at him.

Ed looked up. 'Ah, here.' He laughed softly. 'I suddenly feel incredibly inadequate.'

'Where were you all morning?' Bridey demanded of Ferdia.

'Knocking down a wall with a lump hammer!' He grinned. 'It was cool.'

'He thinks he's all that,' Robyn said. 'It's cute.'

'What does that mean?' Dilly asked.

It means Robyn fancies Ferdia.

'He looks like a man from a magazine,' TJ declared.

'A model!' Bridey said.

'Don't tell him,' Jessie pleaded. 'He'll rear up on us.'

It was too late. They'd grabbed Jessie's *Vogue* and found an ad for Armani aftershave. 'Ferdia!' They tapped the page with wet fingers. 'You look like him.'

'No, his hair needs to be wet.' Dilly was studying the picture. 'And he needs water drops on his bosoms.'

'Get in the pool,' Bridey ordered. 'You need to have swimming pool on you.'

Ferdia obliged, then sat on the edge as they fluttered around, styling him, using their fingers to comb his wet hair back from his face.

Vinnie grabbed the magazine. 'You have to sort of half close your eyes. Yes, like that! You look so stupid!'

Urgently Tom said to Cara, 'Mum, can I have your phone? Thanks.' Then, 'Ferdia, make love to the camera.'

Tom clicked off picture after picture. 'You need to lift one of your legs.'

'Like this?' Ferdia hoisted one leg high into the air and the kids dissolved.

'No, your foot on the ground and your knee bent. Yes, like that.'

'Glorious!' Dilly cried. 'We're in raptures.'

'What's this aftershave called?' Nell asked.

'Poo!' Dilly shrieked, then laughed so much she tumbled onto a lounger, where her small, solid body convulsed with hilarity.

'Smelly!' Tom cried.

'Smelly poo.'

'Fart,' Vinnie called. 'Fartface!'

'Gobshite,' Liam suggested, but apart from a barely audible *Ah, now* from Johnny, he was ignored.

'Fartface,' Ferdia declared, then gave a wildly overdone smouldering look. 'By Armani.'

The kids screamed with delight, so helpless with laughter that they decided to tumble on top of each other.

When so many children had climbed onto Jessie's lounger that she was balanced right on the edge, she got off and shoved two together. 'Now there's room for all of us.'

Dilly, TJ and Bridey clambered onto her, their damp little bodies squirming until they were comfortable. All that could have made Jessie happier was Saoirse joining them, but Saoirse was temporarily lost to her. There was no point even thinking about Ferdia. Ferdia was a man now.

'Any room for me?' Johnny asked.

'Course!'

Fresh squirming started, as everyone got comfortably tangled again.

'Whose leg is that?' Jessie rubbed her foot against someone. 'It feels really hairy. Is it Daddy's?'

This prompted screams of laughter from the girls. 'That's Dilly's leg!'

'And she's not hairy!'

This is all I want, Jessie thought. All I ever wanted.

'Sorry, Mum!' TJ accidentally elbowed Jessie in the ear. 'Are you okay?'

'Fine, fine.' Happier than I could ever have imagined.

Sixty-Nine

Late afternoon, as the heavy air vibrated in the heat, Cara was halfway between awake and sleeping when her phone chimed softly.

'What's that?' Saoirse raised her head groggily.

'Nothing. Sorry.'

It was time for the second of her three daily, hospital-mandated snacks. She had to eat every three hours to keep her blood-sugar levels steady, thereby foiling any ambush attempts by cravings. But eating when nobody else was, felt embarrassing. Even the word 'snack' made her uncomfortable: it was what kids in kindergarten got given, not grown women.

Worst of all, she wasn't even hungry, which felt like the greatest waste of calories ever.

In the kitchen, searching for her bag of raw nuts, she opened a cupboard—and stumbled across a stash of Italian biscuits. In fright, she slammed the door shut but not before she'd glimpsed images of thick chocolate, mini-marshmallows and crunchy hazelnuts.

Her heart was thumping. She hadn't been looking for biscuits—she hadn't even known they were there—but still she felt guilty.

Processed sugar wasn't part of her eating plan. Not yet. And maybe never.

Shocked with herself, she moved away. How come she'd opened the very cupboard that was packed with biscuits? Was she trying to sabotage herself?

Peggy hadn't wanted her to come on this holiday: it was too soon to put her into an environment she couldn't control. Cara had been confident that she wouldn't lapse. Now, though, she understood Peggy's concern.

'What?' Ed had walked in.

Her lips felt numb. 'I . . . aaaah . . .'

'What's happened?' His eyes flicked over and around her, as if he was expecting evidence of a binge.

A terrible thought occurred. 'Did you come here to spy on me?'

They still hadn't fully recovered from the terrible things they'd said after her seizure. They were polite and pleasant but it felt to her that they were both acting.

'I came to see you were okay. Finding your snack and all.'

He looked surprised, then wounded. Suddenly she felt ashamed. 'Sorry, sweetie.'

Johnny appeared, followed by Dilly, TJ, Vinnie and Tom. More people were straggling behind them. All at once the entire household was passing through the kitchen, drifting back to their rooms for a snooze.

Ed moved towards Cara, but she slipped away. 'I'd better ring Peggy.'

He had to let her go because Peggy was the person Cara trusted to keep her on the straight and narrow. Nothing could get in the way of that relationship.

As his wife disappeared up the stairs, Ed stood in the kitchen wondering if he'd ever felt so lonely before. For the last five weeks, terror had invaded his dreams: Cara could have died. It rocketed him into wakefulness with a gasp and a pounding heart. *She's dead.*

His life had become like Sliding Doors. In one version, the real one, Cara was still alive. In the other, she'd died on that Friday night.

He was experiencing this holiday through the prism of the second version. Even though she was here, alive, he understood how close death was. Everyone was attached to life by the most slender of threads. It was just crazy good fortune that they didn't snap, snap, snap, one after the other, sending people tumbling into the void.

He couldn't stop watching Vinnie and Tom—Vinnie creating mayhem in the pool, Tom reading under a tree—and thinking how different this holiday could have been. *Your mum could have died. You'd still be here and she wouldn't.*

Not that he could tell her any of this. She was trying to get better: he couldn't burden her.

'Are you okay there?' Johnny was looking at him with concern. 'Come up the town. We'll have a drink with Marcello. Man stuff! Well, we can pretend. Liam, are you on for it?'

'No espresso,' Johnny said to Marcello. 'If we're "talking about our feelings", we need beer.'

'Ah, stop,' Ed said. 'I can't spill my guts to order.' Besides, these men wouldn't understand. He and Cara were different from Johnny and Jessie, from Liam and Nell, from any other couple.

Before he'd met Cara, all three of his long-term girlfriends had dumped him. He wasn't serious enough—about life, about his career, about them . . . In the early days of a relationship, he'd be lauded for his easy-going attitude but eventually that would curdle into angry charges that he was 'detached' and 'too independent'.

He'd always been okay in his own company, even as a kid. Growing up, he had idolized his older brother Johnny. But when he'd noticed how hard Johnny worked to make everyone love him, his hero-worship had mutated into something nearer to pity.

As an adult, he was comfortable going on solo holidays. He'd strike up conversations on trains, in bars—he'd talk to anyone and he was always okay. By the time he'd met Cara, he was thirty-two and had the reputation of a nice guy who was not to be taken seriously. All of that had changed when he climbed a ladder at a house party. That night, the higher he got, the more frightened he became. Then the woman at the foot of the ladder had called up to him, 'I've got you. You're safe.'

Out of nowhere, Ed felt something totally new: he craved the safety she promised.

From the word go, he had thought Cara was extraordinary. But when he'd been extolling her qualities to his brothers, Liam had laughed and said, 'True what they say, right? Love is blind.'

After his fury had abated, Ed got it: to most people, Cara was unremarkable. But she'd unlocked his capacity to love. With that heart-rush of devotion had come matching vulnerability. He'd never wanted anyone else.

Cheating happened, he knew. Some of his friends were loyal, some had lapses, some were habitual fuck-boys . . . He had his suspicions about Johnny—not that he would ever ask. If Johnny was cheating, he did *not* want to know. Himself, though, he was a straight arrow.

The beers arrived and Ed filled Marcello in on his and Cara's story.

'Say something,' Johnny said. 'We think you're very wise because you have a deep voice and a foreign accent.'

'She is doing a rehab?' Marcello asked. 'This is a positive.'

But it wasn't.

Ed had hoped some childhood trauma would quickly be identified and plucked out, restoring Cara to instant normality. Instead, the hospital's recovery plan seemed to be a trial-and-error process where his wife gradually re-forged a relationship with food. Worse still, she'd become secretive about her 'recovery'. All these years, he'd been her partner-in-crime in her overeating: hiding chocolate, retrieving it.

Now, when she was—allegedly—getting well, she'd cut him out. It hurt him and it scared him.

It felt that they were further away from each other than when she'd been throwing up several times a day.

Outside the villa, Nell waved her iPad above her head. Seriously, the Wi-Fi here was shite. It was the worst to bitch about Wi-Fi when you were in actual paradise, but she needed to FaceTime Lorelei to see how things were going on set at the Liffey Theatre.

She'd got the job designing *Human Salt* just after the murder-mystery weekend. It had done a huge amount to restore her confidence.

'What're you doing?'

It was Ferdia at the door of his little house.

'Trying to get a signal.'

He opened the door wide. 'My bedroom has the best Wi-Fi in the whole place.'

She felt awkward about going in there. He was a young bloke—God only knew what he'd been up to.

Ducking into his living room, she ran up the shallow stone stairs to his bedroom and tried not to look at his sheets or the clothes strewn on the floor. It didn't smell too bad: no smell of feet or sweat or . . . self-pleasuring. Suddenly she wanted to giggle.

'What's so funny?' His head had appeared around the doorway.

'No. Nothing.'

'You like a drink? I've cider!'

'Sure.' Why not? It was nearly six o'clock.

Ferdia was right about the signal. She connected immediately.

'Lorelei, sorry about the lateness. Crappy Wi-Fi. How's it all going?'

'We can't have the giant water tank. Health and safety.'

Ah, shite. She'd feared as much but Nell was ever the optimist.

'But we can have five smaller ones in a line. We've done a mock-up—'

'Show me.'

Lorelei demonstrated the line of smaller water tanks. 'Taken together,' she said, 'it could still look like the sea.'

Nell wasn't sure. It was frustrating not to be there. 'Let me sleep on it. Maybe something will come to me. Thanks, hon, talk soon.'

'Any time you need the signal,' Ferdia said, once she was back downstairs, 'come over. So you're working again?'

'Yep. I got back on the horse—'

'Like I said?' He sounded pleased.

'Oh? It was you, right! Yep, got a gig for the theatre festival. Not as big as the one I was working on in Mayo, much smaller budget, but the work is interesting. I'm excited about it.'

'It must be frustrating being here and not there?'

'Yes—' She caught herself and flushed. 'Who wouldn't want to be here? The most beautiful place ever. And Liam and I are going to the Uffizi on Tuesday. Does it get any better?'

'I wasn't throwing shade. I was just . . .'

'. . . being nice?'

'Yeah!' He grinned. 'Being nice.'

'That's new.'

The grin vanished. 'I've been behaving differently for a while now.' He sounded hurt. 'More mature.'

Now that he mentioned it, he didn't seem as touchy as he'd used to. Must be Perla's good influence. And he'd been great that night in Gulban Manor, helping Cara. 'You *are* different,' she said. 'I'm sorry,' she added. 'I'm too caught up in my own stuff.' Encourage the lad, why not? 'You coming up to the procession later?'

Santa Laura was having some religious festival.

'Sure,' he said. 'Wouldn't miss it.'

She looked at him carefully.

'I mean it. I'm not being sarcastic.'

After dinner, when all the kids had run off, Jessie set her elbows on the table with purpose. 'Okay, can I talk to you about a thing? Last weekend in September? Harvest?'

'What is it?' Nell asked.

'Festival,' Johnny said. 'A new one, only been on the go for the last two years.'

'Is that the one in a forest in Tipperary? But it's really—'

'Nouvy,' Jessie jumped in. 'Yes!'

'I was going to say upmarket.'

Ferdia laughed. 'It's not nouvy. It's cool, boutique, eco-friendly.'

'Grown-up,' Jessie insisted.

'For people who can't hack hardship. The tents have actual beds.'

'But the bathrooms are shared. All the same, they're so, so clean.' Jessie's face took on a dreamy expression. 'They've outdoor showers, wooden bathtubs in the forest fed from hot springs, fairy lights strung through the trees . . .' To Nell, she said, 'You'll love it.'

'What? Am I going?'

'If you'd like. Here's the deal,' Jessie said. 'Pop-up PiG cookery school with René Redzepi's ex-sous-chef doing free demos. I need volunteers.'

'To do what?' Liam sounded sceptical.

'Lure people in, pass around the food, then data-capture. Basically, persuade people to give up their email. There's going to be twelve thousand well-off notion-y types gathered in one place. Ideal customers for the cookery school.'

'I've a lot going on.' Again from Liam. 'Doing my course plus pretty much managing a busy bike shop for shitty pay.'

'No one's making you,' Jessie said, a hint of vinegar to her tone. 'The guys from work would kill to come, but family gets first dibs. You'll have plenty of time to go to gigs or have your chakras realigned or smoke some really strong blem and lie flat on your back outside your caravan, looking up at the stars and talking shite for six hours . . .' This last part was directed at Johnny.

'You can take an acting workshop,' Ed said. 'Or listen to Angela Merkel talking to the head of the IMF or go swimming in the river—'

'*Nudey* swimming.' Bridey had reappeared.

'It was only *one* nudey woman,' Jessie said. 'And I think she was just confused.'

'It sounds amazing,' Nell said. 'Even the non-nudey swimming.'

'And your accommodation would be free.'

'Is that when we stayed in the caravan that looks like a cottage?' Dilly had also slunk back to the table. 'Oh, Nell, you must come. It's *glorious*. The kitchen table turns into a bed. It's magic. Bridey says it's unhygienic.'

'It *is* unhygienic!'

'Are you going?' Nell asked Cara.

She shook her head. 'I'd love the music but I don't do well in the outdoors. Camping, even glamping, it's not for me. And it's the same weekend as my friend Gabby's birthday. Ed goes, though.'

'Line-up is always amazing.' Ed was scrolling through his phone. 'This year they've got . . . wow, Hozier, Janelle Monáe, Duran Duran, hah! Are they still alive? Laurie Anderson, Halsey . . . Someone usually does a secret gig. Jessie, count me in.'

'And me,' Ferdia said. 'I'm going anyway. Me and Perla—'

'What?!' Jessie jumped on this information. 'Since when?'

'Since a few weeks ago.'

'I'm on for it too,' Nell said.

'You'll be working.' This from Liam.

'Last weekend of September? No, my play will have opened. I'm in. Won't it be cold, though?'

'Amazingly, no,' Johnny said. 'The last two years it's been blazing sunshine, like they have their own micro-climate.'

'Maybe they get some fighter planes up there to burst all the rainclouds, like Putin does before a big parade,' Ferdia said.

'*Maaay*be.' Jessie was thoughtful. To Ferdia, she asked, 'Are you *sure* it's not nouvy?'

Seventy

'What if I have a heart attack?' Johnny asked.

'You won't,' Liam scoffed.

It was Monday morning, another shiny yellow day. Johnny, Liam and Ed were gathered at the breakfast table, consulting a big fold-out map.

Nell arrived. 'I'm having one more coffee before the pool.'

'Nell,' Johnny said. 'Protect me from your husband. He's making me go on a killer cycle tomorrow.'

'T-tomorrow?' Nell suddenly had a very bad feeling. 'What do you mean?'

'He's making us cycle fifty-five kilometres, up steep hills, in the heat.' Johnny's tone was cheery.

'But tomorrow?' she checked.

'Tomorrow. Tuesday.'

Liam had looked up from the map. 'What?'

Trying to sound jokey, she wagged her finger. 'No cycle for you tomorrow. You've a date with me in the Uffizi.'

Dumbstruck, he stared at her.

'Remember? I booked tickets? It's in our planner.'

He grabbed his phone and checked. 'Shit. Sorry, baby. Totally forgot.'

'Lucky you have me to remind you.' She forced a smile.

'Will it be like the Prado in Madrid?'

'Maybe even better.'

'Oh, baby, *nooooo*.'

Now *she* was dumbstruck. Eventually she managed, 'I thought you loved the Prado? You said you did.'

'I've literally never been so bored in my life.'

She was shocked beyond words.

Jessie, with her radar for drama, had emerged from the kitchen.

'I went because I love you,' Liam said.

He seemed to be waiting for her to let him off the hook.

'But I thought you . . .' Nell was still in shock.

'Ah, Liam!' Johnny scolded.

'I did it because I love her. It was a good thing.'

'But the deal is, you can never drop the act!' Ed said.

'You take it to your grave.'

Everyone weighed in with the same opinion. The tone was jokey, but the mood was tense.

'It's okay.' A wobbly smile inched across her face. 'I'll go on my own. I'll love it.'

'You can't go on your own,' Jessie cried.

'Seriously. I'm super-excited. It's all good.' Before anyone could say another thing, she abandoned her coffee and turned back upstairs.

She lay on the bed. So. This was not good.

A bump at the bedroom door heralded the arrival of Liam. 'Nell, I'm really sorry. I'm a dick.'

She sat up. 'Yep.'

'You know what it's like? Start of something, you'd agree to anything so the person thinks you're cool. Everyone does it.'

'Do they?'

'Yeh. Course. Everyone.' He was energetically defensive. 'I get it, you feel humiliated—'

It was a lot worse than that. 'I'm wondering who I married.'

He groaned. 'Oh, Nell. Don't make a thing of this. It's not important.'

'It's important to me.'

'Seriously, don't be a bitch. You're better than this. Do you still want me to come?'

'Are you insane? That would be the literal worst.'

'Baby, I fucked up. But I haven't done anything that every human on earth hasn't done at one stage. You could look at it another way.'

'And what way's that?'

'That even though you're passionate about something I don't understand—that I actually can't stand—I still love you.'

'No! No way. You don't get to say anything like that ever. I didn't lie about who I am.'

'I didn't lie either. I just—Nell, let's stop this. C'mon, let's go to the pool.'

'You go. I'll be down in a while. I just need to . . . process.'

'You'll be okay,' he said.

She probably would. But how many more discoveries would she have to make about him? Was this how it was for everyone? Was this what they meant when they said marriage was hard? One disappointment and shock after another?

'Ferdia? You in? Can I use your Wi-Fi?'

He opened his door. He was eating an apple. 'Sure. Go on up.' He spoke through a full mouth. 'Y'okay? I heard about the art-gallery cluster.'

'Grand. Just looking for a cheap hotel in Florence for tonight. My Uffizi ticket is for nine forty-five a.m. tomorrow, local bus can't get me there on time. So I'll go this afternoon, stay the night and, bam, be on the spot when I wake up. Except everything's fully booked.'

'Late August,' he said. 'Tourist Central. Why can't you drive? It's only an hour.'

She hesitated. 'Don't judge, but I'm nervous about driving into Florence. They're loons on the road here, and there's all these *rules.* You need a permit for the centre of Florence and I can't do it, not on my own.'

'I'll come with you.'

Another fool. Seriously, who had she wronged in a past life to deserve this visitation of fools?

'I'd like to see "art". Sammie said I was a cultural wasteland. There's a Da Vinci museum as well, with some of the machines he designed. That would be cool. Hey!' He stalled her protests. 'I'm not being nice. I want to go—there's a spare ticket, so let's go. I can even drive.'

'I don't know . . . I'd better talk to Jessie.'

'I'm twenty-one. Nearly twenty-two. I'm not a kid, Nell. If we're "talking" to my mum, shouldn't you "talk" to your husband?'

She scoffed and rolled her eyes. 'Seriously, I need to okay this with Jessie.'

'Then I want to "okay this" with Liam.' With a swaggery walk, led from the hips, he said, in a deep, dorky voice, '"Hey, Liam, seeing as you're a selfish arse to your wife, I'm guessing you won't care if I drive her there." Ha-ha, that'd be funny.'

'You don't like him, do you?'

'Nell, I utterly fucking hate him.'

A thought occurred. 'Aw, Ferdia, no! Are you doing this to get back at him because of Sammie?'

'I'm totally not. I want to visit the gallery because I want to visit the gallery. Nothing shady.'

She felt mistrustful. 'You might get bored. I don't want to have to stop mid-tour because you've had enough.'

'If I get bored, I can leave. We have phones! I'll wander the streets of Florence, without a plan, like in a movie.'

'You might meet a girl who's leaving Florence on the five p.m. train. You could fall in love for the day.'

'I'm *so* there for that. But basically you can stay in the gallery until they kick you out. Okay?'

Nell was still feeling doubtful. 'I need to talk to Jessie about the car. I don't think you'd be on our car insurance, so you'd have to borrow Jessie's.'

'Okay, let's do it.' With a flourish, he ushered her to the door. '*Andiamo.*'

'If it's the driving you're worried about, we could get you a car and driver,' Jessie said to Nell. 'Do-I-Amooze-You could probably sort it.'

'I couldn't deal. I wouldn't know what to say to the man. I simply couldn't.'

'Okay. Ferdia can drive you. But, Ferdia,' Jessie was stern, 'you can't change your mind half an hour in and start whinging that you're bored.'

Nell expected him to kick off but he simply said, 'Maybe Nell could bring colouring books and crayons for me.'

Which was so unexpected that Nell exploded with laughter.

'So it's decided?' he said. 'Right, I'm off to be waterboarded by Vinnie.'

Jessie held Nell by the arm until he was fully gone, then hissed, 'Find out what happened between him and Barty, will you? Good girl.'

Cara was standing at the marble food sink, washing lettuce leaves for lunch, when Johnny appeared.

'How's things?' she asked.

He seemed uncomfortable. 'Grand.'

'Are you okay?'

'Look. I want to apologize. We've asked a lot of you, me and Jessie. Doing our accounts and that. If all the stress pushed you over the edge, you know . . .'

She'd been hoping for a chance to extricate herself. Here was her opportunity and she needed to be brave. After a breath, she said, 'Would you mind if I stopped doing your monthly accounts? I feel slightly . . . uncomfortable. Knowing all that stuff about your money.'

'Sure. Grand. Of course.' Johnny looked mortified. 'Sorry for—'

She put a hand on his arm. 'Let's not make a thing of it. Anyway,' she managed a smile, 'the pair of you never even look at them.'

'But we knew if we were in terrible trouble you'd tell us. So, with the Airbnb, could you give me a lesson in running it?'

'I'm okay to keep doing that. It nearly runs itself. Hassan does the heavy lifting. All I do is throw an occasional eye over it.'

'Well, that'd be great, but if it ever gets too much, just—'

'I will. I promise.'

After an awkward pause, he blurted, 'It's going great, isn't it? The apartment?' He sounded so proud that she had to laugh.

'Yep. Bookings nearly all the way to October.'

'November!' he said. 'I checked earlier today. Barely a day free between now and then.'

'Congratulations.'

'I keep refreshing the calendar to admire it,' he said. 'I feel so . . . Would the word be *validated*? Reading the nice reviews, I feel, yeah, *warm* on the inside. When they say the location is great, I think how smart I was to have bought it all those years ago. I feel like a savvy biznizzy man. So that's all okay then, is it? Thanks, Cara, thanks.' Full of smiles, he left the kitchen.

Cara resumed her lettuce-washing, her hands trembling slightly. That went okay, she thought. She'd been brave.

But poor Johnny.

Then, *What is he planning to do with all that money?*

It wasn't much later when Jessie came in, dumping her old-fashioned shopping basket on the worktop. 'Do you know what they have in Fausto's grocery store up the town?' she exclaimed.

'What?'

'Fuck-all! Pure fuck-all.' Jessie cast an anxious look about. 'Any of the bunnies here?'

'Am I a bunny?' Tom popped out from the pantry, where he'd been holed up, reading.

'Course you are.' Jessie grabbed him and planted several quick smackers on his head. 'But you don't judge.'

'It's just a word,' Tom said. 'The F one. It's got no moral value in itself. Dad says.'

'That's grand,' Cara said hastily. 'But you're still not to say it.'

'I'm not saying Fausto's shop isn't lovely,' Jessie said dreamily. 'It's like a movie set. Soft yellow paper sacks of semolina flour, dusty cans of chestnut purée, four gazillion jars of preserved lemons . . . But a box of Rice Krispies? Not a chance. I managed to get bread, wine and ice-cream, all the major food groups. But we need a visit to the big supermarket on the Lucca ring road. We'll be grand with bread and cheese for lunch today. Salad from the garden?'

'And we're making the pizzas for dinner.'

They'd been there less than forty-eight hours but they'd already slipped into an easy routine: a late breakfast, followed by pool time. A light lunch, more sunbathing, a snooze, then dinner, usually up in the town.

'I'll go to the big supermarket tomorrow,' Cara said.

'Good woman.'

Seventy-One

In her bedroom, as Cara hit Peggy's number, her first morning checking in to St David's came back to her.

'Date of birth?' the female admissions clerk had asked, then stopped typing and looked up as the office door opened. A man in a shirt and tie had come in, looking flustered. 'Peggy wants her letters.'

'Those.' She pointed with a pen at a pile of paper.

'Thanks.' The man took a sheaf of pages and hastened away.

'Sorry. Give me that date again.'

When all of Cara's details were input, the clerk pressed an intercom and spoke: 'Can somebody come and get one of Peggy's?'

Then to Cara, 'You're with Peggy.'

'Who's Peggy?'

She seemed surprised. 'Peggy Kennedy. Your counsellor.'

The way Peggy was being spoken about implied she was *important*.

A security woman materialized. 'I'm here for one of Peggy's.'

Cara was led along shiny-lino corridors, through set after set of double doors, en route to this Peggy. The hospital looked clean and well-maintained but it was old and austere. *I should be at work right now. Instead I'm a patient in a psychiatric hospital.*

It was impossible to believe.

'Everyone seems scared of Peggy,' she said to the security woman.

She'd expected, at the least, to get a smile out of her. But the woman said stiffly, 'She's very highly respected.'

Cara burnt with embarrassment. She'd only been trying to make small-talk.

'Here we are.' The guard ushered Cara into a small room, then promptly left.

Cara sat in one of the two armchairs. Apart from a low table, the room contained nothing else. *What am I doing here? What's gone wrong in my life? How could I have avoided this?*

In came a short woman with curly hair, probably in her late fifties, wearing an A-line skirt and a pale pink blouse. The kind of woman who might be described as 'cuddly'. 'Peggy Kennedy.' She extended her hand and gave a quick, brisk squeeze. 'You're Cara Casey? So what has you here?'

'. . . Haven't you been told?'

'I'd rather hear it from you.'

Oh. Okay. 'So . . . on Friday night, I had a small seizure. It looked far worse than it was. It was just a bit unlucky. But my husband panicked, so here I am.' She paused. 'Everything feels a bit Kafkaesque to be honest . . .'

Peggy looked blank.

'I mean, as if I've been incarcerated for something I didn't do.'

'I know what Kafkaesque means. Tell me about your bulimia.'

Cara revised her opinion. Peggy wasn't cuddly. At all. 'It wasn't really bulimia. It was just a temporary thing and I've stopped now. I hadn't realized people were so worried about me.'

'So? Fear of food? And love of food? Hatred of your size? Overeating when you're angry, anxious, stressed or lonely? Eating in secret? Once you start eating sugar you can't stop? Guilt after overeating? Promises to yourself to eat normally? How's that sounding?'

Defiantly, Cara said, 'I barely know any woman who has a normal relationship with food or her body.'

'But not every woman has a seizure as a result of her disordered eating.'

'Yes, but it wasn't really a—'

'You. Could. Have. Died,' Peggy enunciated.

'I couldn't have.'

'You could have. You still could, if you carry on like this.'

'I've stopped.'

'You'll start again, without proper help.' Peggy raised her palm. 'Don't tell me you can control it. You can't. I know a lot more about this than you do. Now you're thinking you know yourself better than I do. Once again, you're wrong.'

A cold trickle of fear leaked through Cara. Peggy's confidence was a worry. What if she was right?

But she probably wasn't.

Every weekday for the following four weeks, Cara had seen Peggy for an hour and had had every one of her preconceptions shot down in flames.

When Cara said, 'Eating disorder to me means anorexia', Peggy had responded with, 'Eating far more food than your body can digest, then making yourself sick, that's an eating disorder.'

When Cara said, 'I ate too much because I'm a pig with no self-control', Peggy said, 'You've an illness. You became addicted to the dopamine your brain produced every time you overate. It's exactly like being addicted to drugs.'

When Cara said, 'Don't eating disorders happen because of traumas?' Peggy was blunt: 'Not necessarily.'

Peggy was opinionated and non-negotiable. She wasn't entirely unsympathetic, but she didn't pull any punches.

As well as daily one-on-one time with Peggy, Cara had sessions with a dietician in which she had to dismantle all her dyed-in-the-wool beliefs about food: carbs were not the work of the devil; skipping breakfast wasn't a great idea. She was shown videos on how craving cycles worked, how willpower was useless. She learnt about the chemical changes in human brains when a large amount of food flooded into the digestive system. She was told that it was an act of self-hatred to fill her body with food it didn't need and couldn't digest.

Sessions with a cognitive behavioural therapist offered her healthier ways to manage her stress and anxiety.

Every day that month she was loaded up with so much information that she was too tired to resist all the parts she didn't think applied to her.

Five weeks later, she still didn't like Peggy, but she trusted her. Peggy wanted her to 'get well'.

Even though Cara still didn't really believe that she *wasn't* 'well'.

Seventy-Two

Nell necked a triple espresso in the silent kitchen. No one else was up, not even Jessie.

Outside, grapefruit-coloured mist hung, like gauze, in the air. The sun, barely risen, was just starting to warm the land. Ferdia, in a pair of cargos and a crumpled shirt missing half its buttons, was waiting by the car. 'All right?'

'Yep.'

'Music on?'

'Too early.'

For about forty minutes, the roads stayed empty. Nell leant against her window, stunned by so much beauty, watching the fuzzy edges of the world burn away in the heat of the sun.

Without much warning, they reached the surprisingly horrible outskirts of Florence. Traffic slowed almost to a standstill.

'Don't worry,' Ferdia said, the first words either had spoken. 'We'll be there in time.'

'Okay.' Maybe they would. What could she do anyway?

'When we get to the gallery,' he said, 'we start at the top floor—it's where all the best stuff is—then work our way down. Okay?'

She smiled. He'd obviously read TripAdvisor too.

'Every time you see a Ladies, use it. They're few and far between.'

'What if I don't need to go?'

He flashed a grin. 'Try anyway. We can't bring food or drink in. I've got protein bars we should eat before we start.'

'You've done your research.'

'Up all night, making the most of my high-quality Wi-Fi.'

As they advanced on the centre of Florence, winding though ever-narrowing streets, the traffic was a snarly, beepy nightmare. Every centimetre of road space was aggressively contested. Ferdia was doing his best to hide his anxiety but his face was white and his hands on the steering wheel were so tense she thought his bones might break the skin.

A car from a side-street inched its way into their path, its bumper almost touching theirs. Nell was braced for some sort of showdown, but Ferdia laughed and held back. 'Go for it, if it means that much to you.'

Her shoulders slumped with relief. Not long afterwards, they descended a slope into an underground car park.

'We're here? Wow.'

'See?' Ferdia said. 'Driving is no bother.'

'They're terrifying, those Italians. I couldn't have done that last bit.'

'I wasn't scared.' He laughed. 'Apart from when I was.'

'Only because you're young. The young feel no fear.'

'Nah. It's because you're used to driving with an old man. An old man who's an arse!'

She gave a wobbly smile. 'Ferdia . . .' She eventually said, 'Liam's my husband. He's going through painful stuff with his kids. I know you've issues with him, but can we not?'

'You're over him forgetting about today?'

'Yep.' It was complicated but she no longer blamed Liam. It was the fault of her own unsustainable expectations.

'Okay,' he said. 'I won't say anything again.'

'Are you pissed off with me?'

'No.' He sounded surprised. 'Why would I be?'

'. . . People think this is a fake because her beauty is so modern. Different standards of beauty in the 1400s . . .'

'. . . Caravaggio painted people from life's margins. He used a sex worker as a model to paint the Mother of God, and his patron went bananas . . .'

'. . . At first look, it's a painting commemorating a great battle, but see where the spears are pointing? At a hunting scene. There wasn't any battle, it was a lie and this painting exposes it. Art being political.'

From room to room they went, Nell deconstructing dozens of paintings for Ferdia. 'Am I talking too much?' she asked.

'No! I'm enjoying it, maybe not the way you are. Dilly's phrase—you're "in raptures", right? But it's interesting.'

'You're sure? Grand. Oh, my God, it's *Primavera*. Very famous work by Botticelli. Look at the flowers, can't you almost smell them? Literally five hundred different plant types in this painting. Botanists come to study plants that are now extinct. Ed might be interested.'

'Ed's interested in everything.'

As they moved into the next room, Ferdia nodded at a crowd clustered round a painting. 'What's that?'

'Oh.' She took a breath. 'Botticelli's *Birth of Venus*.'

'Even I've heard of that!' He moved closer to get a better look. 'She looks a bit like you.'

WTF?

'I didn't mean the . . . no-clothes thing,' he blurted. 'I meant—' What had he meant? 'Her hair. Her hair reminds me of yours.'

'*Ooo*kay.' Her look was wary.

'And, of course, the giant shell attached to her feet.'

'Ha-ha. Grand.' It was all okay again. 'We keep going? Oh, cool, here's Titian. See this one? Some rich dude commissioned this of his wife and . . .'

'. . . Same doggo as the earlier painting. So definitely the same woman . . .'

'. . . See the difference in Michelangelo's palette? Much more vibrant than Botticelli's? It revolutionized colour—you're sure I'm not talking too much?'

'Stop asking,' he said. 'If I've had enough, I'll wait in the café. Keep at it.'

'. . . Caravaggio painted people who actually looked like people. He didn't flatter his subjects . . .'

Abruptly the stream of information stopped. Nell said, her tone awe-struck, 'In the next room is Caravaggio's *Medusa*. I've loved it since I was fifteen, I'm so excited right now, I can't even . . .' She took a deep breath. 'Okay, let's do it.'

He followed her towards a round painting, protected by a glass case. Nell stood before it, silent for a full minute.

'Tell me,' he said.

'The emotion. The horror in its eyes. He—or it might be she—has just realized that it's dying. It thought it was invincible. Can you feel it?'

He could, actually. 'The poor bastard.'

'Yeah, but it went around turning people to stone.'

'It's just had its head cut off!'

'Ha-ha-ha. Right.' Then she was back to staring in wonder. 'The realism of the snakes. Over four hundred years old . . .'

*

'Okay,' Nell said. 'I'm done. Let's get some food.'

In a nearby café, Ferdia asked, 'Did you enjoy it?'

'Oh, my God!' she exclaimed. 'I *loved* it.' She would have preferred to be there with Liam. She'd never again have a day in an art gallery with Liam. That was already in their past. But beauty helped heal the wound.

'So what next?' Ferdia asked. 'The Da Vinci museum?'

'If I see any more art my eyes will burst. C'mon, let's walk it off, see Florence.'

Out in the crowded, sunny street, a man was playing an accordion. After a moment, Nell recognized the theme from *The Godfather* and her soul withered. She and Ferdia skimmed a look off each other. They were clearly thinking the same thing: that Florence was like a stage set; that this man had been paid by the Tuscan Tourist Board.

'Your man looks—' Ferdia said.

'I know.'

'But. Look at all these statues.'

In the street, raised on marble plinths, stood several sculptures.

Ferdia stood before a male nude in white marble. 'Is this the statue of *David*?'

'A reproduction,' Nell said, 'but, yes, that's him.'

They studied the statue. Nell gave Ferdia a cheeky look. Echoing what he'd said earlier, she said, 'He looks a bit like you.'

'Oh, yeah? The nudiness? Ah, it's the hair, right?'

'And the giant lump of marble stuck to his foot.'

'He's had a bit of manscaping done, by the looks of things.'

'And,' Nell was looking at the small genitalia, 'it must have been cold, the day it was sculpted.'

Then, embarrassed, 'Come on.'

They started walking, heading away from the centre, with no plan, past seven-storey buildings in every gradation of yellow, from buttercup to straw, tottering over narrow, pedestrianized streets.

Seventy-Three

Johnny and Ed exchanged a look. *For God's sake, don't laugh.* But it was difficult not to. Liam had pushed the pace all morning. Ed had kept up but Johnny loitered far behind, huffing and puffing and hating every second.

Then, about ten kilometres from home, Liam gave a sudden howl and skidded to a halt, claiming to have 'done something' to his back. They helped him, wincing and swearing, to the shade of a tree. Johnny flung himself down beside his brother.

'I might never be able to get up again,' Liam mumbled.

'At least you can cure yourself,' Ed said, distributing bottles of water. 'With your massage stuff.'

'No, I fucking can't! How would I reach? How could this just have happened out of nowhere? I wasn't doing anything to my back!'

'It's just the way of things,' Ed said. 'You try to disaster-proof your life. But the thing that causes all the trouble is something you'd never even thought about.'

'How d'you mean?' Johnny sounded anxious.

'Just. I worried about money, about being away for fieldwork, about Vinnie being a bit wild. Any of them could blow up our lives, I thought. But Cara having a seizure because of an eating disorder? Never saw that one coming.'

'Thought we were talking about my back,' Liam said. 'How did this conversation become about you, Ed?'

'She's getting help,' Johnny said. 'She'll be fine.'

'You know your friend—is it Andrew?' Ed asked Johnny. 'With the alcoholic wife?'

'Grace? *Yeeeess?*' No wonder Johnny sounded wary: this was not a story with a happy ending.

Andrew had been—everyone was agreed on this—'very good to Grace'. He was the one who'd rung around on the mornings after, making Grace's apologies, when she'd made a drunken show of herself the night before. To alleviate her need to drink so heavily, he'd taken her on holiday, got extra childminding help and tried to remove all stress from her life.

After years of her trying and failing to get things under control, Andrew had left her.

Then she stopped drinking.

Andrew stayed gone. She stayed sober.

'Moral of the story, he was enabling her,' Ed said. 'My second-worst fear is that Cara doesn't stick to this. If she starts again, I don't think I can stay with her.'

'But she's not well!' Johnny was horror-struck. 'You can't abandon a person who isn't well!'

'If I stayed, she'd think there were no consequences. She'd probably keep doing it.'

'What's your first-worst fear?' Liam asked.

'That she dies.'

'Yep,' Liam said. 'Could happen.'

'But probably won't,' Johnny said quickly. 'Things often get worse before they get better. But think positive. That's what you do.'

People were always telling Ed that he was a positive person, but, right now, hope was in short supply.

Early afternoon, the villa was quiet. Johnny, Ed and Liam were on their crackpot cycle, Nell and Ferdia in Florence, Saoirse and Robyn at a day spa, and Cara, Vinnie and Tom had gone to the big supermarket in 'the real town', nine kilometres away.

'Mum?' Jessie was on her way to the pool when she was summoned by Dilly, who was in a head-to-head conference with TJ and Bridey. 'Are Violet and Lenore still our cousins?'

'Of course, honey.'

'Could we FaceTime them? Now?'

Jessie didn't see why not. Admittedly, it had hurt that the two girls hadn't come to Italy but she and Paige had always got on. In the early days of the separation, Jessie had wanted to maintain their friendship, but Liam had asked her not to. ('I feel like an even bigger failure, her being nice to you, but not to me,' he'd said.)

That had been hard. But, out of loyalty to Liam, she'd backed off.

This was different: this was about the children. Their relationship mattered.

'Violet and Lenore are at camp this week,' she reminded Dilly and TJ. 'Maybe they're not at home.'

'Can't we try?'

What time was it in Atlanta?

'Seven thirty-nine in the morning.' Bridey had read her mind.

'Okay.' Jessie had decided. 'I'll message Paige and see what she says.'

Within seconds Paige had pinged back: Sure!

'Okay!' Jessie exclaimed. 'We're on.'

They went to Ferdia's bedroom and dialled up.

Then there they were—Violet, Lenore and Paige, their smiling faces filling the screen. A clamour of talk broke out, everyone speaking at once.

'Why didn't you come to Italy?' Bridey demanded.

'TJ!' Violet called. 'Do you still wear boys' clothes? Because so do I!'

'No way!'

'Lenore, I got a unicorn squishy!' Dilly waved it at the screen. 'I could get you the cupcake one with my holiday money!'

'Dilly, I *have* the cupcake one!' Lenore squealed.

Jessie filled up with a painful mix of love and sadness. This was what happened when people split up, but obviously the bond was still there between the kids.

'Jessie.' Paige beamed. 'What a surprise. Is everything okay?'

'Totally. Just, we missed you guys. I'm so sorry we couldn't make it work with the Italy dates but—and maybe I'm out of line here—but would you maybe think about the girls coming to Ireland for Hallowe'en?'

'Excuse me?'

Oh, God, boundaries. Backtrack, backtrack.

'Sorry, Paige. It was just an idea. So that the girls could see their cousins. But it's not my business. I'm sorry.'

'Jessie.' Paige tried to cut through all the voices. 'Jessie! Jessie. We've got to go now. Nice talking to you all. Say goodbye, girls.'

The connection was cut.

'What? No! Wait!' Bridey, TJ and Dilly erupted in confusion. 'What happened? Mum, what happened? Ring them back!'

'They had to go.' Jessie strove for the right words to restore calm. 'They only had a few minutes before they went to their camp.'

'How do you know that?' Bridey was very suspicious. 'Show me the message.'

'She doesn't say it in words but it's an adult thing. It was implied.'

TJ burst into a storm of weeping.

'Oh, bunny.' Jessie gathered her up.

'They don't want to be friends with us any more!'

'They do, they do! They were just busy.'

Jessie had *no* clue what had just happened. Had she been out of line in suggesting the Hallowe'en visit? That must have been it. They probably already had plans. *Me and my interfering, control-freak ways.*

As soon as she got some privacy, she'd apologize to Paige, try to patch up this omnishambles. If she parked the bunnies at the pool—What was that?! She'd spotted something or someone through the trees. Then it came into full view: a man in dark clothing.

'Sweet Jesus.' She felt the blood leaving her face. 'It's Do-I-Amooze-You.'

'What?'

'Giacomo. Coming up the path.' Muttering to herself, 'Worried we were getting too relaxed, so he's here to remind us what fear feels like.' It was no surprise that Giacomo was visiting now, when Johnny was many hard-cycling kilometres away.

'He's scary,' Dilly said.

'Don't I know it!' Then, 'Ah, he's not.' She couldn't frighten the bunnies. 'It's just his way. But whatever you do, kiddos, don't complain about the Wi-Fi.'

'What might happen?'

'Let's not find out. Bridey, get the bottle of Baileys. It's up in my room.'

She looked out again. Christ, he was nearly upon them. How did he do that? He seemed to relocate from spot to spot at enormous speed, but she never actually saw him move.

Standing at the front door, the girls lined up behind her in the dim hallway, she wondered if the discount in the rent was actually worth this.

'Aha-ha-ha! Giacomo, what a *sorpresa*! *Entrez-vous, venite.*' Whatever the fecking word was.

'*Buon giorno, bella signora,* Jessie.' Poker-faced, he bowed his head and gave her the bottle of grappa that she'd come to dread, then bestowed a double kiss.

Stepping over the threshold, he removed his black cap and looked down at the girls. '*Le piccole signorine.* He-he-he.' He gave a warmth-free smile.

'*Buon giorno, Signor Giacomo,*' Bridey said. 'We are having a nice holiday in your house.'

'The Wi-Fi is very good,' TJ blurted.

'Aaaaah.' Giacomo studied her coldly. '*Bella ragazza*. He-he-he.' He pinched her ear as she gave Jessie a terrified look.

'Good girls,' Jessie's voice was high-pitched. 'Off to the pool now. Don't drown.' To Giacomo she said, 'Come in. Sit down. Although it's your villa, you can sit where you like, ha-ha-ha. May I get you a drink?'

When Cara returned from the supermarket, Jessie was lying on the couch. 'I've been Giacomo'd,' she said, weakly.

'How did he know to come when no other adult is here?!'

'His network of spies . . .' She groaned. 'Cara, I'm jarred. I had to have three glasses of grappa, which was *disgusting*. My head is spinning and my muscles ache from fear.'

A razor blade of guilt—yet another—sliced Cara's soul, cutting into the cross-hatch of recent, raw wounds. 'The things you do for us,' she said. 'Don't think we're not grateful.' If it wasn't poor Jessie being pestered by Do-I-Amooze-You in order to get a cut-price holiday for all of them, there were countless other reasons for Cara to feel guilty.

Weighing heavily was all the financial damage she'd done with her food drama. To her intense relief, the Ardglass had continued to pay her during the time she'd been 'sick'. But Ed had got Scott to cover for two weeks so that he could support her, forgoing half a month's salary.

Worse, though, was the cost of her treatment. Their health insurance would pay for about half of it. The rest they'd have to cover themselves. In addition, she'd be seeing Peggy once a week for the next year and that would have to be funded from her own pocket. She desperately wished she hadn't let any of this happen.

Seventy-Four

Mid-afternoon, Ferdia and Nell bought *gelato*, ate it in a shaded park and uploaded a gazillion photos to Instagram. Then Nell lay under a tree, resting her head on her satchel. 'Right, I'm just going to close my eyes for a few minutes.' Within seconds she'd fallen asleep.

When she woke up, the shadows were lengthening. 'What time is it?'

'Twenty to seven.'

'Sorry!' She'd been asleep for too long. 'We should get going. Have we any water?'

As he passed a bottle, she spotted some lines of script inked onto his inner forearm. 'What's that?'

'It says, "IOU one red pastille, Love Dad." Dad wrote me that note, a few days before he died. The inkman copied his handwriting.'

'You gave him your best-flavoured sweet? But he promised he'd give it back. That's lovely! What was he like?' She stopped herself. 'Sorry, I'm not awake properly. Too personal.'

'It's grand. I'm good. Like, I don't really remember him. Just kid's stuff, he was big and calm. But he was stern too, much sterner than Jessie. Not mean or shouty, but when he said no, I knew he meant it.' He shrugged. 'He was only human. If he was still alive, we mightn't get on at all.'

'And maybe you would. You were six when he died? Did you understand what had happened?'

'Not really. One day he went to work like normal and just never came home. Mum and Grandpa and everyone kept telling me that he was in Heaven, but for the longest time I believed he'd be back. Then one day just like all the others, I got it. He was coming back *never*. It just . . . It was a shock. I felt like a train that had been knocked off the tracks.'

'Oh, God . . .'

'For a while I wouldn't go to school, then Mum said I'd have to repeat the year. I didn't want to be the poor sad boy with the dead dad, so I copped on, went back, did the work. All grand.'

'You got back on the tracks?'

'Totally. Slightly different, like a train with a dented wheel. But that's everyone. We've all lost someone or something. It's bizarre—my head knows he's gone but I don't think my body does.'

'How do you mean?'

'You know when you're about to go out but you're waiting for other people to be ready? How you get your muscles ready to move? Like, the backs of your legs, you sorta tense them, so you can stand up quickly? That's how I feel about Dad. I'm braced, still expecting him. It's part of me now. I think it'll always be part of me.'

'Oh, God, that's so sad.'

'Seriously, it's not! I'm fine. And we're all a bit buckled, right?'

'*Bella coppia!*' a wheedling voice said. '*Innamorati!*'

Nell looked up. 'Oh, no.'

An aggressively smiley man wearing a wicker basket bristling with cellophane-wrapped roses had descended on them.

'*Bella signora.*' He'd plucked a rose from his basket and insisted that Ferdia take it. '*Per la bella signora.*'

Ferdia was flustered.

'*Rosa.*' The man persisted. '*É aumentato por amore!*'

'*Quanto?*' Nell reached for her purse.

A flash of ten fingers, then Nell thrust a note at him. It disappeared with impressive speed and the rose was being thrust at her. '*La bella signora.*'

'For him.' She pointed at Ferdia. '*Bello signor.*'

After a split second, the man rallied. 'Women's lib! Women's lib! *Bacio, bacio!*'

'No *bacio.*' Nell thought this was hilarious. '*Grazie, signor. Arrivederci!*'

'*Bella coppia,*' he said, and swung away, looking for his next target.

'Don't give out to me,' she said to Ferdia. 'The poor man, trying to earn a few quid.'

'What's "*bacio*"? "Kiss"? Why would I give out to you? How come your Italian is so good?'

'I downloaded a course. Just the basic basics.'

'Good on you.' He was looking at his rose. He was slightly sheepish. 'I've never been given a flower before. It's nice. Thanks.'

'Right, let's go home.'

'I'm starving. Do you mind if we get some food?'

He was her driver: she could hardly mind.

'Mum told me about a place, just round here . . .'

The heat had gone from the day and the light was mellow. Ferdia led them through the streets, following his phone. Stopping outside a plain double door, sounding doubtful, 'It should be here.'

The door opened, seemingly by itself, and to Nell's confusion, a smiling man in a suit said, '*Signore Kinsella, Signora McDermott, benvenuti,* welcome.'

They stepped inside and the noisy city disappeared. The floor was marble, the walls a yellow distemper, and overhead a multi-vaulted ceiling was adorned with frescos. This was some sort of palazzo. Restored, obviously, but genuine.

The smiling man led them to a madly baroque couch beneath an elaborate chandelier and said, 'Please. Sit. I will check on your table.'

As soon as he'd gone, Nell hissed, 'Ferdia, this is too fancy. Let's go.'

'No. Jessie arranged this.'

'But that's . . . I'm embarrassed that there's this big effort to cheer Nell up. I'm good. And even if I wasn't, it's between Liam and me.'

'Grand. Be touchy if you want. But I need my dinner.'

'This really isn't me. And I'm dressed all wrong.'

'Naw. Your giant shell is ideal. And I'm no better.' He pointed at his loose, low-hanging trousers and thin, worn shirt. 'C'mon,' he coaxed. 'She means so well. Can't you do it, just for her?'

Smiley Man had returned and, almost in a trance, Nell followed him along a black-and-white marble-floored hallway, past statue after statue, into a serene garden, where fairy lights twinkled in the twilight. Invisible water pitter-pattered nearby.

She had a sense of floating past many waiters who beamed and beamed, truly delighted for her that she was there. Jessie had probably paid them to smile, but still.

Their table was next to an ornamental pond, in which a sculpture of a nymph floated on a giant ceramic lily leaf.

'Cider for the *signora*.' One of the army of smilers placed a glass before Nell. 'And Orangina for the *signore*.'

'I can't function,' Nell whispered. 'How did they know about the cider?'

'Jessie. How else? Which means I haven't a hope of getting any alcohol.'

'Have some of mine.'

'Ah, no.' His teeth flashed white in the half-light. 'I've to drive us home.'

'Menu for the *signora*.'

Nell took one look and exclaimed, 'Ah, here! Mine has no prices. I can't do this. I've only got thirty-five euro with me and the smiles alone are probably going to cost us that much.'

'I don't have prices either. Don't go bananas but Jessie is paying.'

She put her face in her hands. 'This is the worst. My stuff with Liam is my stuff. And fancy food is wasted on me. I like Ryvitas, for God's sake!'

He scanned the menu. 'Look, there's normal stuff, they've lasagne!'

'It's probably made with gold leaf. I'm happy with a cheese scone. And maybe a bucket of teacakes.'

'The Marks & Spencer ones?'

'In a perfect world. But I'm on an Aldi budget and they're nearly as nice.'

'Probably no cheese scones or teacakes here, but try to enjoy it?'

'Wow, I'm ungrateful.' Then, 'What's going on with you and Barty?'

He blinked. 'That was *some* change of subject. You asking for a friend?'

'Ha-ha. I won't tell Jessie anything. But what's going on?'

'We had a fight, me and Barty. A big one. About Jessie—Mum. Barty said about Auntie Izzy saying she was a slut.'

Nell's eyes widened.

'It wasn't the first time. But it's not what I think any more. That's all I said, that I believe Mum. It kicked off World War Three.'

'Wow. Do you think you and Barty will work it out?'

He took a breath. 'Maybe not.'

'Oh, Ferdia! You're not having a great time of it. Sammie gone, and now Barty.'

'I'm okay about Sammie. She's great, but we're not meant to be together. Barty, I'm not as okay.' He shrugged. 'But at least Granny and Grandpa still love me.'

Suddenly she was curious. 'What are they like?'

'The literal best. Grandpa Michael is the person I love most on this earth. He's not just my grandfather, he's my friend and, yeah, probably father figure too, all of that. Like, he's *interested* in me. And non-judgey. He doesn't try to solve my stuff, but just spilling it out to him takes the badness away. When I told him about the break-up with Sammie, he said, "You'll be better by the time you're married." Exactly what he used to say when I was a kid and I'd fallen off a wall or something.'

'He sounds great.'

'Ellen's cool too. She's . . . *soft.* Like a granny should be. When I was about eight, I got the chicken pox. Mum couldn't take time off work, so I was sent down to them. It was like time-travel. I stayed in Dad's old room, the TV only had two channels and the food was, you know, bread and potatoes and apple tart. We read lots of books—Granny said they used to be Dad's.'

'Everyone should have grandparents like them. You'd want to meet Nana McDermott.'

'Scary?'

'I can't even.'

'Yeah, but Granny Ellen could be tough too. Granny and Grandpa won't talk to Mum or Johnny. Izzy and Keeva won't either. Because of', he gave a dismissive wave, '"long ago and far away" stuff. When Saoirse and me used to go down there, as kids, there had to be a—What do you call it in diplomatic terms? An intermediary?'

'A "neutral party"?'

'Someone like Keeva's husband, or Mrs Tempest the neighbour. Mum would bring us to Granny and Grandpa's door but Mrs Tempest would let us in. That way Mum and the Kinsellas never came face to face.'

'That sounds . . . awful.'

'Nah. We got used to it.'

It was eleven o'clock when they got back to the villa.

Liam's face was like thunder. 'Where have you been until now?'

'Florence, dude,' Ferdia said.

'Doing what?'

'Looking at art.'

'Until now?'

'We went for food.'

'Where?'

'What does it matter? This isn't cool, man.'

Jessie rushed in. 'Bunnies! You're back! How was Palazzo dell'Arte Vivente?'

'Is that the name of the restaurant?' Nell asked. 'It was utterly amazing.'

'Wait, what?' Liam demanded. 'You were at the Palazzo dell'Arte Vivente?'

'But, Jessie,' Nell said, 'let me give you the money for the dinner.'

'The Palazzo dell'Arte Vivente?' Liam repeated. 'How did you get a table?'

'There isn't anything to pay back,' Jessie said. 'The chef is my friend. Well, maybe friend is overstating it but—'

'Oh, Jessie! Well, I'll pay you back somehow.'

'No.' Jessie grasped her wrist. 'I owe you big-time. For . . .' she mouthed '. . . sorting out Ferdia and me.'

'Have I got this right?' Liam raised his voice. Jessie, Nell and Ferdia finally paid him some attention. 'You,' he nodded at Nell, 'and . . . him had a free dinner in Palazzo dell'Arte Vivente?'

In the silence that followed, Nell asked, in a small voice, 'Is that a good thing? A bad thing?'

'Oh, for fuck's sake!'

Seventy-Five

Liam seemed in better form in the morning. 'You had a good day yesterday?'

'I loved it. I know it's not your thing but it made me so happy. I think I'll go back and see—'

'. . . I didn't have a great day.' His tone was pointed.

Oh. His cycle. 'What happened?'

'My back. Could be a pulled muscle. Could be something worse.'

'Should you see a doctor?'

'Ah, no.' He waved away her concern.

Well, he couldn't be that bad, so. 'I'm going back to Florence, to the Da Vinci museum, probably tomorrow,' she said. 'It's some of his inventions—they've been constructed from his drawings.'

'I read about that place. Sounds okay. I think I'll come with you.'

'You don't have to. Ferdia says he'll drive me.'

'I'll drive you.'

'But Ferdia wants to go.'

'And so do I.'

They couldn't both go. Not together.

She found Ferdia by the pool. 'Ferd?'

He glanced up. 'Y'okay?'

'Liam wants to go to the Da Vinci museum.'

'Oh. Right. I'll give it a miss, then.'

She was grateful he wasn't being a brat about it. 'I'm sorry.'

'Nah! All grand. It's good he wants to go.'

'Yep.'

'Maybe he thinks Mum will sort him out with his dinner at the Arte Palazzo place.'

'Ha-ha, maybe he does.' She smiled, then stopped abruptly.

As she walked back to the house, her phone rang. It was Perla. Perla knew she was in Italy, so this was sort of weird.

'Nell. I apologize for calling you on your vacation. Are you having a wonderful time?'

'Totally. Aaah, is everything okay?'

'Everything is fine. But I would like to speak to Ferdia and his phone is powered off.'

'Oh. Okay. Let me get him for you.'

She hurried back to the pool. 'Ferdia? Perla for you.'

'Oh? I must be out of coverage.'

Nell loitered, waiting for her phone. She would have liked to know what they were saying to one another—yeah, she was *curious*, even if it wasn't any of her business.

'Thanks.' Smiling, Ferdia bounded over and returned the phone. 'I, aaaah—'

She could feel some sort of explanation coming and she didn't need to know.

'Perla and I are—'

'Good for you.'

'The thing is, we're—'

'Grand.' She smiled. 'All grand.'

In the heavy late-afternoon heat, all the loungers around the pool were occupied. The sound of cicadas filled the air. Jessie picked up her phone, she'd got a WhatsApp. Her heart beat faster when she saw it was a reply to her self-abasing message to Paige: **I'll FaceTime tomorrow, 2 p.m. your time. Don't tell Liam. Don't have the kids with you. Xx**

She'd ended it with two kisses. That must mean Jessie hadn't totally destroyed things.

'Cara?'

'Mum? Everything okay?'

'Fine. Just ringing for a chat.'

They'd always spoken regularly but her mum's calls had sharply increased since her seizure.

'I'm fine.' Cara pre-empted the question. 'Don't worry.'

'Worry? Me?' Dorothy made scoffing noises. 'How's the villa and all? Fabulous?'

'Fabulous. But it's the same one as the two other times.'

'And you're okay with the food?'

'Yes, Mum.' She wanted to sigh.

'And you're all set to go back to work on Monday?'

Now she'd got her. This morning she'd woken at around 5 a.m., suddenly hit by the enormity of returning after five weeks off with a mystery ailment. 'Oh, Mum, I'm mortified. I feel so embarrassed.'

'You shouldn't be,' Dorothy said. 'You're sick.'

'Mum.' She cradled the phone and whispered, 'Please don't say that. I hate it. I'm not sick. I was just a . . . I lost control for a while. But even with everyone knowing that, I want to die of the shame.'

'People are very understanding these days. Much better than they used to be.'

'Mmm.' Maybe they were, with proper conditions like bi-polar or drug addiction. But with her propensity for overeating and puking, there wouldn't be the same kind of absolution.

'And are you getting any . . . *urges*? With the *gelato* and all that?'

'Honestly, no. Mum, there's nothing wrong. I just, I don't really know, lost control for a while. But I'm fine now.'

'Well, that's great. How's everyone? The Lovable Eccentrics? My favourite son-in-law? And', her tone softened, 'Jessie?'

'All grand. Bye, Mum. See you next week.'

'So,' Robyn stood up and called out, 'who wants to go to the designer outlet mall?'

'The one near Siena?' Jessie said. 'Not me. It's wall-to-wall junk.'

'Oh.' Robyn's tone was cool. 'Saoirse and I need someone to drive us.' She twinkled at Ferdia, who studiously ignored her.

To everyone's surprise, Liam said, 'I'll take you.'

'Oh! Thank you, Liam.'

'You're welcome. Tomorrow do you?'

'It'll have to be Friday,' Nell interjected. 'We're going to the Da Vinci museum tomorrow.'

'Oh, yeah. Friday, then.'

'You coming, Nell?' Robyn asked archly. 'To the outlet?'

'I'm good. I'm not a shopper.'

'You don't say.'

Robyn and Liam laughed, then Saoirse joined in.

Sitting in the shade with her book, Cara wondered if she'd be invited. Nope, didn't look like it. She was literally invisible to Robyn, not even worth mocking. It was sort of funny.

'So maybe this afternoon, we'll go back to the spa,' Robyn said. 'Get a deep tissue mass*aaaaaaaaage*.' She ran her hand up and down her smooth thigh.

'Hey, I can massage you,' Liam said. 'I need a guinea pig to practise on.'

Cara was stricken with shock. He couldn't *possibly* be serious.

'Hey!' Ed snapped. 'Your back is injured. You can't massage anyone.'

'Yeah, but—' Liam looked irritated. Then he said, 'I guess I can't.'

Cara flashed Ed a small grin and they exchanged a silent conversation, which went, *Can you believe that fool?* and *You were a hero* and *You didn't think I'd let him get away with it, did you?*

Ed's answering smile was very sweet. For a joyous moment they were back to normal.

'Mum,' Dilly said to Jessie, 'why is he massaging the guinea pigs?'

'No, bunny, he's—' 'The March of the Valkyries' blared, startling everyone.

'Jesus,' Liam yelped, holding his chest as Jessie grabbed her phone.

'Loretta! *Cara mia! Bene. Sì, sì. Bene. Fantastico! Grazie mille.*' She ended the call and announced to everyone around the pool, 'Ha-ha, I spoke entirely in Italian, Loretta spoke entirely in English. Anyway! There's a wedding up the town at five p.m. If we're there for five thirty, we'll see the bride and groom coming out, we can *gettare* the confetti! Who's on for it?'

'Ed,' Cara said.

Ed was a well-known lover of weddings.

'Melt,' Liam called.

'Not ashamed,' Ed replied.

He insisted that making a public commitment before your peers was a defiantly optimistic act. Accidentally stumbling across a wedding always made him happy.

Cara wanted to go too, but she was due a snack at six o'clock. She could bring something, maybe a banana. But having to eat in front of people would, once again, single her out as a special case.

Was this what her life would be like for ever? Having to plan everything? Being a freak? Well, it would be better if she just made her peace with it. She had all her limbs, she could see, hear, talk—something far worse could have happened to her.

*

Only Liam, Saoirse and Robyn stayed behind. Poor Saoirse, Cara thought. She was usually a sucker for an Italian wedding. Robyn was a malign influence.

As they approached the little stone church, Nell exclaimed, 'Oh! So beautiful.'

Her attention had been caught by the pastel blue, old-fashioned Cinquecento camper van, festooned with white ribbons and flowers.

'Is that the getaway car?' Ferdia asked.

'I think it's called the wedding car.' She laughed. 'But yeah.'

Standing in the sliver of shade provided by the church several pouty girls were dolled up to the nines, in high, high heels, fanning themselves and looking pissed off. Quite a distance from them lounged a cluster of very young men, smoking and looking uncomfortable in their shiny new suits.

'Why aren't they inside?' Cara asked.

'Feck alone knows!' Jessie's eyes were sparkling. 'Italians are gas. You'd swear they were at a murder trial, not a wedding.'

Automatically Cara checked out the size of the girls. Skinny, skinny, skinny—not skinny. There was one girl jiggling a grizzling baby and she was really quite hefty.

For a moment, there was relief—then the familiar wave of judgement. She shouldn't do this. Not to herself and not to other women.

But, she wondered, was it easier here in Italy? When you had a baby, was it acceptable to be bigger?

Probably not. The Western world subjected all women to the same beauty standards.

Suddenly a swell of organ music reached them, followed by a murmur of activity. The boys were extinguishing their cigarettes with elegant swivels of their new shoes, the pouty girls were no longer pouting, and a number of older women had appeared, seemingly from nowhere, carrying baskets of white paper petals. One of the older women gave Vinnie a handful of petals. '*Gettare*,' she urged, making throwing gestures. '*Gettare*.'

'*Gettare*, my bumhole.' In disgust, he passed them to Cara.

The bride and groom appeared on the front step, young and beautiful.

'*Bella! Bravo!*'

Suddenly everyone had confetti and was flinging it joyfully at the newly-weds. As a blizzard of paper petals rained down on them, Cara watched Ed, his happy face, his eyes that gleamed with unshed tears. He was a great person. He was a brilliant father. He saw the best in people, without being a doormat. His openness to life was remarkable, his positivity rare. Her feelings were in a mess right now, but she knew she loved him.

As the last paper petal hit the ground, Vinnie cried, '*Gelato!*'

There was a surge towards the ice-cream shop. Cara hung back and ate her banana.

Seventy-Six

Nell's eyes opened. It was the middle of the night but she was suddenly fully awake. Beside her, Liam was still deep in sleep.

She didn't know what had woken her—then she did: something was terribly wrong between her and Liam.

The knowledge howled at her: Liam was almost a stranger now, a person she barely liked. He kept disappointing her. His every action was that of a much more selfish man than the one she thought she'd married. She kept disappointing him, simply by being herself.

More horrible truths flung themselves at her: she'd ignored warning signs, she'd got married too soon.

When her mum and dad had told her to wait for a bit, they'd been right.

This couldn't be happening. This couldn't be real. It was like the nightmare she'd had a couple of nights ago, except that this time she was awake.

Dark orange light gleamed under the shutters. The sun must be coming up over all that beautiful countryside. Here she was, in one of the most perfect places on earth, and the contrast between that and the wasteland within her was horrifying.

Their love was lost, gone, dispersed. What could she do? How could she fix this?

It was tempting to wake him up, to talk. But that would make it real.

The next thing she knew, her face was being dotted with kisses. She must have gone back to sleep. Lemon-coloured light flooded the room and there was Liam, smiling down at her. All of her fear had evaporated and her relief was so great she was almost ecstatic. 'Liam, I had a nightmare.'

'You should have woken me, baby.'

'It was like a waking nightmare. I thought we didn't love each other any more.'

'We totally love each other. But this is my fault.' He looked sad. 'Bumpy few days. I was such a dick about your museum.'

'It's okay. The fear is gone now.'

'I'm so sorry. I guess we know each other a little better.'

'I guess we do.'

'Bunny.' Jessie was at Ferdia's door. 'I need your Wi-Fi.'

He stepped back, giving her a clear path to the stairs that led up to his bedroom. 'Work away.'

Her look was wary. She was still suspicious of the new nice him and he felt shitty about it.

'I can just go on up?' she asked.

'Sure. You need privacy?'

'Ah, no . . . I'm just FaceTiming with Paige to eat humble pie. I was interfering again.'

Ferdia remained downstairs on his laptop. Jessie connected to Paige and, after a flurry of hellos, she said, 'Paige, I'm so sorry for sticking my oar in—'

Paige's voice: 'Jessie. Hold up. We need to talk about Italy. What did you mean about the dates not working?'

'The girls have camp and couldn't come.'

'Come where?'

'To Italy. The house in Tuscany. Where we are now.'

'I don't know what you're talking about.'

'Liam messaged you months ago. Inviting the girls. But the dates didn't work.'

'Liam didn't message me one single thing about Italy.'

'But . . .' Jessie was struggling to keep up. If this were true, it was completely awful. How much could Ferdia hear of this? The bedroom didn't have a door she could close.

'Liam wouldn't commit to dates for the girls to come to Ireland. Said his job is too busy.'

'Paige . . . I don't know what to say. I'm mortified. It was wrong for me to interfere, but we all love you.'

'Liam doesn't.'

'The rest of us, though, we love you and the girls. But I don't know where we should go from here?'

'O*kayyyy*.' Paige gave a long, heavy sigh. 'Liam and I need to have a conversation. And I need to process. We'll work it out. Thanks for caring. Love you, Jessie.'

'Love you too, Paige.'

Jessie ended the connection and sat looking at her hands. She felt light-headed.

'Mum, what the hell?' Ferdia had run up the stairs.

'You shouldn't have listened.'

'He never invited his kids?!'

'No.' Then, 'D'you think Nell is in on it?'

'Nell? She hasn't a clue. She's all about protecting Liam because his life is so tragic.'

Jessie's head was awhirl. 'I don't know what to do,' she said. 'How to fix this.'

'Mum.' Ferdia's tone was careful. 'I don't mean this in a bad way but it's between Liam and Paige.'

'But he's lied to all of us.' Jessie sighed. 'Maybe I shouldn't have invited the girls. It's just that the bunnies miss their cousins.'

'Your heart was in the right place.'

'Ferd.' She was suddenly urgent. 'You can't tell anyone about this, okay? We shouldn't know this. I won't even tell Johnny, not till we're home. It would cause an atmosphere here. Okay?'

'I can keep my mouth shut.'

'Look at you, all grown-up.' She gave a sad little laugh.

'Speaking of which, you want to know what happened with Barty?'

'Well, aaaah, yeah.'

'It'll probably upset you. I'm sorry about that.'

'Tell me anyway.'

He laid it out and she listened without comment.

When he'd finished, she said, 'I messed up so badly with the Kinsellas. I'm sorry for how it's hurting you.'

'Ah, Mum, stop.'

'I feel strange.' Cara spoke into the phone. 'In my head I know that I love people or that I should be happy but the feelings aren't there. I sort of feel . . . nothing.'

'You're numb,' Peggy said. 'You've been playing fast and loose with your brain chemistry. Now it's sorting itself out. Trust me, you won't be numb for long.'

'You're not exactly reassuring me.'

Peggy laughed. 'Fight today's war today. Leave tomorrow's war until tomorrow.'

Nell marvelled as cogs began spinning, moving every part of the apparatus. This was a flour mill, but also here were flying machines, a tank and a water pump. Da Vinci's vision was incredible. He'd used techniques that, nearly six hundred years later, were still relevant to her work today.

Liam hovered at her elbow. 'Look,' she said, in delight. 'See how the drawings were so accurate?'

'You're having a good time?'

'Oh, God, *yes*.' Then she realized that that hadn't been what he'd been asking. He wanted to know how much longer they were going to be there. 'Are *you* having a good time?'

'*Yeaaah*. Just my back isn't great.'

Exasperation flooded her. Why had he come? Ferdia had offered. Ferdia had *wanted* to be here.

'You'd like me to hurry up?'

'That's not what I said.'

She tried to ignore his silent but evident impatience, but she had only so much stamina. 'Come on, so.'

'We're leaving?' He sounded delighted.

'After we've been to the gift shop.'

'*You?* Mrs Anti-Consumerism?'

Without answering him, she headed out, scanned the shelves and found what she was looking for. 'Just need to pay for this.'

'What is it?'

'A little flying machine. One of the designs. For Ferdia.'

'*What?*'

'To thank him for Tuesday.'

'Oh, yeah?' Liam looked displeased. Not angry but irritated. 'And where's my thank-you?'

'You want a thank-you? Would you like a little flying machine too?' She was being sarcastic, which wasn't like her.

He gave her a strange look. 'Whatever. So what do we do now? I need to eat.'

'We can take a wander, see if we stumble across a nice place?'

'So? Palazzo dell'Arte Vivente?'

'. . . What do you mean? We'd have to book and stuff.'

'Jessie hasn't sorted it for us?'

She was astounded. 'Not that I know of. Did she say she would?'

'I don't know. I just thought, if she did it for Ferdia, she'd do it for me.'

'But, baby . . .' She felt ridiculously guilty. 'I didn't know anything about it the other night. It was all between Ferdia and Jessie. I don't know what to say.'

'Fuck it. We might as well go home.' He stalked away up the street.

'Liam!' A hundred thoughts were tracking through her head. Should she ring Jessie? Was Liam right to be angry? Could she fix this?

No, she decided. No and no.

On the drive back to the villa, Nell knew he meant her to be intimidated by his silence. Or perhaps feel guilty that she hadn't made his day spectacular. But she felt neither. Liam was like a kid, nearly as bad as ten-year-old Vinnie.

When they reached the villa, he parked the car with jerky motions then gave the door a hard slam as he got out and shot up the stairs.

There was no one to be seen, so Nell went down to the pool, looking for a friendly face.

'You're back early,' Cara exclaimed. 'How was it?'

'Nice. Thank you.' Because it had been nice. Bits of it, anyway. 'Do you know where Ferdia is?'

'You could try his little house?'

She headed back up the stone path and knocked on Ferdia's door.

He opened it immediately. 'Hey, you're back! Come in. How was it?'

'Amazing. What are you doing, lurking up here like a vampire?'

'Working. I'm doing a—'

'I got you a little thing in Florence.'

'You did?' He sounded surprised.

Shyly, she gave him the model. 'It's only small. Just to say thank you for Tuesday and sorry about today.'

He opened the box.

'It's one of Da Vinci's designs,' she said. 'A flying machine. It moves and all.'

'Look at that! She gives me flowers. She gives me planes.' He opened his arms wide, and uncertainly she took a step back. *He's going to hug me.*

It was unexpected. And yet it wasn't.

She let him wrap his arms around her. It was hard to know how it had happened but she and Ferdia had become friends.

Seventy-Seven

Late on Friday afternoon, there was a knock on Ferdia's door. 'Ferd? Can I come in?'

It was Saoirse. 'Course. What's up?'

She crept towards the couch and sat down, curling her legs into herself. 'I feel a bit . . .' Tears began to trickle down her face. 'Robyn. She doesn't like me.'

Saoirse was probably right, but he didn't want to add to her misery. 'What do you mean?'

'I get on her nerves and she keeps saying she's bored. I don't know what she expected—I *told* her this wasn't Shagaluf. But today was weird. And horrible. Everything I tried on in the outlet, she said I looked fat.'

'You're not.'

'I actually know that, she was just being a bitch. But her and Liam, they were talking to each other and, like, blanking me. I'm sure they were laughing at me.'

Fury stirred in Ferdia. 'Based on what?'

'She sat in the front of the car, beside him. They were talking in quiet voices and laughing. But when I asked what was up, they said, "Nothing, nothing" in that fakey way.'

'Mother*fuckers*.'

'What should I do?'

He sighed. 'Probably nothing. People like her—and him—if you call them on stuff, they'll full-on gaslight you. This is our last night, just get through it. Stick with me. And when you're back home, just never see her again.'

'But, Ferd, what about Liam? He's our uncle. I can't never see *him* again.'

Jessie waited until everyone had ordered before she said what she always said on the last night of their holiday. 'Bunnies? Can we go round the table and say our personal highlight?'

A chorus of groans was her answer.

'It was *swimming*,' TJ said. 'It's always swimming.'

'Excuse me,' Tom said politely, 'but my highlight was actually *not* swimming.'

'Swimming and *gelato*,' Vinnie shouted.

'Thank you, Vinnie,' Jessie said. 'I know you all laugh at me—'

'I don't,' Dilly said.

'It'll come,' Bridey said.

'Tell us *your* highlight,' Johnny prompted Jessie.

'Having all my bunnies together. Our tribe of bunnies. There was one day when every bunny came down to the vegetable garden with me and we picked tomatoes. You don't know how happy that made me. Thank you all for that.'

'Thank you, Mum,' Bridey said. 'For paying for everything. For all the *gelato* and stuff.'

'Daddy did too.'

Bridey's look was disparaging.

'Johnny? Your highlight?'

'I'm up to six espressos a day now without feeling like I'm about to have a heart attack.'

'You really put the work in.' Jessie felt great, great affection for him. And pride, yes, *pride*. 'You deserve the results.'

'Ferd?'

Ferdia stared off into the middle distance. 'It was all good. But if I had to pick one thing—'

'*You do*,' Dilly murmured.

'Sorta, like, the total *point* of "highlight".' Bridey was lofty.

'— I'd have to go with seeing the *Medusa* in the Uffizi!'

'Really?' Jessie was astonished, then alarmed. What if Ferdia turned into an art lover? She'd have to make herself into one too!

'I was going to say that!' Nell was glowing. 'I've loved it here. So much beauty, and cool people, thank you so much! But my very best bit was the *Medusa*.'

Ed said, 'It's been heartening to see Italian market gardeners turning away from pesticides.'

'Ah, *Ed*.'

'And the wedding,' he added. 'That was brilliant. Cara?'

'Not having to make fish fingers and chips forty times a day. All the cooking you did, Jessie, seriously, thank you. Basically, having nothing to do except read and drink wine was just *looooooo*vely.'

Gloomily Liam said, 'My most memorable moment was the crappy Italian road banjaxing my back.'

Even though Saoirse was next, Robyn piped up, 'Liam was my highlight.' She slid him a sideways smile. 'Thanks for driving me to the outlet so I could get Sergio Rossi fuck-me slingbacks at sixty per cent off.'

'Language!' Bridey snapped. 'There are children present!'

Quite, Jessie agreed. Whatever happened next year, Robyn wasn't coming.

'Saoirse?' Jessie was gentle. She suddenly felt the full extent of Saoirse's misery: she'd had a hard week.

'Just, you know,' Saoirse mumbled, 'all of it. The sunshine and that. Thanks, you guys.' Her voice trailed off.

Jessie's heart twisted. She knew exactly how her beloved daughter felt: uncool and wrong, the object of a joke, rather than a fully fledged human being. Saoirse's time would come, just as Jessie's eventually had, when she finally made real friends, when people saw her 'flaws' as assets. But until then, Saoirse would feel lonely and foolish. She would get crushes on people who pretended to love her back, not because of who she was but for what she could do for them. Jessie remembered it well. But then she'd met Izzy and Keeva Kinsella and everything had dramatically improved.

Seventy-Eight

From the very first Friday evening, so long ago, when Rory had taken Jessie and Johnny 'down home', Izzy and Keeva had been nothing but lovely. That night, the three of them had shared a bedroom, Jessie in one single bed and the sisters topping-and-tailing in the other. They stayed awake until the small hours talking about *everything*.

Lying in the dark, Jessie related her stories of Burmese Cat Man and Amateur Flute Player and was delighted to reduce them to helpless mirth.

'I thought *I* had the funniest story ever!' Keeva howled. 'But you win!' Then she told her about the local lad who'd sidled up to her and said, with heavy suggestion, 'I could do great things with your three acres.'

'Anything going on with you and Rory?' Izzy asked.

'Not a thing.' Because there wasn't, not back then.

'Or Johnny?'

'Nor him either.'

'"Hey, Johnny,"' Keeva said, in a squeaky voice. '"How come you're such a big hit with the goils?"'

Once again, the three of them burst into a storm of laughter.

'I don't even know why I'm laughing,' Izzy complained. 'What's funny about that?'

'It was an *ad.* You don't remember? For Coke, I think. You're probably too young.'

'*Is* Johnny a big hit with the girls?' Izzy asked.

'Oh, *yes*.'

'Don't be at him, Izzy,' Keeva chided.

'Ah, *Keeev-eeeee*!'

'She's a brat,' Keeva said to Jessie. 'She flirts with every man she meets. But she's only leading them on.'

'Having some fun. That's all I'm doing. Doesn't do any harm. Hey! Should we get biscuits?' A shape that was probably Izzy swung herself out of bed.

Keeva made a strangled noise. '*Care*ful, you larky article. You kicked me in the face!'

Squeaking noises came from Izzy, as she rocked with hilarity.

Jessie felt tears of laughter trickle into her pillow. She hadn't enjoyed herself this much in, like, *ever*.

It had been a turning point in Jessie's life.

Less than two weeks later, Rory stood at Jessie's desk. 'Izzy just rang,' he said. 'She says you're to come to Errislannan on Saturday night.'

'Oh!' A gorgeous warmth lit up her chest. 'Will Keeva be there? Will you be there?'

'That's the idea. And Johnny.'

'. . . Well, *great*!'

As far back as then, the three Kinsella kids had already as good as moved out of home: Rory had his flat in Dublin; Keeva stayed with her fiancé Christy in nearby Celbridge five nights out of seven; and Izzy was already looking for a place in the city. But at least once a month, especially if they'd had a hard week, they rang around each other and descended on Ellen—Johnny and Jessie usually in tow—looking for some mothering.

After they'd been fed, Jessie and Johnny would join in the tussling for the best spot on the couch. They'd watch films, maybe go to the local for a quick drink, and spend the following day visiting the pups or supporting Celbridge in the GAA. On those weekends, Izzy and Keeva always shared a bedroom with Jessie, lying awake until four in the morning, talking and laughing. Jessie was finally living out her teenage fantasies, of having close friends, confidantes to whom she could tell anything.

As time passed, she began meeting up with Izzy and Keeva in Dublin, without Rory or Johnny.

Izzy rang one Thursday afternoon. 'Shops? After work? I'm looking for boots and I need you to ride shotgun.'

Humbly, Jessie said, 'I'm not great with fashion.'

'But you'll give it to me straight. If I want to buy high-heeled boots that make my legs look like pipe-cleaners, you'll tell me. C'mon, Jessie.'

Jessie felt high with happiness and, in order not to disappoint, did exactly what Izzy had asked, and said, 'Pipe-cleaners', when Izzy tried on a pair of pointy-toed boots. Izzy was slightly knock-kneed, as if her limbs were too long for her to manage. 'But,' Jessie added, 'there's nothing wrong with pipe-cleaners. I'd love long, skinny pipe-cleaner legs.'

'Nah.' Izzy stared at herself critically. 'No good. I look like a spider.'

She actually did, with her shaggy dark hair and long, thin limbs. But such a lovable, fun spider.

'C'mon so. Let's go for a drink. And next time, we're going shopping for you. Let me and Keeva know when you've been paid.'

'Oh! Okay. How about Saturday?'

'Saturday it is.'

They met at 10 a.m., and Izzy told Jessie, 'We've decided you're not making the most of yourself.'

'*She* decided,' Keeva corrected. 'I think you look fine.'

'You're just a bit . . .' Izzy said. 'Too many suits? Ya know? You need new clothes. Jeans.'

'I have jeans.'

'But they're too . . . What's the word? Neat? Polite. Stop ironing them, Jessie. You'd look great in a wrecked pair.'

'Would I?' She was breathless with a new, daring vision of herself.

'Yes!'

Jessie looked to Keeva. Keeva was the voice of reason. 'Would I?'

'You would. Also, can you change your hair? Would it kill you to get highlights?'

'No! No, it wouldn't.' Jessie was so eager to oblige. 'Where should I go?'

Over time Jessie began to make more girlfriends—her flatmates, some people from work. She felt she'd finally become 'real', normal, just like other people. Izzy and Keeva had seen her potential and given her the confidence to be herself.

They became even closer when she began going out with Rory.

'About fecking time,' Izzy said. 'We were afraid Johnny would get there first. Not that Johnny isn't lovely, of course.' She wiggled her fingers across the crowded pub at him. With a dazzling smile, she mouthed, 'Wouldn't kick you out of bed for eating Tayto, darlin'!'

Keeva was the best person in the world: she was solid, reliable and good. But Izzy was the one people noticed: high-spirited, spontaneous and generous, everyone wanted a piece of her.

Straight out of college, she began working in personal wealth management, a banking job that required a lot of schmoozing and socializing. Informal and funny, she was nothing like her polite, polished colleagues and was a great success.

Jessie was initially shocked, then impressed, at the rate with which she got through boyfriends. No sooner had she declared an interest in someone than she was reporting to Jessie, 'Ah, it didn't work out. Plenty more fish!' Occasionally when a man disappointed her, her spirits were—briefly—dampened, but never for long. It wasn't until she was twenty-seven, and Jessie and Keeva were already mothers of young sons, that Izzy met Tristão, a Brazilian banker who lived in New York.

Tristão was stocky and *immensely* handsome.

'What? I wasn't good-looking enough for you?' Johnny complained to her.

Tristão was a big hit with the rest of them. He'd come to Errislannan, eat Ellen's rhubarb tart, play with baby Barty and Ferdia, and spend Sunday afternoons standing on the side of a wet and windy GAA pitch, just like the rest of them. His English was perfect and his sense of humour impeccable.

Once a month Izzy flew to New York for four days, then two weeks later, Tristão would come to Ireland. The transatlantic thing seemed to work for them, probably because they both had so much energy: Izzy could get off the plane and go straight into work. Their holidays were always strange and amazing: travelling on a camel caravan through Uzbekistan; ten days spent tracking polar bears in Alaska.

'I thought I was very daring going to Vietnam,' Jessie had said.

Now and again there was talk that Izzy might move to New York permanently but then she'd say something like 'Changed my mind. I like Ireland too much.'

Over four years, she and Tristão split up at least twice, but always got back together. Their relationship might have been unconventional but it suited them.

Seventy-Nine

'Don't stop!' Jessie held onto Johnny's hip bones, as he drove in and out of her, with the speed of a jackrabbit.

'Are you . . . ?' he grunted.

'Not yet! Go faster.'

Propped on his arms over her, his hair was dark and slick with sweat. A drop landed on her face and she touched it with her tongue. She was absolutely *loving* this. *Why* didn't they do it more often?

They'd gone for a late drink to say goodbye to Loretta and Marcello.

'So sad we will not see you for another year.' Loretta had sighed, stroking Johnny's cheek.

'Are you flirting with my husband?' Jessie asked. 'Or just being Italian?'

'Flirting,' Loretta said. 'He is sexy man.'

'That eejit?'

'To me he is not an eejit,' Loretta said. 'He is sexy man. I love Marcello, but if I have one night free of my marriage, I would choose Johnny.'

'If *I* have one night free of *my* marriage,' Marcello said, 'I would choose Johnny also.'

'Lord save us,' Johnny bellowed, embarrassed. 'Is it swingers ye are?'

'He charms me,' Loretta informed Jessie. 'And simply, he is . . .' she twirled her fingers around Johnny's face and torso, her Italian hands painting an eloquent picture '. . . hot. Yes, he is hot.'

All of a sudden, Jessie agreed.

Johnny had picked up a bit of a tan, which made his eyes brighter and his teeth very white. Unlike Marcello, a squashy bear of a man, Johnny seemed lean and strong. Not tall, but a lot of power in those hips and thighs . . .

Seeing her husband through the eyes of another woman had her hurrying through the farewells and pushing him back down the hill, into their bed, for a no-frills fuck.

'No!' she'd objected, as he'd planted a line of butterfly kisses from her stomach to her nipple. 'No fiddly business. Get right to it. Now!'

He tore off his clothes and slid straight into her, and she let herself yelp, 'Oh, God!' with a rare abandon.

'Tell. Me. About. It,' he said, matching each word with a thrust.

When he slowed down and began varying his strokes, she howled, 'No!'

She didn't want finesse, she didn't want skill, she just wanted to be fucked. 'Just keep doing exactly what you're doing.'

Tonight she wanted to come while he pounded away on top of her, but his breathing changed, he was making that sound that always indicated the end was in sight.

'Hold on,' she ordered. 'Think about the dip in Kilkenny's profits!'

'Are you nearly . . . ?'

'Yes. Yes! Yes! Yes!'

Afterwards, star-fished across the bed, she murmured, 'That was fucking fabulous.'

'Telling me.' He rested his hand on her hair.

'Worried your arms would give out,' she said. 'But fair play, you stayed the course.'

He made a noise that might have been a snore.

'You always had good upper-body strength,' she said, dreamily.

On the last morning, Johnny lay by the pool, finishing his Lee Child. He loved Jack Reacher. Sometimes he wished he *was* Jack Reacher. Jack Reacher was afraid of nothing. What he found immensely satisfying was that the Lee Child book was always just long enough for his holiday. He was heading into the home stretch with both his holiday and his book. He'd finish it later this afternoon, on the plane, shortly before they landed.

How many other writers could promise that?!

None, he was prepared to bet.

Jessie swished by and said, 'Look at him there, happy out, reading his book.'

'I *am* happy out,' Johnny agreed.

Nell, too, was lying by the pool. She wasn't really a sunbather but she felt flat and disinclined to activity. End-of-holiday blues.

Ed and Ferdia were in the water with all the kids, trying to shove each other off pool floats. Ferdia seemed to be coming off the worst of it. Although he was probably letting them win.

'You're trying to kill me,' he yelled, swimming to the side. 'Recovery time!' Straightening his arms on the edge of the pool, he hoisted himself out with smooth grace. He shook the water back from his hair and wiped his eyes. When he saw Nell, he laughed, his teeth very white. 'Little feckers nearly had me drowned.'

Putting down her book, she smiled into his face, his eyes, his spiky black eyelashes.

A strange joy filled her.

He got to his feet and his shadow moved over her, while drops of cool water fell from his body onto her hot skin.

Oh, holy fuck, the *lines* at Dublin airport. It looked like the whole of Ireland had come home from holidays today and were ahead of them in the passport line. Johnny's mood nose-dived.

He got out his phone to see if anything had happened while they'd been in the air. Jessie said, 'Put that away, I've something to tell you.'

Words to strike dread into anyone's heart. 'I don't know, babes,' he said. 'I'm feeling a bit post-holiday suicidal—'

'I was talking to Paige. During the week. I found out something bad.' Succinctly she laid it out for him.

'Oh, God.' He moaned softly. 'That's . . . oh, Jess, that's bad. Is it any of our business, though? I don't know.'

'I don't know either. I don't know what to do.'

'Nothing,' he said urgently. 'Do nothing.'

'Okay. You're right. There's another thing. I found out why Barty didn't come on this holiday.'

'Oh?' He was instantly alert.

As Jessie related the details of her conversation with Ferdia, Johnny's dismay mounted. 'Good for Ferdia, standing up for you. But how serious is it?'

'Serious, he says. They might never be friends again. I'm sorry, babes,' she said. 'I know you're upset. I'm upset too.'

His life, which only a day ago had seemed sunny and fulfilling, all of a sudden looked like an assault course: children and dogs and planes and meetings and chefs and piss-ups and DHL and mystery shoes and jaunting cars and stern phone calls from the bank and a secret bank account, which, despite all the people staying in the apartment, was filling up far too slowly.

*

'Oh, there's ours!' Nell exclaimed, as a suitcase emerged from the mouth of the conveyor-belt.

Contemptuously, Ferdia watched as Liam let her drag their bag off the belt. Liam's 'bad back' seemed to ebb and flow to suit him.

Now Nell was going from person to person, thanking everyone for an amazing holiday—Dilly, Tom, even Robyn. She spent a long time with Jessie, talking and laughing. Then it was his turn. Eagerly he stepped forward, only to receive a brief, awkward hug. 'Thanks, Ferdia, I'd a great time.' Her eyes slid past him and that was it.

Crushed, he watched her leave.

Six Weeks Ago

MONDAY, 31 AUGUST

Dublin

Eighty

Maybe the centre of Dublin might be shut because of a terrorist threat. Not a *real* one: Cara didn't want anyone hurt. But she'd really appreciate something to prevent her from showing up to work today.

Since as long ago as last Wednesday, leaking anxiety into her final few days in Italy, she'd been dreading this morning. She'd have given anything to have this first day over and done with, to have had an encounter with every one of her colleagues and endured the unavoidable awkward hello. Even better, to be about a month down the line, when everyone had forgotten about her mysterious absence.

Blow-drying her hair and doing her chignon took half an hour. She spent almost as long on her make-up. She moved from room to room, checking her foundation in different lights, watched by Vinnie and Tom, their mood sombre. They didn't know the details but they knew some bad stuff was going down.

'Are there any ball-y bits on my face?' she asked Ed. 'I need to look efficient and together.'

'No ball-y bits. So. Breakfast?'

Her stomach heaved, but she needed to eat. Peggy had warned that being back in the situation where she'd done most of her bingeing might act as a trigger.

'I'll make porridge,' he said.

But when she sat at the table, the steam from the bowl rising towards her face, her throat closed. She stood up. 'Yeah, look, I'll go.'

Ed pulled her against him. 'You're the bravest person ever. Today will be tough, but you're strong enough. And we're all behind you.'

'Do your best.' Tom parroted what she usually said to him on school sports day.

'Starting work again is a huge deal,' Ed said. 'One step closer to normality.'

Walking to the Luas stop, her apprehension intensified. Cripes, a Luas was already hurtling towards her. Couldn't it have had the decency to give her a few minutes?

With a loud swish, the doors opened right next to her, almost as if they were making a point. She got on, feeling as if she'd boarded the train to Hell.

Within mere moments, or so it felt, she'd arrived in town. Most of the carriage poured out at the St Stephen's Green stop. On rubbery legs, she walked the short distance to the Ardglass.

Once she was inside, the hotel felt subtly different. During the last five weeks, it had been getting on with life, experiencing a thousand tiny events a minute, without her. Ducking her head, she hurried through the underground corridors, heading for the locker room, to change into her uniform. A couple of people passed—a chef, an electrician: she nodded, gave half-smiles and kept moving.

Outside the locker room, she took a breath, praying it would be empty.

Henry had phoned on Saturday, allegedly to see how she was doing, but also, she suspected, to check if she really was returning. He'd said that her colleagues at Reception had simply been told she'd been ill. Anyone with half a brain would know that Cara's illness wasn't physical, not like pneumonia or cancer. It was obviously mental-health related—and the shame was killing her.

Full of foreboding, she pushed the door open. Ling was inside.

'Cara!' She launched herself across the room and wrapped her arms around her. 'Welcome back! Are you feeling better?'

'Yep. Yes. Totally. It was no big deal—' She stopped. She'd been gone for five weeks, leaving her colleagues to pick up her slack: it would be all kinds of wrong to tell them it had been no biggie. 'Sorry for leaving you guys in the lurch! But I'm completely better. Back to my best!'

'Cool! Okay, well, see you upstairs.'

As the door swung shut behind Ling, fear overwhelmed Cara. She was a hard worker, a person who took their job seriously. This was the first time she'd realized how much she valued being seen as reliable, respectable, even. Now that that part of her identity had been compromised, she was mortified.

The door opened once more. This time it was Patience. 'Welcome back, Cara. When you're in uniform, can we have a quick chat? Henry's office.'

So, no cosy fireside chat with a silver coffee pot for this debrief?

At least her uniform still fitted. That was something to be grateful for. Her stomach in knots, she went to Henry's office.

Raoul was there, with Henry and Patience.

'Shut the door and sit down. How are you feeling?'

She sat up straight and smiled. 'Fine. Excellent.' Then she blurted, 'I'm so sorry. I'm so embarrassed. It was a one-off, a blip, a moment of craziness.'

'More than a moment.' Henry was smiling, but still.

'I can't apologize enough.'

'You're ill,' Henry said. 'You don't need to apologize for being ill.'

'It's not an illness, not really.'

'You were out on *sick leave*.' Henry let that hang in the air.

Oh.

'How can we support you?' he asked. 'To prevent a relapse?'

'I won't relapse.'

'You've been out on sick leave,' Henry repeated. 'We have a duty of care.'

Suddenly Cara saw the dilemma. The reason she hadn't been sacked was because she was 'ill'—which meant she was a potential liability, prone to relapse. This was, this was . . . *bad.* 'I need to eat every three hours.' She spoke very quickly. 'Only a snack, it won't take me away from the desk for more than a minute or two. I'll see a therapist once a week. On a Friday. If I work through my lunch, can I leave an hour early?'

Henry looked at Raoul. 'Can she?'

'Should be possible.'

'And that's all you need from us by way of support?'

'No more disappearing to the bathroom downstairs?' Patience spoke for the first time.

Feeling as if she might die of shame, Cara whispered, 'No.'

'You were our best receptionist,' Patience said. 'We would be sorry to lose you.'

There was no doubt about it: that was a warning.

No, it was a threat.

'If anything changes,' Henry said meaningfully, 'you will let us know immediately.'

It wasn't a question and it wasn't concern.

'We won't throw you straight into the deep end on your first day back.'

'Oh! But I'm keen to work. To work hard. You can depen–'

'For the next few days, you'll shadow Vihaan,' Raoul said.

Vihaan. Only five months ago, he'd been shadowing *her*. But she had to swallow the humiliation. Bit by bit, the new reality was dropping and clicking into place: she would never again be trusted the way she'd once been.

She'd been so, so good at her job. It had given her a huge amount of pride—and it was gone.

If she had come to work as normal on that Monday after her seizure, no one at work would ever have known anything.

Now she was damaged goods and she would be that way for ever.

'Today was probably the worst day,' Ed said when, white-faced and stunned, she got home that evening.

She nodded, too shell-shocked to speak.

'How can I help?' he asked. 'Whatever you need from me, I'll do it. Anything.' He was all fervour.

But he could never understand the immensity of her loss.

'You've got to let me help you,' he said.

'I need to go to bed.' That was all she knew.

'Go up, put on a hotel show and I'll bring you some dinner.'

Eighty-One

Bing-bong noises alerted Liam to a FaceTime call from Violet and Lenore.

I won't answer.

But it was a couple of weeks since they'd spoken.

Christ, though, these stilted chats were the worst . . .

To his shock, the person on the screen was Paige. Despite everything, he was panicked: were his daughters okay? 'What's up?' he asked quickly.

'So the girls were invited to Tuscany?' Paige said. 'And you didn't tell me.'

Fuuuuuuuuck.

'Who were you talking to?' Liam asked. 'Jessie, right?'

'You lied to Jessie about me. Said I couldn't change their camp dates. I knew *nothing*.'

'Not what I said.'

'It totally was.'

'Listen up, Paige. Jessie's trouble. Her fetish for having everyone together, she doesn't mind exaggerating to get what she wants.'

Paige sighed. 'I am so glad I'm no longer married to you.'

'Back atcha.'

'Why didn't you tell the girls?'

'Because it was a bad idea. You wouldn't have come, right? Without you, those two kids are, well, they're basically *pathetic*. Hey!' He spoke over her protests. 'No judgement—'

'No judgement?!'

'They'd have been scared and shy. Am I right? By the end of day one, they'd have been begging to go home to you.'

'They would have been with their cousins. They love them. And you know what breaks my heart? They love you too. Spending a week with all of you guys in that villa, they'd have been over the moon. But you're too selfish to let that happen.'

'I wanted them here, hundred per cent. I miss them like crazy. But I knew they couldn't hack it. Better to shut the whole thing down before you paid for plane tickets.'

'So nice to hear that you miss them. Because they're coming to you for Christmas.'

'. . . For how long?'

'Four days. Maybe a week. I'll talk with Jessie.'

'Paige, no.' He couldn't have that. 'You need to discuss this with me. I'm their dad.'

'So act like it.' She hung up.

He was furious with embarrassment, snared in a lie and affronted that Paige and Jessie had talked behind his back about *his kids*.

Keeping his separate worlds entirely compartmentalized mattered. A medium-sized collision had just happened and he didn't like it.

Nell really did *not* need to find out about this.

This fucking family! Why did they have to be so enmeshed?

The situation with Jessie needed to be made right. An abject apology often went down well . . . but attack was usually the best form of defence.

He rang Jessie. 'I hear you were talking to Paige.'

'Oh!' She sounded shocked. 'Um. Yes. In Italy. The bunnies missed their cousins.'

'Look, Jessie. Couple of things. Paige was married to *me*. Her kids are my kids. My relationship with her is much more important than your relationship with her. You get me?'

A squeak of dissent escaped her. 'She's my friend—we're friends. We have a relationship—'

'Second.' He spoke over her. 'You got one version of things from Paige. But that wasn't the full picture. It's much more complex.'

After a pause, her confusion almost audible, she asked, 'What *is* the full picture?'

'All due respect, Jessie, that's none of your business.'

That shut her up.

'Two sides to every story, Jessie. Remember that. Nell obviously knows the whole story.' He wanted that to have impact. *Leave Nell out of this.* 'There's no need for this to become a *thing*. Like, you're cool, Jessie. But maybe butt out of situations that you don't know enough about. Okay, gotta go.'

He cut the call. That should stop her shopping him to every single person in the family. Particularly Nell. Things had been choppy enough lately: they didn't need another situation.

After Liam had hung up on her, Jessie sat in silence for at least sixty seconds. She realized she was shaking. Yet, for all Liam's self-righteous conviction, she still believed Paige's version. As for Nell, did she really know this maybe-true-maybe-not 'whole story'? Hard to say. Was there even such a thing as 'the whole story'?

Maybe Liam *was* telling the truth.

Even if he was lying, his relationship with Paige *was* more important than hers.

Besides, Liam was the one who lived in Ireland, not Paige. Liam was the one she had to see at least once a month.

You choose your battles.

But Johnny needed to know. It was difficult, being caught in a situation between her husband and his brother, but she'd created it by interfering. Did it matter that her motivations had been good?

'Johnny?' She ran down the stairs. 'Need to talk to you.'

His face went white. 'What?'

Taking care to avoid judgement, she laid it out dispassionately. 'Liam is right,' she insisted. 'I shouldn't have got involved. But Liam and me, we're good now.' Well, they weren't exactly best friends, but it would be okay, in time.

'Okay,' Johnny said.

'Are you upset?'

'No. I mean, Liam's a bit of a . . . But. It's all grand.'

'So?' Peggy said. 'How are you?'

'I'm—' Cara got no further before she was overtaken by a storm of tears. She cried and cried, ripping tissues from the box and pressing them to her drenched face. 'Sorry.' Her voice was thick. 'I just—' A fresh bout shook her.

Whenever she thought it had run its course, it began again. It was hard to believe she had so many tears in her.

After several minutes, Peggy asked sympathetically, 'Why are you crying, Cara?'

'Work,' she choked out. 'They're watching me. The whole time.'

All week, Raoul, Patience or Henry had hung around Reception, under some flimsy pretext or other, but in reality assessing her. Watching and wondering.

'The way they look at me!' This made her cry even harder. 'Like in the movies, when a person is a traitor or a—a—double-agent. And a person on the inside suspects. That's how they look at me now. Like I'm a traitor.'

'And this makes you feel . . . ?'

'Heartbroken. I'm—I'm *grieving*, for the trust they once had in me.'

'You're no longer numb?'

'I've too many feelings now. You know what they made me do all week? Shadow Vihaan! *I* trained *him* and he's as embarrassed as me.'

'How are you getting on with the other receptionists?'

She tore another tissue from the box. They must have talked about her, wondering where she'd been during those missing weeks, but no one had asked and she didn't know how to tell them. 'All those unspoken questions and explanations . . . It's so awkward. And I've become so bubbly! I'm adding a gazillion invisible exclamation marks to every sentence so I'm all "No problem!!!" this and "No problem!!!" that and it's *exhausting*.'

Eighty-Two

When the front door slammed, letting her know that Liam had left the apartment, Nell exhaled shakily. Being with him was excruciating. Since that last morning in Italy—only six days ago, although it felt like a lifetime—her head had been a war zone.

Two separate, terrible things had happened. Terrible thing one: Liam—her husband, the man she was meant to love—she suddenly couldn't stand him. He had a mean streak a mile wide and every bad thing in his life was someone else's fault.

It had been the weekend in Mayo that had broken them apart, she admitted to herself. What he'd done to Sammie had been so insulting that, even though Nell had tried to condense it into something small enough to hide from herself, it wouldn't disappear. The spite on his face that night haunted her. Even though he'd been drunk and upset, it felt as if she'd seen the real Liam.

Even before Mayo, he'd been weird. In the fancy hotel at Easter, he had made 'jokey' comments about how much she drank, or how gross her second-hand clothes were. And it had been downhill from there.

The second terrible thing was, she'd got a thing for Ferdia. More than a thing. Borderline obsession.

Ferdia, a *kid*. Her nephew. Sort of. Even if he was actually only a step-nephew by marriage.

She took her iPad and googled 'Inappropriate Relationships'. Several stories popped up.

My husband made a pass at my daughter.

My husband had an affair with my son's wife.

Nell scrolled past these.

I'm in love with my stepson.

This one. She clicked the link and devoured the details.

The woman in the piece was thirteen years older than her stepson. Nell was less than nine years older than Ferdia, so this woman was worse than Nell.

The stepson was eighteen, Ferdia was nearly four years older and four years was a *lot* at that age.

Whenever the age difference she read about was bigger than the one between Ferdia and her, she felt like less of a pervert . . . Nine years, though.

Next Friday was his birthday and he'd be twenty-two, so then she'd only be eight years older than him.

But playing those games was bullshit. She knew that. She just wanted to pretend for a while.

The only thing keeping her from totally losing her mind was her job. The day after they'd got back from Italy, she'd gone in and worked for thirteen hours straight. Every day since, same. As a project, it was *not* easy. But when she was engrossed in trying to work things out on set, she wasn't beating herself up for being a terrible person.

Plus, double bonus, it was keeping her out of Liam's way.

When, though, had this crazy crush on Ferdia started? Because, for the longest time, she'd just thought he was a spoilt fool. Was it in Mayo that she'd first felt *weird* about him? Just after Liam had blown bubbles in Sammie's face? Ferdia, like some hot romantic lead, had been holding Sammie in his arms, murmuring soothing, tender words into her hair—and Nell *definitely* remembered feeling a pang then.

Then, jump to that crazy murder-mystery country house when Ferdia had been so great about helping Cara. Between the two of them, they'd maybe saved Cara's life. That had to be a pretty intense bonding experience.

It must have been then that she'd decided he was sound.

But the wheels had come off good and proper during the sun-filled week in Tuscany.

Even then, she'd thought, objectively, he was hot but *fancy* him? No way.

It wasn't until that last day when, in a single heartbeat, he'd shifted from being a kid she was fond of to a man she was *lit* for. Her fingertips literally throbbed from needing to touch his face. She wanted to taste his beautiful body with her tongue, to kiss him full on the mouth, for the palms of his hands to slide along her skin and for his voice to say her name again and again.

Stunned was how she'd felt: confused, ashamed, afraid. It had been the literal worst.

Saying goodbye at the luggage belt, she was so scared she'd lunge and start eating the face off him that she couldn't even look him in the eye.

What she needed to remember was that these feelings couldn't be real.

Sure, they *felt* real, but they totally, absolutely, weren't.

Four Weeks Ago

FRIDAY, 11 SEPTEMBER

Ferdia's birthday

Eighty-Three

'Jessie?'

'Mmm?' She was trying to jam another bottle of beer inside the door of the fridge.

'Is Barty coming today?'

'What?' Concerned, Jessie switched her attention from the beer to her husband. 'No, babes. They still haven't made up.'

'But it's Ferd's birthday.' Johnny looked woebegone.

Helplessly she gazed at him. Since they'd come back from Italy—almost from the very moment they'd landed at Dublin airport—all their recent closeness had just vanished.

'Sweetie.' She kept her voice gentle. 'Are you all right?'

'I'm grand. All grand.'

He obviously *wasn't* grand. He was morose, maybe even depressed. But Johnny didn't talk about stuff. He could be contemplating jumping off a bridge—sitting on a girder, staring down into the choppy water!—and he'd still be insisting he was fine.

'Johnny,' she said tentatively. 'You can tell me anything. I'm your friend.'

'Yeah,' he said, sounding vague. 'I know.'

'I'd do anything for you.'

That wasn't exactly true. She'd implied that she'd 'think about' changing their business model and she hadn't.

Okay. She was scared about making changes, but the time had come. She hadn't a notion, though, where to start. However, her friend Mary-Laine, who knew more about running a business than Jessie ever would, could probably advise her.

No time like the present. She grabbed her phone. 'M-L? Howya, missus, meet me for a drink after work on Monday? Quick chat about business stuff.'

'Okay. That wanky new bar in Smithfield?'

'Oh, *God*. We're too old, they'll laugh at us.'

Mary-Laine remained silent. Mary-Laine wanted to go to that bar and Mary-Laine never blinked first.

'Oh, *all right*.' Jessie said. 'Six thirty?'

'See you then.'

'Sorry I'm late.' Cara sat down opposite Peggy. 'Sorry.'

Peggy's face was pleasant but quizzical. After a period of quiet had elapsed, she said, 'Is there a reason? For you being nearly fifteen minutes late?'

'Getting away from work wasn't easy, then across town through Friday rush-hour, you know how it is.'

But no one had prevented her from leaving work on time. She hadn't wanted to come here today, that was all.

Peggy was eyeing her with interest. 'How are you, Cara?'

'Fine.'

'What sort of fine?'

'Oh, you know. Just fine. Good.'

The thing was, during the week she'd realized she couldn't do this any more—be the woman with the mortifying illness. She'd already lost far too much from this whole debacle. She wanted her life to return to the way it used to be— cutting ties with this hospital and stopping seeing Peggy. And after enough time had passed, nearly everyone would forget this blip had ever happened.

'How was work this week?' Peggy asked.

'Good. Fine.'

'Last week you felt sad and angry because you felt they no longer trusted you.'

'This week's been a lot better.'

It hadn't. The humiliation of shadowing Vihaan had stopped but there was still a *mood*: horrific levels of perkiness from both her and the other receptionists as they tried to obscure the strange fact that she'd disappeared for over a month with a mystery illness.

She was still being watched by Raoul, Henry and Patience. Whatever they'd been hoping for from Cara, they clearly hadn't seen it yet. Which had become manifestly clear yesterday.

The Spauldings were the couple from Hell. Before her sick leave, Cara had been the only one trusted to wrangle them. Admittedly, she'd been nervous as the time of their arrival approached. This was the first real challenge she'd faced since her return to work, and if they were particularly mean, she couldn't be sure how she'd cope.

Standing at the front desk, with their iPad and keys, she discreetly did one of her breathing exercises, to try to calm down, before their arrival.

In for four, out for seven, in for four, ou–

Raoul appeared, followed by Madelyn. 'Who has the Spaulding keys?'

'Here.'

'So.' Raoul picked them up, along with the iPad, and gave them to Madelyn. 'Keep smiling. Say yes to everything. Off you go.'

Vihaan's head jerked around to stare, Ling gasped and Zachery's eyes bulged with amazement.

It seemed to happen in slow motion and Cara felt her face freeze with shock. Madelyn avoided looking at her, but it was clear she was embarrassed.

Trying to calm her breath, which was quick and shallow in her chest, Cara realized she'd never actually been told that the Spaulding check-in was hers. But because it had always been her job in the past, she'd assumed it still was. The humiliation was almost enough to crush her. That was the moment when she'd decided that this had gone far enough.

Peggy was watching her with the same intent focus. 'That's a big change between last week and this week.'

Cara smiled. 'All back to normal.'

'How's your eating plan?'

Cara sat up straighter, on much more solid ground. 'Good. Like, great. Seriously, it's seven weeks since the, um . . . seizure and I've stuck to the plan. I don't even *want* chocolate or sweets! I'm finding it really easy.'

So easy that the conviction there was nothing wrong with her had strengthened. If she was really a compulsive overeater, surely she'd *never* have lasted that long.

'You might need to keep an eye on that,' Peggy said. 'You wouldn't want to get complacent.'

'I'm not complacent,' she said. 'I'm saying your plan works.'

Peggy shook her head. 'What you're trying to say is that there's nothing wrong with you.'

I don't think there is.

'Nobody wants that stigma,' Peggy said.

'You're right.'

But by now she was almost convinced she *hadn't* an eating disorder and it felt dishonest to be a patient of this hospital.

'How are you and Ed?' Peggy asked.

Cara flinched. It was impossible to put it into words. Sometimes she was angry with him for setting this whole circus in motion. Mostly, though, they couldn't seem to connect in their old, effortless way. They were trying to communicate but it was as if they were both sealed inside individual soundproofed bubbles.

'Peggy, can we finish here for today? I'm absolutely shattered.'

'Twenty minutes early?' Peggy gave her another of those gimlet-eyed stares. 'So? Next week?'

'I can't. Vinnie. Has an appointment. With a specialist. About his possible ADHD.'

'Let's fix another time next week.'

'Sorry, I can't. They've been so good to me in work and it doesn't feel right to ask for more time off.'

After a silence weighty with disapproval, Peggy said, 'Addiction is a disease of denial. It tells you that you don't have it.'

'Uh-huh.'

'This time two weeks?'

'Absolutely. This time two weeks.'

As she got up to leave, Cara felt a pang. Peggy had been very kind to her. She felt sad that she wouldn't be meeting her again.

'See you tomorrow,' Nell called to Lorelei.

'Where you going? It's only six o'clock!'

'Nephew's birthday dinner.'

'So you take a half-day?'

'Ha-ha-ha.' She was *so* nervous. 'Bye.'

It's cool, it's cool, it's cool, she thought. *I've totally got this. Just show up, say happy birthday, give him the gift, then go play with the kids. No one will guess anything.*

At home, she let herself in. 'Hey,' she called out to Liam. 'Let's go.'

But he looked bedded in for the evening.

'You really going to that prick's birthday?' he said.

She took a breath. 'Liam, they're family.'

'Not yours.' He'd been trying to hurt her. If only he'd known. 'I'm not going,' he said.

'Well, I am.'

He frowned. 'Wha-at? Really? Driving or cycling?'

'Bus.' She felt too wobbly to chance driving or—more insane still—cycling through rush-hour traffic.

'Wow.' His back was still tricky after the holiday. 'I'd love to be able to jump up on the bike and get a good cycle in.'

'You'll be better soon.'

'Since when were you a doctor?'

'Hurry up, Mum,' Vinnie said, as Cara let herself into the house. 'We're ready to go to TJ's.'

'Hello, sweetie.' Ed kissed her. 'How did you get on with Peggy?'

'You know, Ed . . .' This could be a good time to drop it lightly into the conversation. *There's no need for me to see her. I think I'll stop.* 'I'm feeling fine. I don't need to keep going.'

'Honey.' He looked haunted. 'She's your lifeline, you absolutely have to—'

'But I'm doing so well. No compulsions. I'm back to normal.'

'Please don't stop. Not yet. Sticking with Peggy will give you a much better chance of not relapsing.'

She wished he wouldn't say words like 'relapse': he made it sound so much more serious than it was.

'Honey, I love you so much.' He looked dog-tired. 'But if you start with the food again, I'd have to leave. If I stayed, I'd be enabling you—'

'That's not going to happen.'

But today was clearly too soon to change his mind.

When she'd skipped a few sessions and was still sticking to her plan, she'd have proof that she really was better. She'd tell him then.

Outside Jessie's house, Nell faced facts: Perla would be here. Since this insanity had kicked off, she'd become crazy-jealous of Perla. But she could *not* let it show. A deep breath, a slow exhale, then she was okay to ring the bell.

The sound of running feet came thumping down the hall. 'Nell's here!'

The door was wrenched wide and Nell was swept into the kitchen by a flotilla of the younger cousins.

. . . There he was, taller than everyone else. She couldn't look at him.

No sign of Perla yet.

'Nell, Nell, Nell!' Jessie grabbed her in a hug. 'Have some wine. Hey. Where's Liam?'

'His back is still bad . . .' She made herself focus on Ferdia. 'He says sorry.'

'Covering his ass?' He smiled. 'You do know you're *waaaaay* too good for him.'

Her face flooded with heat. 'Happy birthday.' She gave him a chunky box.

She focused on his fingers as he carefully unknotted the ribbon and slid his nail under the Sellotape. Every movement of his beautiful hands had her mesmerized.

'What's in here?' Easing away the Sellotape, he gave her a quizzical look.

Methodically he peeled the wrapping paper off the box and removed the lid. Inside was a hand-carved toy car, a sleek walnut Chevrolet, which kicked off a clamour of awe.

'Where did you get it?' Jessie cried.

'Summersgate market.'

She'd spent too many hours there, when she should have been working, trawling the curiosities at the stalls, looking for something special enough.

'So you've given me a plane,' Ferdia said, 'and now a car!'

'It's from Liam too.' Hah. Liam didn't even know about it.

Ferdia ignored that. 'Birthday hug?'

She had to step into the circle of his arms, as if he were as safe as Dilly. The heat of his chest travelled through the thin fabric of his shirt, then through her top.

Tentatively she touched his back, but when her fingertips felt the knobbles of his vertebrae, she stepped, too quickly, away from him. To her relief, the arrival of Ed, Cara and the kids shifted the focus.

Still no Perla—not even when Jessie laid several platters of Korean dumplings on the table and there was a sudden scramble for chairs. Maybe she wasn't coming. Jessie wouldn't have dished up the grub if they were waiting for more people.

Patrolling with the wine, Johnny stopped at Ferdia. 'More?'

'No. Pacing myself.'

'Big sesh tonight?' Ed asked.

'Gig in the Button Factory. You should all come.' His glance skimmed around the table and snagged on Nell.

'My gig days are long behind me,' Cara said. 'If I don't have a seat, my suffering is unquantifiable.'

'Old age comes to us all,' Ed said.

'And we're too young,' Bridey piped up.

'But Nell could go,' Dilly said. 'She's the right age.'

'Do, Nell,' Jessie insisted.

'Do,' Ferdia said.

'Ha-ha.' She didn't know if she was being humoured. 'I've got work tomorrow.'

'On a Saturday?'

'All the days right now. Only eleven days till opening night. Anyone wants free tickets, let me know.'

'How's it going?' Jessie asked.

'Good.' She paused. 'I think. If nothing goes badly wrong between now and a week next Tuesday, we'll make it.'

Once she'd made her escape from Jessie's, she rang Garr. 'Where are you at? Meet me? In about forty minutes?'

'What's up?'

'Tell you when I see you.'

'I'll be in the Long Hall.'

When she arrived, Garr had a drink waiting.

'I . . .' She hardly knew how to get into this. 'I feel like I don't love Liam any more.'

The great thing about Garr—maybe about men in general—was that they didn't start telling her what they thought she wanted to hear. Triona, for example: she'd have said, 'Of course you love him! It's just a phase.'

'Did something happen?' Garr asked.

'A few somethings but I don't know that they're deal-breakers. Maybe I just know the real him now. This is awful, but I actually don't like him. I married him too quickly, Garr. It was bullshit. Nana McDermott was right. And it's not fair to him.'

'Talk to him.'

'I've tried. He said we're just getting to know each other better. But the more I know him, the less I like him. I feel like a terrible person.'

'You need to tell him what you've told me.' He paused. 'Not word for word. Maybe ease up on the negative stuff. You can probably fix this.'

'You think? I feel so guilty about his family—they've all been so sound. I *love* Cara. And Jessie, too, even though she's stone mad. Ed is great, and Johnny is funny. And the *kids*. Dilly, TJ, Vinnie and Tom. Even Bridey. Saoirse is a sweetie. And—' She stopped abruptly.

'What?' Garr asked.

She couldn't speak.

Garr's face was all disbelief. 'Nell . . . Jesus Christ, is something going on between you and the young lad? The son? Your *nephew*?'

'No. No. No way. No.'

'Nell, *what*?'

'Garr, it's horrific. I'm . . . sort of . . . *obsessed* with him.' Tears were pouring down her face. 'I'm scared out of my mind. Am I mentally ill? Is this a thing?'

'But what age is he? Nineteen? Twenty?'

'Twenty-two. I'm nearly nine years older than him, Garr. But it's not illegal. Falling in love with your nephew. I looked it up.'

'Oh, *Nell.* Lemme ask, which came first? Going off Liam? Or getting a thing for the nephew?'

'Going off Liam.' She needed that to be true. If she'd lost interest in Liam because she'd got a thing for Ferdia, what kind of a person was she?

'Do you fancy your man? Or . . . ?'

' "Fancy" isn't the word, Garr. I want him so much it's . . . *insane.* I think he's good, his heart is good. He was an eejit and now he isn't. And he's funny and lovely . . .' She cleared her throat. 'Anyway, he has a girlfriend.'

'Stay away from him. I totally mean it: stay the hell away from him. And sort your shit out with Liam.'

'Thanks, Garr. I'll do that.'

The Button Factory was dark, crowded and very noisy. Had she lost her damn mind? Besides, she'd never find him in this chaos. But there he was, pushing through the people, his gaze intent on hers.

'Nell.' His eyes glowed. 'You *came.*' He took hold of her face, the palms of his hands rough and soft against her cheeks. Moving so close that they were breathing the same air, he asked, 'Are you on your own?'

She could see the pores of his beard, the slight chapping on his lips, how his dark eyelashes clumped spikily together.

'Let me get you a drink.'

She was seized by fear. 'Ferdia. No. Sorry. I should go.'

The surge of panic propelled her through the crowds and out of the front door. In the busy street, she dodged and swerved, putting distance between them, her heart hammering.

Her phone buzzed with a text. Please come back. She moved faster, trying to breathe away the anxiety in her chest. Her phone began ringing. She shouldn't talk to him, she couldn't go back. This was scary and dangerous.

What had he been doing, holding her face and looking at her like that?

Maybe he was drunk. Stoned? Just being friendly? Looking to get one over on Liam? Anything was possible. The important thing she needed to keep remembering was that as of *right now*, at this *exact* moment in time, she'd done nothing wrong.

I'm safe. I'm still a normal person. I haven't done anything bad.

If she crossed the line, she'd create a whole world of pain and regret. Not just for herself, but for other people, especially Liam. He deserved better.

Walking fast, she focused on Garr's advice: to sort her shit out with Liam.

They needed to talk about the expectations they'd had of each other. They needed to adjust to reality and—maybe—be honest about their disappointments.

Communication was vital, everyone was always saying that—when they weren't going on about marriage being 'hard work'.

There was also the matter of his baggage: Liam had two daughters whom he never saw. That had to be eating away at his self-esteem.

By the time she'd reached home, she'd made a decision: she wasn't giving up yet.

Eighty-Four

She was embroidering a barcode onto a ticket for the opening night of *Human Salt*. It was fiddly, intricate work, so easy to get wrong, and she had several hundred more to do . . . A hand on her naked hip surprised her. Fingers were pitter-pattering along the top of her thigh, lightly touching off her most sensitive spot, and moving away again. Hot breath on her face, then a voice said thickly, 'I let you sleep as long as possible.'

Adrenalin spiked, moving her from the anxiety dream into grim reality. Liam was in the mood for sex. They hadn't done it since they'd got home from Italy. It was no accident: she'd been keeping out of his way, up early and home late. The few times he'd put the moves on her, she'd been blunt about how knackered she was.

Today, though, he'd obviously decided she'd had enough of a rest.

Going through with this would be a challenge. Right now, Liam was just a man with an erection who wanted to have sex with her body. If she refused, it would trigger a crisis. Which she didn't want. Not after last night's decision that there was still hope for them.

I am agreeing to this.

I am consenting.

I am doing this to buy myself time.

She closed her eyes, tried to disappear into her head and reminded herself that she was giving Liam permission to do whatever it was that he was doing.

It was over quickly. Panting, he lay on top of her. 'What about you?' he asked.

'I'm fine. Tired.'

'Grand.' He toppled onto the mattress and within seconds was snoring.

'Should I wear my boots?' Saoirse called, to the household at large.

'It's sunny!' Bridey said.

'But it's September—it's autumn. What if autumn arrives while I'm out and I've to come home in the cold in my sandals?'

Johnny kept his head down, afraid that Ferdia or Saoirse would ask for a lift to Errislannan.

Something about this, the turn in the seasons, made him remember other long-ago Saturdays when it had felt as if he practically lived down there.

After Rory's death, he'd been given his own key and an open invitation. Almost every weekend, he'd driven there, had a quiet dinner, then watched Saturday-night television, reassuring in its crapness. Sometimes Keeva dropped in, sometimes Izzy came by, but often Johnny sat there alone with Ellen and Michael and no one seemed to find it odd. Being with Michael had made Johnny feel slightly less weirded out by everything.

If, for any reason, Michael had to leave the house, Johnny followed him like a faithful dog. When a last-minute ticket-checker was needed for the GAA quiz night, both Michael and Johnny rose from the couch simultaneously. Johnny was quite content to spend ninety useless minutes sitting next to Michael in a draughty porch, watching him tear tickets in two.

When the Kinsellas' nearest neighbours were short-handed on a night's lambing, both Michael and Johnny got up, put on wellingtons and crossed the fields to the barn, where Johnny obediently yanked lambs into the world.

All the same, he wasn't doing so well. Even he recognized that.

At work things, people made polite enquiries about how he was coping without really wanting the answer. He'd perform a palatable version of grief: a soft, wry smile, a sad shake of the head and some platitude, like 'You learn to live with it.'

But the truth was, he'd scare people if he told them how he really felt.

One night, at an industry party, he crossed paths with Yannick, a man he hadn't seen since Before. He liked him—he'd always seemed warm and easy-going.

'Johnny, how have you been?'

There followed that weighted pause, the unspoken words: *Since Rory died?*

Johnny had had too much to drink and strange thoughts began to leak from his mouth: 'I . . . ah. Yannick . . . You know that painting of the man holding his face? Is it called *The Howl*?'

'You mean *The Scream*? By Munch?'

'Maybe I do. The other day I saw it on an oven-glove—I know, an *oven-glove*. Aren't people mad?' He gave a bark of a laugh. 'Anyway, I saw it and for a split second I thought I was looking into a mirror.'

Yannick's pupils flared in alarm. He wasn't sure if he was meant to laugh.

'Where do we come from?' Johnny asked. 'I don't understand any of it. We get born and we do some stuff and then we die and . . . *why*?'

'I see . . .'

'Does it make any sense to you?' Johnny realized he was pleading. Abruptly he stopped, made himself smile, and said, 'I'm doing okay, Yannick. How are you?'

He struggled on, and one Saturday, not long before the first anniversary, when the leaves were turning red and orange and the air had an autumnal chill, Johnny drove to Errislannan and found Izzy at the kitchen table doing a Sudoku. 'You're supposed to be in New York.'

'I broke it off with Tristão. Planes, lemon-scented towelettes . . . Johnny, suddenly my life seems so *flashy*.'

Johnny understood. Rory dying had bumped each of them out of their habitual groove and caused them to re-examine how they were using their short, precious days.

'Those fancy holidays Tristão and I went on . . .' Izzy said '. . . all I was doing was experiencing sensations.'

'Nothing wrong with that.'

'There is if that's all it is.' Fiercely she said, 'Johnny, I want to live in one place and get on a plane twice a year. I want to be part of a community and have a husband and children. I want to be in a book group and join the neighbourhood watch.'

He said nothing. If that was what she wanted, that was what she wanted.

'What about you, Johnny? You're not getting any younger.'

He wanted the same things Izzy did. Over the years, he'd had relationships, some of them looking like they'd go the distance, but whenever it had come to crunch time, he'd backed away. During this time, his feelings for Jessie had risen and fallen. His longing would reach a peak, then ebb away, and for months, maybe even years, they'd be back to being mates. During those spells he was certain he was finally done with it all. But it kept recurring. So much so that he'd wondered if he should just accept that it would continue to afflict him occasionally, as if he were a person prone to chest infections. Meanwhile, he'd got himself a name as a heartbreaker. In his more self-pitying moments he felt that was undeserved, but there was no denying that actually he had, albeit temporarily, broken one or two women.

Every time another one bit the dust, Izzy would joke, 'No one's ever gonna measure up to me, Johnny Casey. You might as well just make your peace with it.'

They'd always been that way, him and Izzy, sparking off each other. Once upon a time, when they'd all been so ridiculously young and carefree, he and his housemates were woken at 3 a.m. by a persistent ringing on their bell.

When a bleary Johnny had opened the door, Izzy was outside, laughing. 'Open wide, as the bishop said to the actress!'

'What're you doing here?'

'Curiosity,' she said. 'Where's your bedroom?'

He'd tensed. He fancied her but he was besotted with the entire Kinsella clan and he didn't want complications.

She had already disappeared up the stairs. 'Feck's sake, Johnny Casey,' she called down. 'I don't want to *marry* you. I just want a ride. C'mon!'

In his room, she kicked off her boots and unzipped her jeans.

'Yeah, but . . .'

'Stop over-thinking things.'

In the morning, she was just as breezy. 'Nothing happened, okay? We don't want an atmosphere around Ellen's dinner table.'

'Yes. Yep.' His relief had been huge.

Next time, *he* showed up at *her* home.

Over the following few years, they made occasional booty calls on each other. Sometimes a flurry of several in one month, then a long time without anything at all. Eventually it petered away entirely.

In the months after she had broken up with Tristão, a routine developed, where most Saturday afternoons, Izzy and Johnny came to Errislannan and stayed until Sunday evening. Ellen would load them up with home baking and they would indulge in gentle pursuits like Monopoly and Risk. If there was a birthday or some sort of celebration, Jessie visited with Ferdia and Saoirse. As would Keeva, Christy and their kids. They'd sing and eat cake and carry on around the appalling absence in their lives.

Johnny was still Michael's little helper. When Christy's van broke down, even though Johnny understood nothing about engines, he went along to help.

During the snow, when a tree fell across a neighbour's gate, Johnny helped Michael chainsaw it away.

It was Liam who eventually challenged Johnny. 'Wait a minute, you're nearly thirty-five. You spend your downtime sleeping in a single bed in your dead mate's parents' house. You need to man up.'

But Liam hadn't a clue: too young and too hard.

'Or are you, like, depressed?' Liam had asked. 'Go see the doctor, get some tablets and get a grip.'

Weeks later, Johnny looked up the signs of depression. Coincidentally he saw he did have some of them but there was no need to see a doctor: time would take care of him.

Eighty-Five

Monday evening after work. Both speaking urgently on their phones, Jessie and Mary-Laine arrived at the hipster bar at exactly the same time.

'Gotta go.' Jessie hung up, then hugged Mary-Laine. 'Thanks for this.'

'There's a table.' Mary-Laine pounced, then waved over a waiter.

'Gin and tonic,' Jessie said to him gratefully. 'In a giant round glass—you know the one I mean? With loads of ice.'

'Same for me,' Mary-Laine said. 'You had me at "giant round glass".' Then to Jessie, 'So what's up?'

'Who would I talk to about changing the business to online?'

Mary-Laine frowned. 'You want to do that?'

'Not really,' Jessie admitted. 'But Johnny does.' She hesitated before confiding the next part. 'His birthday is coming up. This will be his present. Look, I know!' She forestalled Mary-Laine.

'I didn't say a thing!'

'You're thinking he doesn't deserve anything after the total shambles he organized for *my* birthday—'

'I felt sorry for him, if you must know.'

'And you'd be right. But, look, I'm over it now. This means a lot to him. But I don't know where to start.'

'Talk to a management consultant.'

'I don't know any. And I don't know who to trust.'

'Karl Brennan. He's the absolute best.'

'Well, thanks!'

'The only thing is, he's sort of . . . *awful.* Handsy. Creepy. Always having children with different women. Oh, thank *God*, here come our giant drinks!'

'It's like a goldfish bowl.' Jessie admired her enormous round glass, then clinked with Mary-Laine. 'To gin.'

After a glorious swallow, Jessie said, 'Remember when gin wasn't cool? What was *wrong* with us?'

'We hadn't a clue.' Mary-Laine gulped a mouthful and sighed. 'Christ, that's lovely. They're trying to make whiskey a thing now, but I don't think I'll ever like it.'

'Why would we, when we have gin?'

'Should I "reach out" to Karl on your behalf?'

'I actually feel like singing a song about how much I love gin,' Jessie said. She pulled back to study her giant glass. 'These must be stronger than I realized.'

'I've nearly finished mine.'

'That's because we're businesswomen! Energetic self-starters. Do. Reach out. But in *strictest confidence*.'

'Strictest confidence it is.'

'If Karl Brennan says yes, what do I do?'

'Meet him. Take him for lunch. Keep it light and chatty.'

'And he's the best, you say.'

'Brilliant. Unfortunately. Now's the time to get him, before he ends up in rehab. Or perhaps prison for some sort of sexual pestering.'

'Should I be worried?'

'Nah, be grand. Just don't try to save him. He has . . .' she lapsed into a thoughtful pause '. . . a repulsive sort of charm.'

'Repulsive charm. Gotcha. Are we getting another fishbowl of gin?'

'I'd better go. Thanks for the gin.'

'Thanks for the info.'

Jessie was scoping out the street, looking for her taxi, when her phone rang. Unknown number.

'Jessie Parnell? Karl Brennan. Mary-Laine was on to me.'

'That was quick. Did she explain?'

'Some. We should meet. Is now good?'

'Christ, you're dynamic! Is that a management-consultant thing?'

'Always.'

'I'm on my way home. Tomorrow evening?'

'Jack Black's in Dawson Street. Seven o'clock? Email me your accounts for the last three years. I'll text the address.'

'Cara,' Raoul said. 'A word.'

What *now*? Today had been absolutely insane. Zachery was sick so they were down a receptionist. Plus every possible thing that could go wrong had gone wrong. Guests arriving early. A departing guest developing a strange stomach complaint and being too ill to leave. A half-empty bottle of red wine accidentally spilling on the white carpet of the Honeymoon Suite forty minutes before the happy couple arrived.

Cara had been firefighting for hours. No sooner was one drama resolved than another blew up.

Just now a guest who'd checked out this morning had called saying they'd left a pair of diamond cufflinks behind in a drawer—but the new guests were already in situ, with a Do Not Disturb sign on the door. The caller had talked wildly of injunctions and it took every fibre of Cara's energy to persuade him to calm down.

The phone rang again, as Raoul said, 'Don't answer. What about your snack?'

'My . . . ?' Oh, my God, her *snack*. She felt sick with embarrassment. 'What time is it?' It was two fifty-five p.m.: she hadn't eaten in almost six hours.

'I'm fine. Too busy to be hungry. Anyway . . .' She indicated the phone.

'Henry says you have to eat.' Raoul sounded irritable. 'We've a duty of care. But be *quick*.'

It seemed easier to comply than to stand there and argue, so she hurried towards the stairs, to eat her handful of nuts in the locker room.

'Where are you going?' Madelyn looked angry. And well she might. It was hours since anyone had even had a bathroom break.

'Be back in a second.'

Cara scooted away, but not before she heard Ling say, 'Where's she off to?'

Several lone men haunted Jack Black's, all looking a little post-work desperate. But the one who stood out sported sharply cut, silver-fox hair, a paunch, bloodshot blue eyes and a look-at-me suit with a faint but worrying metallic sheen.

Don't be Karl Brennan.

'Jessie?' Mr Dodgy Suit asked. 'Let's grab a table!'

'Before we go any further, are you very expensive?' Jessie asked, when the drinks were ordered.

His smirk was lazily confident. 'I charge in six-minute intervals. My rate.' He scribbled a figure on a piece of paper, like he was in *The Wolf of Wall Street*, and slid it across to her.

'Not your *hourly* rate?' She had to check. 'I'd better talk fast. Retail is dying, so everyone keeps telling me. Online is the future. Change or die.'

'Yeeeaah. Something tells me you're not crazy about making this change.'

'My husband's the one who wants to.'

'What's worrying you?'

'A lot,' she said.

'Meter's running.'

Quickly she spilt it all out: her fear of the banks, her fear of irrelevance, her fear of losing everything. Her belief and pride in the current set-up, her conviction that her chef-pestering was a lucrative endeavour.

'I did something similar for AntiFreeze,' he said. 'Bespoke, high-end adventure clothing operating from a lone store in London. It was all about the personal—hand-fitted boots, goggles, everything. Converted the entire business to online. Managed to recreate some of the one-to-one dynamic, using computer scanning, instant messaging. Not perfect, admittedly. But turnover is up by over 2000 per cent.'

'That sounds . . . hopeful. What now?'

'I send you a contract. You pay a retainer. I'll look at your accounts, do my research, pull together a few different proposals.'

'Will they work? I won't go out of business?'

He rolled his eyes. 'I'm good. I never said I was bullet-proof!'

'How long will it take? I'd like to have something for Johnny's birthday, which is four weeks away.'

'That's insane,' he said. 'Too soon.'

'So how long *will* it be? Because at your six-minute rate, I'll be bankrupt if it goes on much longer than that.'

He laughed. And well he might. 'Not every second of my time is chargeable. I'll be waiting on information to get back to me. Now and again, taking some downtime.' Another of those slightly repulsive smirks.

'Ballpark?'

'Six weeks, maybe eight?'

Well, it was a start. The expensive contract would make a lovely birthday present for Johnny, ha-ha.

In the taxi home she rang Mary-Laine. 'I met him.'

'He try to lure you to a lap-dancing club with his twenty-three-year-old girlfriend? No? You got off lightly. You must really love Johnny Casey,' Mary-Laine said. 'Putting yourself through this for him.'

'I really must.'

Eighty-Six

Cara ducked into SpaceNK and, within seconds, was testing foundation colours on the back of her hand. This was like skipping school—the same sense of freedom coupled with fear of being caught.

At four o'clock she'd left work because today was Friday and that was what everyone expected her to do.

But she wasn't going to Peggy so she had a free hour to do whatever she liked.

On Monday or Tuesday, she'd call Peggy's assistant with an excuse for next Friday. Something, anything, it didn't matter. She was an adult woman, a free agent: she wasn't obliged to see Peggy. The week after, she'd write a letter, bringing the whole charade to an end.

It wasn't an easy decision: she'd grown very fond of Peggy. More importantly, she didn't want Ed to worry. But she *knew* she could do this. She would be okay. There would be no more overeating, then vomiting. It was gone, done, in the past, and she was absolutely certain she had the strength to keep things that way. All she needed was enough time to prove it.

When she got home, Ed sounded anxious. 'How was Peggy?'

'Mmm,' she said, trying to sound positive, without actually saying anything. 'Grand.' Lying to Ed felt all wrong. But it was too soon to tell him the truth. He'd panic. He'd go straight into Follow the Instructions mode and insist that she return to Peggy quick smart.

Getting her life back to the way it used to be would require careful handling. There were a few obstacles to manoeuvre. But by patiently dismantling the unnecessary scaffolding that had been constructed around her, she'd get there.

Seventeen Days Ago

TUESDAY, 22 SEPTEMBER

Eighty-Seven

'Nell! Nell!' It was her dad, squeezed into his one suit, accompanied by Nell's mum, looking blow-dried and glam.

She crossed the lobby of the Liffey Theatre to them. 'It's only six thirty, you pair of eejits! We don't start for another hour.'

'We didn't want to be late,' Angie said. 'Big night for our little girl.'

'Will I understand the play?' Petey asked. 'No? Grand. I won't bother trying, so.'

'How're you feeling, love?'

'Anxious. Knackered. Excited. Listen, I've to do some last-minute checks. I'll meet you in the bar. Lorelei is up there with her fella.' Nell had offered freebies to all her friends, as was the norm, but because the festival was on, Triona and Wanda were the only ones who could be there.

It was actually a relief that Garr wasn't coming—because Ferdia *was*. At the end of last week, Jessie had texted:

Any tickets left for your opening night?

Nell had replied: **For you, always. How many you like?**

Jessie answered: **Two be okay? Me and Ferd. He's your biggest fan lol!**

What the hell did that mean? She'd reread it a million times, *agonizing* over the meaning. Particularly the 'lol'—was it meant to be sarcastic?

But Jessie wasn't like that.

In the bar, Petey said, 'It's twenty past, should we go in? Where's Liam?'

'On his way,' Nell said. 'You four go on in and I'll wait in the lobby for Jessie.'

'Are you all right?' Petey asked. 'You're very nervy-seeming.'

Bloody right she was nervy-seeming. She was a total wreck. And praying that Liam didn't turn up at the same time as Ferdia, interfering with any chance of talking to him.

Here came Jessie now! Nell's heart was thumping in her chest.

Behind Jessie, she spotted Saoirse.

Why was *she* here? No one had mentioned her and there wasn't a spare ticket. Unless . . . no. It couldn't be . . . Had she come *instead* of Ferdia?

'Nell!' Jessie descended, and pressed a bottle of something on her. 'Congratulations!'

Feeling crazed with disappointment, Nell submitted to an over-excited hug from Jessie, then Saoirse. 'How many tickets do you need?'

'Two, thanks—me and Saoirse.'

'Just . . .' she cleared her throat '. . . you'd mentioned Ferdia?'

'Oh, I did, didn't I?' Her vagueness was almost unendurable. 'No, he's up to something with Perla so—'

'Grand. Fine.' She forced a smile. 'You two go on in. I'm just waiting for Liam.'

Once she was alone again, the loss felt like vertigo. She'd been so tightly wound, so *ready*, that she couldn't cope. She'd wanted eye-contact with him, a chance to piece together what exactly had taken place that night in the Button Factory.

Yeah, well, she knew now what had happened—absolutely nothing. He wasn't here. In fact, he was out with his girlfriend. What else did she need to know?

'Nell, you should go in.'

'What?' Still stunned, she turned.

An usher was by her side. 'Need to go in now, honey. They'll be starting.'

'Oh. But I'm waiting . . .' Then she made her decision: feck Liam. It was gone half past seven. He was legit late. Why wait any longer?

The lights dimmed, the screen rose, the play began. Nell had a lot of arm-squeezing and people leaning forward in their seats so that they could smile encouragingly at her. Making a concerted effort, she tried to concentrate on what was happening on stage. She'd already sat through this six times, but you never really knew if everything worked until it had a paying audience.

It was Not Bad. Maybe even Quite Good. But she was sad about the props they hadn't been able to afford, the little tweaks here and there that could have improved everything.

Her self-berating concentration was broken as people near the aisle stood up. Liam had arrived.

'Sorry,' she heard him whisper, as he pushed past them. 'Sorry. Sorry.'

It was seven fifty-six, almost half an hour late.

He finally reached the empty seat beside her. 'Sorry,' he whispered. 'Chelsea being a bitch again.'

She acknowledged his arrival with a small chin incline. Her eyes didn't move from the stage.

At the interval, they piled into the bar.

'Congratulations,' Triona said.

'Yeah, totally,' Wanda echoed. 'It's really good. Your work, I mean. Innovative.'

'Not a *baldy* what's going on,' her dad said. 'But it's a solid-looking construction. Couldn't fault that. I'll get the drinks in.'

'I don't know the right words,' Angie said. 'But you're so clever. You have such imagination.'

'A genius is what she is,' Jessie declared.

'She is.' Saoirse hugged her.

'So, you're not going to believe it,' Liam announced. 'Chelsea, right? Told her I needed to leave early. Told her *why*. So I'm there, in the shop, it's ten past seven, no sign of her. So I text, I need to leave. Tell her, you need to be here, to do the till and lock up. And she texts back, says she knows nothing about it.'

'She'd forgotten?' Angie sounded scandalized.

'My arse she had. She's just a bitch.'

'Oh, Liam, you really need to get out of that place. The sooner you qualify as a massage person, the better.'

Nell felt as detached as if she were watching a movie.

Liam turned and placed his hands on her upper arms. 'I'm so sorry, baby.'

'It's fine.'

'Really?' He seemed uncertain.

'Fine.'

At 6.35 a.m., Nell woke again. Once more she reached for her iPad. Since 3 a.m., she'd been dozing on and off, refreshing the media sites, desperate to know what kind of reviews *Human Salt* would get.

Finally, Wednesday's newspapers were live.

Her stomach fluttering with fear and excitement, she clicked on the *Independent*'s review of the theatre festival.

Nothing.

She scanned it more slowly, just to be certain her anxiety wasn't making her miss something.

Still nothing.

The disappointment was brutal.

She moved on to the *Irish Times*.

'Anything?' Liam had woken up.

'Not in the *Indo*. Or, by the looks of things, the *Irish Times*.'

Now he was clicking and studying his screen. 'Small mention here in the *Mail*.'

'Show me.' She lunged at him.

'Sorry, baby. Nothing about you.'

She insisted on reading it. 'An adequate production,' was the conclusion but there was no mention of her or her set.

Because she'd got such good reviews for *Timer*, she'd been desperate for further recognition of her work. She couldn't help it.

'Another mention, tiny, on RTÉ.ie,' he said. 'Nothing about you again.'

She had to read that one, too, before she believed him.

It was mad to get hung up on reviews. A bad one could destroy your confidence, just as a good one could have you mistakenly thinking you were the Second Coming.

Her own opinion of her work should be the only one that mattered. But she kept googling and clicking, a few wisps of hope hanging on. Eventually she sighed and gave up.

'Nothing else?' Liam asked.

She shook her head, too disappointed to speak.

'It's the festival.' He sounded sympathetic. 'So many shows on. They probably don't have the reviewers to get around to everything.'

'It's grand,' she said. 'I did good work and that's all that matters. And maybe there'll be something in the *Ticket* on Friday.'

Liam sounded irked. 'Why does it matter so much? Like, you're always working. Or thinking about work.'

'Not always. I—' Surprised, she stopped. 'You know it's important to me.'

'Actually, no. When I met you, you said that money didn't matter.'

That wasn't what she'd said. Or thought. Ever. Money wasn't her motivation. But she was very ambitious. Confused, she said, 'They're two different things—money and work. Working makes me happy.'

'I don't believe this.' He seemed angry. 'You sold yourself to me as easy-going, relaxed—'

'*Sold* myself?'

'Just a phrase. Don't get up in my grille.'

She was too dispirited to fight.

'Seriously, though,' he said hotly, 'last summer when we went up the west coast on the bus? You weren't working then. Or talking about it.'

'Because there wasn't any. Nothing new was casting. But I told you the very first night we met how much my work means to me.'

'Nope. No memory of that. Just this cool girl, loving life.'

'But, Liam . . .' Again, she stopped. Back then he'd obviously decided she was some sort of skippy, free-spirited, unworldly type. Any evidence to the contrary jarred with who he'd decided she was.

No wonder he was pissed off with her.

'Hey.' His tone was friendlier. 'Why don't I give you a massage? Practice for me and it might relax you.'

Hah. The massage would last about two seconds before he had a hard-on and it became foreplay.

She didn't want to fuck. Even the idea of him touching her gave her the giant ick.

The day after an opening night was always weird: nervy exhaustion mixed with anti-climax. Suddenly, after weeks of working twelve hours a day, there was literally nothing to do. Unless the reviews were great, Nell knew there was no way round this dip in her mood. It had to run its course.

She and Lorelei had a text back-and-forth, where they propped each other up with assurances that they'd done their best. The director emailed her thanks. Triona and Wanda WhatsApped to tell her again how great she was.

And Liam was still hanging around.

She was anxious that he'd stay home all day, trying to convince her that sex would cure her of her micro-depression.

She was more and more worried that his bad attitude would piss Chelsea off enough to sack him.

There was no denying the practicalities here. *One* of them needed to be generating some dosh.

Right now, she was convinced she'd never work again.

When, at nearly midday, he *finally* left for work, relief flooded her.

On the couch with Molly Ringwald and her iPad, she escaped online. She did a quiz on Buzzfeed, then at least twenty more, before falling asleep, only to be woken at 10 p.m. by a WhatsApp from Perla: **Saw *Human Salt.* So good! Your set is clever. See you at Harvest at w/e.**

Her phone beeped again. Another WhatsApp. This time from Ferdia.

Hey! Perla and me just out from *Human Salt.* You're a genius, the set was the best thing about the play. (Not dissing the play.) See you at the not-nouvy festival!

They'd gone together.

They'd gone together, just the two of them. On a date. Being loyal and nice to Nell because she was the one who'd introduced them.

All day, tears had been threatening and, finally, she cried. For the failure of her marriage, the disappointment about her play and, most of all, for her giant stupid crush on a twenty-two-year-old boy.

Two Weeks Ago

FRIDAY, 25 SEPTEMBER

Harvest Festival

Eighty-Eight

Just like the previous time Nell had had a positive review, Garr gave her the good news, this time via a WhatsApp at 8.07 a.m. on Friday morning: ***Irish Times*** **loving your work. See** ***The Ticket.***

'Liam!' She nudged him awake. 'Open the *Ticket*. Garr says there's a mention! Oh, God, here it is!' She scanned the text, 'Blah de blah, dialogue, acting . . . Oh, here we go! "Nell McDermott's set is original and surprising. Rapidly becoming the go-to designer for innovation on a shoestring. It would be interesting to see what she'd pull off with a decent budget. In the world of Irish set design, she's one to watch."' Her face was full of wonder. 'That's me they're talking about, Liam. Me! I'm one to watch, Liam. Me!'

'Congratulations, baby.'

She scooped up Molly Ringwald and twirled about the room. 'Your mama is one to watch! Bet you didn't know that now, did you?' She doused the cat with kisses.

'Don't get too carried away,' Liam said, from the bed. 'The world of Irish set design is a very small one.'

Abruptly she stopped. 'You're pissed off! You'd be happier if they'd said I was shit.'

'Bollocks.'

No, it wasn't.

Maybe it was . . .

A silent stare-off ensued, then Nell swung off to the bathroom.

'Come on,' Nell said. 'Grab your weekend bag and let's go.'

Liam made a face. 'Yeah, you know, I'm not feeling it.'

Startled, tripping over her words, she said, 'This isn't just a jolly we can opt out of. Jessie needs us to work.'

Irritably he said, 'She's got *dozens* of minions down at that festival.'

'We said we'd be there for her.'

'And I've changed my mind. My job is a nightmare, I'm studying on my own time for another career, and I'm expected to work for free on my weekend off.'

There were a hundred ways she could shoot this down, but suddenly she didn't care. 'Well, I'm going.'

'What? *Why?*'

'Because she's depending on me.'

'No, baby, don't. Stay here with me.'

'Will you even tell her you're not coming?'

'You're really going? Then you tell her.'

She stepped into the kitchen and rang Jessie.

'Nell?' Jessie answered. 'Y'okay?'

'Grand. But, Jessie, Liam isn't . . .' Why should she cover for him? 'Liam won't be coming to Harvest.'

'Is it his bad back?'

Jessie was so willing to give Liam the benefit of the doubt that Nell felt a huge rush of love for her.

'His back is grand. And I'm still coming.'

'You don't have to. I can get—'

'I want to. I'll text Ed, see if he'll give me a lift down.'

Cara let herself into the house to find Ed in the hall, his backpack at his feet, keen to get going to Harvest.

She could have been home an hour earlier, instead of floating around Brown Thomas. But it was still too soon to tell him that she'd stopped going to Peggy. Another few weeks should do it.

'Honey, go,' she said. 'Have a great time.'

'The car's being temperamental,' he said. 'I hope it survives the journey. Sorry to leave you all alone with this pair.'

'Don't be sorry. I'm going out tomorrow night.'

Vinnie and Tom would be spending the night with Dorothy and Angus.

'I know. I just . . .'

'If you're worried I'll go on some mad binge, I can tell you that I won't.'

'I didn't mean . . .'

'It's fine, it's fine.' She tried to wave away the acrimony. 'I'm sorry.'

'I'll call you.' He still looked unsure. 'Have a great time with Gabby.'

'You have a great time too.'

When he'd gone, she put the boys in front of a movie and a giant bowl of homemade popcorn and slid on her headphones. One of her favourite YouTubers had just uploaded their stay in the Haritha Villas, Sri Lanka, literally walking her through every stunning step of it. It was over the top but oh-so-fabulous.

After that she immersed herself in a duplex suite in the George Cinq, then a luxury tree-house in Costa Rica . . .

'Mum.'

'*Mum.*' Her leg was being poked. She lifted off one of the earphones. Vinnie was yelling, 'MUM! Movie's over. Ice-cream!'

'Okay. Take it easy, sweetie.' She moved to the kitchen and rummaged around in the freezer. 'What flavour? Pistachio?'

'*No!*'

'I'd rather die,' Tom said primly.

'Chocolate?'

'Yes!'

Three small scoops in two small bowls, that would do them. As she shut the freezer door with her hip, she automatically licked the scoop. Oh, my God, it was so intensely delicious that she felt light-headed.

In the living room, she watched the boys devour their ice-cream.

Sugar was not something she could avoid for ever. At some stage, she'd have to start eating normally again. Now was as good a time as any.

Back in the kitchen she got herself two medium-sized scoops of chocolate ice-cream. Then sat down and ate them.

Nothing bad happened.

Eighty-Nine

Harvest boasted impeccable eco-credentials. Indeed, no sooner had Ed parked his car than Nell had counted two, three . . . no *four* Teslas.

'This crowd really *are* eco-sound,' she said to Ed.

'Yeaaahhh.' He sounded doubtful. 'All the same, Jessie says they kicked off big-time when the helipad was scrapped.'

It was almost eight in the evening, the light was dimming, and dozens of people were crossing the field, heading for the entrance, carrying—even in the gloom Nell noticed this—very sleek-looking weekend bags. A *lot* of Louis Vuitton.

Almost as soon as she was through the gate, a troupe of samba dancers, about thirty strong, kitted out in full carnival regalia, went dancing by, their feathered headdresses swaying.

'That's the pop-up Mardi Gras,' Ed said.

Mesmerized, she watched them go.

Ed was consulting his app. 'Jessie and the gang are at the Singing Vegan, which is . . .' he looked around and pointed '. . . this way.'

As he led her past tents and stages, through groups of beautiful girls, covered with glitter, she wondered if Ferdia had arrived yet. The eruption of longing was shocking. Even if he were there, he'd be with Perla.

You really need to get a grip on yourself.

Now they were passing through a cluster of street-food vans from around the world, set against a giant cine-screen of the Brooklyn Bridge. You could almost fool yourself you were in New York. It was stunning.

'This isn't the *half* of it,' Ed said. 'As well as the bands, there's so much fun stuff, mad stuff, dance lessons, candle-making, tantric something or other . . .' They turned into a narrow street with small, vibrantly coloured 'buildings'. They looked Nepalese, or perhaps Andean. Just façades, but so convincing.

Following his app, Ed said, 'The Singing Vegan should be right . . . here!'

So it was. They opened the door and there were Jessie, Johnny and what seemed like an army of children. But after the frenzy of hugging had died down, Nell registered that only Bridey, TJ, Dilly and Kassandra were present. 'Where's, um, Saoirse?'

'Not coming,' TJ said. 'She's got a new friend. A Goth. She cut her fringe *really* short and says she might dye her hair navy.'

'Ill-advised, imo,' Bridey said. 'That means "in my opinion".'

'We miss her,' TJ said. 'But what can you do?'

'That's sad.' Clearing her throat, Nell aimed for a deeply casual tone. 'And Ferdia?'

'Coming tomorrow with Perla.'

Perla. God. How sorry she was that she'd ever introduced them. But how could she grudge Perla happiness?

'You like to see your tent?' Dilly asked.

'Or would you like to eat?' Jessie asked.

'The tent.'

'C'mon.' She was swept out of the door by all the females of the group.

'At first it will seem far—' Dilly said.

'— and confusing—' Kassandra said.

'— so if you get lost, look up for the tower. You see it?'

'Head for there. Then you can ask a man.'

'Not any man. They must have the uniform—we're nearly there!' Then, 'This is your tent,' Dilly declared. 'Isn't it adorable?'

Adorable was exactly right: a cosy cone-roofed space with pink-hued lanterns strung across the ceiling. It even had a real bed, made from carved wood, adorned with patterned pillows and mohair throws. A solid-looking chest-of-drawers sported an old-fashioned wireless.

'Shoes off!' Bridey said. 'Now try the carpet.'

The ground sheet was covered with three overlapping rugs, which felt deep and luxurious.

'Because Uncle Liam isn't here, Kassandra and I will sleep in with you,' Dilly said.

'Thank you. I accept, with pleasure.'

'Is there room for me?' Bridey asked.

'No!' Dilly yelled.

'Of course,' Nell said.

'Uncle Ed's tent is over there,' TJ said. 'His isn't as fancy. That's because he's a man and men don't care about any of that shi–' she threw a hunted look at Jessie '— stuff. And Perla's is down that way.'

'You don't have your own bathroom,' Bridey said. 'But they're not far—'

'— and they're not disgusting.'

'Let's show her the magic bathtubs!' Jessie ducked back outside and led the way through the rows of tents.

'They're outside,' Dilly said. 'But hidden in the trees, so nobody can see your bum. There's one, over there.'

'See that giant water-jug beside the trees?' TJ asked Nell. 'With the tulip drawn on it? That's the tulip bath.'

TJ moved closer, stuck her face between two tree trunks and yelled, 'Hello? Is anyone in the bath being nudey?' She paused, appearing to listen.

'You can just check the app,' Jessie said. 'That'll say if it's occupied.'

'But I like shouting,' TJ said. 'Tell us NOW because we're COMING in.'

Nobody answered. 'They didn't say they *weren't* there. So let's go in.'

Linked between TJ and Dilly, Nell was led into an enchanting little space. In a circle surrounded by dense foliage, a deep bathtub sat on slate flooring. Simple shelves made from tree branches sported towels and soaps.

'You like?' Jessie asked.

Nell breathed, 'I *love.* You're literally having a bath in a forest.'

'When you book it,' Jessie said, 'they'll run the bath, so it's all ready when you arrive. And the water's great for your skin because it comes from hot springs.'

'But not smelly!'

'Can anyone use this?' Nell asked.

'Course. Look on the app, see if a bath is free—there are seven—and put your name down! Easy! Let's get Daddy and Uncle Ed. We'll sit in the enchanted garden and we'll plan our gigs and stuff for tomorrow.'

'Jessie, give me my orders,' Ed said.

Jessie produced her iPad.

A shoal of people in patterned bodysuits fluttered by, wearing wings lit up by LED strips.

'Who are *they*?' Nell stared after them as they flickered off into the night.

'Just people being fireflies,' Johnny said.

'I love it here.'

'I hope you'll still love it after you've worked six cookery demos,' Jessie said. 'Three tomorrow, three on Sunday, at ten, twelve thirty and four o'clock, each forty-five minutes long. Float around with a tray of food, have a chat. If they seem friendly, ask if they'd like to be on our mailing list. No need to be pushy. If they're not keen, be nice and move on.

'Just you two will be doing the ten a.m. and twelve thirty sessions. But Ferdia and Perla will be there for the rest. If you can get to each demo fifteen minutes early that would be great. Apart from that, your time is your own.'

'But everyone is coming to Momoland at five thirty,' Dilly insisted. 'A girl band. K-pop. From *Korea*! Oh, Nell, they're so cute.'

'We love them,' Bridey said.

'There's nine girls,' Dilly gushed. 'They all have different hair.'

'They're too girly,' TJ said. 'But I like the songs. And sometimes their videos are funny.'

'It's bubblegum pop,' Dilly said.

That made Nell laugh. 'What do you know about bubblegum pop?'

'It's what Ferdia said.' Defensively, she declared, 'And there's nothing wrong with it. I'll teach you the moves.'

Furtively, Jessie leant very close to Nell. 'You want to come to the burlesque dance class tomorrow afternoon?'

'Ugh . . . no.'

'But don't you feel the pressure? To keep adding to your sexual skill set.'

'Like, *no*. We're not performing dolls. Sex should be an equal, loving thing between two people.'

Jessie looked perplexed. 'I struggle to keep up. I thought all young people did porn-star sex.'

'Maybe I'm not young.'

'You *are* young.'

'Don't forget Ferdia's thing,' Bridey said. 'That's at one thirty.'

'What thing?'

'In the brainy-people's tent. He's talking about free tampons for Perla.'

'And other ladies!' Dilly corrected her. 'Not just Perla.'

'Didn't you know?' Jessie frowned at Nell. 'I thought you would. He's "raising awareness about period poverty".'

Johnny buried his face in his hands. 'Of all the causes he had to pick. He's doing it on purpose to mortify me.'

'That reaction of yours is exactly why it needs to be done!' Then Jessie muttered, 'Mind you, I'm a bit mortified myself.'

'I didn't know.' Nell was stunned.

'He's been pestering politicians, pharmacy chains, journalists, all kinds of people. He was working on it while we were in Italy—I was sure he'd have told you. It's very worthy. Mind you, he can knock it off now he's back in college. If he doesn't get a decent degree, I'll kill him.'

Nell was stabbing at the app, trying to get details—and there it was. 'Make Period Poverty History'. Apparently, Ferdia Kinsella and Perla Zoghbi were hosting a panel discussion at one thirty tomorrow in the Lightbulb Zone, where the literary and political talks took place.

This was . . . *astonishing.*

Suddenly it was all too much for Nell. 'Hey, do you mind if I go to bed now?'

'Aren't you coming to make memories at Janelle Monáe?' Dilly asked.

'Too tired for memory-making tonight.' She squinted at Dilly. 'You're eight years old. Don't you need to go to bed?'

'No. I'm—What did that lady say I was, Mum?'

'Precocious.'

'That word. That's what I am.'

Nell found her tent and tumbled into bed without ringing Liam to say goodnight. If he complained, she'd pretend her phone had no signal.

Ninety

Johnny and Jessie were flanking the work station, keeping an apprehensive eye on Anrai McDavitt, who was as famous for his outbursts of rage as for his skill with a scallion.

Nell began circulating, iPad in hand. Pestering punters was daunting. Some were ultra-serious about food and cooking and did not respond well to any light-heartedness. Others were merely passing the tent and had popped in to be scornful. 'Heard about your man. What is it with chefs and anger management?'

Everyone willingly gave up their info but, even so, Nell was relieved when it was over.

'How d'you get on?' Johnny asked.

'Johnny! You should be given an award for all the excellent talking you do. You make it look effortless and it is *hard*.'

'Any oul eejit can do it.'

'They totally can't. It is *killer*.'

'Peasy.' Ed had appeared.

'That so?' Johnny asked him. 'How many people did you get?'

'. . . Ah. Four. No, three. Feck, I forgot to ask the last man for his email.'

'*What* were you talking about?'

'Mammals unique to Madagascar. Did you know that—'

'No. And I don't want to. Nell, how many did you get?'

'Thirty-one . . .'

There was only an hour and a half until they were on duty again, but she was so full of nervy anticipation about seeing Ferdia that she had to do something—anything—to keep her from going bananas. She looked at the programme. What was on now?

'Whatever you're doing now, can you take the bunnies?' Jessie swung by, looking harried.

'Y'okay?'

'Grand. Just, *chefs*, you know.'

Slightly late, Nell arrived at the Lightbulb Zone. It was crowded, all the seats were taken and some people were sitting on the floor. Ferdia was standing on the low stage, lanky and dishevelled, the sleeves of his shirt rolled up. '. . . Abolishing Direct Provision is the endgame,' he was saying. 'That's going to take work. The current system, where Ireland seems unattractive to asylum-seekers, suits our government. Only when the weight of public opinion becomes too great will change happen.'

Mic in hand, he was pacing slightly, looking like a hot young politician on the campaign trail. Nell felt horribly in love with him.

Beside her, Dilly whispered, 'He looks like a *man*.'

'He *is* a man,' Bridey hissed.

'No! Like a man off the TV. One we don't know.'

'. . . Sanitary protection costs approximately ten euro a month. Which is six per cent of the annual allowance women in Direct Provision get from our government. It's a lot.'

He was loose and rangy, relaxed in his body. People were *listening*.

'One of the reasons sanitary protection for periods isn't free is that people are uncomfortable talking about it.' His laugh was soft. 'Yeah, you know you are.'

An appreciative wave of laughter rose.

'Not so long since I was mortified too. You're probably thinking I've some neck talking about period poverty. But the reality is that the public purse is controlled by men. If men don't ally themselves with this issue, the chances of change are reduced.

'Seriously, men need to get past their embarrassment. It's a bodily function that happens to fifty per cent of the earth's population. For the men here today, this analogy might help. Imagine you stepped in a puddle. Your sock is wet and your shoe is wet. You're far from home, so you have to walk around all day with your wet sock and your wet shoe, the cold seeping into your skin and bones. Your friends might laugh at you because you were so stupid to step in the puddle in the first place, so you say nothing. Now imagine that happening for up to seven days in a row . . . and that it will happen again next month. And the month after. And the month after that.'

'Being a woman is the worst,' TJ said quietly. 'The literal worst.'

'In living memory,' Ferdia said, 'it was considered a bit off for heavily pregnant women to be out in public. Or they were draped in circus marquees, loose enough to hide their "condition". Now? A woman who's nine months pregnant can wear a bikini without anyone batting an eye.

'But taboos don't bust themselves. That change happened because enough women ignored the unspoken law. With this issue, the more it's talked about, *especially by men*, the more we normalize it. Asking for free sanitary care for women in Direct Provision will kick off a lot of whatabout-ery: what about homeless women, what about women in refuges, what about women with low incomes? Here's the deal: in a perfect world, sanitary protection would be freely available to all. But we've got to start some place, some time. Thank you for listening.'

He finished, to applause and one or two whoops.

Next, Perla told her story, but Nell couldn't concentrate. As soon as the event ended, she hopped up, wove through the people and intercepted Ferdia as he jumped down from the stage.

'Nell!' He smiled.

Almost angrily, she demanded, 'Why didn't you tell me you were doing this?'

The smile vanished. 'I started a few times, but something always got in the way. I didn't want to be all performative about it. You know? I didn't want you thinking I was doing it for praise.'

'Wow.' Then, 'You've changed.'

'I've been telling you.'

'You were great up there.' Her chin wobbled. 'You were amazing.'

'So what's everyone doing now?' he asked. 'Food? I just need to get my charger from my tent.'

'Where is it?'

'Opposite yours. I'm in with Ed.'

She was confused. Maybe, for the benefit of the kids, he and Perla were pretending they weren't sleeping together.

'What?' he asked. 'You look . . .'

'Just wondering why you're not in Perla's tent?'

He looked startled. 'Perla's tent? Me?'

'Aren't you . . .' She paused. She could barely say the word. '. . . together?'

He seemed mystified. '. . . We're working together on this project—Wait! You actually thought we were . . . Do you mean *together*-together?'

She was irritated at how unlikely he thought it was. 'Why not? Or is she "too old"?'

'... Um, Nell? Why are you pissed off?'

'I'm not pissed off.' She was close to tears. 'But it's not cool that you think she's too old to be, like ... She's only twenty-nine!'

'I said nothing about her age! I think she's amazing, but it's just not that sort of ... thing.'

'Sorry.' Tears had leaked onto her face. 'I've had a weird week. Sorry.'

Nell lay on her bed, listening to the various Caseys outside her tent.

'We need to be there early so Dilly and me can see,' Kassandra wheedled.

'Five minutes everyone!' Jessie clapped her hands together. 'Then we go to Duran Duran. Yes, I know it's very early, but who wants Dilly and Kassandra to cry?'

'Me!' Bridey said.

'I wouldn't mind either,' TJ said.

'Bunnies!' Jessie gasped. 'No!'

Nell was exhausted. Being happy and dance-y would be impossible. She had too much to process.

So when Jessie called, 'Time!' she stuck her head out of her tent. 'I'll catch up with you all in a while.'

Jessie gave her a hard look. 'You okay?'

'Grand.' She forced herself to smile. 'Fine.'

When their voices died away, she stuck her head out again, just to be sure they really were gone. Furtively, she emerged and headed for the woods, moving in the opposite direction from the main stage. She'd cut back down to it in a while, when she could cope.

Overhead, a tangle of branches formed a canopy, which muffled all sounds of the man-made world. The sun was going down, but a meandering path through the trees could still be seen. Out of nowhere, in a clearing, a tiny wooden house materialized. Startled, she came to a sudden halt. Gingham curtains hung at the fairy-tale windows and the little front door was painted red. Before Nell's surprised eyes, the door opened and a woman in a long, shimmery dress, with glittery stuff in her hair, came out. 'Hello there.' She smiled. 'What brings you here?'

'Ugh ... going to the gig.'

'Funny route to take.'

'I wanted some time to think. What are *you* doing here?'

The woman smiled. 'I'm from your future.'

This was creepy. It was getting dark now and who knew where she was?

But the woman laughed. 'I love saying that line. It's so dramatic. No, no, you're grand, I'm Altfy—A Letter To Future You. I'm on the programme. Take a look.'

'What do you do?'

'I give you a pen and paper. You write a letter to yourself—well, to the person you'd like to be in a year's time. You describe your life then, all the good things you'd like, all the bad stuff you want sorted out. Then we stick on a stamp and post it to you in a year.'

'Why would I do that?'

'Brings positive change to a life.' She paused. 'So they say. When you write down what you want, it helps you focus on the important stuff. Allegedly.'

'How much does it cost?'

'Nothing. Included in your ticket.' A bundle of pages was passed to Nell, along with a pen. 'They located me off the beaten track,' Altfy announced. 'So that only those who needed this would be led here. Which I *get*. But I've only had six people all day. And no Wi-Fi.'

'That sounds, um, boring?'

'You have *no* idea. Anyway, plank yourself under a tree and work away. Don't over-think this. Be optimistic.'

As she faced the blank page, Nell was nervous. This felt like a big responsibility. If she got it wrong, she felt, her future would turn out to be a shambles. 'I'm scared,' she called to the woman.

'Ah, it's only a bit of fun.'

'How do I begin it?'

'You could write "Dear Future Me." '

Dear Future Me,

I'm writing this, in my present, where I'm very scared. I don't think I love Liam any more. I promised I'd love him for ever, and I know nobody really thinks marriage is for life, but in fairness, ten months is pretty poor and I don't like myself very much.

But in the new present, things are okay. I left Liam . . .

What?! She threw down her pen.

Had she really written that?

Altfy looked up. 'Keep going,' she said. 'Think happy endings.'

You were scared sick, but it was totally the legit correct thing to do.

'How do I know I'm doing this right?'
'No wrong way to do it. Think positive.'

Liam's doing good, these days. He qualified as a massage person, he left the bike shop and he probably has a new girlfriend because he's Liam.

Your work is good too, Nell. You've been working steadily since this letter and you've just done a commission for Ship of Fools in the theatre festival.

Feck it, why not shoot for the stars?!

Nobody was badly freaked out when you left Liam. It was news for, like, five minutes, then everyone moved on. After a while even the Caseys didn't care. They stayed friends with you. Jessie said that once a Casey, always a Casey, so you still get invited to things and you're still best buds with Dilly, TJ and Bridey. Also Jessie and Cara.

Also, Ferdia.

Your lunacy passed. You were insane for a while, just because of the whole Liam thing. It seemed easier to think you didn't love Liam any more because you'd fallen for someone else. Instead of facing the fact that you'd got married too fast. To the wrong person.

Soon as you left Liam, the feelings for Ferdia just disappeared.

This made Nell feel suddenly very sad.

Well, not exactly disappeared. They changed. You found you wanted to be good friends with him. Because you have a lot of common interests, like.

He finished his degree and you didn't ruin his life.

Nell found she was writing faster and faster.

Now he has a job doing good work for a woke cause and he's happy. Your age difference seems less and less, the more time passes.

You are still very, very good friends. Very close.

She was scribbling at speed now.

You see him a lot and none of the Caseys mind, not even Liam, and none of your friends think it's weird and they all like him too and think he's cool. And if he has a girlfriend you don't mind, you think she's class.

Suddenly aware of how self-obsessed she was being, she wrote,

Garr is getting great work and everyone knows what a genius he is. Wanda, Triona, all of my mates, they're living their best lives. Perla's case was heard. She and Kassandra got refugee status. Perla is a GP *now and it's all good.*

Who else was there? Jessie. But Jessie had no problems. Cara, though.

Cara's eating disorder is cured and she's happy. Mum and Dad are grand and so is Brendan, even though his values are a bit fucked and all he wants is to be minted. Everything is good and fine, and life is going well for everyone I know, and I'm not obsessed with Ferdia any longer and that is good and everything is good.

Maybe she should stop now. She'd established that, in the end, everything would be okay.

Good luck, Nell!
From me to me

'I'm done,' Nell said. 'Quick, an envelope, before I lose my nerve.'
'Write your address and I'll do the stamp.'
But who knew where she'd be living next year? Next *week*?
She wrote her parents' address, then surrendered the envelope.

'Cara!' Delma exclaimed. 'Hi!'
She led Cara into an alcove off the main restaurant. 'We're hidden in here. I guess they didn't want twenty drunk women upsetting the date-night crowd.'
'Are we the first?' She barely knew Delma and had always found her a little too much.
'Yep. So!' Unashamedly Delma checked her out. She scanned every inch of Cara, from her face to her ankles, looking for . . . what exactly? 'You don't look too bad at *all*!'

Cara felt the blood drain from her face.

'Yeah, heard about your little adventure. Look, Cara, could happen to any of us. Ah, here's Gwennie.'

'Cara!' Gwennie exclaimed, wafting booze into her face. 'Wasn't sure you'd show up tonight.' Then, a reassuring shoulder squeeze. 'You're doing great.'

'Cara!'

'Oh, hi, Quincy.'

Quincy gathered her in a clumsy hug. 'Fair play to you.'

It was a long time since she'd seen this group, probably not since Gabby's birthday last year. If every single one of them was going to make a big thing of her 'eating disorder', she didn't think she'd last the night.

'Cara, how *are* you?'

'Heather, hi. All good. You?'

'Please tell me the name of the tablets.'

'What tablets?'

'They must have given you something to stop the overeating? I need them too. Swear to God, if there's chips in the house, I literally cannot stop eating them. Am I right?'

A woman called Ita, whom Cara barely knew, steered her into a corner. 'They're idiots. Insensitive bitches, they understand nothing. You need to take care of yourself here. You've a killer disease. Fuck them. Do you hear me? Fuck them. You have an illness that can kill you, so if you need to get up and leave, to keep yourself safe, you do that!'

That actually felt worse than all the others put together.

'Um, thanks.' Cara extracted herself as she spotted Gabby. She grabbed her. 'Gabby, who did you tell?'

'No one. Well, Erin, obvs. And I *might* have mentioned it to Galina. Because she's always going on about her weight. Trying to tell her she actually didn't have a problem, not, you know, compared to you.' Gabby looked contrite. 'Oh, God, I'm really sorry. I didn't think she'd tell everyone. But you're okay now, right?'

'. . . Right.' If she left now, everyone would say she'd gone home to eat herself into a coma. (*She can't help it, it's an illness, you know.*) Pride meant she had to stick it out.

And surely, when they sat to eat, it would all calm down.

But as the time passed and the alcohol flowed, people became more intrusive, not less.

'. . . I've never made myself puke,' Milla was droning on to Cara, 'but I've *wanted* to. Lots of—'

Janette shoved her way in and sat on Milla's lap. 'Cara, don't take this the wrong way but why aren't you thinner?'

'Excuse me?'

'Like, isn't it the same as anorexia?'

And on it went. As soon as the chair next to Cara was vacated, another woman arrived, keen to probe.

'Dessert?' the waitress yelled, above the drunken hubbub. 'Who wants to order dessert? Yourself?' She looked at Cara.

'Tiramisu, please.'

'Are you *allowed*?' Celine yelled from further down the table. 'You're *bulimic*.'

'I'm fine.' Cara managed a smile.

When her tiramisu arrived, everyone watched Cara with the same avid interest as if she were swallowing fire. Casually, without any evident enjoyment, she ate four or five forkfuls, then abandoned it with about a quarter of the slice left.

'Jesus, fair play,' Delma said, impressed. 'I could never do that.'

Cara waited, braced for a craving to kick in. Even if she got an urge to eat all the cake in the world tonight, she wouldn't give in.

But nothing happened. She was fine.

Nell wandered back the way she'd come. It was properly dark now. Maybe she'd see if one of those outdoor bathtubs was free.

All seven were up for grabs. Looked like no one wanted to be having a bath on a Saturday night. Nobody but her. She booked on the app, then wandered along until she found the narrow break in the trees. Slipping into the dark green copse, hot, fragrant water steamed silently into the night air. Fresh waffle towels sat on a low, rustic-looking stool and a robe hung from wooden slats. The slate flooring was dry and faintly warm to the touch. Everything gave the impression that, literally seconds previously, a team of people had been dashing about, making it perfect for her, but there wasn't sight or sound of a single human.

The lanterns strung through the branches gave off a pale yellow glow. On a shelf made from the branch of an ash tree stood five glass jars of hand-labelled bath salts. Nell threw in a handful of Ocean Mineral, which turned the water blue and milky, then stripped and climbed in, shuddering at the sudden warmth.

As her body floated, she looked up at the tangled branches of the trees and was grateful that she could still appreciate their beauty. She was going to leave Liam. When she got home tomorrow night.

Maybe he'd once again promise to do better, but it would change nothing.

She was grateful he'd been so horrible. It would be much worse if he was a nice man whom she'd simply fallen out of love with.

Liam would be fine, that was for sure. She suspected that all the blame would be put on her, and his next girlfriend would be treated to stories of his crazy ex. But none of that mattered. What she needed now was to extricate herself from him, and from all of the Caseys. Then this obsession with Ferdia would evaporate.

She'd miss them. But she'd had a life before and she could build a new one.

Floating on her back, her ears in the water, she heard a faint voice calling, 'Nell?'

Quickly she sat up, displacing water with a loud sluice.

'Nell?' The disembodied voice was coming from just outside the circle of trees. 'Are you okay?'

'Ferdia?'

'Mum sent me. She's worried. Are you okay?'

'Grand,' she called. 'Changed my mind about the gig.'

'I'll tell her. Sorry for disturbing you.'

This was nuts, them shouting at each other in the dark, through the trees. 'Listen, come in. I'm decent.'

Suddenly, he was in the copse.

'Well, I'm not *decent*.' She was very nervous. 'But the water isn't see-through. Sit down, move the towels.'

He sat on the mini-stool, determinedly avoiding looking into the milky water. 'Sorry,' he said. 'Jessie was worried about you. Because of Liam being a no-show . . .'

'How'd you know I was in here?'

'Your name is on the list.'

She pressed herself against the side of the bath, supporting her face on her folded arms. His elbows rested on his knees. His hands were so beautiful. His thin knobbly wrists and raw knuckles seemed achingly vulnerable to her. God, she had it bad.

'I'm leaving Liam.' It was out of her mouth before she could stop it.

'What?'

Oh, God, no. 'I shouldn't have said that. Liam should be the first to know.'

'Did something happen?' Ferdia asked. 'Did you find out . . . something?'

'I found out that I don't love him any more. Isn't that enough? I'm a terrible person. Ferdia,' Nell said urgently. 'You can't tell *anyone*. Not until I've told Liam.'

'You can trust me. A million per cent.'

Unblinking, they gazed at each other in the shadowy light of the lanterns.

'Are you single now?'

That was so unexpected, she actually laughed. 'God, I don't know. I have no fecking idea.' Then, 'Who wants to know?'

'Me.'

Oh.

He swallowed hard. Croakily, he said, 'Just putting it out there. Nell, I think about you all of the time—'

'You do . . . ?'

He moved his chin up and down. He looked miserable.

'What . . . ? Happened? When?'

'Maybe . . . Dilly's first communion? I knew it wouldn't have been Liam's idea to give the money to Kassandra. It had to have been yours. Just . . . your passion, your values, the way you walked your talk. It's how I wanted to live.'

'I thought you didn't like me.'

'I thought I didn't too, if you wanted to be married to Liam. Then the weekend in Mayo, you told me to volunteer somewhere. So I did. Because I wanted to impress you.' Then, quickly, 'But now I'm doing it for real. I mean it, I'm committed to it. Remember when Perla was doing that talk? You walked in and *bam*! The most beautiful woman in the world. Ton. Of. *Bricks*. I nearly lost my mind.'

'But so soon after Sammie . . . ?'

His smile was melancholic. 'Sammie knew before I did. On the train home from Westport, she called it. I knew I thought you were cool, I didn't know then there was more to it. But Sammie loves you. It's all good.'

He winced. 'Then Italy. That was agony. My birthday, same. But you came to the Button Factory, I'd had a few drinks, I couldn't hide how I felt. Why were you there, Nell?'

Because I didn't have the stamina to keep resisting.

Abruptly, he looked depleted of everything. 'Just tell me, is there any chance? For me? For us?'

'Pass me a towel?'

Startled, he pawed around on the slate floor. Unfolding the towel to its full width, he got to his feet. She rose from the bath, water draining off her body, into its embrace, then let him wrap the towel around her and secure it with a chaste tuck near her armpit.

He offered his hand, to help her to step out, but she shook her head. While she was in the bath, with some sort of a barrier between them, she'd felt they were safe.

Hesitantly, she reached for him, pulling his body against hers, drawing his face closer. She shut her eyes, felt his breath on her skin, then his mouth on hers, slow and aching and tender. His hands were in her wet hair and the kiss intensified, becoming more urgent.

If they didn't stop soon, she would start fumbling at his jeans. She'd wrap her legs around his waist and let him slide into her. Or she'd pull him into the water, tearing at his clothes . . .

Holding her tight, tight, tight, pressing her hips against his, his gaspy, ragged breath loud in her ear, he whispered, 'Get out of the tub, Nell. Please.'

'No.' With an effort, she pulled away.

Abruptly, he released his hold of her. Then, moving to the treeline, he pressed his arm against a trunk and tried to catch his breath.

'Ferdia,' she said. 'This is the scariest mess of my life. I can't deal. I need to take care of things with Liam.'

'Nell. I think I'm in love with you.'

'Cop on!'

'No, you cop on. There's something special here between us. We both know it.'

'I'm nine years older than you. I'm married to your uncle.'

'*Step*-uncle. By *marriage*. And nine years is nothing. Sam Taylor-Johnson is twenty-four years older than her husband. Yeah. I've been googling all that stuff.'

'What about Jessie? I respect her, I really like her, she'd freak out . . .'

'Hey, we're all adults here.'

'Yeaaah, you know, we're kind of . . . *not*. You're still in college.'

'In eight months I'll be done.'

'I can't trust myself because I was sure I loved Liam.'

'Because he was coming along, like, all Mr Perfect, pretending he loved art and that. Me? You thought I was a—a spoilt kid. Because I *was*. But I've been on a steep learning curve.'

She pressed her lips together. Until she'd talked to Liam, she couldn't promise Ferdia anything.

He sighed and shrugged. 'Look, you know how I feel. It's up to you. If you want me . . .'

Then he was gone.

Nell dried herself slowly as the bathwater drained away. That was not cool. It shouldn't have happened. None of it. No matter what Ferdia said, he didn't really love her: he was simply young and idealistic. Likewise, the feelings she thought she had for him—the longing, the physical attraction—they were just a weird by-product of this crazy emotional upheaval.

Leaving Liam and ending their marriage were going to be tough: all of her focus and energy would be needed. She just had to trust that when everything was done, she'd be madly relieved that nothing had happened with Ferdia.

Apart from that one—let's be honest here—fucking *amazing* kiss.

Ninety-One

'Mum.'

'*Mum.*'

'MUM!'

A sharp finger dug into her upper arm. 'Ouch!'

'Wake up,' Vinnie yelled. 'We're home from Grandma's!'

Cara opened her eyes and had to shut them again. Everything hurt. Her head, her jaw, her shoulders, even her feet. 'What?' she croaked.

'I need money.'

Memories of the previous night came flooding back. Gabby's birthday. That horrific meal. The humiliation of everyone whispering about her. She'd only had a couple of glasses of wine. Why did she feel as if she had the worst hangover of her life?

'Money,' Vinnie repeated.

Slowly, every muscle aching, Cara managed to sit upright in bed. She'd obviously caught a virus. 'Is Grandma here?' she whispered.

'She's gone to play tennis.'

'Get Tom for me,' she croaked.

'Money first.'

She managed to open her eyes. 'Get. Your. Brother.'

Vinnie backed away nervously and returned moments later with Tom.

'The thermometer,' she instructed Tom. 'It's in the box in the bathroom. I'm sick.'

But her temperature was normal. She didn't understand.

She felt as if she'd done ten Pilates classes back to back.

Was it because of last night?

Maybe. She'd felt under attack, so she'd clenched all of her muscles, trying to make herself so small that she'd disappear. Worse than the physical pain was the terrible depression that had descended on her, seemingly out of nowhere. Everything felt broken and strange—her friendships, her job, herself and Ed.

She could not have got out of bed if her life depended on it. As the day went on, the boys made her toast and a cup of tea, which they presented with the same pride as if they'd just managed to split the atom. She couldn't summon the praise they so obviously expected.

Early evening, waiting for Ed to get home, they climbed into bed with her and put on *Wreck-It Ralph*. Tears began leaking down her face. Soon she was gasping and struggling for breath.

'Stop,' Vinnie said, not unkindly. 'Please, Mum, stop. Mums don't cry.'

Dropping her weekend bag in the hall, Nell found Liam in the living room. Anxiety buzzed in her stomach, making her feel sick. He needed to know *now*. Common decency said he deserved that.

'Hey, you're home!' He moved to get up to kiss her but she waved him back down.

'We need to talk.'

It was a surprise when he replied, 'Yep, we do. I'll go first. I've quit my job.'

Nell felt the blood drain from her face. 'Whatnow . . . ?'

'Yep.' He was cheery. 'Just seemed obvious. Trying to work and study, it's too much, was making me narky. And seriously, baby, all the grief I get from that place, for so little cash, what's the point?'

This can't be happening.

'Only thing is, we'll be living on whatever you make. You'll be supporting us—just for a while. That's okay?' Softly he said, '"For richer, for poorer", right? Baby, don't look so shocked.' His smile was gentle. 'We'll be grand. Exams are only a couple of months away. Soon as I qualify, I can start charging people. Might take a while to build up a clientele, but we'll be grand.'

She'd written *nothing* about this in that stupid letter to herself.

'Now what was it you wanted to talk about?'

'Oh . . . ah. Nothing.' How could she land all this on him now? 'Not important.'

Johnny whipped his belt from around his waist and threw it into the plastic tray, along with his wallet, his briefcase, his laptop and his iPad.

'Any liquids?' the woman asked. 'Anything in your pockets?'

Johnny jingled around, burrowing for change. There was something about the woman, the twinkly way she watched him, that reminded him of Izzy. He threw a clatter of coins into the tray and moved on, but suddenly his mind was cast back to the past, more than thirteen years ago.

Izzy had called him at work. 'I need a plus one,' she'd said. 'For a gala night, a work thing.'

It was about ten months since she'd broken up with Tristão and it seemed to be permanent. 'Will you come with me?'

He barely had to think about it. 'Sure.'

The function took place in a shiny marble-and-gold hotel in the middle of nowhere. The long evening eventually finished, and without consultation, they went to Izzy's room and had sex. Johnny was thirty-five now, older than he'd been during those carefree encounters of their early twenties—and a lot sadder. But when he was caught up in the sensation of Izzy's skin, her mouth, her hands on him, he felt normal—a man, a human animal, doing what he'd been programmed to do.

In the morning, with Izzy sprawled unconscious across the sheets, her long legs entangled with his, he wondered if she belonged in his bed. Did he belong in hers? Izzy was very special but she was vulnerable. *He* was vulnerable.

When her eyes finally opened, she said, 'I shouldn't have bothered booking you a room.'

'We didn't know this was going to happen.'

'C'mon, Johnny.'

He was shocked at his own naïvety. 'Izzy, you're one of the most important people in my life. I care about you too much for us to be . . .'

'Fuck buddies? Grand. No worries.'

'So we're okay?'

'*Course* we're okay, ya big thick. We're Izzy and Johnny, we'll always be okay!'

A few Saturdays later in Errislannan, on a blustery October afternoon, they pulled on their wellies and went out for some air. As they cut through the fields, the light was already fading. Winter was on its way.

The faint humming noise from the electric fence prompted Izzy to say, 'Remember when we used to push each other into it?'

'Yeah.' It raised a faint smile.

'That was what counted for fun back then. We were mental.'

'Well, *you* were.'

'Ha-ha. Here, isn't the sky beautiful?' She looked up at the streaks of lilac and mauve. Then, 'Johnny? I've something to say. Is there . . .' She stopped and started again. 'Johnny, I think there could be something between the two of us. Something serious.'

His heart dropped like a stone. No way had he seen this coming. *I can't hurt her.* 'Izzy . . . I think the world of you.'

'Course you do.' Said with an echo of her old swagger. 'And that night in the hotel . . . right?'

He felt he was slipping and sliding, trying desperately to grab on to the truth before it was swept from him. He'd thought they'd had an admirably adult, emotions-free fuck, but for Izzy, he was fast realizing, it had been a meaningful romantic encounter.

'You said you didn't want us to be fuck buddies,' she said.

'I did. But . . .' He'd meant they shouldn't be sleeping together at all.

'Is there someone else?' She had stopped walking and was staring at him.

'Izzy, listen to me, I'm in no state to have a girlfriend.'

'It's been nearly two years, Johnny. We've got to try.' She managed her familiar, optimistic smile. 'Promise me you'll think about it.'

But the right words just wouldn't come.

'Hey, Johnny Casey,' Izzy had demanded down the phone. 'Are you avoiding me?'

Yes. 'Nah. Work. Mad busy.'

Since her proposition that day, being with Izzy had made Johnny feel shitty and weird. He'd realized that you couldn't go round sleeping with just anyone. Actions have consequences. He'd started skipping his Saturday nights in Errislannan. One here, two in a row there. He'd just missed three on the trot, his longest yet.

'Look,' she said, 'I've obviously thrown a scare into you. The "you and me" thing was only an idea. A bad one. I didn't mean it.'

'Ah, sure, I *know* that.' Jesus Christ, the *relief*.

'Off my rocker there, for a while. None of us are exactly in tip-top condition now, are we? I'm sorry for putting the wind up you.'

'Nah. You haven't. Seriously work *is* mental.'

Funnily enough, that was the truth. Jessie kept pushing forward, working herself harder and harder and dragging everyone else with her. She was currently fixated on finding premises in Limerick.

'Come down this Saturday, though,' Izzy coaxed. 'We all miss you. I'll ring Jessie and tell her to give you the weekend off.'

'Right, so, do that!'

A huge load had lifted from him. Suddenly he was springing around, full of energy.

As it happened, a couple of days later he drove Jessie to Limerick to view potential premises.

The site looked promising, good enough to get the architect involved. Jessie was too tired for another round trip the next day: her nanny could spend the night with Ferdia and Saoirse, and Johnny was okay to stay the night because he had nothing on that evening. Because he never did.

They booked into a small hotel, then went for a sandwich. Johnny saw Jessie to her room, then checked there were no intruders hiding under her bed. He was almost out of the door when she said, 'You only wanted me because your buddy did.'

He could have left it at that—a short laugh, an admission that that was the kind of dickhead he was.

Instead he said, 'I do want you.'

Because, yeah, he did.

Hadn't he recently learnt that actions have consequences, that he couldn't live his life having sex with anyone and everyone?

But this was Jessie.

Flushed and delighted, she was suddenly unbuttoning his shirt, and although he tried to pretend it wasn't happening, he wasn't stopping her either. And sometimes he had to wonder just what kind of man he was.

Eleven Days Ago

MONDAY, 28 SEPTEMBER

Ninety-Two

From his breathing, Nell could tell that Liam was already awake.

Neither of them had a job, so neither had any reason to get up. It was a depressing realization. 'It's everyone's dream to skip work on a Monday morning,' she said, 'but when you've no choice . . .'

Liam rolled over. 'I know what will make us both feel better.'

No. She slithered across the sheets and clambered from the bed.

'What?' He looked baffled. 'You don't want to?'

What should she say? 'I'm sorry.'

'Is it your period?'

'No . . . I'm just . . . sorry.'

'You just don't want to?' He seemed shocked. 'Don't you fancy me any more?'

'I just don't want to right now.'

'I don't get it.'

She shrugged nervously. She needed a reason to be out of the flat. The two of them trapped there together day after day felt dangerous.

In the living room, she rang her dad.

'Nellie, what's up?'

'Have you a job on right now? Can I help out? I don't need to be paid much.'

'Who are you and what have you done with my daughter?'

'Dad. Yes or no?'

'. . . Yeh. Big house in Malahide. Look, are you all *right*?'

'I just need to be doing something. That's all.'

'Don't tell me, so. Your mother will get it out of you and she'll tell me. You could cut out the middle man and . . . No? Rightio. You want to start tomorrow?'

'Thanks. Text me the address.'

'I could just tell it to you. Seeing as we're talking to each other. Why do we have to click every fecking thing? Can't I just—'

'Grand. Fine. Tell me.'

She heard Liam slam out of the apartment. With enormous relief, she climbed onto the couch with Molly Ringwald, got her iPad and googled, 'I got divorced and I wasn't even married a year.'

It was amazing how often this happened. There were couples who had discovered on *literal honeymoon* that it was all over. For some, the wedding preparations had been so elaborate and time-draining that the happy pair hadn't exchanged a civil word in months. When they'd found themselves marooned together on a tiny strip of sand in the Indian Ocean, they'd discovered that actually they couldn't stand each other.

Then there were the women who had 'panic-married': afraid they'd never find the perfect man, they'd decided they could put up with some substandard specimen. Only to realize that, actually, they couldn't . . .

Nell devoured each story, taking particular comfort from the ones most similar to her: basically that they'd got married too quickly, before they knew each other properly. 'It's too easy to tune out the details at the start.' That *really* resonated.

There was no point in blaming Liam. This was on her. She'd willed him to be Mr Fabulous and she'd refused to listen to those who begged her to be cautious.

Why had they got married? What was the big fat hurry? Liam had wanted it, but so had she.

She'd thought it was exciting—that was what it was. That it made her seem interesting and grown-up.

Now she remembered actually saying to her dad, 'We can always get divorced.' She'd been joking but, subconsciously, had she sensed that this was not something for the long haul?

She hadn't left Liam. Because if she had, the entire Casey clan would have been in uproar. She'd seemed so certain on Saturday night. But something had obviously changed after she'd arrived home. Had she decided to give him another chance? Realized she still loved him?

Whatever it was, Ferdia felt like shit. Hands down, these had been the hardest few days in forever.

On Sunday evening, when they'd all got back from the festival, he'd been holding his breath, waiting for the news to break that she'd left Liam. Nothing happened, so, feeling uneasy, he went to bed. The next morning, still no word. He went to college, trying to style it out, but checking his phone every ten minutes.

All he got was a big fat nothing. Every. Single. Time.

Tuesday, same. He was distracted, jittery and utterly fucking miserable.

The worst was that he had no one to talk to. *Especially* not Nell.

Whatever she decided to do—or not—he had to be cool: texting or calling would be stalker-y.

Who knew if she'd have a thing with him even if she left Liam? But while she was still married, there was zero hope.

It was crushing him. He felt abandoned, as if he'd lost someone precious. Which was insane, because he'd never actually had her.

Wednesday morning now. Still no news. For the first time, he admitted that there would likely *be* no news. This was his life now. He needed to carry on, act As If. Keep putting one foot in front of the other and eventually he'd get over her.

Up in the house, the breakfast mayhem was under way.

Jessie thrust a plate at him. 'Bunny, toast, it's going spare.' Then, to the younger kids, 'Go now or you'll miss the bus.'

Ferdia looked at the slice of toast. His mouth was dry. He literally couldn't eat. 'Mum?' he croaked. 'When's our next family get-together?'

She flicked a look at Johnny. 'His birthday. A week next Friday. Dinner here at the house.'

'Who's coming?'

'Usual. Us. Ed, Cara and the nippers. Liam and Nell. Why?'

'Just wondering.'

She was all set to interrogate him further, but her phone beeped.

Zipping past, she took a glance. 'From Nell. Liam's looking for bodies to practise his massage on.'

'Wha-at?'

'His massage course.' Jessie was impatient. 'He needs volunteers.'

Nell was going in to bat for Liam? This really didn't sound good.

'I'm too busy,' Johnny said quickly.

'It can be any time over the next seven weeks.'

'Even if I had all of eternity, I'm not having a massage. Doesn't anyone ever consider how unnatural it is? One person scrubbing away at another person, like they're trying to get dog wee out of the rug?'

'When did Camilla wee on the rug?' Jessie glared.

'It's fixed now.'

'Grand. I'm also too busy,' Jessie said.

'*So* not loving the idea of a massage from Uncle Liam.' Saoirse made an *ick* face.

'Ferd?'

'Seriously? You *know* what I think about that dick.'

'He could ask Robyn.' Saoirse's voice was soft. 'I'm sure she'd enjoy it. They both would.'

As Jessie descended the stairs into the gloom of Jack Black's, the barman spotted her and reached for the gin bottle. *No.* Gin was for evening times, not for ten thirty in the morning.

There, at a sticky table, sporting yet another of his wacko suits, was Karl Brennan. In a different person, his reliability might be impressive but today, their third meeting, Jessie wondered if he actually slept there.

She shook her head at the barman. 'Just water, thanks.'

'But you always have gin!'

My God, these men with their fragile egos, looking for positive endorsement simply for remembering a person's drink. Which was (a) their job. And (b) hardly the most challenging prospect when she was literally the only woman she'd ever seen in this small, desolate bar. Which, for her own sanity, she'd renamed Last Stop Before Rehab.

'Bit early for gin,' she said, which caused two men at separate tables to give her startled, wounded stares.

'Ms Parnell.' Karl gave an over-formal nod. 'Always a pleasure.'

'Mr Brennan.' Jessie pulled up a stool.

She had no experience of management consultants but suspected Karl Brennan was wildly atypical of the breed. For a start, he seemed to do a lot of daytime drinking. Also, evening drinking.

His suits belonged to the lead singer in an eighties band.

As did his hair.

But his ability to focus on the very things she thought were important heartened her. He'd asked for this meeting to drill down into her chef-pestering. Her suspicion was that he was many things—most of them bad—but there was a chance that, in his repulsive, dysfunctional way, he might be a genius.

'Ed, no! I'd have to shave my legs. And maybe put on fake tan.'

'What? Why?'

'For Liam to see me without my clothes on . . . I would *die*.'

'But didn't Peggy say you've to start being kind to your body?'

'Yes, but . . .'

. . . It was almost three weeks since she'd seen Peggy. In a few more weeks, she'd be able to tell Ed.

'How about you tell Liam you're nervous?' Ed suggested.

'I don't think he'd care.'

'He'll be dealing with all kinds of people, if he ever qualifies. This'll be a good opportunity for him. And for you.'

She could not *bear* to be massaged by Liam. He was not a good man. She wasn't quite sure when she'd arrived at that decision but she felt it intensely.

He was a bit of a lech—in Tuscany he'd been ogling Robyn *non-stop*.

She didn't think he was a kind person. She sometimes wondered if Nell was too young and too dazzled by him.

But if she kept resisting this massage suggestion, there was a chance that Ed might do something like ring Peggy to get her to intercede. And *that* would be a disaster.

'Okay,' she said. 'I'll do it.'

'Cara says you can massage her,' Nell said.

Liam winced. 'No. I can't deal, not with her.'

'Why not?'

'Super-judgy person.'

'She's totally not. She's so sweet.' It was a huge effort to get herself under control. 'When you qualify you'll have to work with people you don't love. All part of your training.'

'I'll only work with people I like.' He noticed her sceptical look. 'What? I'm good at this, Nell. I'll be able to pick and choose my clients.'

This was like being in a bad dream, trapped with Liam until he passed his fucking exams.

Thanks to him, she'd lived rent-free for a year. Fairness said she should shoulder the financial burden for the next couple of months. A tougher person would have just walked away. They'd have told him he was a fool for jacking in his job and leaving himself with no income. But that wasn't who she was.

As soon as he was earning again, she could leave, so the only thing she could do was round up plenty of bodies for his massage practice. Which was a *lot* more difficult than she'd expected. His nearest and dearest weren't exactly knocking the door down. And she literally couldn't bear him to touch her.

Her obsession with Ferdia was still eating away at her. If they were insane enough to start anything, who knew what chaos it would kick off? Horrible visions bothered her, of him crashing out of his degree, both of them living in penury, hated by all the Caseys, then eventually by each other.

She'd probably see him on Friday of next week for Johnny's birthday. It would be absolute torture.

Four Days Ago

MONDAY, 5 OCTOBER

Ninety-Three

Liam's massage table was in Violet's bedroom.

'Sit down.' Liam waved Cara towards the pink rocking chair. 'Just need a few details here. You on medication? Injuries I need to be aware of? Any other pertinent info?'

'No medication. No injuries. But I'm . . .' she coughed '. . . out of my comfort zone.'

'This is a professional environment, Cara. Think of me the way you'd think of a doctor.'

That didn't help: she was also embarrassed whenever she revealed herself to a doctor.

Liam stepped from the room, leaving her to undress. She clambered onto the table, tugging at the towel, desperate to cover as much of herself as possible.

Lifting her face from the headrest, she bleated miserably, 'I'm ready.' Then she replaced her face and admired Violet's carpet.

In he came, whisking the towel down to her waist, carelessly splashing oil across her back. Some drops ricocheted into her hair, which she had only just washed. His cold hands landed on her skin, making her entire body pop with goosebumps. Immediately he was kneading and knuckling as if he were a washerwoman by a brook, laundering a badly soiled bedsheet.

He was energetic, she'd say that.

Soon her skin felt as if it had been scorched with a lighter. He appeared to have landed on a particularly stubborn stain on her right shoulder. Jabbing both of his thumbs deep into the tissue, it felt instantly bruised. His knuckles dragged back over the same area and she wasn't sure she could endure it.

This is what it's like being tortured, she thought. Lying down, being subjected to unbearable agony.

Except when you're being tortured you don't have to pretend you're enjoying it. You're allowed to shout and beg for mercy.

God, here he came again with the knuckles.

'Um, Liam,' she coughed again, 'I'm finding the pressure a bit intense.'

'Yeah?' He sounded surprised. 'Probably cos you're not athletic. Right?'

'Yep,' she muttered, hot with humiliation.

'Okay. Toned-down version specially for you.' There was an expectant pause.

'Thanks,' she mumbled, into the headrest.

Off he went again, the pressure less brutal, but at no stage actually pleasant. When he reached her thighs, he spent what she considered far too long on them, lifting and squeezing her cellulite, as if it was Play-Doh slime. She was certain there was no benefit in this, that he was just amusing himself.

There he went again, lifting it and letting it wobble-flop back into place.

Eventually she had to turn over, so he could work on the front of her body. But when he made a move towards her stomach, she could take no more.

'Okay,' he said. 'That's you done. Wow, you needed that.'

She smiled anxiously. *Please get out and let me get dressed.*

'You are literally the most tense person I've ever touched.'

Fuck off.

'So how was it?' he asked.

'Good.'

He continued to look at her.

'*Very* good.' Then, in a flash of inspiration, 'Dreamy.'

'That *is* good! Great.' His smile was wide. 'Cool. Any suggestions for improvements?'

She shook her head. Please could he just leave the room and let her put her clothes back on.

'Dreamy,' he repeated. 'And no need to improve. I'm totally killing this!'

Three Days Ago

TUESDAY, 6 OCTOBER

Ninety-Four

The sound of a ringing phone startled Nell so much that she wobbled on her ladder. No one rang anyone these days . . . It must be an emergency! She grabbed her mobile.

'Jessie? Y'okay?'

'Nell, sorry for ringing. Johnny's birthday dinner, Friday night? I'm not sure it's going ahead.'

'Oh. Okay.'

Maybe she should be relieved: being in the same space as Ferdia, behaving as if he was nothing to her, would she even be able?

But a jittery thrill shot through her whenever she'd thought of Friday.

Jessie was talking quickly. 'Michael Kinsella—you know, the father of my first husband, Rory? My father-in-law? We just found out he's in intensive care, a heart attack. Johnny's in bits. Michael was like a father to him, a proper one, I mean, not like that psycho Canice. Ferdia and Saoirse are very upset too.' Then she added, 'And I'm not doing exactly fantastic myself.'

'That totally sucks, Jessie.'

'So a birthday dinner in two days looks unlikely.'

'Forget about all that. Just mind Johnny and . . . the kids. And yourself.'

'Okay. Thanks. Bye, bunny.' She was gone.

Nell took a deep breath. Ferdia had told her how important Michael was to him. So . . . should she ring him?

As a friend?

But she'd put ten tough days into weaning herself off him. Any contact would reset the counter to zero.

Okay. Not calling him. Totally not calling him.

Emails, Jessie thought. She'd answer emails.

She glanced across at Johnny. Simultaneously, he looked up. 'Should we—'

'Ring Ellen? No.'

'But—'

No, they couldn't.

Ellen's husband might be dying. The poor woman must be going through hell. They had no right to distress her further.

'I could ring Ferdia?' Jessie suggested.

'Will he even have his phone on? If they're all in intensive care?'

'I'll give it a go.' But his phone went to voicemail and she hung up.

Early afternoon, Ferdia rang back. 'He flatlined twice. A balloon was put in to unblock his artery, and he got a temporary pacemaker. His chances are only thirty per cent. If he survives until tomorrow night, they'll have a better idea.'

That really didn't sound great . . . 'How's everyone?'

'Ah, you know.' Ferdia sounded awkward.

'Can you tell them—' Jessie stopped. 'Thanks, bunny.'

She related the facts to Johnny, who responded with a curt nod. Her heart sank. He was so upset. Though she wasn't anything like as cut up as he was, this had stirred up a lot for her too: protective sorrow on behalf of Ferdia and Saoirse; empathy for Rory, how hard he'd have found this, if he were here. Most of all, memories of that part of her life when she'd been so young and happy, when Izzy and Keeva had made her feel 'real'.

She'd long ago stopped yearning for a reconciliation. It was uncomfortable—and embarrassing—to be estranged from her former in-laws, but she got on with it. Today, though, she was overwhelmed with nostalgia—they really had had the best of times. Today she missed them terribly. Particularly Izzy.

The call from Ellen to Ferdia had come just before seven that morning. Ferdia and Saoirse had raced around, preparing to go to the hospital.

Jessie was in the kitchen making breakfast for them, when Johnny said quietly, 'Should I go too?'

Shocked, she realized that Johnny must be expecting—even hoping—that a life-and-death drama would trigger a reunion. In fact, a tiny pocket of hope had also survived for her.

But the life-and-death drama was here and a last-minute deathbed love-in was looking increasingly unlikely. The only solution was for them both to undo everything that had happened since Rory's death.

Jessie neither could nor would do that.

If she had grieved Rory the way the Kinsellas had wanted, she would never have married Johnny or had three more children. The family and the life she had now simply wouldn't exist. But remembering how she'd broken the news to them, it was hard to believe her own insensitivity. She'd sat in their living room and said, 'I think I was meant to be with both of them, first Rory, then Johnny.'

Which was utter bullshit. But in those gorgeous early days of sex, sex and more sex with Johnny, some handy part of her subconscious had silenced her guilt with whispers of *Meant To Be.*

Michael, Ellen and Keeva had responded with aghast silence. Izzy had erupted in tearful fury.

'What is *wrong* with you?'

Jessie knew about Izzy and Johnny's long-ago hook-ups. Like, everybody had known. It was never any sort of deal, because Izzy slept with everyone. So did Johnny, for that matter.

Izzy had always been cheerfully dismissive, saying things like 'No man for *ages*. Apart from a ridey night with Johnny Casey, but he doesn't count.' In matters of the heart, Izzy was admirably resilient. Funnily enough, although she'd told Jessie about her most recent hook-up with Johnny, she'd said nothing about her suggestion that they give an actual relationship a go. Johnny had been the one to tell Jessie.

She'd read nothing at all into Izzy's omission—life had changed, priorities were different.

Now, through unstoppable tears, Izzy had gasped, 'Rory is gone, you've taken everything, and we have nothing.'

Jessie had gone cold. She'd just realised that Izzy was in love with Johnny. She didn't know when Izzy's feelings for him had turned to love, but they clearly had.

She *adored* Izzy—admired her, respected her, loved her, was in awe of her. Now she'd wounded her. Rory's family were never going to be thrilled about this development between her and Johnny but she'd had faith that they'd eventually make their peace with it. This was a whole different problem.

Panic took hold as she wondered how to fix it. *I'll have to let Izzy have Johnny.*

But I love him.

And we're having a baby.

I should let him choose.

But, no, that's absolute nonsense. I love him, he loves me. It's not a handbag that Izzy and I are tussling over.

All four Kinsellas had seemed much angrier with Jessie than with Johnny.

'There's two of us here', Johnny insisted loudly. 'I'm just as much to—'

But Izzy hissed, 'Shut up, Johnny,' and spoke over his attempts to blame himself.

Even as Jessie and Johnny had slunk from the house, Michael had shaken his hand and Ellen had grabbed him in a wild, tearful embrace.

All Jessie had got was how-could-you glares.

As soon as she got home, Jessie called Izzy. Izzy hung up on her.

Jessie rang back. She called again the following morning. Izzy hung up again and again and again.

Apart from Johnny, Jessie had no one to confide in now.

Comfort came from an unexpected source—her own mother.

Dilly Parnell was, by nature, a low-key person. It took an awful lot to get her chatting animatedly. But hearing about Johnny and Jessie did the trick. 'To be given a second chance with love! That's a great blessing. And another baby on the way! But, tell me, how are Michael and Ellen taking this?'

With a rush of relief, Jessie unburdened herself, 'They're awful upset. So's Izzy and Keeva.'

'That's to be expected.'

'But they're blaming me much more than Johnny. As if I was some heartless seducer. Women always get the blame.'

'They're not thinking with their proper heads,' she said. 'They think you stole both of their sons.'

'I stole nobody!'

'When you married Rory, you took him away from them. While he was in your "care", he died. Now you've taken their—What's the word? Replacement. Surrogate?'

'Ma, that's not logical. I'm getting blamed for . . . And I'm surprised, because they're such lovely people. Decent.'

'They're grieving. You've had the luck to meet a man who might be Rory's equal. But they'll never get a replacement son or brother. And what about Johnny and Izzy?'

'I didn't think it was anything. But Izzy, her heart is broken. Maybe I should let her have him.'

'Don't be cracked. Anyway, you don't mean it.'

She didn't: her survival instinct had kicked in.

'You're alive again,' her mother said, 'and you like it.'

*

Over the following weeks and months Jessie continued to click off texts to Izzy, pleading her previous ignorance about Izzy's feelings for Johnny; she sent emails full of abject apologies; she handwrote letters in which she swore she'd do anything Izzy wanted. Except give up Johnny.

Izzy ignored everything.

It was well over a year before they even clapped eyes on each other again: one of Michael and Ellen's meticulously choreographed weekend handovers of Ferdia and Saoirse had slipped off its tracks. Mrs Templeton, the neighbour who most frequently acted as the go-between, was bedbound with pneumonia. It was Izzy who opened the door and let Ferdia and Saoirse into the house. Her glance slid over Jessie, in a way that was both dismissive and scathing, then the door closed.

It shook her, being that close to Izzy, feeling her hostility. On the drive home, she cried.

Then, from the back seat, eight-month-old Bridey began squawking and her heart lightened.

She wished she hadn't hurt anyone; she wished she and Izzy were still friends. But in this life, you get what you get.

Now Johnny stole a look at Jessie across the office. For many years, missing the Kinsellas had been a low-level thing, frequently so faint it barely registered. But since that rainy Sunday back in June, when he'd driven Saoirse and Ferdia to Errislannan, that had changed.

He'd let Ferdia and Saoirse out of the car, done a U-turn and driven back along the narrow country road, heading for home. He'd gone barely fifty yards when he heard a muffled rhythmic noise, music with a heavy bass. A shiny, burgundy-coloured Range Rover Discovery was booming its way towards him.

There wasn't enough room for both cars to pass: one of them would have to pull in and, from the attitude of that yoke, it would have to be him.

Suddenly his heart was pumping pure adrenaline—Izzy was the other driver.

It was years since he'd seen her. He watched her face change as she recognized him; abruptly her car stopped, blocking his path.

All of his muscles tensed, waiting for the confrontation.

Then she smiled.

One Day Ago

Ninety-Five

He loves his grandpa, he must be in pieces, he'd want me to call.

But . . . What about Liam? What about my principles?

Yeah, but I can meet Ferdia just as a friend . . .

All day Wednesday, Nell back-and-forthed in her head.

Now it was Thursday morning and the mental table tennis continued with no let-up.

She realized that if she didn't call, the agonizing would go on into infinity: if she rang him, it would stop.

Grand, she thought, awash with relief. *I'm doing it.*

He answered after half a ring. 'Nell?'

'Ferd.' She exhaled, just from the pleasure of saying his name. 'I heard about your grandpa. I'm really sorry. How's he doing?'

'Still hanging on. If he survives the next thirteen hours, he should be okay.'

'Oh, God. Right. Fingers crossed.'

'Yeah.' Then: 'Nell? Meet me?'

'Okay.'

'You will?'

'Totally.' Why else had she rung?

But where?

It couldn't be a bar or a coffee shop. Dublin was too small—someone was bound to see them. *Obviously* it couldn't be in Liam's apartment and *obviously* it couldn't be in Ferdia's granny flat.

What about her parents' house? No. That would be super-scuzzy. Garr's place? No. It was wrong to involve any other person.

A fleeting thought zipped across her mind: this house she was decorating? Only like the sketchiest plan ever but it had given her an idea. 'What about Johnny's Airbnb flat? If someone isn't booked in there today.'

Silence followed.

She was worried now: had she gone too far?

Then he said, 'How would we get in? He must have a key in the—'

'I've a key. From painting it in the summer. I never gave it back. Well, I tried but Johnny said a few of us should have one in case Cara lost hers.'

'From what Johnny says, it's really busy, nearly always booked.' She heard him clicking. 'The chances of it being empty are . . . Here we go. No. Someone's there today. But looks like tomorrow it's empty?'

Fuuuuuck.

'Nell?'

Was she doing this? *Really* doing this?

'Okay.' Her voice wobbled. 'What time?'

'Checkout is at twelve.' He had to clear his throat. 'Should we give it a couple of hours to make sure they're properly gone?'

'So . . . ? We'll meet each other there at two o'clock?'

Nothing was going to happen. Not in that way. They were better than that.

Ed had just moved over to the left-hand lane when his car engine began making alarming choking noises. Hitting the brake, he bunny-hopped to the hard shoulder and hoped to God his AA membership was still in date. The engine was emitting evil-looking black smoke and he sensed that it was game over for the ageing Peugeot.

Not ideal in terms of timing. It would never have been ideal, but at the moment, because of the expense of Cara's illness, they were more strapped than usual. If they needed a new car, she was likely to plunge into a fresh bout of remorse.

He wished she wouldn't. He got it: she felt profoundly guilty. But it had happened, she was getting well, and it was time to move on.

Maybe the car would be okay. Broken fan belt, something small like that . . .

But when he lifted the bonnet, bluish flames jumped up at him, immediately burning faster now that they had oxygen.

He strode quickly away down the hard shoulder, putting as much space between him and the car in case it decided to blow up. Never mind ringing the AA, he'd better ring the Fire Brigade instead.

'The car's buggered.'

'What?' Cara looked up, shocked. 'Seriously?'

'The engine went on fire on the M50.'

'Oh, Ed! Were you okay? Promise? So . . . Does this mean we need to buy a new car?'

'Afraid so.'

Oh, no. 'How much?'

'Could probably get an okay second-hand one for about ten grand. Bank loan?'

She shook her head. 'It's only a month since we got an overdraft.' To cover expenses they couldn't currently pay. Expenses that were her fault.

'Could we get a new credit card?' He sounded exhausted. 'Pay for it with that?'

'Ed, the interest rates . . . It would be almost as bad as a loan shark.'

They were both silent. She couldn't ask her parents: they didn't have it. He couldn't ask his: they wouldn't give it.

'I could ask Johnny for a loan?' Ed suggested.

'Maybe.' She hadn't done their accounts for a couple of months—perhaps they'd suddenly got a grip on their spending?

Then there was always Johnny's Airbnb account: there was plenty of money in that.

'Okay,' she said. 'Ask him. The worst thing he can say is no.'

'Johnny.' Jessie's tone was halting.

They'd had a strange evening at home, she and Johnny floating in separate orbits, suspended in an atmosphere of imminent catastrophe. Ferdia and Saoirse were still at the hospital. They hadn't rung in hours. Soon they would know if Michael was going to make it.

Despite their falling-out, Jessie still thought of Michael with great affection. He'd been a lovely man and the best father-in-law you could wish for. She hoped he'd survive but a solid seam of acceptance ran through her: sometimes people died. Both her dad and her mum had. And Rory. She knew better than most . . .

Those who hadn't experienced the death of a parent—and Johnny was one—had an innocence that flew in the face of reality, an expectation that life would still deliver a fairy-tale ending. All the same, she knew the last two days had been really tough going for him.

He was half watching some car show. Jessie took the remote and muted it. 'Just for a second,' she said. Then, 'Babes, we made our choice. It was a good one, we've been happy.'

Johnny remained silent.

Maybe if she articulated the truth he was trying to face, it would help. 'We've been hoping that, if we waited long enough, they'd forgive us.'

She didn't really mean 'we': she hadn't been convinced of the possibility for a long time. But she didn't want to risk humiliating him. 'I'm not so sure it's going to happen.'

'Okay.' His voice was barely audible.

She wanted to say more, something to give him comfort or courage, but maybe she'd said enough for now. She presented him with the remote. 'Watch your cars.'

As if she was keeping vigil, she sat with him.

The car show ended and another began—this must be the car channel. How could there be enough car shows to fill an entire channel?

Her phone vibrated. Ferdia!

'Bunny?'

Beside her, Johnny's phone rang—it felt as if every phone in the house had suddenly starting ringing. 'Yeah?' Johnny got to his feet and left the room.

Ferdia said into her ear, 'Mum. Grandpa's going to not-die, the doctor says. Like, not yet, you know what I mean? His vitals are returning to normal. Saoirsh and me are coming home now.'

'Great. Great! Drive safe. See you soon.' She hung up and called, 'Johnny!'

She found him in the hall. 'That was Ferd. He says Michael's going to be okay.'

Johnny put his face into his hands. Silent tears leaked from his eyes.

Today

Ninety-Six

'You're okay to do this?' Raoul asked Cara.

'Totally.'

Billy Fay was on his way from the airport and Cara had asked if she could check him in.

'Madelyn can manage,' Raoul said.

'Trust me.' She made herself smile. 'Let me.'

In the six weeks since she'd returned to work, Billy Fay had stayed at the Ardglass twice. Madelyn had taken care of him on those two occasions.

Everyone was still walking on eggshells around her.

But she had a plan. It was time to be her own hero. If she managed to banter her way through Billy Fay's insults—while still remaining professional and polite—it would boost her opinion of herself. Even if her colleagues didn't know the details, they were bound to pick up on the improvement in her self-esteem.

In her idealized version of events, she'd take Mr Fay to his suite. When Anto, or whichever bellboy, brought up his luggage, asked where he'd like his bags, her most ambitious imaginings had her saying, in light-hearted tones, 'Remember, last time I checked you in, you suggested that Anto shove them up my butt? Is that still your favoured place?'

Hard to know how he'd respond but her intention was to smile, smile, smile, and keep talking. 'You told Anto to stick them up *his* butt. He said it was too small, so you suggested that he stick them up mine instead. You must remember, it was so funny!'

And then, 'So, Mr Fay, do you need anything else? Or should I just get out now—fat bitch that I am?' Finishing up her perfect scenario, she'd give a cool smile and swing out of there, leaving him gulping like a dying fish.

It was a delicate tone to strike, but it could be done—Anto managed to be both cheeky and respectful. All Cara had to do was be a bit more Anto.

Billy Fay *might* find it amusing. Maybe. Bullies often dropped the front when their victim stood up for themselves. Or he might find himself shamed into better behaviour. Not entirely impossible.

There *was* a chance that he'd lodge a complaint. But she could insist that they'd simply been sharing a laugh. That he'd instigated some light-hearted teasing and she'd responded in kind. That she'd been demonstrating how good a sport she was . . .

It was potentially risky. But, technically speaking, she wouldn't be in the wrong. All she had to do was act innocent and keep on acting it.

She might even become a *cause célèbre* for bullied receptionists the world over—the very idea made her smile—and Billy Fay would be black-listed at every five-star hotel on earth.

There was a teeny, *teeny* possibility that she might lose her job. But it was genuinely very small. And at least she'd have regained some self-respect . . .

Anxiously, she paced back and forth behind the front desk. Her phone buzzed. A WhatsApp from Jessie: Johnny's birthday dinner tonight back on! 7.30

Oh, no! The sudden crushing disappointment! She loved Johnny, Jessie, all of them, but in her head she'd already eased into an uncomplicated Friday night, watching TV in her pyjamas. Instead she'd have to summon gallons of adrenalin, which had already clocked off for the weekend, hoist her energy up from the basement and hold it above her head until about ten o'clock tonight.

Her internal line rang, making all of her nerve endings frizz.

'Incoming,' Oleksandr, the doorman, said. 'Mr Fay.'

Taking the key and the iPad, she went to the front step and watched Billy Fay push his way out of the car, as if he was trying to escape a chokehold. Then he thumped his flat-footed way up the steps. Honestly, he had some nerve calling *her* fat.

'Good afternoon, Mr Fay.' Her mouth made dry, popping noises.

Without answering, he lunged for the elevator, Cara in his wake.

'I would ask how your journey was.' She strove to sound pleasant. 'But as I remember, you prefer silence.'

The look he gave was perplexed. Suspicious.

'The McCafferty Suite.' She opened the door and bade him enter. 'Your usual. Your mini-bar has been stocked with the American beer you like. The bathroom has extra towels—'

Here came Anto. 'Where would you like your bags, Mr Fay?'

Now! *Now!* This was her moment, when she stood up to the fat-shaming creep, when she handed him back the shame he'd foisted on her.

Last time you suggested that Anto shove them up my butt? Is that still your favoured place?

But when she opened her mouth, the words wouldn't come out.

She needed them to be said. Her self-respect depended on it.

'On the rack,' Mr Fay muttered. 'Whatever.'

Anto dropped them and scooted away.

She could still say it, there was still time . . . She heard her voice say, meekly, 'Would you like me to take you through the room's features?'

'No.' He sounded tired and bad-tempered. 'Just get your fat ass out of here.'

Quick! Say something now. Anything!

Time slowed down. She stood, motionless, in the middle of the room. He frowned, looking at her with mild curiosity. Her mouth opened again: this time she was going to say something.

'I need to take a nap,' he said.

Her mouth shut. Her body moved. Then she was out in the corridor, with the free-falling desolation of anticlimax.

She'd only gone a couple of steps when fury at having squandered her chance blazed in her. She was raging at herself—for being a target, for being a coward.

She couldn't *bear* feeling this way. Ravenous emptiness and hunger erupted, filling her with a great roar. She had a desperate need for food and more food, to pile it into her, to muffle this appalling discomfort.

Was *this* what Peggy had been talking about? The connection between unbearable feelings and the desire to numb herself?

Probably. She'd just never seen it before.

Did this mean there really *was* something wrong with her? Call it an illness, an addiction, the name didn't really matter. Whatever it was, she'd thought she had a handle on it, and she clearly hadn't.

What had she been *thinking* with her crazy plan to challenge Billy Fay? She could never have pulled it off. He was too sure of himself—and she . . . wasn't . . .

A swirl of dirty emotions was sucking her down into the dark and she wanted to binge and vomit.

Well, she did, but she didn't. Her feelings craved a painkiller but she already felt terrible loss. Afterwards she would wish she hadn't done it.

The solution, when it appeared, felt like balm on a burn: she'd ring Peggy and plead for an appointment. Today, if possible.

She stepped into a quiet nook between two bedrooms and rang the hospital. The switchboard operator said, 'Mrs Kennedy is with a patient.'

Of *course* she was with a patient, but Peggy had been so consistently available in the past that the let-down was disorienting.

'I can connect you to her voicemail.'

'Okay. Um, no, wait, it's all right.' She wondered if she should ring Peggy on her mobile. Peggy had said she could, but that had been back when she'd been Peggy's client.

Actually, *patient*: that was the word. She'd been Peggy's *patient*.

Could she call while she was with another patient? Wouldn't that be terribly wrong? But if she didn't get to talk to her, she was going to go out and buy far too much food, then eat it.

Peggy's appointments began on the hour and lasted for fifty minutes: if she called her at about five to two, she might pick up.

But when Cara made the call at five to two, Peggy's mobile went straight to message. Quickly she hung up.

'Cara,' Raoul said. 'Two o'clock. Your lunch.'

It was all over. She had no more say in this. She had no more fight.

Except there was no place she could do it. 'Her' little bathroom in the basement was far too risky. She considered the ladies' room in another nearby fancy hotel. But that wouldn't give her the privacy she needed. Wildly, she considered renting a hotel room—which was such an extreme idea that sanity began to return.

From the far side of the busy street, Ferdia watched the door, waiting for Nell. He'd arrived early, feeling like he was losing his damn mind. She wanted to see him. That must mean *something*—

The heavy Georgian door opened from the inside and he tensed in readiness. Maybe she was already there. But the woman emerging from the building wasn't Nell. For a moment the confusion was too much. What the hell . . . ? What was *Izzy* doing here? Dropping in on a mate?

Seriously? What were the chances that Izzy had a friend who lived in the same building as Johnny's flat? There were only six apartments in that place, *waaay* too much of a coincidence.

Izzy cast a quick look over one shoulder, then the other, then stuck her arm out and hailed a taxi. She jumped in as if she couldn't get out of the place fast enough.

This was not good. This was so not good. Then the door opened again.

And the person who came out was Johnny.

Fuck.

Ferdia's heart thumped painfully.

Johnny repeated the same furtive over-the-shoulder checks Izzy had, then, just as she had, flagged down a cab.

It was obvious they'd been together.

What the hell had they been up to?

And what kind of stupid question was *that*?

Poor Mum. That was his overriding thought. This would *ruin* her.

He'd often wondered about Johnny. In the past, he'd decided he was a cheater, because believing bad things about him had felt good. Lately, though, he'd liked him better. Just because he literally *never shut up* didn't mean he was a player.

But Ferdia had been wrong: the world was bigger, badder and far darker than he'd ever realized.

Ninety-Seven

I should have bought new underwear. Are we going to have actual sex? I wish I'd worn deodorant. Wait, I didn't bring condoms. I shouldn't be meeting him. Why did my hair have to go bushy when I need it to be beachy-wave? It was okay until I combed it. Will he have brought condoms? What will I do about Liam? This is crackheadery and I am losing my mind.

Would he be literally lurking outside on the street? Hey, maybe he wouldn't show at all.

No. He was not going to change his mind: she was certain about that.

The street curved around and now she could see the building. Ferdia wasn't there. But as she got nearer, she spotted him across the street, wearing a long dark coat and clumpy lace-up boots, looking like an elegant tramp.

Forcing her body to carry on as normal, she got the key from her satchel. On the edge of her vision, he was crossing the road.

The key wouldn't fit into the latch. Oh, God, *no*. Had Johnny changed the locks? With trembling hands, she tried again. It slipped in, twisted easily and, with relief, she fell against the heavy door, pushing it open. Stepping into the hallway, Ferdia was behind her. She could actually smell him—fresh sweat, cold day, washing powder and a slight hint of mustiness, probably from his coat. Her skin goosebumped.

The door shut and the bright, chilly street disappeared. In the dim hallway, the only light came through the fan-shaped window above the lintel.

Nell turned to him, their glances locked and fear flared though her. This was insane.

'It's okay.' He sounded really pretty sure about this.

'The flat,' she said. 'It's on the first floor.' She gave him the key. 'Can you . . .'

'Uh . . . Okay.'

He had no trouble with the lock, she noticed. His fingers were all confident slides and turns. He gestured her ahead of him into the hallway and the door echoed shut behind them.

So? What now? A friendly chat? 'How's your grandp–'

'Getting better.' He spoke quickly. 'I didn't say because you might have cancelled on me. So why'd I have to open the door?'

'Because it can't seem like I'm, you know, taking advantage of you.'

'Nell, could you please not?' He sounded exasperated. 'I'm hardly a teenage boy. I'm a man.'

'Okay . . .'

'And what's even the issue? You're married. You're not leaving your husband. Why are we here?'

Technically, you *asked* me.

But feck it. I didn't show up so you could cry on my shoulder. Might as well be honest with myself about it.

'Why do you think?'

'Oh. Kay.'

Her chest contracted so tightly that her breath was happening in short, sippy gasps.

He moved his hands to her body. Slipping his thumbs along her hip bones, he pulled her against him and, oh, my God, this was *on.*

Their lips touched in a clumsy bump. In anguish, he clutched her jaw. 'Did I hurt you?'

'No, no.' *Please don't stop!*

It became a kiss of slow and aching sweetness.

Oh, God, I remember thiiiiiiis.

Her hands slid under his big coat and around his narrow, narrow waist. Slowly pushing her palms along his stomach, she loosened his shirt from his trousers so she could touch his cool, bare skin.

It was the sudden rush of cold air that told her they were no longer alone.

Disentangling herself from his arms, she turned.

Cara. Cara was there.

Cara's gaze moved from Nell to Ferdia. She looked beyond shocked.

'What are you—' Nell gulped. Then she saw the shopping bags in Cara's hands.

Visible through the thin plastic were packets of chocolate biscuits, multipacks of Twirls, colourful bags of jelly sweets.

'Oh, Cara, *no.*'

Cara turned and stuck her foot through the door before it closed. She twisted out through the space, Nell following, then Ferdia.

'Cara, it's okay—'

Cara hurtled down the steep staircase, going far too fast. With several steps still to go, she stumbled, then fell, bumping herself against the banisters and steps, cracking her head smartly against the oak post at the bottom. Biscuits and sweets skittered across the polished wooden floor.

'Cara!' Nell had reached her. 'Oh, God, are you okay?'

'I'm fine.' Cara was agitated.

'Take a second.' Ferdia laid his hands on her shoulders. 'You banged your head really hard. Can you see properly?'

'I'm fine, I'm fine, I'm absolutely fine.' She was already trying to stand.

'We can take you to A and E.'

'I'm fine. Sorry for interrupting you. I thought it was empty. I checked the bookings . . . But I'm going back to work now.'

'But . . .' Nell gestured at the food on the floor '. . . is there someone you could talk to? Your therapist or someone?'

'Yep, yes. Can we just pretend none of this happened? Sorry, you two.'

She'd slipped towards the door. It slammed shut behind her and the dust motes vibrated in her wake.

Nell stared at the chocolate and biscuits scattered on the floor and realized that the mood was completely gone.

Ferdia began gathering up the stuff. After a moment, she joined him. Instead of recommencing their blissed-out kissing, she felt as if they were two conspirators clearing up a crime scene.

'I'm worried,' he said. 'That was a bad bump.'

'Maybe I should go after her.' A breath, then she said, 'You know, I think we should leave. This doesn't feel good.' She looked helplessly at the packets in her hands. 'What'll we do with these? Leave them in the apartment for the next people?'

'I suppose. Yeah. Look, something weird. Johnny was here earlier. Just before us. He was with Izzy. You know, my aunt?'

Her eyes flicked from side to side as she thought through the implications. 'Oh, my God, *no*. Poor Jessie.' Then, 'Are you okay?'

'It's bizarro. Just, poor Mum. And we're all seeing each other tonight for his birthday. We'll be doing some Oscar-winning acting.'

Cara pushed through the Friday lunchtime crowds, making her way back to the Ardglass. Her head was swimming. Ferdia and *Nell*? Nell and *Ferdia*?

Affairs happened, everyone knew that. But those two?

Although . . . was it *that* unlikely? They were closer in age to each other than Nell was to Liam.

She wondered if Nell was going to leave Liam. If Cara were somehow unlucky enough to be married to Liam, she'd leave him . . . A wave of nausea swept through her. What on *earth*?

Her stomach calmed, then leapt again. Now her head was thumping.

The utter irony if she puked now!

Weirdly, the need to overeat had vanished. Seems like catching your nephew and your sister-in-law in a sexy clinch would do that to a person. She decided to ring Peggy one more time—and, to her surprise, this time Peggy answered.

'Cara?' There was a smile in her voice.

'I'm sorry I stopped coming,' Cara blurted. 'But can I start again?'

'Of course.'

'Would you have anything free today?'

'Not today. Let me see.' After some clicking sounds, Peggy said, 'Tuesday, eight a.m. I know it's early.'

'That's great.' Did she just slur her words? A little bit?

'Cara?' Peggy asked. 'You don't sound too well.'

'I whacked my head a few minutes ago.'

'Mmm, that's not so good. Do you think you could be concussed?'

Briefly Cara saw double. 'Really, I'm fine.'

'Concussion can be very sneaky—'

'I'm fine. Thank you. See you on Tuesday.'

Anxiety flared in Ed when he discovered Cara was in the house when he got home. 'Why aren't you at Peggy's?'

'I bumped my head. Work sent me home.'

Please let her be okay. Please don't let them be pissed off with her.

'You cancelled Peggy? You'd better see her twice next week. Make another appointment.'

'I've got one.'

'When?'

'Tuesday. Eight a.m.'

'Really?'

'Really.' She offered him her phone. 'Call her if you'd like.'

'Sorry, honey, I . . .' *Was afraid you'd stopped going to her*. Now he felt guilty. 'What happened to your head? How did you bump it?'

'. . . A wooden sign. Fell on me.'

'That sounds odd.'

'Life is odd,' she said.

'What about tonight's dinner? You able for it?'

'What did Johnny say about loaning us the money?'

'He said he'd see.'

'Then we need to be there. Really, I'm fine.'

He wasn't sure. But there was too much to worry about so he let it go.

Now

Ninety-Eight

Johnny launched into a fit of energetic coughing—a bit of bread down the wrong way. But the chat around the long dinner table carried on. Lovely. He could die here, literally *die*, on his forty-ninth birthday, and would any of them even notice?

Jessie was his best hope but Jessie was off in the kitchen readying the next elaborate course: he could only hope he survived to eat it.

A sip of water didn't help, tears were streaming down his face, and *finally* Ed asked, 'You okay there?'

Manfully, Johnny waved away his concern. 'Bread. Down the wrong way.'

'Thought for a minute you were choking,' Ferdia said.

'That'd be a shame,' Johnny croaked. 'To die on my birthday.'

'You wouldn't have died,' Ferdia said. 'One of us would have tried the Heimlich manoeuvre.'

'You know what happened recently?' Ed asked. 'Mr Heimlich? The man who invented the Heimlich manoeuvre? Finally, at the age of eighty-seven, he got to do it on someone.'

'And it worked?' This was from Liam, right down at the end of the table. 'It'd be a bit mortifying if he did it and then the person died.'

Liam really did bring the snark to any situation.

'Like Mr Segway,' Ferdia said. 'Said they were totally safe, then died on one.'

'In fairness,' Ed said, 'his only claim was that you'd never fall over on one.'

'So what happened?' Johnny, despite his resentment, was interested.

'He accidentally drove one off a cliff.'

'Oh, God.' Nell dissolved into giggles. 'Started believing his own publicity?'

'Got high on his own supply,' Ferdia said.

'You'd know about that.' Liam threw his nephew a dark look.

Ferdia glared back.

So the feud between those two was on again? What was it this time?

He'd ask Jessie, she'd know. Here she came, carrying a trayful of sorbets.

'Palate cleansers!' she declared. 'Lemon and vodka.' She resumed her spot at the head of the table.

'What about us?' Bridey piped up. 'We can't *possibly* have vodka, we're *far* too young.'

'On it,' Jessie said.

Course she was, Johnny thought. Fair play to her. Never dropped the ball.

'Just lemon for you guys.'

Bridey issued stern instructions to the younger kids that if their sorbets tasted 'in any way funny' they must desist from eating them with immediate effect.

Jessie resumed her spot at the head of the table. 'Everyone okay?'

Cheerful noises of assent rose, but when the hubbub quietened down, Cara said, 'I'm bored out of my skull.'

Good-humoured chortles ensued and someone murmured, 'You're funny.'

'I'm not joking. I am bored to *tears*.'

Jesus Christ, was she serious?

'I mean, *sorbets*?' Cara asked. 'How many *more* courses do we have to sit through?'

Okay, Cara had one or two issues. To put it mildly. But she was a sweetheart, one of the nicest people he'd ever met.

Johnny's gaze went nervously to Ed—it was his job to keep his wife under control. If that wasn't a very sexist thought and, yes, he admitted it was. Ed looked stupefied with confusion.

In an attempt to pull things back to normal, Johnny adopted a lighthearted tone. 'Ah, come on now, Cara. After all the work Jessie has done . . .'

'But the caterers did it.'

'*What* caterers?' someone asked.

'She *always* has these things catered.'

Jessie would never use caterers. Cooking was her thing.

Up and down the table, the mood was one of scandalized commotion. Why was Cara—normally the loveliest person—saying such stuff?

'How much have you had to drink?' Ed asked Cara.

'Nothing,' she said. 'Because I had that bang—'

'— on the head!' Ed finished her sentence and his relief was audible. 'She got a bang on the head earlier. A sign fell off a shop and hit her.'

'That's not what happened.'

'We thought she was okay.'

'You *wanted* me to be okay,' Cara said. 'I knew I wasn't.'

'You should go to A and E!' Jessie was struggling to recalibrate to her default nurturing and bossy personality. 'I insist you go this very moment. Why are you even here?'

'Because Ed needs Johnny to loan him the money,' Cara said.

Right on cue, Jessie asked, 'What money?'

'From the other bank account,' Cara said. Then, 'Oh, God. I wasn't meant to say that.'

'What bank account?' Jessie asked. 'What loan?'

'Cara, the hospital, right now.' Ed stood up.

'Johnny . . . ?' Jessie asked.

However, he still had something in his arsenal. 'Jessie? What caterers?'

Ferdia glared at Johnny. 'You're really doing this to her?'

'I'm entitled to know.'

Ferdia's tone had many layers. '*You?* You're entitled to nothing.'

In Johnny's stomach, eels of dread slithered. *Ferdia knows. But how?*

Pinned by the collective gaze, Jessie looked panicked. 'Yes, okay, yes!' She sounded exasperated. 'Caterers. Sometimes. So what? I've five children, I run a business, there are only so many hours in the day and—'

Cara stood up. 'I'd better go to the hospital before I fall out with every one of you. Come on, Ed.'

'Hey, Cara, do you *really* like my new hair?' Eighteen-year-old Saoirse sounded wobbly.

'Don't ask me that!' Cara said. 'You know how much I love you.'

'That means it's bad?'

'Oh, sweetie. That fringe makes your face look like the moon.'

At Saoirse's devastated expression, Cara said, 'I'm really sorry, Saoirse, you shouldn't have asked me . . . But it's only hair, it'll grow back. Come on, Ed.'

'Cara, before you go?' Liam leant forward, his eyes narrowed. 'Did you *really* think that massage I gave you was . . . What was the word you used? "Dreamy"?'

'I hated it. Forget being a masseur. You are *terrible*.'

'Hey!' Nell jumped in to defend her husband. 'He's doing his best.'

'Why are *you* bigging him up?' Cara asked.

Suddenly, Liam was scrambling to sit upright. He smelt blood. 'Why wouldn't she back me up? Tell us, Cara, come on, tell us.'

'Cara, come on.'

'No, Cara.' Nell's voice was sharp.

'Bridey!' Jessie was urgent. 'Take the kids up to my room. Put on a movie. Go!'

Even as TJ, Dilly, Vinnie and Tom were being ushered out by Bridey, Liam was demanding, 'Tell me.'

'Don't!' Nell said. 'Cara, it'll come back on you too.'

'Tell me,' Liam's tone was urgent, 'why my wife wouldn't stick up for me.'

'No. I'm not saying any more—'

Nell suddenly spoke up. 'Liam, stop it. I was at Johnny's flat today.'

'Doing what?' Johnny sounded scalded.

'Meeting Ferdia.'

'Unbelievable!' Johnny exclaimed.

'Hey!' Ferdia yelled at him. 'I saw you too!'

'Where?' Now it was Jessie's turn to sound panicked.

'Mum, I'm very sorry.'

'Hold the fuck on,' Liam croaked. 'Nell? Nell, you were in that flat with . . . *him*?' He threw his head at Ferdia.

Jessie was still addressing Ferdia: 'What did you see?' Her face was the colour of parchment.

'Johnny and Izzy,' Ferdia said. 'Coming out of the flat. I'm sorry, Mum.'

'Nell?' Liam asked again, his voice deadly calm. 'What were you doing with that little prick?'

'*You* can't be angry at Nell.' Saoirse was in tears. 'I know about you and Robyn.'

'*What?*' several voices demanded.

'Is it true?' Ed asked Liam, who shrugged in irritable assent.

'She's a teenage girl!' Ed exploded. 'Almost a child.'

'She's no child.'

'Johnny?' Jessie seemed on the edge of tears. 'Were you really in the flat with Izzy?'

'It wasn't what it sounds like.'

'Cara,' Ed interjected. 'Why were *you* at the flat?'

'I thought it was empty.'

'But why were you there?'

'I needed to eat. Chocolate. Then . . . you know.' Her scratchy irritability faded to nothing.

'I see.' Ed sounded calm. He stood up. 'Well, that's that.'

After

Friday Night/Saturday Morning

I don't belong here, Nell thought. *I never belonged here.*

Everyone was caught up in different crossfires of accusation and defence.

Most horrible of all was Liam and Robyn. She was so painfully young, only a kid. Not that Liam's cheating balanced out Nell's. She felt doubly ashamed: as if she were also to blame for his behaviour. Or perhaps for not noticing.

Suddenly Nell's survival instinct kicked in: she needed to leave, pick up Molly Ringwald, clear all of her stuff out of Liam's apartment and find a place to sleep tonight.

Ferdia was tensed in his chair, watching her. Meaningfully he glanced at the doorway into the hall.

Discreetly, she slid from the room, Ferdia following. 'We need to get your things out of his place,' he said. 'We need to go now.'

'It's better if I do this alone. If we left together this—*this* would escalate like crazy. Everything's gone insane. Can we just . . . take a moment? Let everything calm down. See how things are tomorrow.'

'But where will you stay tonight? Who'll help you to pack?'

'I'll call my mate Garr. It'll be okay. Please, Ferdia. If we both disappear now, it'll make everything extra-crazy. I'll message as soon as I'm sorted.'

He was reluctant to let her go and panic was rising in her. 'I really have to go,' she said. 'I'll be okay. And, Ferd, don't let anyone put the guilts on you. Nothing happened with us.'

'It would have if Cara hadn't arrived.'

'But she did.'

Outside she hailed a taxi and found her phone. 'Garr. Serious shit has gone down. I'm leaving Liam, like right now. Any chance you can—'

'I'll meet you there.'

'I hate to ask but can I . . . Just for tonight?'

'Stay as long as you like.'

But she couldn't do that. He lived in a shared house: there were other people to consider.

'Grab my work stuff.' She scooted past Garr, piling things into a nylon sack. 'Portfolios, models. I need it *all*.'

'Can't you come back tomorrow?'

'I don't trust him. He might chuck it out.'

'Even though he was with that young girl?'

A wave of disbelief made her dizzy. 'Isn't it the most messed-up thing ever?'

'What about you and the young lad?'

'Don't ask me. I'm too goofed to have any clue. I just need to find a place to live and get calm. Priorities.'

When Rory died, Jessie's one consolation was that she'd never again have to live through something as bad. Her dad's passing was painful. Her mother's was worse. The wound of being cut out of the Kinsella inner circle had taken a while to heal. Giving up on having a sixth child had, for a patch, been oddly unbearable. But nothing had ever come close to the visceral punch of Rory ceasing to exist.

Over the years, whenever a big drama had blown up, her second or third thought was, I've already survived the worst thing that could happen.

It had made her feel safe. Almost lucky.

But this—tonight—was as bad as Rory, that same light-headed combination of disbelief and stone-cold certainty: something terrible had happened. She didn't want it to be true, but everything had already changed for ever. Once more, the jigsaw of her life had been thrown up in the air and she had no idea where the pieces would land.

For all their tussles about money and work, she'd believed she and Johnny were solid. Suddenly she felt in freefall.

After all these years, Johnny and Izzy? Her shock was profound—she knew this because she felt as if she were dreaming. Through past experience, she'd learnt that this was how the unbearable was borne: her helpful brain muffled her perceptions so that appalling reality only impacted in manageable drops.

But despite her brain's best efforts, waves of fear kept heaving through her. This—Johnny cheating. With Izzy—it had a humiliatingly inevitable feel.

Even though she was shocked, a voice in her head was saying, *Oh, yeah, it's bad but it's not really a surprise.*

The mistake she'd made was thinking she had grown out of being the person whom others mocked. She'd got used to being broadly happy. But the wheel of life was just going to keep on turning until it delivered her right back to the person she had always been.

It wasn't just her and Johnny who'd fallen apart tonight. The entire *family* had imploded.

Sadder still, in this whole mess, was that Cara was once again bingeing and puking. Her body wasn't able for it—and neither was Ed.

'Mum.' Bridey broke into her introspection. 'Movie's over. It's ten past eleven. Where will I put Vinnie and Tom? In my bed? I can sleep with Saoirse? You put Dilly to bed, and I'll do TJ.' Then, 'Dilly, behave for Mum. Bad things happened tonight.'

Quickly, anxiously, Dilly crossed to her bedroom and pulled her duvet to her chin.

'Good girl,' Jessie said. 'Go to sleep.'

'Mum . . .' Dilly said, as Jessie's tears splashed onto her. 'Your crying is falling off your face!'

'Go to sleep. Everything will be okay.' You shouldn't lie to children, but now wasn't the time for the truth.

Downstairs, Johnny was at the kitchen sink, up to his wrists in soapy water. 'Babes, please.' He abandoned the washing-up. 'Just let me explain. Nothing happened—'

'But it did.'

'Not like . . . Look. Yes. I know. But can I just explain—'

'Why? You, Izzy, apartment, secret meeting, secret *bank account*. I can join the dots.'

'Please listen.' Johnny talked quickly. 'A few months ago, in the summer, I gave Saoirse and Ferdia a lift to Errislannan. I bumped into Izzy. Totally random. Expected her to be pissed off, she was . . . friendly. Few days later, she sent a friend request.'

'And you *accepted*? Without telling me?'

'It was delicate. You wouldn't have wanted me talking to Izzy. *But!*' He spoke over her uprush of complaint. 'I was trying to find out if they still hated us.' His mouth sounded clacky. 'Without straight out asking. I thought if she trusted me first, it would give both of us a better chance with all of them. To be friends again.'

'But we were fine without them.'

'I thought you wanted . . .' He looked confused.

'It would have been nice if we were all pals again. But you know . . .'

He seemed dismayed. 'I thought we were both still . . . hopeful. I guess you dealt with it better than I did.'

'And then you started fucking her.' Tears began, once again, pouring down Jessie's face.

'All we did was talk.'

'Have you been using the apartment for lots of . . . *Christ.*'

'I swear to you that all we did was talk.'

'That's the oldest line in the book. Oh, Johnny. I *trusted* you.'

The smell of urine, trolleys wedged tightly together and orderlies literally running from cubicle to cubicle.

Cara had been triaged within an hour of arriving but a steady stream of new arrivals suffering from knife wounds, heart attacks, burns and beatings had pushed her paltry little concussion way down the list.

Another gurney rushed past Cara and Ed, bearing a man with evident head injuries.

She took a breath. She felt faint.

'Oh, yeah, that's right,' Ed said. 'You were out for the count last time. You missed the show.'

His tone sounded strange.

'Second time in three months we're in an emergency department because of your hobby.'

'But, Ed . . .' Her earlier hair-trigger irritation had entirely vanished. All she was now was confused. 'I'm ill. It's an illness.'

'Not so long ago you were telling me there was no such thing.'

Her thoughts were too muddled and slippery to hold on to.

'Cara Casey?' A man in scrubs called.

'Here.' She sat up.

'It's going to be a while.' He looked at Ed. 'You should go home.'

'I'll stay.'

After the orderly had moved off, Cara said, 'Thanks, honey.'

She took his hand in hers. Deliberately, carefully, he disentangled it. '*Ed?* I don't understand.'

'Because you had a bang to your head.'

'But you sound like *you*'ve had one.'

'I told you I wouldn't go through this again. I'm only here because concussion can be serious. Soon as you're okay, you're on your own.'

'But, Ed, I didn't do it. The eating and throwing up.'

'You would have if Nell and Ferdia hadn't been there.'

'Yes, but . . .' Then, 'Nell and Ferdia. Can you believe it?'

Ed remained silent.

Nell's haul of belongings was so small that it took only one trip to unload the taxi outside Garr's house. 'Wow.' She actually had to laugh. 'Back where I was living the night I met Liam. Life is funny.' She stashed Molly Ringwald in Garr's bedroom, which had been a sitting room in a previous, more prosperous, household. 'None of the current crop of housemates are allergic, are they?'

'If they are, they'll soon let us know. Anyway, don't worry about it tonight.'

'So, any spare blankets? Maybe a pillow?'

'Sleeping on the floor? Don't be mad. It's a double bed.'

It wouldn't be the first time. A few years earlier, they'd made a tentative shift from friends to lovers. It lasted mere weeks before they admitted it had been a mistake. They'd been lucky to have successfully engineered a reversal.

She messaged Ferdia: **Staying with my friend, Garr. I'm okay. Hope you're okay. Talk tomorrow x**

'You texting Liam?' Garr sounded concerned.

'No, just . . .'

'Oh, the young lad.'

'It was nothing like you think,' Johnny said urgently. 'We sent each other the occasional message. Light, jokey stuff. Cat gifs.'

'*Cat* gifs?' Jessie said. 'You hate cats!'

'I do. But . . . Jessie, can you look at the messages? You'll see there was nothing like that.'

'Sure I'll look at your *light, jokey messages*.' Then, 'Whoops, Jessie, looks like I accidentally deleted them.'

'Why would I do that? I wasn't doing anything wrong.' He scrolled along his screen. His hands were shaking, she saw. Well, he'd been caught cheating: was it any surprise?

'Just read them.' He thrust his phone at her.

Izzy's first message said: **MAD bumping into you in Errislannan last weekend**

It had been sent four months ago. Fear reverberated, like the clang of a giant bell. Izzy had been back in Johnny's life for all this time and she hadn't had one clue.

Johnny had replied, **Funny alright**

Jessie felt sick. 'What does she look like now?' This was an important question.

'I dunno. The same.'

She glared at him and he said defensively, 'The *same*. Lots of hair. Tall.'

In the next message, Izzy, in recognizably Izzy fashion, said, **That's some piece of shit you're driving**

Ha-ha, Johnny replied, **least I don't look like a drug dealer**

'What's her car?' Jessie asked.

'Discovery.'

'Ugh.'

Next was a cat gif from Izzy. Then Johnny sent Izzy an attachment about an armed robbery in Kildare, captioned, **You up to your old tricks again lol**

'Lol?' Jessie furrowed her brow. 'You're a "lol" person now?'

Another cat gif from Izzy. Jessie would never have seen her as a cat person. Life really took people in some strange directions . . . She spotted her own name and her heart nearly jumped out of her throat.

Jessie's 50th this weekend, Johnny had written. **Doing murder mystery thing in fancy hotel**

Izzy hadn't commented. Nothing from her for an entire week. Then she sent a photo of lambs in a farming championship, followed by a little back-and-forth between Johnny and her about how busy they were.

I'm always on a plane, Johnny wrote.

Ha-ha me too. Never settled down with the babies and the book club

Jessie spotted her name again. **Off on my summer holiers with Jessie and the kids. Tuscany**

Izzy's next message wasn't until ten days later. **Ouch!** With an emoji of a footballer.

'What does this mean?' Jessie asked, distressed because she didn't understand.

'Football?' Johnny said. 'Liverpool must have been beaten that day. I can't even remember.'

'Johnny.' Her voice was faint. 'I can't believe this. All of it.'

'I didn't do anything.'

'You did. I can't believe . . . You and her, best friends.'

As she read the stream of messages, many were so bland she thought they must be code.

Nice weekend? Johnny had asked in late August.

Down in Errislannan.

Sounds great. How's everyone?

Grand

Whenever Johnny mentioned Jessie or their kids, Izzy made no comment.

'She still hates me,' Jessie said.

'I was trying to find out . . .'

For the thousandth time, Jessie reminded herself that, back in the day, before she'd started sleeping with Johnny, she'd had no clue that Izzy wanted him. This wasn't her fault. If she had known, would it have stopped her?

Maybe.

And maybe not. Life is rarely black and white, and how could she ever know now?

Thinking out loud she said, 'I won a competition that I didn't even know I was competing in.'

'It wasn't a competition,' Johnny said. 'I loved you. I only wanted you.'

'Except when you wanted her.'

'That was a million years before. And you *know* that, Jessie, you know it.'

Watching Jessie scrutinize the messages from Izzy, Johnny's heartbeat hurt his chest.

After an exchange featuring several laughing emojis, Izzy had messaged, **It would be good to see you IRL**

Cautiously, Johnny had bounced the ball back into her court, by replying, **It would**

A few days later, she'd said, **So are we meeting up?**

He hadn't known what to say because he still hadn't a clue what she wanted from him. Trying to get a steer, he said, **What were you thinking?**

Drink after work? Someplace city centre

No. He didn't want to meet her in a public place where he could easily be seen. If word got back to Jessie before he knew how Izzy felt, it was open to misinterpretation. To put it mildly. But neither did he want to lurk with Izzy in shady corners, like he was up to something scuzzy.

He replied, **Thinking Errislannan would be better**

City centre suits me. Then, Errislannan too far to drive on a school night

He didn't buy it. The drive wasn't that long.

It was clear that both of them were being cagey. He didn't want to meet her in public and she didn't want him anywhere near her family.

They were at an impasse, and while he was in Italy, he'd decided he was no longer sure this was worth bothering with. But the day they got home from holidays, Jessie told him about Ferdia falling out with Barty. It troubled him deeply. He felt as the ties remaining to the Kinsellas were becoming fewer and fewer, and the thought that soon none would be left made him persist.

So he messaged: Any other suggestions?

She replied: You know what? We could prob have a drink at Dublin airport? Sometime when we're both travelling? Seeing as we both almost live in the place

It wasn't a great suggestion. Airports were in constant motion. He had wanted their first face-to-face to be in a peaceful place, where he could ask her about Michael, Ellen and Keeva. And even though they both complained about 'almost living' in Dublin airport, he suspected it would be a monumental challenge to pin down an overlapping time when they were both in the vicinity.

It was then that he'd started thinking about his apartment. It was in the centre of the city but it was private.

Limited availability, however.

He *could* reserve it for himself, but that started to feel like a whole other thing. Despite his hopes for a reconciliation with the Kinsellas, it seemed easier, safer, just to let things slide.

A week elapsed quietly. Then ten days, two weeks . . . Then Michael Kinsella had a heart attack and Johnny found out about it from Ferdia.

Nothing from Izzy. Not a word.

That first day, he rang her several times and her phone went to message again and again.

He was deeply shaken. He'd thought he and Izzy had recovered plenty of their old easy intimacy. But it wasn't just Izzy he was upset about, it was all of them.

Ferdia's intel said that Michael likely wouldn't survive, and Johnny was confused: he'd always thought that *at some stage* he and the Kinsellas would be okay again. How could that happen if Michael died?

On Wednesday and Thursday he brooded on everything, moving back and forth along his memories, like fingers up and down the keys of a piano, wondering how he could have averted that long-ago falling-out.

In the middle of it all, Ed had texted, asking if he could borrow ten grand. He was so distracted that he gave a vague **I'll have to see** as a reply, then promptly forgot about it.

Suddenly, around nine o'clock on Thursday night, Jessie's phone buzzed, the family WhatsApp chimed and Johnny's phone started to ring. The person calling Johnny was Izzy and he went light-headed with hope and dread. Either Michael had died or . . .

He hadn't.

The relief of that, coupled with Izzy considering Johnny meaningful enough to be told, rocketed him back into hope. This was fixable. All of it.

Izzy said, 'We really need to meet up soon!'

And his response was, 'Yes! Remember my old apartment on Baggot Street? Hold on a sec, I just need to check . . . Wait, this is great. Tomorrow? One o'clock? One thirty?'

'Okay. One thirty. See you there.'

Jessie appeared before him to tell him the good news, which he already knew, and he was so overwhelmed with hope and guilt and the past accelerating into the present that weak tears dampened his face.

It was almost 5.30 a.m. and she was already better by the time it was confirmed that Cara had had a concussion, which was why she'd said those cruel, out-of-character things.

As Ed drove them home, the previous night began revisiting her in bursts of vivid imagery. Telling Liam that he was a terrible masseur. Oh, my God, dropping Nell and Ferdia in the shit. Admitting that she'd been all set for a food binge. Upsetting Saoirse, whom she loved so much, by saying she had a face like the *moon*. Instigating some revelation about Johnny and Izzy Kinsella . . .

It was hard to fathom—actually horrifying—the damage she'd unleashed. She had a lot of apologetic calls to make as soon as people were up.

In the darkness, Nell looked at her phone: 5.35 a.m.

Three missed calls from Ferdia.

She was finding it hard to believe that she'd gone ahead and met him in that apartment. Last night—my God, was it *really* only last night?—when their thing was revealed to everyone around the dinner party, the spell had broken.

Everything seemed entirely different this morning. She felt older, wiser, far less starry-eyed.

She must have been temporarily *crazy*. Ferdia was *waaaaay* too young for her. To think that if Cara hadn't shown up, they'd definitely have fucked.

She liked Ferdia. Objectively she could see that he was hot, but her feelings for him had reverted to the way they'd been before Italy. He was only a kid. She'd got an insane crush on him because her marriage was falling apart. Maybe he'd be on the same page as her, realizing that there was nothing real here. She needed to call him but couldn't summon the nerve yet.

There was nothing from Liam, not a text, WhatsApp, nothing. She wondered if she'd ever hear from him again.

None of it had played out like she'd hoped. She'd expected that when 'the end' eventually showed up they'd be civil to each other. But *her* business with Ferdia and *Liam's* with Robyn . . .

She couldn't deny her sadness: the initial sweetness with Liam had turned very ugly. And Robyn was so astonishingly young that she felt ashamed of Liam.

What wacko way had the planets been aligned last night? Every marriage around the table had hit the skids.

'You okay?' Garr whispered. 'Will I turn on the light?'

'Thanks.' She was very grateful to have him to talk to. 'I cannot understand how I got married and eleven months later it's over. Who *does* that? I've been thinking about all the *stuff* when people split up. The two names on, like, a mortgage, bank account, bills? Liam and I own litch nothing together. His ex-wife pays for the apartment, but the bills are in his name. I paid half of them but nothing document-y connects us.'

'That's probably good,' Garr said.

'Mmm, yeah. But it's not really *normal*. Anyway. Soon as it's a sensible time I'm gonna call Mum and Dad, see if they'll take me in while I look for another place.' Weakly she punched the air. 'So winning at life.'

'Stash your gear with them, but you can stay here if you want.'

'*Could* I? That would be the best. Just for a couple of weeks.'

'Whatever you need. What will you do about the young lad?'

'I feel so bad about him. He's . . . great. But he's too young and I'm obviously a bit mad, and starting a thing with someone else would be the worst.' She eyed her phone. 'I need to tell him.'

'Do it. I'm getting a glass of water. Room's all yours.'

'Oh, *God*.' Then, 'Okay.'

Ferdia answered immediately. 'Nell? Are you okay? Can we meet?'

'Ferdia. Ferd. Listen, I need to say this. You and I, we need to stop. I've got to sort my head out.'

'Uh. Um. God . . .' He sounded shocked. 'I thought we were going to—'

'That's my bad. It's like I was insane for a while. Now I'm sane again and I don't like the way I've been acting. I don't understand it. I need to stay out of relationships.'

'I was hoping—'

'I know. I'm sorry. But you'll get over it quickly. You're—'

'— young. So people keep telling me. I wish we'd had a chance to . . . But, hey, okay. I get it. Just, you're great.'

'And you're great too. You're the best.'

'Okay. Gotta go.'

Quickly she hung up, feeling almost euphoric that this unpleasant thing had been done with dignity.

At about 6.30 a.m., Ed and Cara got home to a cold, empty house. Exhausted, they traipsed up the stairs and into their bedroom.

'Do you need anything?' he asked.

'I'm fine.'

'Try to get some sleep. I'll wake you in four hours, just to check you're okay.'

'. . . Aren't you coming to bed?'

'Not in this room.'

Then she'd known. She waited.

'I'm leaving you,' he said gently. 'You know that?'

She nodded.

'I'm sorry.' He began to cry.

'Sweetie, don't. Please. It's okay.'

Something strange had happened to her over the last several hours, as if weeks of tension had come to a head, then burst, blowing away all her self-hatred, her resentment at being labelled, her distance from Ed. For the first time in months, her love for Ed, the real, unsullied version, had rushed back in, like a delayed high tide.

She'd also had an unprecedented overview of her problem with food: she had no control. She couldn't fix herself—and Ed couldn't fix her either.

'If I stayed,' he said, 'I'd be complicit . . . The most important thing is that you get better. For you and for the boys. More important than me or us or . . .'

Lots of people wouldn't understand his actions—they'd think he was deserting her when she most needed help. But she wasn't one of them. Being without him was going to be horrible. Right now she was unable to imagine the depth of the loss. But this was all her own doing. Some part of her had known they were going to end up exactly here. He had told her he couldn't cope with her starting again—and he'd never been one to fling around meaningless threats.

From the very first time she had lied to him about Peggy, they'd been headed towards this very outcome. She'd known it and she hadn't been able to stop.

'Get some sleep, honey,' he said. 'I'll be next door.'

'Morning, Mum! All fine, but bit of bad news. Liam and I have broken up.'

'Nell, love.' Angie's voice was soft. 'Everyone has big, shouty arguments. You think it's the end of the world but—'

'Seriously, Mum, we're done. We'll be getting divorced.'

'Oh, Nell! How can we help? Hold on, Dad wants to know what's—' Nell heard Angie's muffled voice say, 'Nell and Liam have split up. They're getting a divorce.'

Then Petey's muffled reply: 'I never liked the chap.'

Petey took the phone. 'Ah, dear. Ah, dear, dear, dear, Nellie. That's sad now, so it is. Are you okay? Because that's all that matters. Lookit, that wedding of yours at the North Pole probably wasn't even legal. There was a thing on *Joe Duffy* about people taking their kids to see Santy there and even the snow wasn't real, never mind the elves. You can live with us. We can do the TV bingo together, like we used to.'

'Dad, you're the best. But I'm going to kip at Garr's place.'

Petey's brief silence spoke volumes. 'Garr?' he demanded. 'Hold up there, Nellie! Is there something you're not telling us?'

'Dad, don't be a plank. Garr's my best friend.'

'And Angie McDermott is *my* best friend.'

In the background, Nell heard her mum say, '*Niall Campion* is your best friend.'

Jessie woke up from a Xanax-induced sleep. She was crying. Johnny was there, up and dressed, with a mug of green tea for her. She didn't know where he'd slept last night, but most probably on the couch.

'Angel.' He touched her wet face.

'I've no friends,' she gasped, with tears.

'I'm your friend.'

'You're not. This person who was my best friend once-upon-a-time and now she hates me and you've been meeting her, and even if you weren't sleeping with her—and how do I know that?—you still shouldn't have been messaging her all friendly and funny, with your old in-jokes and lols.'

'Only because I hoped she might be our friend again. *Our* friend.'

'But I didn't need it. You went behind my back. I'm so sad.' Jessie's tears began again, seeping and spilling down her face. 'I thought you and me were on the same side.'

'We *are*. I was doing it for both of us!'

'Tell me.' She sat on the bed and looked into his face. 'Have you had sex with her? Even a quick one-off for old times' sake?'

'*No*.'

'You were always slippery. You could never keep it in your pants.'

'A long time ago. I'm different now.'

'Those messages you showed me, they could be fake. You could have another phone with the real stuff on it.'

'You know I haven't. I would never do that to you. Even simple logistics back me up. On Friday, I left the office at one ten, I was back at five past two. In that time I did two taxi journeys in lunchtime traffic. It would have been a very fast fuck.'

Jessie had also calculated Friday's timings and concluded that there hadn't been much time to do anything. Also, the tone of the messages, it wasn't flirty.

But none of that made any real difference to how she felt.

'You were messaging her without me knowing anything. You betrayed me and, Johnny, I can't handle it. I feel like I have nobody.'

'You have me.'

'Explain to me again about the bank account.'

'A bank account for the income from the Airbnb. Kept separate from the rest of our stuff, just in case we hit the skids financially. If the bank ever decided to call in our overdraft or cancel our cards, that money might have kept us going until we were back in the black.'

'You were that worried?'

'Weren't you?'

'Why wasn't it a joint account?'

'. . . Because I didn't want you to know about it. Unless . . . until it was necessary.'

'Why? Because I'd have spent it?'

'. . . Well. Maybe. Yes.'

Last night she'd been certain it was his running-away money. This morning she believed this version of events, but it still made no difference.

'I want you to leave. The house, I mean. I want you to live somewhere else. Not with me.'

No one else would understand why this was such a big deal. They'd think that Johnny had wanted to reconnect with an old friend, at a time of crisis, and there was nothing wrong with that.

'Jessie, I swear to God—' He was white with panic.

'There is nothing you can tell me that will make this okay.'

'What about . . . but what about the kids?'

'I didn't create this mess and sometimes with kids all you can do is feed them and keep them safe from physical harm. You leaving isn't ideal—'

'You mean, you kicking me out isn't id–'

'You meeting Izzy Kinsella *on the sly* isn't ideal. You pretending *you like cats* isn't ideal. But it's happened.'

'Please, Jessie.'

'Michael was going to be okay. I don't understand why you wanted to see her.'

'It was that thing of, you know, you get a big scare, then a big relief. I just got carried away.'

'No. You wanted me and you wanted the Kinsellas and you thought you could have both.'

Cara was awake. The house was noiseless. No sounds of kids playing came from outdoors.

Her phone said it was twenty past nine.

It was surprising how calm she felt. She'd always thought that if Ed left her she'd literally be tearing her garments with grief. But right now her soul was silent. Perhaps because it was still merely theoretical. But in six weeks' or four months' or two years' time, it would be agony.

All of these thoughts rolled around, like smooth pebbles between her fingers.

She found him in Vinnie's room. 'Honey,' she whispered.

He turned towards her and his eyes filled with tears.

Pulling back Vinnie's duvet, she got in, pushing herself into his warmth. She had never loved him more and her calm acceptance began to shatter.

'It's the best thing I can do for you.' He pulled her tight against him. 'I can't be your warden. Only you can do this for yourself.'

'Honey, I didn't *actually* do the bingeing and—'

'You would have if Nell and Ferdia hadn't been there.'

'. . . I could have changed my mind at the last minute?'

He shook his head.

He was probably right. 'Ed, I'm sorry . . . So much. For all the damage . . .'

'You couldn't help it. You're an addict. You weren't able to accept help.'

'Maybe I will now.'

'The kids,' he said. 'Can we try and keep things as normal as possible?'

'Of *course*. What will we tell them?'

'The truth. Although that might be a hard one for them: you're sick, so in order to help you, I'm leaving.' A fresh spasm of weeping shook him.

'We can't tell them a lie, like we've drifted apart. Can we tell them the facts? They might get it.' She took a breath. 'Ed, is this really happening?'

'Don't.' His voice was thick. 'It's all so sad. When should we tell them?'

'Now? We could bring them home and tell them now.'

'Okay. And then I'll have to go.'

Nell steeled herself to ring Jessie. There was every chance she wouldn't answer—but she did.

'Jessie.' Nell raced through the words in case Jessie hung up. 'I'm very sorry about me and Ferdia. Nothing much happened, if that's of any help. You've been so kind, taken me into your family, and I've embarrassed you, caused mayhem and I'm just, like, *really* sorry for all the crap.'

'I didn't see it coming.' Jessie sounded nothing like her usual dynamic self. 'I don't know what to feel. So much happened last night, and this is only one thing I'm trying to . . . Look, you're both adults, you can do what you like. But he's my son, you're my sister-in-law. Although I'm guessing not for much longer?'

'. . . I don't think so.'

'We were all mad about you,' Jessie said. 'Everything's gone to shit and it's . . . I'm finding it very hard. I have to go. Take care, good luck.'

'Thank you. You too.' Nell hung up. That had been brutal. But it could have been much, much worse.

Moments later, a text came from Liam: Lawyer up, bitch

She was shook. But he was just posturing. She hadn't a penny, neither had he: there was nothing to tussle over. She sat and waited for her insides to stop shaking.

'Liam says I can stay with him.' Johnny was hoping that *now*, surely *now*, Jessie would change her mind.

''Kay.' She carried on emptying the dishwasher.

'And when would you like me to leave?'

'Now.'

'Right now?' Two fifteen on a Saturday afternoon?

'Yes.' She suddenly became irritable. 'Right now. When the fuck else? Next effing spring? Go!'

He deliberately packed almost nothing, so that he had plenty of reasons to keep returning home, then drove to Liam's.

'How are you?' he asked Liam.

Liam shrugged.

'You and Nell . . . ?'

Extravagantly, Liam rolled his eyes.

'It's over?' Johnny asked.

'Of fucking course it's fucking over! I wouldn't touch that tramp ever again!'

'And you and Robyn?'

Liam smirked. 'Me and Robyn.'

'. . . You don't think she's a bit young for you?'

'If you want to stay here, you'd better keep those thoughts to yourself.'

'Okay. Which room can I have?'

'Either of them.'

Johnny looked in at Violet's bedroom. Very pink. Then Lenore's. Even more pink. 'I'll take Violet's,' he called to Liam. 'Just unpacking my stuff.'

'Don't get too comfortable,' Liam replied. 'This is only very temporary.'

Moving a family of velvet pigs out of the way, Johnny put his various chargers on the bevelled little dressing table. He was still in a state of shock. It was barely more than twenty-four hours since he'd buzzed Izzy Kinsella into his apartment building and his life had collapsed.

At the time, his hopes were once again being slowly, painfully hoisted but he was no longer entirely convinced that persisting with Izzy would be worth it. He couldn't get past the fact that none of them, not even Izzy, had bothered telling him when Michael had gone into hospital. That said, it was an urgent, stressful time for them. And Izzy *had* rung as soon as the news was promising.

But Ellen hadn't called. Michael, on his sickbed, obviously hadn't summoned Keeva and whispered a hoarse *I want to see Johnny.*

He'd kept bumping against painful pockets of probability: *I don't matter to them and I thought I did.*

Yesterday, Izzy had come bounding up the stairs, her curls hopping. She'd brushed past him into the living room, rattling a steel beaker onto the low table, thrown her coat onto the arm of the couch and flung herself into the tub armchair.

'Fancy chair.' She twinkled with mockery.

'That's me,' he replied. 'Coffee?'

'Got my own.' She nodded at the beaker. 'Happy birthday. So? How are you?'

'Jesus, you know yourself. Thanks for last night's call.'

'Yeah.' She exhaled long and hard. 'It's been the longest few days. I can't believe it's only Friday. Do I look horrific?'

'You look exactly the same.'

'"Exactly the same"?' She sounded offended. 'The Johnny Casey I know can do better than that.'

'You look lovely.' He shifted in his chair.

He needed to stop this chit-chat. He'd endured four months of playing out a line without moving anything on. It was time to do some straight-out, bald-y asking. 'So Michael's definitely getting better?'

'He won't be running a marathon anytime soon, but . . . I thought he was a goner. When they said he'd be okay,' her face lit up, 'the relief was like, ha-ha, being on drugs.'

'That's how I felt when you rang.'

'You were one of the first people I thought of. I guess something this serious shows you what's important.' In a quieter voice she said, 'I've missed you.'

Here we go. 'Me too.' He was energetically cheery. 'I've missed you all. That's why . . . As you said, a shock like this puts things into perspective, so, Izzy, is there any chance we could move on from the past?'

'Could who move on?'

'Could all of you—you and Keeva, your mum and dad—forgive me and Jessie?'

Izzy's gaze roamed over his face. Her mouth opened, as if to speak but she closed it again. Then. 'We could be friends, Johnny. You and me.'

Oh, shite.

Well, his instincts had already been telling him this was a bust.

But had he played her? Had she played him? Were they both to blame?

His heart heavy, he said, 'You know that Jessie and I have always thought the world of you.'

Her face froze. After a long moment of silence, she said, 'Honest to God, Johnny Casey, you giant chancer.'

He sat, sheepish and mortified. Putting her through this was downright shabby.

'I think we're done here.' Sweeping up her coat and coffee flask, she made her way to the hall and slipped through the doorway.

As she turned towards the stairs and disappeared from view, her knowing smile, that familiar despairing shake of the head, might have been genuine.

Leaning against the shut door, self-loathing, like sour milk, washed in his stomach.

Neither of them had got what they wanted.

This was over. Done. Finished.

'You left her?' Johnny yelped.

'You *left* her?' Liam demanded. 'Ed, what the fuck is wrong with you?'

'For once, Ed, could you just not . . . not . . .' Johnny sought the words '. . . not be weird?'

'Can you stop shouting at me? Just for a while?' Ed said. 'Which is my room?'

'Seriously,' Liam said, 'don't get too comfortable here. Either of you.'

'Thanks a fucking bunch,' Johnny said. 'Thanks, *bro*.'

'Paige might kick me out.'

'Right. That's . . . Yeah, that wouldn't be great.'

'Have you really left Cara? Have you told your kids?'

Ed could hardly bear to think about it. 'Yes.' It had been even worse than he'd expected.

Vinnie had cried. His little hardman of a son, crying because his daddy was leaving.

Tom had asked anxious, suspicious questions: 'What sort of sick are you, Mum? Are you going to die?' And 'Dad, you're supposed to mind her if she's sick.'

'I have to get strong by myself,' Cara said.

'But it's only for a while?' Tom insisted. 'You'll come back when she's better? Mum, you will get better.'

Who knew whether she would or not?

'You've really done that to your kids?' Liam asked.

Kettle, pot. But whatever. This was better than Cara having another seizure. At least this way both of their parents were alive.

Monday

'God almighty,' Petey said to Nell, 'you're jet-propelled today. Splitting up from your husband obviously suits you.' Then, 'Did I upset you there? I was only—'

'Stop. I'm fine. Give me something else to paint.'

There had been no contact from Ferdia. This was good, great even: it had cut out a lot of emotional noise, clearing her thinking.

She got it now: her fixation on Ferdia had happened because her subconscious was trying to distract her from what an arse Liam was. Things made sense and she liked that.

Jessie filled the kettle, tears streaming down her face. Cat gifs! *Cats*. They were dog people, a dog family!

Rummaging around, trying to find spaghetti for the kids' dinner, she heard the front door open. Johnny appeared and she called down the hall, 'You don't live here any more.'

'Just picking up some clothes for Berlin. Going tomorrow.'

Good. It had been strange and awful sitting opposite him in the office today. 'How long for?'

He came into the kitchen. 'I'll be back Thursday evening.'

'You need to get another job,' she said. 'We can't work together. You're great at your chatty charming-Johnny thing. You'll get something.'

Money, that was a problem, she acknowledged. It had been a problem before and it was a bigger problem now. But she would wait until Karl Brennan delivered his report . He might suggest something helpful.

It was ironic—or was that what irony meant? She'd always been afraid to assume, since poor Alanis Morissette had been so humiliated all those years ago—that she'd consulted Karl Brennan to placate Johnny, but now he might provide the financial solution to facilitate their split.

'You knew she hated me. You should never have met her.'

'I didn't know anything. I was afraid to ask too soon. When I *did* ask, I made it clear that you and me came as a job lot.'

'She didn't want me.'

Anguished, he said, 'I'm sorry you had to find that out.'

'She only wanted you. And not as a friend.'

'I should never have—I hate myself . . .'

'Try being me. I feel unloved, friendless, left out, abandoned, humiliated and stupid.'

Tuesday

'If you've lost nothing,' Peggy said, 'why would you change?'

Cara nodded in agreement.

Ed had had no choice.

But it was so, so sad.

Her thoughts were way more evolved than her feelings. In theory she agreed with Ed but emotionally she was an ocean of tears: she could cry for ever.

And yet things could be worse: the logistics of their separation weren't as devastating as they might be for other couples. As things stood, for three months of the year Ed was away during the week. She and the kids were used to it. They coped.

Then there were Dorothy and Angus. They were mad about Vinnie and Tom and always available for baby-sitting, doctor's visits, any emergencies.

Ed needed a place to live: finding the money for that would be a challenge. But Ed didn't need material comforts—he'd happily sleep in a cupboard.

'I've broken his heart,' she told Peggy. 'I've broken mine. If I do everything you tell me to do, how long before I'm better?'

Peggy laughed.

'Piece of string?' Cara asked.

'Yep. *Aaaand* don't do this for Ed. Don't do it to fix your marriage—'

'Do you think it's fixable?'

'It's not for me to say. What I'm saying is, you have to park all of that. If you want to get better, then do it for you, Cara.'

In a way she felt that she had already lost too much to bother with any of this . . .

'You get one precious life,' Peggy said. 'Why not try and have a contented one?'

. . . but she had her sons. And she had herself.

They were good reasons to try.

Wednesday

'Nell! Watch out! The jayzis architrave!'

Dumbly she looked. The yellow eggshell she'd been rolling onto the walls had dribbled onto the white gloss woodwork. She hadn't even noticed. 'Sorry, Dad.'

'You're a liability today. What's up with you?'

What was up was that her giant fucking crush on Ferdia had come back, like a cold-sore she'd thought was healed.

At Johnny's birthday, her utter mortification had efficiently corralled her feelings: it was crystal clear how terrible her flirtation with Ferdia had been. That conviction had lasted all over the weekend and into Monday.

But yesterday it hadn't seemed *so* terrible.

And this morning, it didn't seem terrible at all. Small matter of an age difference and, yeah, they'd met in a way that wasn't strictly out of the meet-cute playbook. But *so fucking what?*

Thursday

Into the ether Nell sent an experimental, **Hey.**

The aftermath of adrenalin and fear made her pull Molly Ringwald hard against her chest.

'Are we watching this movie?' Garr asked.

'Yep. Let's go.'

Molly squirmed away, leaving a layer of ginger hairs on Nell's shirt. The poor cat was shedding fur by the handful, probably due to stress. If they didn't get settled soon, she'd be completely bald.

Which was looking increasingly likely. Nell had been viewing places every evening after work: for a thousand different reasons they were all unsuitable, sometimes disastrously so. 'Hold on two seconds.' She went to the cupboard under the stairs for the Hoover. She scooted around Garr's room, vacuuming up Molly's latest fur deposit.

'Okay. Done. Hit play.' She took a sneaky side-glance at her phone. Nothing.

The movie had won an Oscar for best cinematography, but she kept giving her phone sneaky peeps. Nothing, nothing, nothing, nothing—then a curt **Hey**

Happiness flooded her and it must have been obvious because Garr gave her a look. 'The young lad?'

'Garr?'

'Yeah?'

'Could we not call him "the young lad"?'

Garr looked surprised. 'Uh. Sure. Grand. Whatever.'

'His name is Ferdia.' She clicked out: **You good?**

After another long wait, he replied: **What can I do for you?**

Ohhh! She almost laughed.

But he was right. She'd told him they were finished before they'd even started. What was he meant to do?

She clicked out, **Are you over me?**

The answer zinged back: **Yep**

On Thursday night, having got off a flight from Berlin, Johnny automatically drove to the family home.

It was only when he parked the shitmobile outside the house that he remembered he didn't live there any more.

He let himself in anyway. He wanted to see his kids.

Also, ever the optimist, he thought it was only a matter of time before Jessie let him back.

'*Daddy, Daddy, Daddy!*' The girls were delighted to see him.

Jessie poked her head out of the living room. She looked confused. 'What are you doing here?'

'I, ah . . .' He shrugged. 'Wanted to see the bunnies.'

'You can't just drop in with no notice. We need a schedule.'

His blood chilled in his veins. She was as implacable as she'd been last Friday night. For the first time he truly believed that she might not change her mind. Jessie was generally quick to blow up and quick to forgive. But tomorrow it would be a week since that dinner from hell.

The younger kids clamoured for bedtime stories, for him to put them to bed, so he ferried them up the stairs. He took his time, promising that he'd soon be living at home again, just that he and 'Mum need to sort out some grown-up stuff.'

It was gone 11 p.m. when he came back down. Noiselessly, he entered the living room. Jessie was slumped in an armchair, sightlessly scrolling through her iPad. He'd been nursing a sneaky plan that he might hang around and sleep on the couch, the first stealthy foot in the door of his reinstatement.

But Jessie snapped from her torpor. 'Time for you to be going.'

'But . . . This is terrible for the kids.'

She muttered, 'We'll have to sort something out.' Then she began crying again and said, 'You ruined everything.'

'Jessie, I'm begging you . . . Have I ever given you any reason to not trust me?'

'"Lol"!' she said. 'Could you leave now?'

Helplessly, he did.

*

'I fancy him.' Nell addressed Garr's ceiling. 'That's all. And you can't go round having sex with everyone you fancy. Civilization would collapse—people would be riding each other in the streets.'

'Uh-huh?' Garr said.

'It's just simple physical attraction. *Strong* simple physical attraction in this case but I can out-think it. Like, I'm not an *animal* . . .' She shouldn't have said that word because now she was thinking along very animalistic lines. Words like *ripping* and *biting* and *thrusting* ran through her head, accompanied by erotic images of Ferdia, naked and beautiful.

'It's the almost-but-not-quite that's wrecking my head. Two times, we kissed and it got very . . . and then we had to stop. And, Garr, that's not *healthy*.'

'So what would un-wreck your head?'

'Finishing what we started. Just once. That might sound like bullshit, but I genuinely think it would give me closure.'

'Could you *please* just go and fuck him? I can't take much more of your angst.'

'He said he was over me.'

'Yeah, well. Maybe he is, or maybe the man just has some pride.'

'So. Should I call him?'

'No. You should get two empty bean cans and string them on a taut rope between here and his house. Or you could hire a small plane and do a leaflet drop over Foxrock. Yes, Nell, for feck's sake, *ring* him. I'm going out to walk the cat. The room is yours.'

As soon as Garr was gone, she rang Ferdia. She wasn't even sure if he'd pick up.

'What do you want?' he asked.

She was sweating. 'You said you were over me.'

After several beats of silence, he sighed. 'Nell, this is so not cool. You told me what you wanted. It's been tough but I've been doing it. You're playing games with me.'

'I can't be in any sort of thing until my head is sorted. But—' and now she was so incredibly nervous '— could we have one night together?'

'You think this is just about sex?'

'Yes or no?'

'Is it what you want?'

She paused. 'It's hard to know how much I can trust my feelings right now, but . . . yes, it is.'

Another of those long, alarming silences. Then, 'When?'
'Soon. As possible. I can get time off. I'm working with my dad.'
'Okay.' He was immediately all business. 'I'll sort something. I'll text you.'
But he didn't.
Friday passed.
Saturday passed.
Sunday passed.

Monday

Ferdia finally called. He asked, 'You still want to do this?'

'Yes.' Nell swallowed.

'Okay. Tomorrow, can you get the train to Scara? It's down the coast.'

Scara? 'Where the lighthouse is?'

'Yep. Not many trains there because it's small. Could you get the fourteen-fifty out of Greystones? Is it okay if I see you at Scara station? Instead of getting the train with you?'

'Um. Sure.'

'Text me when you're near. I'll be there.'

On Monday evening, Liam looked up as Johnny came in from a work do. 'She still holding out on you?' He seemed irritable.

Johnny swallowed. 'I don't think . . .' He sat and put his head into his hands. 'I'm not sure this is fixable. It's been eleven days, that's nearly two weeks. I think she means it.'

'Nah! When she needs you to pick the kids up from horse-riding—'

'Horse-riding?'

'Or whatever hobby it is that particular day. I dunno, ballet or stuff. She'll need you then. She won't last long without her little errand boy.'

'I'm not her errand boy.'

'You totally are.'

Sudden hot rage burst from Johnny's mouth. 'Shut up, you fucking paedophile.'

'She's eighteen, you prick! Eighteen. *Fuck* you.'

'Fuck you too.'

'No, fuck you, you sap. Your problem is you're scared of Jessie.'

'I'm not.'

'Totally are. You need to man up.' Then, 'Where're you off to?'

*

Jessie was turning off the lights and shutting the house up for the night when the doorbell rang. It was Johnny.

'What the hell?' she said. 'They're all in bed.'

'I'm here to see you, not the kids.'

'What for?'

He followed her down the hall and into the living room. 'We need to talk.'

'Don't apologize again,' she said.

'I won't.' He took an armchair at an angle to hers. 'Because I did nothing wrong.' His conviction surprised her. 'I didn't go looking for anything with Izzy. It felt like a random opportunity that life sometimes drops in your lap. Messaging her, meeting her, I did it for both you and me. I'm *sure* about that. It was a mistake. But I wasn't up to something bad.'

He seemed different tonight, Jessie thought. Nothing like as meek.

'You saw all the messages,' he said. 'And don't start that secret-messages thing again. There aren't any. Nothing sexual happened with Izzy. It literally didn't even cross my mind.'

She was upset by this ardent speech, without knowing why.

'When I was younger, I didn't have any respect, not for myself. Compared to other men—Rory was one of them—I felt like a shallow fool. I was careless about the women I slept with. Careless about a lot of things. I'm ashamed of who I was. But I'm not that man now. I haven't been that man for a long time. I'm a joke to you and the kids—'

'*I*'m the joke. Herr Kommandant and all that.'

'And I'm Johnny the eejit who can hardly lace his own shoes. But—and this is something I've thought about a lot—I'm a decent man. I'm sure. I try my best to be a good father. I live my life around you because that makes me happy.'

'If that was true, you'd never have messaged Izzy.'

'You're hurt by what you thought was in my head. And you're hurt by Izzy not wanting both of us. I'm sorry that my actions caused you that pain.'

'I couldn't give a damn about Izzy—'

'Before all of this, we were happy. Happier than most people. Well, I was.'

'You were worried about money.'

'Everyone's worried about money.'

'Are you still waiting for the Kinsellas to welcome you back?'

'I have my own family now. Finally—and, Jessie, this is the last time I'll say it—'

His confidence was very unsettling. She'd got used to him abasing himself with remorse.

'— I only said "lol" once and I despised myself for it. Plus, I never sent a single cat gif. I'm leaving now. That's the last time I'll say any of that.'

Tuesday

Soon after Jessie arrived in the office, Karl Brennan's name lit up her phone. She answered quickly because he'd probably put his meter on the second he thought about ringing her.

'I'm done,' he said. 'Four proposals for you, lovely lady.'

'How come you were so quick?'

'Because your set-up is so small.'

She bristled and he must have sensed it because he laughed. 'You're hardly Facebook. So, the report includes projections, market research, focus groups ops. Emailing it now.'

Heart beating fast, her mouth dry, she asked, 'How much are you charging me?'

'Oh, Christ, *loads*.'

She hung up and held her breath, until the document landed in her inbox.

There was page after page of figures, percentages and words but she couldn't focus.

She had to call him back. 'Give me broad brushstrokes.'

'It's easier in person.'

'I'll come to your office.'

'Meet me in Jack Black's.'

God, he bloody loved that place. It was probably where he was right now. It probably *was* his office.

To no one in particular, she announced, 'I'm out for a couple of hours. A meeting.'

In the hellhole that was Jack Black's, Karl Brennan had a tall glass of dark liquid before him.

She nodded at it. 'Tell me it's a Coke.'

'A Manhattan.'

It was twenty to eleven in the morning.

'I'm never drunk,' he said, 'and seldom sober.' He hit a key on his laptop and the screen filled with numbers. 'You might need a drink too.'

'Just tell me.'

'Right! Four proposals. One: carry on as you are, with your chefs and your shops.'

'And?' Surely it couldn't be that easy.

'You'll be out of business in two years.'

The blood drained from her face. 'Seriously?'

'Oh, yeah.' He seemed pleased. 'Rising rents, dying retail, all the blah. Next option, seek an equity raise to fund your online arm. Not going to happen. Your moment was twelve years ago. You're too small and too risky for anyone to invest in. And *you* personally are too controlling.'

She swallowed hard.

'Option three: close all of your shops.' He watched her flinch. 'Yeah. All. Of. Them. *And* the cookery school. Release the equity in the property you own. You get to stop paying rent on your leases and you get to stop paying your staff—BTW, your payroll is *insane*. Then you'd be liquid enough to create a decent online set-up. Only problem, brand recognition. Strong in Ireland, trusted, you'll be pleased to know. Rest of the world, not so much. You called it yourself, it's a crowded market place. You'd struggle. You might not make it.'

'The fourth option? I sell my children?'

'Or . . .' His bloodshot blue eyes gave her a sudden speculative look. His imagination had gone to some place she did *not* want to think about. 'Option four: close five of your retail outlets. You get to keep three stores in bigger towns *and* your cookery school, plus you've freed up equity to invest in the online side of things—warehousing, couriering, new staff. What you *won't* have is the cash to get yourself up the Google rankings, and reach more international audiences. Here's the thing, though. Your stuff with the chefs gives you an advantage—'

'I told you that.'

'Yeah, hurray for Jessie. But to optimize, you need a YouTube channel, interviews with the chefs, online demos. This could be the thing that makes the difference. And you need to accelerate. Currently you do four chefs a year. Bump it up to one every six weeks and you could be golden.'

That was *not* going to happen. It already took so much of her time.

'Get a new hire.' He'd obviously read her mind. 'Who elected *you* the only chef-getter in town? I see it all the time with mom-and-pop outfits like yours. You can't delegate. Whole thing comes down to ego. Ultimately it implodes.' He spread his hands on the sticky table. 'There you are. Broad brushstrokes like you asked for.'

There was so much information to process, but the hardest chunk to digest—like a snake having swallowed a pineapple—was that she'd have to change and quickly, when she was already living through so much upheaval.

'Which one would you go for?' she asked.

'Not my gig, is it? But I like a risk. Option three. Put everything online. Might work, might not, but you'd go out in a blaze of glory.'

'Blazes of glory don't pay the mortgage.'

He had a good laugh at that. 'You'll grab on to option four. That route, you'll likely be small-time for ever—no one's going to swoop in and buy you out for billions. But if you become very adaptable very fast, you might actually survive.' He took a long swallow of his Manhattan. 'I need another of these. Are you having a drink? A drink-drink?'

'Yeah,' she said. 'Yeah, I am.'

'What's with your suits?' she asked.

It was three drinks later and she was feeling considerably more optimistic.

'You like them?'

'There aren't words for how much I hate them.'

'I get them hand-tailored in Hong Kong.'

'By who? A—a plumber? A blind one?'

'By *whom*. By a tailor who copies designer's patterns.'

'For really, really, really, really, really, really cheap?'

'. . . Who are you ringing?'

'Shush.' She held up a finger, then spoke into her phone. 'Johnny? Can you stay with the kids this evening? Late. Maybe very late. I'm fine, just out on the piss.' Then, 'I want to have fun. I'll be sad again tomorrow but now I feel nice so can you stay there till I get home? Which will be at—God, I don't know—something o'clock, but promise me you'll stay and mind the bunnies, but don't worry, Johnny, I'm quite drunk but very healthy and see you when I see you, as they say.' Abruptly she hung up.

'What's going on?'

'Me, my husband, my other husband, his sister . . .' Jessie did her best to explain.

Karl Brennan's frown deepened and at some stage he waved for more drinks.

When she finished, he said, 'You're being ridiculous. Nothing happened.'

'How do *you* know?'

'You've just told me what was in those messages. If he was looking for a booty call, he could have had one months ago.'

'He was meant to be *my* friend.'

'So he made a mistake, he got your woman's motives wrong. But his intentions were good. She's hurt you but you're punishing *him*. That's what's going on here.'

Is it?

Maybe it was.

'Are you a decent man, Karl Brennan?'

'No,' he said. 'Definitely not.'

'Johnny says he's a decent man.'

'Maybe he is.'

'Says he's devoted to me. But he's been on my case for ages about changing the business.'

'Even if he was riding every woman in Ireland, he still did you a favour with that.'

Suddenly she felt sad again. 'I'll never forgive him.'

'Are we getting another drink?' he asked. 'Or are you coming home with me?'

'Are you *out* of your mind?'

'That's a maybe?'

She rolled her eyes and, briefly, saw double. 'I'm drunk, I'm vulnerable, my life has fallen apart.'

'That's definitely a maybe. We'll have one for the road.'

It was a bit late now for Nell to become a woman who owned lots of sexy dresses. Anyway, the weather was cold and rainy so, somewhat defiantly, she dressed in overalls, a sweater and her warm padded coat.

But underneath was her new underwear, a lacy gold bra and matching underwear. It was impressive, that sheeny thing they did to her skin.

In fairness, though, this wasn't good, partaking of capitalism just because she was mad about Ferdia Kinsella.

For the last three stops on the rattly old train, she was the only person on board. Now and then the sea heaved into view, a grim, bleak expanse. Above it, in paler tones of grey, the huge sky went on for ever.

Two short platforms and an unattended ticket office made up Scara station. There he was. In his long coat and big boots.

'Hey.' His eyes shining, he took her hands. 'I'm so glad you're here.'

He insisted on carrying her satchel, even though it was her literal handbag. Maybe all of this should be awkward, but he seemed so happy.

'You okay for a bit of a walk?' he asked. 'Seven minutes. I timed it.'

'Where are you taking me?'

'Local B-and-B with a judgey landlady and a crucifix above every bed.'

'And a red-glowing picture of the Sacred Heart in the hall? Cool!'

Moving off the path and across a grassy plain, they were walking into the wind. Squalls of painful rain smacked against her face.

'This wasn't part of my plan.' He sounded stressed. 'I apologize.'

'Seriously, where are you taking me?' *Surely we can't be in a tent? We'll literally be blown away.*

'You'll see in a minute.'

They crested a gentle hill, which dipped into a previously invisible hollow. On the far side, the land began climbing again. Hidden until now by one of those tricks that uneven ground plays was an isthmus of land. On it stood a lighthouse. *The* lighthouse.

'There,' he said. 'That's where we're going.'

A giant metal key opened a thick wooden door. Inside, in a bare-floored entrance hall, he shut out the sound of the wind. Stone steps curved up and around, out of sight.

'They're the worst part,' he said, unlacing his boots. 'Eighty-seven of them. After that, everything's golden. *Andiamo.*'

A metal handrail, attached to rough stone walls, twirled up and up. She began to climb. And climb. Her thighs were turning to jelly.

'Nearly there,' he said. Then, 'We're here.'

'Hold on, I just need to—' She took in a lungful of air. 'I'm . . .' She stopped.

'Breathless?' he asked. 'But we haven't even start—' Then he lost his nerve, dipped his head and pushed into a warm, whitewashed living room, plain but cosy. Two armchairs and a sofa were clustered around a sturdy little table. Playing very quietly was some southern Gothic-y blues she couldn't identify.

'There are other rooms.' He pointed upwards. 'Stacked on top of us. A kitchen, then an, um, bedroom, and right at the top, a bathroom.' He pulled off his overcoat. 'The bath has a view. It's class. You'll see. So. Can I take your coat?' He sounded so polite she almost laughed.

He got to her zip before she did. Holding the tab, he started sliding it down. Too slowly.

Startled she looked at him. Sudden change of mood there. Very sudden. Maybe not so polite after all.

Holding her gaze, he eased her coat zip down its length. The nearer he got to the end, the more leisurely his pace became.

She needed to swallow but her throat wouldn't work.

When, finally, her coat fell open, something happened to them both: a shaky exhale, a repositioning of their bodies.

Moving his hands beneath the coat, he eased it from her shoulders. His thumbs smoothed their way along her collarbones. The palms of his hands stroked down onto her arms.

He hadn't done anything remotely unchaste, yet her body was pulsing.

Her coat fell to the floor, he whispered, 'Nell', and she went weak.

Lifting a thick strand of her hair, he rubbed it between his thumb and fingers. 'I love your hair.' With his other hand he cupped her face.

Their kissing was hot and sweet, romantic and sexy.

'This wasn't supposed to happen here,' he said, hoarsely. 'Not in this room. Can we . . . ?'

He took her hand and led her up more stone steps. On the next floor there was a circular kitchen; above that a small bedroom, with three huge windows overlooking the grey sea. 'It's nicer here,' he said.

The bed was a simple metal affair, with a plain white duvet. The only colour in the room came from a faded Persian rug and a red angora throw. He made straight for the bed and pulled her down with him. 'Sorry for assuming,' he said, his eyes mischievous.

He opened the buckle of the bib of her overalls and slowly slid the strap over her shoulder. Then the other side, running his hands along her, as if she were made of glass.

She opened one of his shirt buttons, then another, until his chest was bare. His inkings dark against his pale, perfect skin, she remembered how she'd felt that day in Italy—the hunger she'd had for him, the shock of it all. This—right now—was exactly what she'd wanted.

Then his hands were roaming under her top. With a sudden snap, he'd opened her bra. This reminded her of teenage snogging sessions. But she and Ferdia weren't kids. They didn't have to stop.

Pulling the shirt from his body, she reached for his zip, but he gently pulled her hands away. 'It'll be over too fast . . .'

He snapped open the row of metal buttons along her hips. Together, they tugged off her overalls, then her underwear.

His dark head moved between her legs, inflicting a row of gentle bites to the insides of her thighs. Using his tongue and lips, he inched closer to her centre while, from the other direction, his hand pressed down hard.

'Ferdia. Can you . . . ?'

He looked up. 'Is it not okay?'

'But . . . I need you. Like, now.'

'Uh. Okay.'

Bumping against each other, he tore off the rest of his clothes, while she ripped open the condom wrapper. Hands trembling, she hurried it on, then slid herself down onto him.

'Go slow.' He sounded anxious.

But she couldn't.

Within seconds, her hair tangled in his fist, he was rearing beneath her, pulling her hip bones against his, saying her name again and again and again.

'Put your hand on it, Jessie.'

'I'm going home.'

'Just for a second. Here under the table. No one will see.'

'Karl, you're repulsive. Perplexingly—that's a hard word to say—you're still sexy. But the repulsive bit wins. And the thing is, the thing, Karl, that I have just remembered—'

'Yeah?'

'Is that I have a very sexy, non-repulsive *husband*.'

'Forty minutes ago you could "never forgive him".'

'Time is a great healer.'

'He *could* have been riding your woman.'

'I didn't believe that for long. I was much more upset about the cat gifs and the great fun they'd been having. No one likes me . . .'

'Don't they?'

'Not really. I'm too pushy. So I hear.'

'Mary-Laine likes you. *I* like you. Gilbert likes you.' He indicated the barman. 'We hear you coming down the stairs, all business in your clicky-clacky shoes and "It's too early for gin." It lifts our spirits.'

'Johnny likes me. That's what I'm trying to say.' She sighed. 'It was horrible, seeing him be so nice to someone who didn't—doesn't—want me. But it's not his fault.'

'I just told you that.'

'He came to see me last night. He was . . . different. Very sure of himself.'

'Uh-huh?'

'He's . . .' She nodded thoughtfully. 'He has brilliant upper-body strength. Always had. Still got it. Not just the upper-body strength, I'm talking about—'

'Yep. Thanks for sharing.'

She picked up her phone. 'If I ask him to come and get me, who'll mind the kids?'

'It's twenty-six minutes past three. In the day.'

She blinked. 'Seriously? This place always feels like it's four in the morning, and I've just been declared bankrupt.'

She put her phone to her ear. 'Johnny? Could you come and get me? I'm in a terrible bar called Jack Black's.' She hung up and said to Karl Brennan, 'He's on his way.'

'You want me to disappear?'

'Oh, God, yes. And you'd better pay the bill—I've to be careful with money now.'

She folded away her laptop, combed her hair, threw on her coat and finished her drink. It seemed like she'd spent almost no time fiddling with her phone before Johnny was jogging quickly down the stairs, his eyes searching for her.

As he crossed the room, she was sure she'd spotted the reappearance of his habitual handsome swagger. 'Johnny.' She stood up.

'Hello.' He sounded cautious.

'Hello indeed.' She linked her arms at the nape of his neck. 'Would you like to stay for a drink?'

He cast a look around. 'No.' Then, 'Definitely not.'

'Correct answer.' She couldn't help smiling, a great, big happy beam. 'I'm so happy to see you.'

'And I'm so happy to see you.'

'Okay, let's go home.'

Nell woke up. Her hair was spread across his chest, his arms tightly wrapped around her. Raindrops rattled against the glass, almost as loud as hailstones. The light had almost faded from the day.

'Are you asleep?' she whispered.

'No,' he whispered back. 'Can I turn on a light? Cover your eyes.' A lamp clicked on and there he was, with his skin and his ribs and those eyes.

'This is amazing,' she said.

'It happened too fast. I'm sorry.'

'Well, you have me for another, about, seventeen hours. You can take as long as you like the next time.'

Softly he laughed.

'How much of a gap do you need?' She answered her own question. 'Oh, yeah, I forgot, you kids need *zero* recovery time.'

'Hah! I think you'll find I'm very much a man. But you need to eat,' he said. 'To keep your strength up for my manly demands. There's stuff in the kitchen.'

'I brought pyjamas. I'm putting them on. I'm shy.'

'Work away.' He pulled on his shirt and trousers. 'I've seen it all already.'

Down in the kitchen Ferdia said, 'I can cook if you'd like. But see what's here.'

She wandered around the circular kitchen, so high above the sea. 'How did you *find* this place?'

'Usual. Online. But it's good?' He felt ridiculously proud. 'For you, it had to be somewhere really special.'

He didn't tell her of the hours he'd spend googling 'not-normal hotels' and 'most romantic place in Ireland'. How he'd dismissed dozens of them for being 'Not Nell Enough'.

'You're not a boutique-hotel woman. You don't do that lifestyle shizz. And you're *so* not a big, glitzy Mum-style hotel person. No shade at Mum,' he added quickly. 'Then I started thinking castles. I could see you striding about on ramparts. Next thing, creepy Google, which knows more about us all than we do ourselves, suggested here. If it wasn't so fucked up it would be cool.'

'It is cool, though. It's so cool.' Nell opened a cupboard and laughed. 'Ryvita! Hello, you blast from the past. I love Ryvita. Peanut butter—and Nutella! Those three things together are the bomb, you have to try some. Did all this stuff come with the house?'

'Mmmm, yeah.'

She poked her head into the fridge. 'Purple cherries! More expensive than gold. I *love* them. Halloumi cheese! Grilled halloumi would be my literal Death Row meal.'

He watched her notice the cans of cider, the Dairylea triangles, the chargrilled artichokes. Her body language suddenly alert, she returned to the cupboard for a more detailed look. Rummaging, she found a jar of Lotus crunchy biscuit spread, four cheese scones and a tub of teacakes—the fancy ones from Marks & Spencer.

'Were you spying into my head?' she demanded.

He shrugged and laughed. 'You actually told me your favourite food. I paid attention. What can I say? I'm obsessed with you.'

'No, don't say that.'

'I've *liked* you—is that acceptable?—yeah, *liked* you for a while. I'm interested in what you like. Not just food.'

She yanked open the freezer, to find two tubs of stem ginger ice-cream. 'Is there anything for *you* to eat?'

'Are you not giving me any of yours?'

She insisted on making him Ryvita, peanut butter and Nutella 'open sandwiches'. 'Do you totally love it?' She watched him.

'Totally.'

'Ha-ha. I'm not so sure you do. This is going to sound like the worst question but . . . is there Wi-Fi?'

'No.' Then, 'You'll be feeling panicky now. It'll go.'

'Ah, I'm grand.' She *had* felt a whoosh of fear.

'The panic will come back, maybe like once an hour. It got me that way this morning when I realized. But you'll get through this.'

'So no Wi-Fi, no Netflix, what are we going *to do* all evening?

'Joking!' she said, as his eyes flared with shock. 'This couldn't be more amazing!'

She surveyed the array of goodies she'd lined up on the table. 'Where do I start? I'll have you.' She selected the teacakes. 'And you.' A bag of Tangfastics. 'You.' A box of Lindt balls. 'And you, obviously.' She pointed at Ferdia. 'Let's go.'

Back in bed, sitting up and eating, Ferdia said, 'Tell me why you do your job.'

'I'd love to! Hah. I think I'm on a sugar-and-carb well-being buzz.'

'Nah. Probably just because you're with me.'

He was being funny but, with a plunge of fear, she thought he could be right. She felt ridiculously happy.

'So I try to create feelings—the set has to convey the emotion of the piece. It usually plays out as a series of challenges. I try to produce creative solutions. Some just don't work, others I have to compromise on, usually because of money. Sometimes health and safety. That's frustrating. But on the opening night, when I see what I've designed and built becoming part of the whole, supporting the play, then I feel . . .' she caught the way Ferdia was looking at her and immediately felt shy '. . . proud. So! Tell me how you're getting on with your stuff.'

'I will afterwards.'

'After what?'

'After you take off your pyjamas.'

'First show me what *you*'ve got.'

He shrugged and popped the top button on his trousers. The head of his erection peeped out.

'That was *quick*,' she said.

He rolled his eyes. 'It's been there for, like, the last forty minutes.'

She laughed with delight. 'Well, let's not keep it waiting any longer.'

'We need to make sure you're ready.'

'Oh, I'm ready.'

'Yeaah, I'm not sure you are.'

'I am—'

He wound his hands through her hair and kissed her. She tried to push him off and go straight to business but into her ear, he said, 'Wait a little while.'

She almost howled. 'You've been riding-ready for the last forty minutes! I want it now.'

But he wouldn't do as she asked. Tender though his touch was, it was also a kind of agony. He played with her expectations, sometimes sliding himself a little way in, but always retreating.

When, after a long time spent suspended in deferred pleasure, he finally filled her, she thought she might die from the intensity of sensation.

'Told you,' he growled into her ear. 'I'm a man.'

Wednesday

Ed was in Liam's kitchen, buttering toast, when he heard the front door open.

It was Johnny.

'It's half seven in the morning,' Ed said. 'You dirty stop-out. You want coffee?'

'No, I'm grand.' Johnny disappeared into Violet's bedroom and Ed followed him. Johnny was unplugging his chargers and flinging them into a bag.

'What's going on?' Ed asked.

Johnny whipped three shirts from the wardrobe and threw them into the bag too. 'I'm forgiven. I'm out of here.' He gave a big smile. 'Going home to my wife.'

'Nice one.'

'Something you should do too.'

'Stop.'

'Seriously. Cop on. Go home to your wife.'

Ed kept his mouth shut. Johnny didn't get it. Almost nobody got it.

The only other person who understood was Cara.

Ed wasn't going home to his wife. Not today. Not tomorrow.

Not ever.

'Ferdia, I need to leave in about an hour.'

Sadness flashed across his face, then he smiled. 'Let's have a bath.'

Right at the top of the house a big tub overlooked the waves.

'Look at the sea,' she exclaimed. 'It's so fabulously dour.'

'Like it's got a grudge against us.'

In the bath, she leant against him, her back on his chest, watching the restless switch and turns of the tides. Their mood had become sombre.

'This really is just a one-off?' Ferdia asked.

'It really is. I'm repeating myself but I need to get my head straight. I've done things I don't approve of. And I don't want to do them again. Me staying single for a long time is the right thing. Like, it's necessary. But being with you . . . it's been the best. Thank you.'

'Nell, if you wanted, I could wait for you.'

This was kind of breaking her heart. 'One day when you're, like, forty-seven and you've lived several more lifetimes, you might vaguely remember this. Same for me. The memory will be happy. But small. A tiny, shiny gem in the mosaic of our lives. That's what we are to each other.'

He nodded silently, his chin touching her head.

'In my mosaic you can be an obsidian,' she said. 'That's dark, nearly black.'

'What are you? Tell me one that's rare and beautiful. Gold-coloured.'

'Citrine? Tiger's eye?'

'Tiger's eye. I like the sound of that.'

After further silence, he said, 'So when you get on the train, we block each other's number, contacts, everything?'

'Yes.'

At the small, draughty station, waiting to say goodbye felt too awful.

'Ferd? It's better if you don't wait with me.'

'I should go?'

'It's just, the whole waving-me-off thing? It feels a bit World War Two.'

'Got it.'

'Bye,' she said. 'Thank you. You're . . . you know . . . great.'

'And you're fucking amazing.'

'But promise that you won't "wait" for me.'

'I won't wait for you.' He was resigned to this, she saw. It was good.

'Tiny, shiny gems?' he said.

'That's it. Tiny, shiny gems.'

Eight Months Later

It was a sunny June evening and a few kids were out playing football on the green. As Ed cycled towards the house he used to live in, he spotted Vinnie, sprinting towards the ball.

. . . And was that *Cara*? Tearing up the grass, just behind Vinnie.

God, it *was*.

It was quite a while since he'd seen her so carefree.

It was . . . great?

Since he'd moved out, they'd kept to their promise of civilized co-parenting. Their only contact was a series of brief, painful intersections, always to do with Vinnie and Tom. The boys spent every second weekend with Ed. These days, he was living in a small caravan in a corner of Johnny's giant back garden. It was an unorthodox solution to his housing problem, but it cost almost nothing and the kids—being kids—loved it.

On a day-to-day basis—work, money, childcare—he and Cara were managing.

Two nights a week Cara went to a support group run by the hospital; Ed spent that time with the kids. But he tended to avoid Cara. It was just too painful.

On a night such as this, when she was going out, she'd slide past him in the hall, with a quick, nervous smile. When, a couple of hours later, she returned home, they'd exchange another wobbly smile. Then he'd disappear.

He never asked questions about her treatment. Whatever Cara did or didn't do, it had to be for her alone. Harsh though it sounded, it was none of his business.

In the house, Tom was at the kitchen table, reading a hefty hardback. 'Hi, Dad,' he said. 'Did you *see* her out there? Football? I feel like I don't even know her any more.'

Ed managed a laugh.

'Ed!' Cara tumbled in through the front door. 'Ed?'

'Kitchen.'

'*So* sorry.' She was glowing. Vibrant. 'Lost track of the time out there.'

Mutely, he nodded. This was the most eye-contact they'd had in months.

'Quick shower,' she said. 'And I'll be off.' Then she frowned. 'You okay?'

He forced a smile. 'Course. Grand.'

' 'Kay.' She hurtled up the stairs. Ten minutes later the hall door slammed shut behind her and she was gone.

Ed switched on the oven to prepare the boys' dinner. His hands had a slight shake.

He and Cara were done. It was over and he knew it.

For the last eight months, he'd trudged through his days, doing what needed to be done. Give him a task and he'd do it. Tell him to show up at a particular time and place and he'd be there. But his future was a blank expanse.

He never wondered if he'd meet someone else. Nor was there any hope, tucked away in a tiny corner of his heart, that one day Cara would be well enough for them to be together again. Life was simply about survival in the short term.

But seeing Cara looking so happy had shattered the walls he'd constructed around his feelings.

He saw now that he *had* been holding on.

He felt *flooded* with loss.

Cara was getting better. That much was obvious.

It looked like she was peeling away on a different path, about to graduate to a bigger and better life. How could he object to that?

As he mechanically slung oven chips and Quorn nuggets onto plates, he was dying a quiet death.

People thought that Cara was weak, especially so since her dramatic meltdown. That he'd been the caretaker in their relationship. But they had it wrong. Cara was the strong one, the only person who had ever made him feel secure. Fourteen years ago, she'd promised him, 'I've got you. You're safe.'

He'd needed it then.

He still needed it.

In a bare room, nine people sat on upright chairs, arranged in a circle.

Peggy was tonight's moderator. She began by inviting a contribution from Serena, a newcomer, followed by a man called Trevor.

When he'd finished, Peggy asked, 'How are things with you, Cara?'

'Aaah. Today I kicked a football around with Vinnie. He was much better than me but to feel so free in my body . . .' To her surprise, tears spilt from her eyes. 'It's new. Good. Something I never thought I'd do again.'

'So what's with the tears?'

'I don't know . . .'

Peggy waited. None of the others dared to cough or shift in their chairs. The silence would endure until Cara found her truth.

Eventually, she said, 'I think I'm becoming a better version of the person I was. And that's breaking my heart because Ed missed out on it.' She paused. 'He deserved to get the best of me. I love him. I feel I'll always love him. And he's not coming back.'

Peggy remained tight-lipped.

After a pause, punctuated by shuddery sniffs, Cara said, 'I wish we got a certificate here, signed by you, Peggy. "Cara Casey is now cured." Then he'd have proof that it was safe for us to be together.' She gave a watery laugh. 'It doesn't work like that, I know.'

Peggy nodded, to indicate *Keep talking*.

'Time is passing too quickly. I hoped that after a few months he'd see I was committed to this. But it's been eight months. I think it's sinking in that this is permanent.'

'How do you think you're doing?' Peggy asked. 'Overall?'

'You'll probably disagree but I think I'm doing okay. Not one binge since Jessie's fiftieth. I haven't missed a single weekly session with you in the last eight months. I've come to every meeting of this group, except for when Vinnie broke his ankle in January. I've obeyed my food plan so much that now it feels instinctive. I don't panic if I have to go out to eat. At the start it felt . . . like there was no joy in eating . . .'

'And now?' Peggy was interested.

'I've got used to it. The dullness of how I eat. No highs. No shame. They're just my meals. I'm lucky to have them but they're not my . . .' she sought the word '. . . my entertainment. Not any more.'

'What would *you* think if someone else in this group said what you've just said?'

Cara was wary. 'I'd say that they sounded like they'd learnt a lot . . . They were in a good place.'

'Good enough to resume a marriage?'

'I suppose, yes.' Then, with more conviction, 'Yes.'

Any hope was shattered when Peggy asked, 'Good enough to survive the end of their marriage?'

Cara pressed her hands over her eyes. 'God,' she whispered. Then, 'Yes. I guess. It's going to be really fucking hard, but yes.'

Peggy smiled. 'There you are. Whatever happens, you'll be okay.'

Ed heard Cara call out, 'I'm home.' This was his cue to gather his stuff and vanish from the house.

Instead, he went into the hall, blocking her from scooting up the stairs. 'Cara?' He indicated the living room. 'Can we talk?'

She followed him in. 'About what?'

He took an armchair. 'About how you are.'

Cautiously, she sat opposite him. 'Doing well. All the right things. Even Peggy says.'

'You looked happy. Earlier. Playing football.'

'I guess . . . yes. I felt happy in my body. Free.'

'*Free?*' Maybe it was already too late.

'Ed. What's going on?' She swallowed. 'Is it time to make this—our split—official? Like, get divorced?'

'Is that what you want?'

'You're the one who left.' Then, 'Sorry. If it's what you want, then okay.'

He decided to risk it. 'No, Cara, I do not want it.'

Her eyes flicked from side to side in confusion.

'Look . . . I want to come home. To you. To the boys, but mostly to you. If that's not what you want, I'll live with it, but—'

'Stop.' She looked stunned. 'Wait. Are you serious about this?'

'Completely.'

'Because I couldn't take it if you're—'

'I mean it.'

'Then, yes. Do.'

'Seriously?'

'Seriously.'

The relief was too much and he began to cry. She was there, climbing onto his lap.

He buried his face in her neck. 'I haven't touched you for two hundred and forty-seven days.' He half laughed. 'Not that I've been counting. I've been so scared without you.'

'There's no need to be scared,' she said.
'Say it,' he said. 'Humour me.'
'But I mean it.'
'Go on, then. Say it. I need to hear it.'
'I've got you,' she said. 'You're safe.'

Acknowledgements

It takes a village, as they say, and I'm immensely grateful to so many.

I need to mention that The Lough Lein Hotel is *inspired* by the dreeeee-amy Hotel Europe in Kerry, where I've had happy Easters with my nieces and nephews. But there are differences; for example, there is no boathouse in the Hotel Europe for 'the young people' to meet up late at night, for shenanigans.

The other hotels (The Ardglass and Gulban Manor) are also invented, as is Harvest festival, the towns of Beltibbet and Errislannan and I took wild liberties with the location of Lough Dan.

Further liberties were taken with the date of the Spice Girls' Dublin concert. Also, with the Fleet Foxes gig. I hope you don't mind.

Various people, very generously, helped me with all kinds of research: Lian Bell, Richard Chambers, Suzanne Curley, Monica Frawley, Ema Keyes, Luka Keyes, Vicky Landers, Petra Hjortsberg, Jimmy Martin, Ann McCarrick, Judy McLoughlin, Fergal McLoughlin, Brian Murphy, Aoife Murray, Stephen Crosby and Rachel Wright. Special thanks to Louise O'Neill. I'm immensely grateful to all of them.

The Goddess that is Nigella Lawson helped me out with some Italian translation. In addition, my friends on Twitter jumped in to assist with all kinds of random enquiries (usually medical questions). I appreciate all the information given and any mistakes or inaccuracies are mine.

One of the greatest ways a person can help is to read the book as I write it and offer insight, encouragement and opinions. I'm deeply indebted to Jenny Boland, Cathy Kelly, Caitriona Keyes, Rita-Anne Keyes, Mammy Keyes, Louise O'Neill (again) and Eileen Prendergast.

Kate Beaufoy deserves a *War-and-Peace*-size tome of gratitude—she read the manuscript in various forms approximately a million times and kept me on track with suggestions, unstinting support and, once or twice, a sound scolding!

You'll have seen the term 'Direct Provision' mentioned in the book. This refers to how the Irish state treats people who are seeking asylum in Ireland, having escaped war or trauma in their country of origin. While they wait for their application for asylum to be processed, they are provided for 'directly', as in their food and shelter is provided for, in one of thirty-six centres around the country.

Their lives are subject to a variety of restrictions and indignities, from being ineligible to work, being unable to cook their own food, sharing sleeping space with people from many different countries and cultures and not being permitted to have visitors. Many asylum seekers live like this for several years.

It's a terrible way to treat people who are already traumatized and I suspect that one day Ireland will feel great shame that we let this happen.

The book also touches on the issue of Period Poverty. Obviously this affects those in Direct Provision, but also many others. My gratitude to Claire Hunt from Homeless Period Ireland who has done great work in this area. (And of course to everyone else working to make sanitary protection free to those who need it.)

My visionary publisher Louise Moore has championed me from day one. As an author, I'm unusually lucky to have such an amazing person to encourage, support and promote me. She gives me all the time I need until I feel my book is 'there'. There aren't enough words in the universe for my gratitude.

Likewise my wonderful agent, Jonathan Lloyd, who always has my back. Louise, Jonathan and I have worked together for over twenty-three years and I owe them my career.

Enormous gratitude too goes to every single person in Michael Joseph: the Sales team, the Marketing team, the Editorial team, the Artwork team. Everyone works so hard and imaginatively to get my books out into the world and I'd like to extend a special thank you to Liz Smith, Clare Parker and Claire Bush.

Likewise, thank you to everyone at Curtis Brown—Foreign Rights, Film and Audio. I'm immensely grateful.

And where would I be without the lovely Annabel Robinson from FMCM, who manages my publicity in the UK?

Or indeed the powerhouse that is Cliona Lewis who takes care of my Irish publicity? PRH Ireland publish me with great energy and enthusiasm and I'm in awe of the achievements of the Sales team, Brian Walker and Carrie Anderson.

Thank you, Gemma Correll, for creating such a beautiful jacket.

This is my fourteenth novel and may I offer deep, heartfelt thanks to you, my readers, for your faith and your loyalty. It's a huge honour to have people who believe I'll write a book they'll enjoy. I *never* take any of this for granted.

The person I'm most grateful to is my husband. He offers unstinting support and encouragement, never lets me do myself down and has unwavering faith in my work even when I've none myself. I don't know what I ever did to get so lucky.

(I should mention that thanks to the menopause my memory has gone to hell; if there's anyone who should be on this list and who isn't, please accept my abject apologies.)

Permissions

Excerpt(s) from WALKING ON WATER: REFLECTIONS ON FAITH AND ART by Madeleine L'Engle, copyright © 1980, 1998, 2001 by Crosswicks, Ltd. Used by permission of Convergent Books, an imprint of Random House, a division of Penguin Random House LLC. All rights reserved.

"I Fought The Law"
Words & Music by Sonny Curtis
© Copyright 1961 Sony/ATV Music Publishing.
All Rights Reserved. International Copyright Secured.
Used by permission of Hal Leonard Europe Limited.

"Girls Like You"
Words & Music by Adam Levine, Henry Russell Walter, Jason Evigan, Brittany Hazzard & Gian Stone © Copyright 2017 Prescription Songs/Songs Of Universal Inc/BMG Platinum Songs/BMG Gold Songs/Bad Robot /Cirkut Breaker LLC/These Are Songs Of Pulse/Sudgee 2 Music/People Over Planes/Sudgee 2 Music. Kobalt Music Publishing Limited/Pulse Songs/Sudgee 2 Music/BMG Rights Management (US) LLC.
All Rights Reserved. International Copyright Secured.
Used by Permission of Hal Leonard Europe Limited.

MARIAN KEYES is the international bestselling author of *Watermelon*, *Lucy Sullivan Is Getting Married*, *Rachel's Holiday*, *Last Chance Saloon*, *Sushi for Beginners*, *Angels*, *The Other Side of the Story*, *Anybody Out There*, *This Charming Man*, *The Brightest Star in the Sky*, *The Mystery of Mercy Close*, *The Woman Who Stole My Life*, *The Break*, and most recently the novel *Grown Ups*. Her journalism, collected under two titles, *Making It Up As I Go Along* and *Under the Duvet: Deluxe Edition*, containing the original publications *Under the Duvet* and *Further Under the Duvet*, are also available. Marian lives in Dublin with her husband.